I AM MALCHUS

D. Charles King

Name: D. Charles King
Title: I am Malchus
By D. Charles King
ISBN paperback: 978-1-953114-24-2
ISBN hardcover: 978-1-953114-25-9
LCCN: 2021918964
Subjects: 1. Fiction/Christian/Biblical
2. Fiction/Christian/Historical
3. Fiction/Christian/Romance/Historical

Author photo credits: D. Charles King, author
Maps photo credits: Mail & More, Mt. Pleasant, South Carolina
Cover photos: iStockphoto.com, used with permission, 2021

Published by EA Books Publishing, a division of
Living Parables of Central Florida, Inc. a 501c3
EABooksPublishing.com

Dedication

To Grant, Henry, Will, and Milly—who have opened new categories in my heart.

Acknowledgments

Mike Davis was the first to read the manuscript. He was much more conscientious in that task than I expected, and the story is better for his scrutiny. Jenny Ramsey also read the manuscript and provided several helpful insights which improved the novel. Bret Lott was helpful and encouraging. To Peter Lundell, I am also grateful. His expertise and recommendations helped me bring the story into its final form.

The people at EA Publishing, in all my interactions, were professional and gracious. Linda Goldfarb was my first contact and her energy and enthusiasm warrant special attention. Rebecca Ford, Kim Autrey, Rhonda Robinson, Jeanette Littleton, Robin Black, and Tanya Shanley were always courteous and efficient. The company, by statement and by practice, has made a purposeful effort to honor our Lord in their business enterprise, and that intentionality was evident in my collaboration with them as we went through the process of bringing this story to print.

I am also grateful to Lynne. Her patience with me is incomprehensible.

D. Charles King

Principal Characters

Characters in regular type are historical; invented characters are in italics. Persons marked with an asterisk are dead when the story begins. Some minor characters are not listed.

Alexander*	Son of Herod the Great by Mariamne I.
Ananias	Damascus resident who brought the blinded Saul of Tarsus into his home.
Ananus	Youngest son of Annas, the former high priest in Israel.
Annas	Former high priest in Israel.
Antipas	Son of Herod the Great by Malthace and the tetrarch of Galilee.
Antipater II	Son of Herod the Great by Doris.
Archalaeus	Son of Herod the Great by Malthace
Aretas IV	Nabatean king.
Aristobulus III*	Brother of Mariamne I, wife of Herod the Great.
Aristobulus IV*	Son of Herod the Great by Mariamne I.
Asriel	*Scribe.*
Caiaphas	Son-in-law of Annas and high priest of Israel.
Claudia Procula	Wife of Pontius Pilate.
Gavriel	*Tutor for Malchus.*
Herod the Great*	Idumean/Nabatean who ascended to kingship in Israel.
Herodias	Herodian princess first married to Herod Philip, then later to Herod Antipas.
John the Baptizer	Prophet who called Jews to repentance; executed by Herod Antipas.
Joseph the Arimathean	Secret disciple of Jesus, who provided a tomb for his burial. (Luke 23:50-56)
Judas Iscariot	The disciple who betrayed Jesus.
Malchus	Slave of the high priest whose ear was healed by Jesus.

Mariamne*   Hasmonean princess, second wife of Herod the Great, murdered because of the suspicion she was plotting against him.

Marius   *Roman Centurion.*

Manaen   Also known as Menahem, "foster-brother" of Herod Antipas and mentioned as one of the disciples and teachers, along with Barnabas and Paul, in Antioch.

Nicodemus   Pharisee who met Jesus at night.

Paul   Formerly known as Saul of Tarsus, the persecutor of the church, who became a disciple of Jesus Christ.

Peter   One of the original disciples of Jesus of Nazareth.

Phasaelis   Daughter of King Aretas of Nabatea and wife of Herod Antipas.

Phillip   Son of Herod the Great, tetrarch of the northern regions, and first husband of Herodias.

Pontius Pilate   Roman prefect of Judea.

Quartus   *Slave and friend of Malchus.*

Sabrina   *Slave to Claudia Procula.*

Salome   Daughter of Herodias.

Sejanus   Roman prefect of the Praetorian Guard.

Stephen   Follower of Jesus of Nazareth and the first martyr of the faith.

Tiberius   Emperor of Rome.

Zuriel   *Commander of the Jewish Temple Guard.*

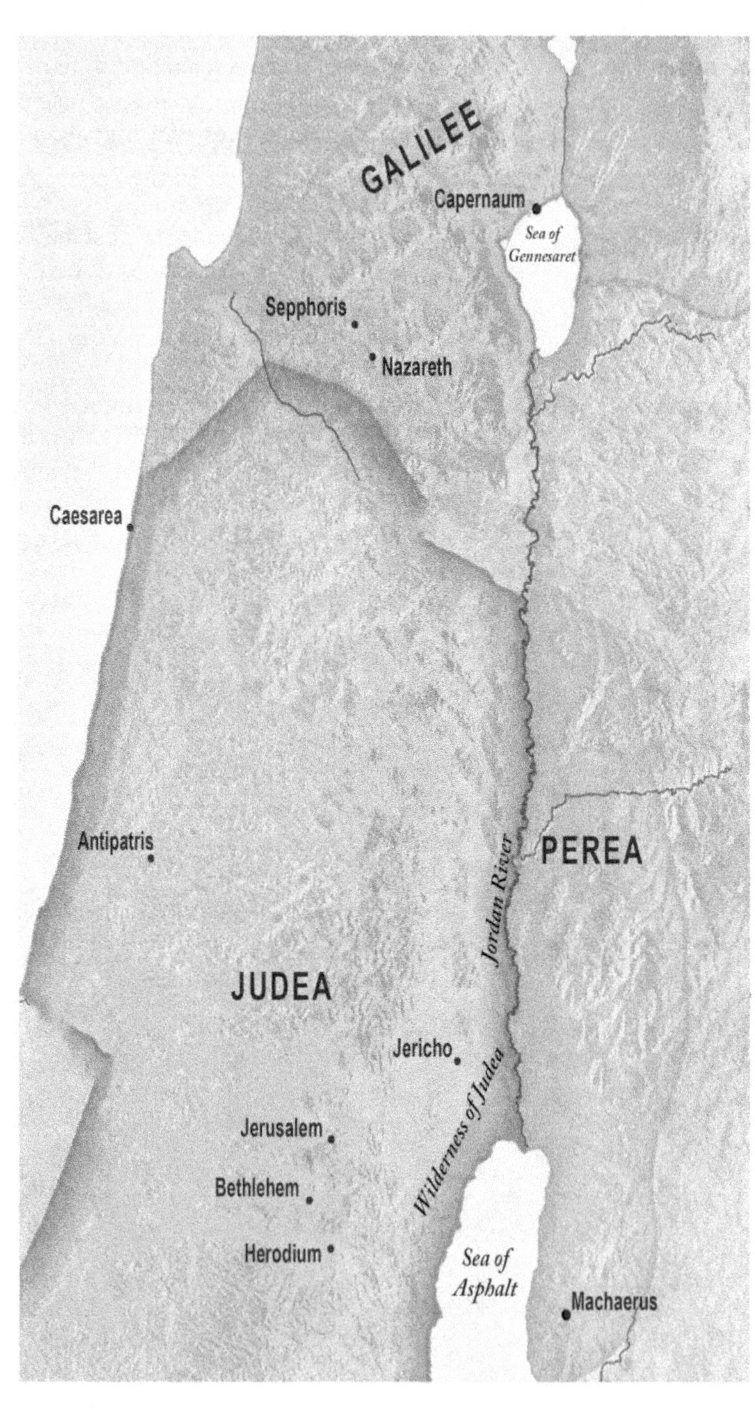

GALILEE
Capernaum
Sea of
Gennesaret
Sepphoris
Nazareth
Caesarea
Antipatris
PEREA
Jordan River
JUDEA
Jericho
Wilderness of Judea
Jerusalem
Bethlehem
Herodium
Sea of
Asphalt
Machaerus

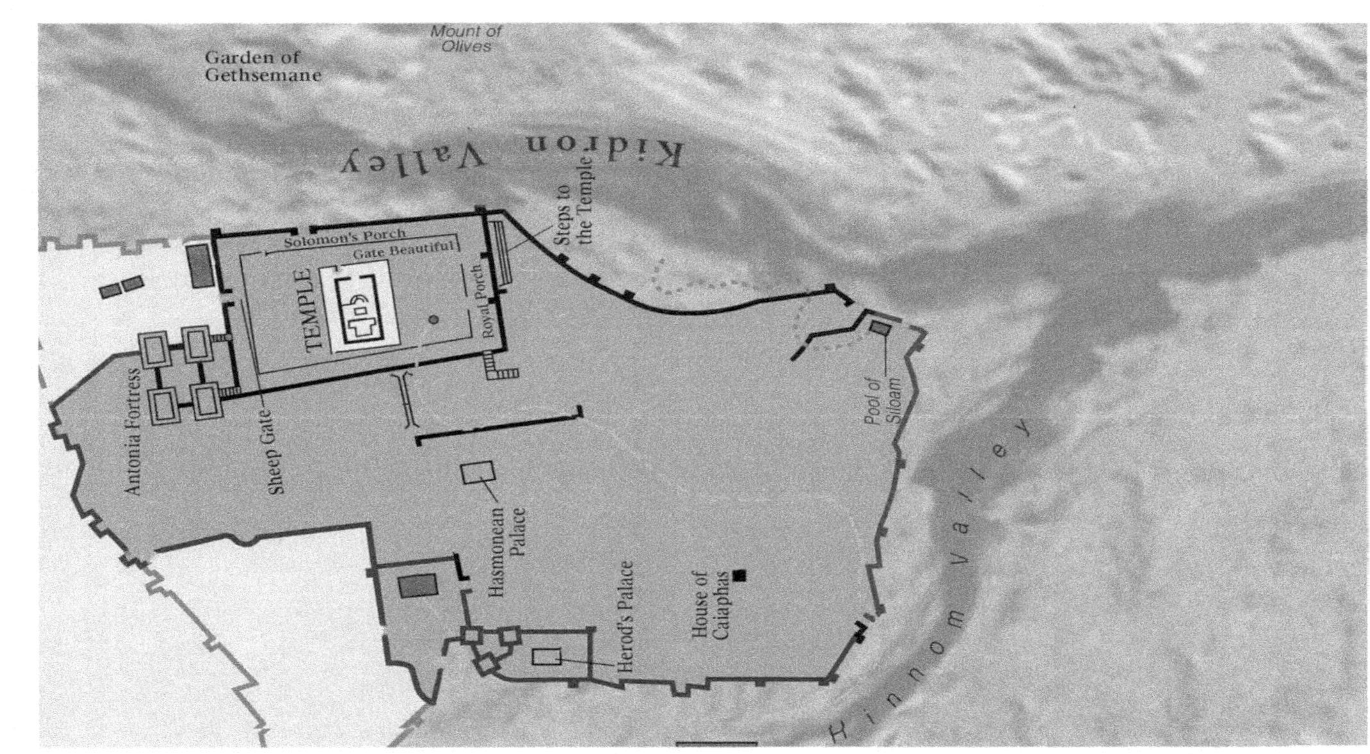

Garden of Gethsemane
Mount of Olives
Kidron Valley
Solomon's Porch
Gate Beautiful
TEMPLE
Royal Porch
Steps to the Temple
Antonia Fortress
Sheep Gate
Hasmonean Palace
Herod's Palace
House of Caiaphas
Pool of Siloam
Hinnom Valley

Prologue

I am Malchus.

You may have heard of me. My name, I am told, still passes the lips of some in Jerusalem—even after these years. *The one the fisherman smote,* they say.

It is an odd identity—*the one the fisherman smote*—but it is my identity. I cannot escape it, nor do I wish to. Even here in Antioch, nearly thirty years later, when the events in Jerusalem at Passover are recounted, some will point to me: "He was there," they will say. "He is the one Peter struck." I smile when I hear this. I also smile when men crane their necks as I pass—looking at my head—trying to see if my ear is intact.

They have heard the story.

I am Malchus. I will always be known as the one struck by the Galilean fisherman's sword. For those who have heard the account of that night in Jerusalem, the altercation in the olive trees across the Kidron from the temple is the one event that identifies me. Sometimes in the Jewish quarter here in Antioch I will hear a whisper, "He was slave to the high priest." A true statement, but I am better known for having my ear sliced by Peter.

Whether my name is familiar or not is no matter. I take no credit.

Can a man take credit for standing in the way of a sword?

Nearly thirty years have passed since that night—the night when the burly fisherman from the Galilee took his sword against me. The world is different now. It will never be the same again. That Passover, those events in Jerusalem, rendered the world a different place. Everything, whether before or after those days, must be measured in regard to those days. For those of us who follow "The Way," those events are central to our convictions. They are the midpoint of our chronology. Events either occurred before or after that Passover in Jerusalem. How improbable that I, Malchus the slave, would have a place in those events that forever changed the world. I am grateful.

Malchus, the one from the north. Malchus the Cherusci. Malchus the tall one. Malchus the slave of the high priest. Malchus, the one assigned to keep order at the temple.

That was how I was known in Jerusalem. Am I still a slave? If so, my submission now comes willingly. But that will come in the telling of the story that changed the world.

Passover is upon us. It will be celebrated here in Antioch, where our fellowship will gather and celebrate redemption. We will speak of the past, and we will speak of the future. We will commemorate the lamb's blood that provided redemption in the days of Moses, and we will celebrate the blood of the Lamb of God that gives us redemption today. We will acknowledge gratitude to the one who brought redemption, and we will extend it to others. Nearly thirty Passovers have passed since those events in Jerusalem changed the world.

The one who touched this world to change it also touched my bleeding head. Would that the rawboned fisherman had hacked me a dozen times—rather than once—that I might have felt his master's healing touch on each wound.

The fisherman was sturdy. His arms and shoulders had been made strong by pulling heavy nets from the Gennareset. They were arms capable of cleaving a man's head—but he was no swordsman. Had the fisherman been as skilled at swords as he was at nets—I would tell no story today. A better aim would have killed me quickly. The difference of the width of two fingers is the difference between a sliced ear and the cleaving of a skull.

We were thrown together as adversaries on that dark night in the olive grove, but we would not long remain adversaries. Who could have supposed that the one who tried to split my head would become my brother? Who could have supposed that we would sup together, share laughter, shed tears together? Such a bond was unlikely, but his strong embrace and his hearty laughter would become common to me. We knew a fellowship few others could comprehend. Our collaboration became well-known among the brethren as we shared bread with them and told the story of those events in Jerusalem.

The brethren always heard our story with delight. "A better swordsman would have split my skull—" I would deride him, "—rather than sliced my ear!" Like a thunderclap his laughter came, quick and booming, as it always did—a thunderous laugh that swelled up from his big chest and seemed to shake the doorframes.

"I am worse than you thought!" he would roar in reply. "My aim was for the son of the high priest, not you!" Whether a man had heard that story a dozen times or heard it new, he found laughter in it—rich laughter, laughter that was pure. Neither Peter, nor I, nor any who heard it ever tired of that story.

I miss him dearly.

I wish we could wrap arm around shoulder—one more time—as we had often done when we recounted the events of that night—when we met first as enemies. Which of us was the more confused that evening on the hill, I do not know. Each had been assigned a responsibility that evening, but neither of us had the will to obey. There we met, two reluctant servants, unsure of our roles, unaware of how our actions would be retold in succeeding years. It was near the olive press on the hill that is banked up opposite the Kidron that we first met. There in the dark night, under the olive trees, the flickering light of two dozen torches showed the fear and bewilderment on our faces. Both of us were confused and afraid, as were those around us. But we would eventually be bound together by the one that night who was neither afraid nor confused.

Will Peter and I embrace again? Will we again clasp hands and laugh together? Peter has left Antioch, summoned to other places, and I cannot be sure he will return. There are others whom he sensed needed to hear his story, which is not his story, but the story of his lord. When he tells that story, others will embrace it. Wherever it has gone, and whomever has told it, the story has been embraced. In a hundred places Peter's story has taken hold and has now become the story of thousands. The fisherman says his hope was a living hope, that it was imperishable. So it was. And so it is—as it finds its way into the hearts of men and women across our world.

Yes, I am Malchus. A curious Antiochian in the marketplace or someone new in the fellowship will sometimes ask, "Are you—?" And I will nod. Sometimes one will look at me as if I should lift my hair to confirm the story. My name intrigues some. They will say, "You are called Malchus. It is the name of a king. Are you a king?"

"I am a slave. Can a slave be a king?"

Is Malchus the name of a king? Some say so. I make no such claim. What my name means I cannot be sure. The one who rescued me gave me the name. She said I was a prince, and I will not contradict her. She is the one who saved my life. She said I was derived from some royal stock in the lands of the north, but in truth, it may have been just a story in her own mind. I was a slave in the house of the high priest when I found my true identity.

"I was a slave who became free—and I am now a slave again," I tell those who ask. Most who hear that are confused. Paul would understand. He was free and allowed himself to be a prisoner. He waits in Caesarea—two years now.

Luke has heard my story. He writes a bigger story, and I am grateful to have a small part in it. "Some men in Jerusalem still remember you," Luke told me. "They say, 'The high priest's slave, the big man, the yellow-hair from the north, the one who kept order in the temple.'"

Nearly thirty years have passed since those events no one can forget. Among those who remember are those who would kill me if given the opportunity. "Do not return to Jerusalem," Luke told me. "The high priests remember you. A man of your stature would not go unnoticed." I have accepted Luke's counsel. I will not return to Jerusalem.

Yet Luke's reports of the city are welcome to my ears. Two trips he has made this past year, asking questions of those who knew our

Lord. Luke is a methodical man. His account, once finished, will be thorough, and it will include my report, but he will not call my name. That would not be wise, he says. He will refer to me as "the high priest's slave."

I will stay here in Antioch, as I have for nearly thirty years. Our movement, *The Way*, has great energy here, and many are joining us. Our detractors here in Antioch have taken to calling us "little Christs." They mean it to demean us, but we have adopted the term with pride.

Manaen is here with us in Antioch. He gives leadership to our movement, shepherding the flock, as our Lord instructed us. Joanna and Chuza, who served Antipas for many years, are part of our fellowship. Luke spends much time with these friends, making notes about the Herods.

Those three were with me in Jerusalem during Passover thirty years earlier. Together we endured those days, when the one we had determined to serve was betrayed. And three days later our grief turned to ecstasy. Now we are together again and together we serve him and proclaim him, the one who gave us new identities. If those opposed to us wish to call us "little Christs", we accept the designation. We hope that will be our true identity. We know who we are.

I do not know my origins, but I know who I am, and I have a story. I will tell it from my first memories.

PART I

Chapter 1
Screams

Screams. Persistent screams. Women's screams. That is what I remember. My first memories are composed of screams.

I was old enough to have memories but not old enough to make sense of them.

Panic and screaming are what I recall—the smell of smoke and the sound of panicked footsteps. Hands tugged at my arms. Clamor, terror, confusion. And the continual screams of women—that is what I recall.

If details are what make a memory—in reality I have few memories. The emotions—and the memory of the emotions—are strong, but the particulars are indistinct. My mind holds no pictures, no colors, no words; it holds only emotions. Panic and fear are my recollections. My mind cannot reclaim the events, but it will not turn loose of the sensations. When I am honest, I have to admit I have no real memories. I have only memories of memories.

The screams endured. Every night in my young life the screams came back to me. They have subsided now. The years have dulled those echoes—but for many years those piercing sounds lifted me from my bed at night. Whose scream was it that inhabited my memory?

I suppose I had a mother. All men do. And I suspect the screams lodged in my memory are hers. If so, it is all I have of her.

Often, in some way, she would come back to me. Something feminine would waken the memory—the timbre in a woman's voice, or an aroma, or that quiet moment just before sleep. These would remind me of her presence I had once known. And it created a longing for something inaccessible. An impossible reunion was what my heart sought. She was gone, taken by the smoke and clamor and terror, and she would not return. Those fleeting moments—when her presence came—those moments touched on eternity, moments when a man senses a desire he knows cannot be attained. Better that he should try to hold smoke in his hands. Despair can sometimes be the sister of memory—and for me, those memories always brought despair.

The clamor and confusion around me—the smoke, the panic, the wailing, the shrill screams—were things I would understand later. Quartus would explain it to me as we sat by our little fire under the pepper trees beside our hut.

"The slavers follow the Roman soldiers to the north-lands," he told me. "Some of the slavers have contracts with the army. They wait until the battle is over and then purchase the captives. Other slavers work on their own. They position themselves near a village and wait until the men go out to face the Romans. Then they raid the villages. These seek children, sometimes women. They do not have the courage to go against men. Straw-haired youth are their preference. That's why they took you." Quartus, like me, was a slave. If he had a similar story, he never told it.

Over the years as Quartus and I sat by our hut, watching the sparks from our cook-fire drift into the open sky, the events of that night would come back to me in small parcels. In my memory, in the midst of the screams and smoke and confusion, I sensed competing hands tugging at my arms. I was pulled away. I felt the pain as fingernails slid down my arms, hands reluctant to release me, then more screams—then darkness. I was constrained. I was thrown into a bag. I pushed against the sides, but my little strength was useless against ox hide. I was dragged across the ground and hoisted on a man's back. The screams diminished, then subsided entirely. The smell of smoke lessened—replaced by the sticky odor of the ox hide and the foul odor of unwashed clothes. The man was running. I bounced with every step. The man's breathing became heavier. I heard other footsteps and the voice of another man.

I managed to open the drawstring of the bag. Pushing my head part way out of the bag, I put my teeth against the man's neck and bit as hard as I could. He screamed, and then I felt the jolt of hitting the ground. His foot caught me in the ribs. I lay on the ground in the bag, my rib-bones in agony. He opened the bag and I saw his face for the first time, gap-toothed and sweaty, full of anger and hatred. Cursing me in a language I did not know, he took a cord and lashed my hands and my feet. Then he took another cord and pulled it tightly through my teeth and around my head and tied it. My ribs were in agony, and I still was working to get my breath. The wailing of a boy came from the bag of the other man. My captor kicked me again before pulling the bag over my body. He threw me on his back again and began walking.

We trudged along and finally stopped. He dropped me to the ground and walked away. A horse whinnied. A second horse responded. The footsteps came back. I was picked up and thrown over the horse. The man, who smelled of smoke and sweat, lashed me to the horse, tugging the cords tightly. The horse started its trot. Wherever I was and wherever I came from, I would never know.

When I was younger, I often wondered about the place from which I was taken. Where was it? What was it like? I heard stories about places where the water pours down the mountains too cold to drink, and the trees grow up to the edge of the sky, a place where the snow piles deep in the valleys in the winter. Did I come from such a place?

I thought about that a great deal when I was younger, but I think about it less these days. It serves no purpose.

The horse slowed to a walk. The men spoke to each other. I could not understand them. We stopped. My bag was untied from the horse, and the man carried me to a tree where he opened the bag. It was nighttime, but I could see we were in a small opening in a dense forest. Large trees spread a canopy over us, but some light from the moon filtered down to the forest floor covered with pine needles and damp leaves. The other man brought his bag beside me and opened it. The boy looked at me and I looked at him. He was older than I but no less afraid.

I tried to bite the hand of the man when he loosened the cord from my teeth, but he slapped the side of my face and put the cord around my neck and tied me to a tree. He squirted some water down my throat. I begged for more but did not get it. The two men went about watering the horses and eating some provisions they had brought. They built a small fire and huddled around its heat, drinking from a wineskin. They laughed coarsely as they congratulated themselves. The fire threw its light on the underside of the trees, but beyond was darkness, and I could not see the sky.

The heavy limbs of the trees hovered over me like ogres, and the damp leaves chilled my bare legs. My hands and feet were tied, and the cord around my neck secured me to the tree. In the quiet of the forest, I remembered the screams I had heard only hours ago. As the memory of those screams became more vivid, I began to cry. I longed for my mother, and I cried.

Curses in a strange tongue came from the huddled figures around the fire, and somehow I understood they were directed to me, but I could not squelch my grief. More curses, louder this time, but still my fear and grief and longing spilled out in my sobs. The man who had carried me rose from the edge of the fire. His large figure was made larger by the fire as he tramped toward me. A muffled rattle of steel accompanied him, the noise of the weapons he carried around his waist. The metallic rattle mixed with the insistent crunch of leaves as he came toward me. He cleared his throat and spat.

I whimpered again.

The blow caught me by surprise. He slapped me across my face, and my head was knocked sideways. I felt the leather cord tightening around my neck. I rolled over in the dirt. Wet leaves held to my face and arms. I tugged at the cord to loosen it. The man stood over me and put his foot on my chest and pressed down. He kicked me again, his foot catching my ribs with all its force. I curled into a ball in the leaves. I was addled. My ears rang. My side burned with pain. The cord went tight around my neck. I was yanked up. My feet left the ground. The slaver had thrown the cord over a limb and pulled me up. With both hands I held the choking cord, but it was too tight. It bit into my neck, tearing the skin. My legs could not find the ground. I thrashed wildly, the leather cutting deeper into my neck. I kicked and struggled to gain air—it would not come. I jerked and pulled at the cord, but it served no purpose. My brain seemed to swell. My head felt as if it would explode. Laughter came to my ears, but from miles away it seemed. Sparks of the fire rose up in the trees, throwing light on the underside of the leaves, but then sound and sight began to slip from me. My brain would surely burst. My kicking legs lost their energy. I spun at the end of the rope. My fingers slipped from the cord. My arms went limp. The world went dark.

Consciousness came back. I was on the ground again, in the thick wet leaves. Air. Air. I needed air. I loosened the cord around my neck and sucked in the precious air. I could taste blood. My ears rang like a dozen drums beating. Even so, I could hear my own gulping throat as I tried to pull air into my chest. The man looked at me, contorted his face, mocking me by making a noise like a baby crying. He laughed again, turned, and went back to the fire, where he and his partner shared more laughter.

My chest continued to heave. The boy beside me looked at me with fear and confusion. I sat with my back against the tree, breathing heavily. The slaver and his companion chewed their meal around the fire. Outside that ring of quivering light on the undersides of the branches, the world was dark. A new pain came in my stomach—hunger, which competed with the pain in my ribs. In the gap of the leaves I could see a thin cloud covering the moon. The insects in the forest found their voices, a steady buzz among the bushes that mingled with the ringing still in my ears. The other boy whimpered in the dark. I put my hands to my neck and felt the stickiness of my blood. The memory of the screams I had heard a few hours before came back to me. A shiver of cold and fear sent a tremor through my body. I almost cried again, but I caught myself. I made a determination—I would never cry again. Crying served no purpose. Crying would not help me. The slaver taught me that lesson. Other pains, other slights, other indignities would come to me as a boy, but I would not cry—not on that journey and not in the coming years. Whatever hardship, whatever pain, whatever mistreatment, I would not cry. It was a promise I would not violate for many years—until that night in Jerusalem . . .

Chapter 2
The Village

The sequence of the next few days is lost to me. How many days and how many nights did we travel? Was it a week? Was it two? We stayed in constant movement during the day. We stopped to eat and sleep when darkness came. Sometimes I was cinched across the back of the horse. Other times I walked, hands bound and the cord around my neck connected to a longer cord, which was tied to the horse. Both were agony. More than once I fell and was dragged in the dirt behind the horse. When I fell, the slaver would slap me and curse me in his language.

My ribs ached with every step. A blue and purple swelling, the size of my hand, developed at the place where the slaver had kicked me.

We traveled through forests, always on an incline either up or down. Our path was sometimes little more than a bridle-path, and sometimes the tree limbs scraped my face as we walked. As we progressed, the trees thinned, and we made our way through pine forests and rocky hills. Each day seemed the same as the previous one. We walked constantly, and I was in constant pain. We crested a hill and came to a wider road. Meadows spread out in all directions with clusters of huts set among small groves. Occasionally a rider on a donkey or a cart would pass us. Once a cart with several grubby boys walking beside it passed by, and they taunted me, shaking their scythes and field tools at me as I walked behind the horse. But the next day a girl sitting with her father in a cart passed by, and I saw her eyes, brown and sad, like a doe's, and there was sympathy in her face.

I was a slave. I did not understand that. I would not understand that until later. But those who saw me knew. Indifference, contempt, pity—these are the ways men and women, even children, look at slaves. The sight of a slave brings out a person's deepest nature, whether good or evil. Ordinarily it was indifference. Often it was contempt. Less often, but occasionally, it was pity.

My ribs became worse. The purple turned black with yellow flecks. Pus began to drip down my side. Flies sucked at the wound. Wakefulness and sleeping became indistinct. The real world and the world of my dreams commingled.

These memories do not come easily. For many years I tried to put them away, and now I try to recover them. A man who has spent years pushing memories off a cliff cannot easily retrieve them.

We came to a village, where I was tethered to a pole. A jumble of odors assaulted my nose—unwashed men, animal dung, the aroma of vegetables stewing in spices. My nose and my ears functioned, but my eyes could not focus. A donkey brayed in annoyance; a metalsmith hammered at his work; men talked. The other boy, tied to a post near me, wailed pitifully. There were others—perhaps five or six tied to other posts. At least one was a girl, because I could hear her crying.

Dozens of villagers surrounded the posts. Some came close enough that I could smell their foul breath. It was market day in this nameless village, but not a common market day. Slaves, I would learn, were not always available on market day. Slaves were a rare commodity than, say, turnips or goats or donkeys. On these special days, when slaves were available, there were greater crowds.

I would learn these things from Quartus, with whom I was destined to share a hut for ten years. Quartus answered my endless questions with unending patience. May God be gracious to him. As we sat on our stools under the twin pepper trees outside our hut, Quartus would explain about slaves and about market days. He told me only a few of those who came to the market could actually afford a slave, but on that day the slaves were for sale, all who were able came to the village. Perhaps only once or twice a year in a village would this spectacle take place. Why would a man come to gawk at a slave when he could not buy one? Perhaps, I suggested once, that some came to compare their respective state with that of the slave. Perhaps a poor freeman, sitting in his meager hut, eating his gruel at night can remember seeing the slave at the market and say: "At least I am not a slave."

A man came near. He pulled my hair to see my face. Sour wine and onions were on his breath. He pushed against the wound in my side. I screamed and kicked, my foot catching him in his groin. He moaned and fell backward. I heard laughter, but the slaver brought his hand sharply across my head, stinging my face. He lashed another cord around my feet. My head buzzed. I could not keep my eyes open. There was no strength in my body. The bartering voices melded with the animal sounds, and I fell into a delirious sleep.

When the slaver slapped me to awaken me, the sun had fallen below the tree line, allowing only the twilight into my eyes. Only a few stragglers remained in the market. I asked for water, but the slaver slapped me again, knocking my head against the post and splitting my lip. I looked around. My eyes had trouble focusing, but I could see the other boy who had made the journey with me was gone, as were the others who had been tied to posts. The slaver hit me again, cursing in a language I did not know.

I would not understand my situation—a precarious situation— until much later: I no longer had value. I had become spoiled goods. A boy so obviously damaged was not a wise purchase. I did not know it, but I was close to death. Those who looked at the gore oozing from my side did not see me as a worthy investment. The slaver had no more use for me.

A persistent hum developed in my brain. Colors whirled through my mind, and a ringing echo pounded through my ears. Then the spinning and the echoes slowed down, and a bright light began to appear. It came closer and became brighter. The pain in my ribs, in my face, in my head, even my hunger and my thirst, seemed to dissolve. Not only did the pain disappear, but whatever is the opposite of pain replaced it. I had the sensation of falling—not falling *off* something, but *into* something. Something composed of light. And then . . .

I dreamed of a presence, a feminine presence, something good and generous and sweet-smelling. I was reluctant to leave the light into which I had fallen, but I sensed a touch, a very tender touch that seemed to encourage me to come away from the light. For weeks I had fought every touch, but this one was different. This touch was not probing. This touch was assuring. The tension in my soul released. For the first time in weeks, the clamor in my mind subsided. With the touch came an aroma—an aroma that prevailed against the smell of unwashed men, animal dung and the spices from the market. And in my spirit I sensed something new. Trust. Why did I trust this one who touched me? I do not know. But I trusted her even before I opened my eyes to see her. Perhaps it was the way she touched me—her soft hands on my arm and then my face. With the little energy I had remaining I raised my head and looked through eyes that would not focus. Though I could not understand her language, something in the lilt and timbre of her voice confirmed she was one I could trust. There is a communication that surpasses words, and I knew I should trust this lady—whoever she was.

Chapter 3
The Estate

"Near dead . . . that's what you were when the lady purchased you—near dead," Quartus would often tell me this, teasing me. "Full price she paid! Why, I cannot understand, with pus oozing out of your side." He would screw up his face in mock disgust whenever he recounted this story, which he often did over the years, always emphasizing that I was not worth the price. He tried to agitate me with his teasing, but I learned to let him talk without responding. "Not likely to live out the day—that's what I thought when I saw you. No bargain, that's for certain. She could have gotten a better price." He would shake his head in disbelief. "That slaver would have sold you for the price of a skin of wine. He had given up on you. Anyone who looked at you could tell that you were not going to survive long." More head shaking. Quartus always concluded the story with a final question: "Did the lady ask my opinion? No. If so, I would have told her, 'Do not buy that boy. He's not worth the price.'"

I came to enjoy the story. Quartus held genuine affection for me—which he could not express directly, but I sensed it in his story about the day the lady bought me and brought me to her house.

"This is not a new story," I would say. "I have heard this story before."

"And you will hear it again," he always answered, "for it bears telling."

I have no memory of my arrival at the house. Reality and the nightmares in my brain were to me the same. My nose and ears came alive before my eyes did. It was *her* aroma I sensed in the village, and now in the house it became more intense, an aroma that carried an essence of flowers and spices and wind-blown fields. Even today when passing through an orchard in the springtime, or the spice-souk in Antioch, my nose will catch a portion of that aroma, and it will evoke her memory, the woman who saved my life.

Attendant to the aroma was a voice—a soft, reassuring voice. There were no words—at least no words I understood, for it would be many months before I could understand the language around me . . . yet I understood what the voice was saying. The voice was encouraging me. It was telling me that I should not die, that I should not give in to the injury that was seeking to kill me.

I would come to know the one who emanated this aroma and who spoke this voice, but at the time of my arrival—while I was in the throes of my fever, she was simply a presence—an angelic presence. And as I gradually awoke from my fever, and as her face came into focus and I felt her soft hand on my face, she was no less angelic.

I owe her everything. I trust God has shown her the same mercy she showed me.

Quartus would explain later that I spent nearly a week in the house with her attending me. Of those days as I faded in and out of consciousness, I have some vague memories, the lady dressing the wound in my side, rubbing cool water on my face, and putting balm on the burns on my neck. The aroma and the voice remained constant—and seemed to pull me back to health.

She had a name, but a name I never spoke. For Quartus and for me, she was simply "the lady." Whenever we referred to her, it was always "the lady" and her husband was "the master."

For all the things I cannot recall clearly, I have a vivid memory of the day that I was entrusted to Quartus's care. I had recovered enough to eat, and the lady gave me soup, which provided enough strength to begin to walk for the first time since I was brought from the market.

I sat on the side of the bed as the lady brought Quartus into the room. He seemed old to me, his hair thinning and speckles of white in his beard—but it was a child's assessment of his age; he probably was not nearly as old as I thought. His was a trustworthy face, with a gentle smile and a head browned by the sun. Spindly legs protruded below his goat-hair garment, cinched with a piece of leather around his waist. His left arm hung at an odd angle because of an accident years earlier. But his right arm was good, although just as spindly as his legs.

"Quar-tus," the lady said to me, pointing at this figure in the doorway and enunciating very clearly.

"Quartus," he said, pointing at himself.

In acknowledgement I tried to say "Quartus," but my pronunciation made them both smile.

Quartus led me out of the house. The sun seemed especially bright that morning. I stepped out the door and surveyed the surroundings of my new home. My master, as I would learn, held a large estate that extended miles around his house, which sat prominently on an open hill, the house and courtyard well-shaded by junipers and fig trees. The house was made of stacked stone with a tile roof. The rocky landscape rose gradually behind the house then fell away in other directions, providing the master with a broad view of his domain. A flat valley the shape of a horseshoe, the open end away from us, extended down toward the village until it rose up again against steep hills, often clouded over. Some of the old men in the village say one of the gods dragged his foot here years ago and scoured out the valley. The story frightened me. I worried that the god might come back again to drag his foot and fail to notice our hut, but after a while, when the god never came, I quit worrying.

Along the upper edge of the scoured-out valley spread hundreds of olive trees—lines of orderly silver ribbons, the orderliness disrupted by a few fig trees whose branches reached higher. They undulated down the valley in the direction of the village and when the breeze caught the leaves, they sparkled green and silver. Grapevines—even more orderly than the olives—grew in the sloping flat between them. Beyond the grapevines lay an open meadow where the master kept a few sheep. A circular pen of stacked stones, waist-high to a grown man, kept them confined at night. A bank of almond trees nestled neatly on the hill just above the main house. Wider out, the master's domain was surrounded on both sides by gray-rock hills, whose sides grew green with pines and hardwoods. Beyond those small hills were greater hills, hills I could not see—hills from which I had come.

The only other significant building on the estate was the stable, which lay a few stones' throws below and beside the main house. Like the main house it was made of stacked stone, but the roof was thatched with river-weeds, not tile. Attached to it was a hut. And to that hut Quartus escorted me.

Ducks scattered as we approached the stacked-stone building. Two pepper trees extended their limbs over the structure and gave it shade. A three-legged stool sat beside a fire-pit adjacent to the stable. Quartus threw back the goat-hair cloth covering the door, which was just high enough for him to make his way through without bending. He motioned me in. One window, crudely shuttered with dry fronds, provided some light. The donkey and the master's horse were given the greater portion of the structure, but one section was given over as a residence for Quartus—and now for me as well. One cot, just inches above the dirt floor, lay in one corner. Another cot, smaller and obviously new, lay in the opposite corner. Quartus pointed to the cot. It was for me. A rough table with a few clay pots and cups sat in another corner. This was to be my home. For ten years Quartus and I would share that square room—four paces in each direction—next to the stable with the master's horse and donkey. And Quartus, my friend with one bad arm, would be my close companion.

Dear, dear Quartus, may the years have been kind to you, and may God have granted you the mercy you deserve for your goodness you showed me. I left you without saying goodbye and that regret haunts me still.

Quartus spent the day showing me around the stable and the nearby orchards. I was fascinated by the ducks and their waddle and their amusing noises. He showed me how to toss grain from a bag he kept suspended from the ceiling. Later we had some soup he heated over the fire-pit, and then Quartus lay on his cot—a custom he followed every day. He motioned for me to follow his example and lie on my cot, but after he fell asleep, I stepped outside to watch the ducks, who clustered around me, seeking more food.

As I stood there, a noise came to my ears. Horses' hooves. I looked down the path that led away from the house. A shiver ran through my shoulders. The last horse's hooves I had heard were those of the slaver. Had he returned? I wanted to hide, but I stood still. The sound of the hooves came closer. I watched carefully. The hoof-sound became louder. My legs trembled but found no courage to run. A horse and its rider appeared on the path. I watched carefully. The horse and the rider stopped in front of the house. The man paused for a moment, sitting in his saddle.

This is an important man, I thought to myself. Somehow I knew the man sitting astride this horse was an important man—and I was very afraid.

There is a certain deportment of men, whether walking or astride a horse, that tells much of the man himself. This was a man with au-thority, responsibility, a man charged with leadership. I could see it in the way he carried himself in the saddle.

He was not a large man, but his authority exceeded his stature. I watched carefully, unable to move. A deerskin vest fit snugly on his torso, and a broad-brimmed hat with a low crown, also of deerskin, kept the sun from his eyes. His riding boots of matching deerskin came to his knees. On his hip, secured by a bull's-hide belt, hung a bronze sword in a silver-studded sheath. He looked capable of using it. He dismounted and looked down the slope to the stable. I stood there, gawking in the full sun, just outside the shade of the pepper trees. His head went to a slight angle when he saw me—as if he were trying to make sense of what he saw. We were not fifty paces apart. I stood without moving, but I trembled again. Was this man like the slaver? I wanted to run, but fear kept me immobile.

Quartus came out of the stable. He ran up the hill toward the man and the horse. He took the reins of the horse. He and the man looked down the hill at me. I was still transfixed, still standing with my arms to my side, still fearful—still sensing, but fighting, the impulse to run. Quartus and the man talked. They talked about me. I was sure of it.

The lady came to the door. The man walked brusquely past her and into the house. I heard an angry voice, which had to be his. Instinctively, I sensed his anger had something to do with me.

Quartus led the horse down the slope to the stable. He avoided my eyes and said nothing. I stood in the same place for some moments, unsure of what to do. I sensed the tension, but did not understand it. Quartus led the horse to the watering trough, removed the saddle, and let it drink. I looked up at the house above us and wondered about this man who had just arrived—and what his arrival would mean for me.

In the full sunshine I shivered. I worried that he would come down from the house to the stable. If he came, what would I do?

He did not come.

The next day I saw him in the orchards, inspecting the trees. He looked at me. The tremble I felt the day before returned. I dropped my head and looked away as he went on down the line of trees. In the succeeding days, as I learned my responsibilities from Quartus, the master never came to the stable, and I never went to the house. For that I was glad. At times, when he was outside the house as I fed the ducks or gathered wood, he would stand on the hill and look at me. I sensed I was being evaluated, and somehow, by the way he stared, I knew this man had power over me.

Quartus would later explain that valuable money had been spent on me, but I had no value. The lady had exceeded her authority. A sickly slave boy could bring no value to the estate. I was a liability, not an asset. The lady had allowed her emotions to override her good sense. She had made this ill-considered purchase in the absence of the master—and she would endure his displeasure.

I longed to see the lady. I wanted to feel her hands on my face and sense that wonderful aroma that surrounded her, and the assurance her presence had provided—but somehow, instinctively, I knew that was not possible. And I understood it was this man, this master, who made it impossible. I had only a boy's understanding, but some things, even for a boy, are sensed, even if they are not understood. This man stood between the lady and me. In some way I did not understand, he would keep us apart. *Will I see her again?* The distance by which we were separated was meager—but it seemed as if she were miles away.

I learned more responsibilities. Quartus taught me patiently, and I took to the work willingly. In addition to feeding the ducks, and gathering their eggs, I learned how to gather the wood and break the twigs into the appropriate sizes for the cooking fires. I helped Quartus water and feed the donkey and the horse—and clean up their manure. I gathered onions and beans into baskets that he took to the house. At night Quartus and I sat on our stools outside the stable as the sun slid behind the hill, turning the sky into a riot of pinks and purples. As the insects began to call to each other in their chirpings, I would see the lamps lit in the house on the hill, and sometimes I would see—or thought I could see—the silhouette of the lady in her window looking down the hill toward the stable where I sat.

Did she pause at the window to look down the hill at me? I was sure of it.

Once, when feeding the horse, I noticed a leather cord hanging on a peg in the stable. It was the one that had been around my neck. Quartus was not one to waste anything, and he had kept it, certain to find a purpose for it.

In late summer, when the figs began to ripen, Quartus showed me how to harvest those sticky-sweet fruits from the dozens of trees in the orchard. I was young and nimble and able to secure many of the figs Quartus could not reach. I took it as a challenge to gather the nearly inaccessible cluster of figs at the top of the tree. Sometimes as I inched along precarious limbs, Quartus assumed an expression of worry on his face. But when I brought the bag of figs down, it was obvious that Quartus was pleased. There were more figs than needed, so he and I ate figs until my stomach ached.

Two days later we were back in the fig grove. I climbed the tallest fig tree and began gathering from the top branches. The limbs swayed as I held to them, and I took a moment to look down the valley. Smoke from cook-fires wafted above the green and brown hills that hid the village from view. Beyond the valley greater mountains rose up against a clouded sky.

Were those the mountains I came from? Is that where the slaver found me? Only a few months earlier had we traversed those mountains, but it already seems years ago. The mountains of my origin, I would understand later, were well beyond my sight, but my young mind had no comprehension of the scale of the world. It even began to seem that those events happened to another person.

I began plucking the ripe figs again, taking care not to squeeze the delicate fruits, placing them carefully in the reed basket hung over my left arm. When I was certain I had gathered all I could in the upper branches, I descended. As I did, I was surprised to see the master himself standing near Quartus. Hands on his hips, he looked up at me. Somehow I knew he was evaluating me. The tremble returned and the basket almost slipped from my grasp.

What is a man worth? How is his value determined? Is there a scale on which a man can be placed to measure his significance? Those were questions that remained residual in my mind, both then and later. Those questions, questions I sensed but could not articulate, would not be answered for me for many years—not until those days in Jerusalem. It was there that one would show me what I was worth.

Neither approval nor disapproval showed in the master's face. He had alert eyes under bushy brows and a mouth set in an expression that was neither a frown nor a smile. He said nothing as he looked up at me, but I felt the discomfort of his gaze. In the deepest part of me, I sensed the truth: *This man can do with me as he wishes.* I thought it best to continue plucking the figs. I did not look down again until I was certain he was gone.

"The master's estate is large," Quartus said. "You could walk one day in three directions and still be on the master's land." Most of the land consisted of broken stretches of meadows framed by wooded shoulders. It was not a rich soil, some of it rocky with great gray boulders the titans had supposedly thrown down eons before, but it was adequately watered by two streams that never dried, even in midsummer.

Some lambs were born in those weeks. Quartus was giddy as he cleaned the newborns, talking to one as if it were a child. I took delight in Quartus' delight and in watching them, only hours old, gain their balance on spindly legs, bleating insistently as they found their mother's milk.

A few weeks later Quartus broke our regular early morning routine. As the sun was rising, he put the saddle and bridle on the horse, and he and I led it up the hill to the house. The yellow light of oil lamps spilled out the windows into the gray morning. He had me hold the horse's reins as he went to the door. I looked at the windows and wondered if I would get a glimpse of the lady. An owl hooted in the woods. The master came out of the house with leather bags. Quartus cinched the bags tightly on the back of the horse. The lady came to the door and waved to the master as he rode away—but she lingered in the doorway for a moment, speaking with Quartus and looking down the hill at me as I stood near.

Later that morning, to my surprise, Quartus led me up the hill to the house. The lady came to the door. She carried a broom and motioned to me to sweep the front stoop. I took the broom and began to sweep. She nodded to Quartus, and he walked back down the hill to the stable, but she stood in the doorway for a few minutes as I swept. I had been at my work only a few minutes when the lady came back to the door and motioned me inside. Three months had passed since I had been inside the house, but the pleasant aroma still pervaded the place, evoking the memories of waking up within these walls and being nursed back to health.

She led me to the back of the house to the dining area where a bowl of stew was waiting. At the end of the table sat a large chair with a bearskin thrown over it. It was certainly the master's chair. I shuddered. What if he returned? But he had taken provisions when he left that morning. He would be gone for a few days.

The lady handed me the spoon and motioned for me to eat. Among the onions and lentils were real pieces of lamb, not just the joints and knuckles that Quartus and I usually had in our bowls. She watched as I chewed those delicate morsels, speaking to me in her gentle voice that I had come to know. In her voice there was a communication that went beyond words. None of the words she spoke did I understand, yet I felt secure.

As I finished every drop of the stew, she brought some flat barley-cakes drizzled with honey.

To this day, when I take a spoonful of honey from the larder, the memory of the lady and that first taste of honey comes back afresh.

Her face took a concerned look as she examined my neck and rubbed aloe in the scar, talking in a soft voice, gentle and reassuring, but with words I could not understand.

Five days I came to the house. The lady abandoned the pretense of my sweeping the stoop—or doing any other chores. Mostly I just sat in her presence as she spun wool into yarn. Her dark eyes, deep and thoughtful, were the shape of the almonds I gathered in early spring. Black hair, when unpinned, fell to her waist. Her arms were bare as she worked. Once she brought me a mirror and showed me the red scar on the highest part of my neck. When she attended to me— rubbing balm on my neck—her hair, like a sheening black waterfall, heavy, as if weight were upon it, draped over my shoulders, its sweet aroma filling my head.

I was a boy without a mother. She was a mother without a boy.

She talked to me as if I could understand her and I listened carefully to try to make sense of this new language. She was fashioning the yarn into a cap. She would often place the material on my head to measure it, and as she did, she would rub my face and kiss my forehead. She would often pinch the leaf from an aloe plant and rub the salve into my neck, where the mark of the slaver's cord was still evident.

Occasionally I spoke a word in the new language, and when I did, her face beamed.

At the end of the fifth day I spent at the house, she gave me the cap, tied it on my head and stepped back to look at me before kissing my forehead again and sending me down the hill.

The next day I was not summoned to the house. That afternoon the master returned from his travels. This would be the pattern that she and I would follow for many years.

As Quartus talked to me constantly, the language gradually came to me. He said it was called "Latin".

The days shortened. We harvested the grapes, and Quartus took a full wagonload to the village. Under gray skies we pulled onions from the ground, knocking the dirt from them and laying them in baskets. Some of the olives had darkened on the limbs, but Quartus told me, "When half are black, we will harvest them." A cool wind blew down over the high mountains into our valley, tearing the few remaining leaves from the trees. Only the olive trees held to their leaves, defiant of the wind. The cap the lady gave me proved its value. Each morning I tied it around my head as I fed the animals. And once again I found some satisfaction—and some appreciation from Quartus—when we harvested the olives, for once again my nimbleness allowed me to shake the olives from the top of each tree. Below me Quartus gathered them in bags. During this harvest the master walked up and down the tree rows, his hands behind his back, looking from side to side, and sometimes looking at me scrambling in the trees, but he never acknowledged me or spoke to me.

"More than before," he told me as he hitched the donkey to the wagon full of olives. "More than before," he acknowledged my contribution to the harvest as he climbed onto the cart to take the baskets of olives to the village. "Before we were never able to gather those on the highest limbs." He paused for a moment as his teasing smile came to his face. "But that does not mean the lady should have paid full price." He called to the donkey, and he started down the path toward the village. As I watched him go out of sight, I wondered if someday I might go to the village myself.

The cool winds became cooler. A few onions remained in the ground. All else had been harvested. With little harvesting to be done, I took the duty to gather wood. I was glad to have this duty that allowed me to go into the edge of the woods and expand the world I knew. At first Quartus joined me, along with the donkey. He would ride, and I would walk into the woods where we would gather wood, using the axe to break it into pieces that could fit in the bag on the donkey's back. But with only one axe, and my having more energy, along with the nimbleness to climb the trees, Quartus eventually gave that responsibility entirely over to me.

Every morning during that winter I put the bridle on the donkey—who always complained in his high-pitched voice—jump on his back and make my way into the woods above the estate. I could fill the bag to its capacity in only a few hours which left me additional hours to explore the hills. Every rocky outcropping, every meager stream, was a new adventure for me as I sought each day some new area to explore.

Once I found a large beech along the stream, put my back against its base, and nestled into its black gnarly roots and sat quietly. Layers of leaves, heavy and damp, the sheddings of hundreds of trees, over more years than I could imagine, filled the floor of the woods. Above, thin ribbons of clouds showed through bare branches. A buzzard soared effortlessly in the highest part of the sky. I felt safe and comfortable and warm.

I returned to that spot when I could. As I sat quietly, the woods would come alive with chattering birds above, and squirrels clambered among the leaves on the ground. Sometimes deer would pass nearby, their ears alert, sniffing the air suspiciously. The foxes seemed less wary than the others, scurrying through the leaves, sometimes pouncing on a mouse or an insect I could not see.

Quartus warned me to be cautious. "Wolves sometimes come down in the winter."

Once, when I had ventured to the top of the hills above the estate, the donkey suddenly brayed in panic. He tugged against his tether, his eyes wild with fear. His nose had caught a scent. I looked at the ridge above me—movement, quick but stealthy. I looked again. Wolves. Three of them. No, four. No, five. My heart thumped. I tried to mount the donkey, but he jerked free and ran away. I ran too, as fast as a boy my age could run, yet it seemed my legs were mired in the ground. Rocks and leaves tugged at my feet. I stumbled once and fell, rolling down a small incline. I looked behind me but saw nothing. I ran again. The forest thinned. I came to the olive grove edging the valley. Still I ran. The grape vines came into view. Still I ran...until I came to the stable. "Wolves," I said to Quartus, barely getting out the words as my lungs heaved. "Wolves."

The dreams were vivid that night. Wolves chased me. Slavers chased me. The wolves became slavers. The slavers became wolves. Both chased me.

I awoke fighting Quartus. "Calm, calm," he said, holding my arms. "There are no wolves here."

From then on I stayed closer to the edge of the woods. My short axe, I knew, would provide no defense against wolves. Still there was plenty of wood available, and I kept the woodpile behind the master's house stacked high. Sometimes when I unloaded the wood at the back of the house, I found barley cakes or dried figs or some other treat just behind the woodpile. And on a few occasions the lady herself ventured out of the house just for a moment, to hand me the treat, always giving me a kiss on the forehead before returning quickly to the house. Once she brought me a woolen undershirt she had knitted. It served me well. It kept the chill off my body as I spent much of each day out in the woods.

Snow filled the valley. The woods around us bore a heavy blanket of pure white, the soft contours of the valley covered in an undulating whiteness.

"The master and the lady have more wood than they can burn in two winters," Quartus cajoled me as I pulled on my cap. "Will you gather more?"

I did not answer him. He was right. No more wood was needed, but the new snow had made the hills more fascinating.

The snow covered my ankles as I led the donkey through the olives, looking behind me to see how our tracks had marred the smooth perfection of the landscape.

But the donkey balked, leaning back on his haunches and braying in deep snorts. In the snow I saw the reason. Among the various tracks in the snow were those of wolves. The wolves had come lower. The snow had driven them down from the higher hills.

I gave up wood gathering. Through the remaining part of the winter, other than feeding the ducks, there was little for me to do, and sometimes in my restlessness, I would look up at the house above me and see the smoke curling above the roof and find some satisfaction that the lady inside was being warmed by the wood I had provided. I would sometimes imagine that I came to the house and sat in front of the fire with the lady—and she would rub aloe on my neck and talk with her gentle voice. But the master did not leave the estate that winter, and I was not summoned. Sometimes in the darkest parts of the night, I would hear the howl of the wolves, as if they were telling us that they were also heirs to these mountains and valleys.

"They have come before. They may come again," Quartus said as he handed me bramble to stack at the gate of the sheepfold. He looked up at the hill covered with snow. "Our pen is adequate to keep the sheep in. . . But it is not adequate to keep the wolves out. Yet we do what we can."

On the coldest nights of the winter, I would take my lambskin cover into the stall with the donkey and sleep beside him for warmth. He didn't seem to mind, but sometimes, during those long nights the dreams would possess me and the fire and the smoke and the screams would come back as if they were real—and I would awake kicking against the slaver in my dreams, and the donkey would move away.

"Helios' journey becomes longer each day," Quartus said, his words rising into a little white cloud in the frosty air as he spoke. I nodded as I squinted, looking toward the brilliantly clear sky. Some snow still held in the valleys and in the ravines, but the almond trees were beginning to put out small hard buds.

Two days later, however, the sky went dark in the middle of the day, and by late afternoon, huge flakes of snow began falling. "It is late for such snow," Quartus said. "But I have seen it before." All day and all night the snow fell. The next morning I stepped out of our hut into snow that came to my knees. The ducks squawked their complaints—the only sound in an otherwise completely silent world. I cleared the ground at the base of the pepper trees and threw the seeds for the ducks there. When I did, I heard a howl up in the woods.

That night Quartus shook me awake. "Wolves," he said, his face close to mine. "In the sheepfold. Put on your clothes. Light the torches."

The crunching snow chilled my feet as we stepped quickly down the path next to the olive trees. Each of us held two pine-pitch torches. The bleating of the panicked sheep filled the cold air. "The wolves fear fire," Quartus said. "It is the only thing they fear."

I held the torches above my head to keep the light from my eyes. A half-moon in a clear sky gave us good light as we ran down the hill. I was well ahead of Quartus when I came to the sheepfold. The dark shapes of the wolves, moving quickly, showed against the snow. The sheep clambered over each other at the back of the pen, the thump of their hooves and their high-pitched bleats mixing with the low snarls of the wolves.

Thick brush, higher than my head, surrounded the sheepfold, but the wolves had made a breach—wide enough only for a wolf, or a boy my size—to fit through. Two wolves had entered the pen. Three or four others were slinking around the edges, their heads low to the snow-covered ground, eyes sparkling as the torchlight hit them.

Quartus came behind me screaming, "Aiyyaa! Aiyyaa!" The volume of his voice surprised me. I had never before heard him shout. One of the wolves ran from the enclosure and gathered with the others, but one remained in the pen. "Malchus, move away! Give the wolf a place to escape."

Why I climbed over the brush I don't know, but when I did the flock shifted to escape the wolf and they knocked me to the ground. Their panicked bleating filled my ears. The torches fell into the mud on the ground. One sizzled out. The other sputtered and regained its blaze as I picked it up. I held it above my head. The flock had shifted again, and the wolf crouched, looking for a victim, but also keeping an eye on me and my torch. The wolf lunged into the flock. A lamb bleated in pain.

"Malchus, move away!" Quartus shouted.

The wolf was slinking slowly toward me, his head down, eyes fixed on me, the lamb twitching in his mouth. Its growl was deeper than I had imagined. Step by step he moved toward me, the growl deeper with each step.

"Malchus, move away!" Quartus called again.

Whether by fear or by recognition I was no match for the wolf, I stepped away from the opening. The wolf rushed through the gap to the flat field behind us. We heard the yelps of the other wolves as this one, the leader, rejoined them. The bleating of the lamb ceased.

At that moment the master arrived, a torch in one hand and a spear in the other. "Only one, master," Quartus said. "The wolves got only one."

The master said nothing. He walked over to the damaged fence to inspect it. The sheep were restless. They jumped about, running from corner to corner.

I stepped out toward the open field. The air was clear and cold, and the moon threw pure sparkling light on the snow-covered fields. The wolves, at the edge of the woods, snarled at each other as they argued over their meager meal. When I turned back, the master was making his way back up the hill to his house.

Quartus and I set about repairing the fence. "They may return," he said. "One small lamb does not fill the bellies of a wolfpack." We repaired the gap in the brush as best we could. A better repair would wait until the next day. I dragged dead olive limbs and we built a fire, which was soon blazing, then sat beside it, blankets pulled tightly around us.

"Not every winter do the wolves come," Quartus said. "Only when the snow is deep. When they come, they take some of the lambs. Last winter the master got a dog to warn us when the wolves came, but the wolves killed him."

We talked for a long time, and I threw more wood on the fire. Eventually we went silent and watched the fire, occasionally looking out over the field for signs of the wolves.

Looking into the fire, I recalled Quartus' words to the master: "Only one. They got only one." My mind went back to events I was trying to forget.

Fire and smoke. A bleating victim. A ravenous thief. Something deep in my spirit was offended by the wolves. But my young mind could not connect the events at the sheepfold with the events of my own life. It would be many years later when I understood why I hated the wolves so intensely—and why I wanted so desperately to kill them.

How long I slept I don't know. The fire's core crumbled, and its soft noise awakened me. Quartus was asleep, the blanket pulled over his head. I looked toward the field. Hardly fifty paces away I could see a dozen yellow eyes sparkling in the dark. I threw more brush on the fire and stoked it with a limb. In a moment the flame quickened, throwing light to a wide circle over the snow. The sheep in the pen stirred. I looked back to the field and the eyes were gone. But we could not keep a fire burning every night.

I moved closer to the fire for warmth and searched the star-sparkled sky for evidence the morning was coming. Some gray had thinned the black sky, promising a dawn within an hour. When morning finally came, and the fire had burned out, I walked into the field, where the lamb's blood stained the white snow.

That day Quartus and I cut dozens of saplings and had the donkey drag them to the pen, where we stacked them to make the enclosure higher and deeper than before.

Even so, less than a week later the wolves returned and stirred the sheep into a frenzy. As they fearfully pushed against the walls, they opened a place for the wolves. As Quartus and I arrived with our torches, the wolves were running away with their small prey in their mouths. Four lambs lost that night, we spent another long night around a fire beside the pen. In the end it was not our skill at building fences that saved the lambs—it was the melting of the snow and the wolves' return to the higher hills.

Spring came. Both we and the valley emerged from our lethargy. The snow melted, and the mud, for a while, made our work more difficult but eventually the ground dried and I followed behind Quartus as he plowed the fields behind the donkey.

That spring and summer passed, and I joined the rhythm of daily and seasonal life of the estate—which was punctuated by occasional trips by the master. He made these trips two or three times each year. Sometimes he was gone for two weeks or more. And as always, when the master was away, I became the guest of the lady in the house.

"Your name is Malchus," she told me, enunciating my name carefully. "That is your name."

I nodded that I understood. "Mal-chus."

"My husband must often go to Rome. Rome is far from here. He must ride two days to get there."

Again I nodded.

"I have never been to Rome myself," she added. "But I think it is the greatest city in the world. Perhaps you will go there one day." She smiled at me.

The lady's unintended prophecy would come true—but when it did, the sound of her lamentation would fill the valley.

I asked Quartus about the lady. We sat outside our hut, our cook-fire dwindling and the stars beginning to fill the clear sky above us. "She was betrothed to the master when she was fifteen years. She is more than twice that now. But she laments she has no children. It is her reproach." He pushed one of the burning sticks into the middle of the fire, throwing more light on our hut and against the underside of the leaves of the pepper trees that hung over it. "She is a gracious lady, and it is a sad thing she has no children." We both sat quietly. "You should be careful, Malchus," he said.

I looked at him to see what he meant.

"The master—" he started but could not finish.

I understood. Should the master discover the affection the lady had for me, it might not go well for me.

Even if I feared the master, I admired him, especially when I saw him atop his horse. He was not a large man, but the way he carried himself, especially his deportment as he sat in the saddle, demanded respect. His shoulders were square, and the bronze sword slapped against his hip as he rode. Anyone who saw him would agree he was an important man. And certainly a man who went to Rome must be important. My young mind wondered about Rome and what he and the other important men in the world talked about there.

The lady predicted I would one day go to Rome. Her prophecy would eventually be fulfilled, but my removal to Rome would bring her no happiness.

I was not often near enough to the master to see his face clearly, yet after a year I noticed a change—the contempt toward me had softened. Quartus confirmed what I thought. "You have proved yourself useful," he said. "You are doing good work, and the master no longer resents you."

I nodded to Quartus in acknowledgement.

"Still," his voice mischievous, "the lady overpaid when she bought you."

In those days the master's words to me were quick directions, "Stack the wood here." Or "Take the onions to the cook house." These commands were made with neither malice nor grace. He spoke to me the way he would have spoken to the donkey, if it had language. Because he owned me, it was in my best interest to obey quickly.

One day several men arrived at the house. They rode fine horses and wore fine clothes and the master greeted them at his door. "Landowners." Quartus said. "They own the estates around us. Our master has the largest estate, but all of them have estates of their own." I nodded that I understood and I wondered what these important men talked about inside the house.

Confined to the estate, I had a simple, understandable life. I cared for the ducks, the horse, the donkey, and the sheep. I tended the groves and gathered wood. I harvested the crops. Food, shelter, and security were provided. I was not mistreated. Yet for some reason, my spirit was not satisfied. The lady made me clothes—better than a slave should have worn—and when the master was away, she called me to the house to spend the day. But often in the evening, when I sat near the brooding fire next to our hut and looked into the embers, discontent filled my spirit.

I sensed I would be called away from this place. Where would that be? What is my destiny? Of that I had no sense.

Chapter 4
The Village

The nearest village to the estate, the site where I had been brought and the lady rescued me, and to which the master often went, lay just beyond a low strip of hills that rose up across the broad valley that extended from the estate. I sometimes saw smoke from the villagers' cooking fires rising above those low hills, and I wondered what life was like there.

During my second summer at the estate, after Quartus had been summoned by the master, he returned to our hut. "In two days we will go to the village."

He and I were busy those two days, bundling the sheep shearings and gathering the vegetables as we prepared the goods we would take to the market. The evening before we departed, a slanting sun threw the last light of the day through the leaves of the olive trees as we stacked bundles of wool into the wagon.

When we loaded, pressed down, and tied the last bundle, Quartus stood on the wagon wheel to look at the cart. "I think it will hold no more. It is all the donkey can bear."

"Let's have our dinner and get to bed," Quartus said. "We must depart two hours before sunrise."

I had difficulty finding sleep. My mind stirred with anticipation of the trip. Although I had no real memories of my arrival at the village two years earlier—still I knew it was the place where the lady purchased me. My troubled mind sought that memory—but could not find it. Eventually I went to sleep.

An hour before sunrise a low half-moon hung over the hills, its light thinning the black sky to gray as I cinched the donkey to the cart. Quartus and I walked beside the donkey, saying nothing to each other as we started down the road to the village. We passed a few huts made of rough stone and reeds with small gardens beside. Nearly naked children called to us as we passed. Honeybees buzzed in the clover. Starlings, seeing our approach, sought refuge in farther trees, showing the sheen of their wings as they banked away from us. The sun came late to the village as it was sheltered by the hills to the east, and we arrived as the first rays of the sun were finding the rooftops.

"The master will meet us at the metalsmith's shop," Quartus said. We pulled the wagon under a poplar tree beside the thin stream that ran alongside the village, unhitched the donkey, gave her some feed, and tied her to the tree.

"Follow me," Quartus said.

The village was just beginning to stir in the early morning as we walked toward the shop. My head went from side to side as I tried to take in the sights—various shops, made of stacked stone and thatched roofs, ringed the village square. A few weed patches grew in the tramped down dirt. Then I saw the posts. A muddled memory returned. Two years earlier I had been tied to one of them. The feelings came back. In my mind I could smell the odors and hear the sounds of two years ago.

"Come." Quartus jerked my arm. "You must follow me."

I was shaken out of my reverie, but I looked over my shoulder at the slave posts, the resurrected memories now fresh again.

The master had not yet arrived. The metalsmith added wood to his furnace. His thick arms were hairless, except for singed stubble. I was fascinated by the tools and the metal items hanging on the walls. "Greetings," he said, his face red from the fire. "Hello, Quartus. Welcome to my shop. That is a strong boy with you. Have you brought wool? My wife and my daughter must make me a coat for the winter."

"We have brought wool for your coat," Quartus confirmed.

"Good. Your master and I haggled about the trade yesterday. There in the corner are the plow points and bridle pieces we agreed on." He shook his head with a smile on his face. "Your master is a hard bargainer—but I need a coat for the winter, and his wool is the best. Come, sit. I will get water as we wait for him."

The master arrived, spoke with the metalsmith, and Quartus and I were directed to bring the bundles of wool from the wagon. As we did, I stopped briefly to look again at the slave posts.

"This will make a rich coat." The metalsmith inspected the wool. "I will put my wife and daughter to work right away."

The master nodded at the plow points and other items in the corner, and Quartus and I understood we were to take them to the cart. I insisted on carrying the plow points, trying to prove my strength. As we passed by the slave posts, I put my burden down for a moment and again looked at those ugly pieces of wood. The delirium, the confusion, the pain came back. Then—

Something hit my head. I crumpled to the ground, dazed. Next to me—a rock the size of my fist. I rose to my knees. The world was spinning. Blood dripped down my cheek. Then I heard the taunts, "Slave boy! Slave boy!"

I raised my head to see four boys, all laughing. They threw more rocks, one caught me in the leg, just below the knee, but the others missed. They continued their taunt, "Slave boy! Yellow-haired slave boy!"

Quartus came running. He stood between me and the boys, shouting at them. They smirked and one threw another rock that skipped by his feet. Out of rocks, they sauntered away, laughing.

Quartus stooped to inspect my head. He used the edge of his shirt to press against the wound on my head. "Come." He helped me to my feet. "We will go home."

We bumped along in the cart for a long time saying nothing until I broke the silence. "Why are some men slaves?"

Quartus did not answer my question. "Let me see your head."

I leaned over and he looked.

"The bleeding has stopped. The lady will have medicine."

We bumped along for a few more minutes. I repeated my question, "Why are some men slaves?"

Quartus took a deep breath. "Some questions do not have answers, Malchus." It seemed that was all he would say, but then, "I think your question is not '*Why* are some men slaves?' but 'Why is *Malchus* a slave?' He looked at me. "Do not think I have not turned that question over in my mind. But I no longer ask it because I do not know the answer." He looked ahead and paused. "And even if I had an answer, what would it change? If I had an answer, would I no longer be a slave? Would you?" He took a deep breath. "We would still be slaves. Asking questions does not change anything. So I quit asking the question. You would be wise to do the same."

We did not speak again until we returned to the estate. The lady fretted over me and washed my hair and put some potion on my wound. She kissed my forehead a dozen times before I returned to the hut.

Winter passed with few events although the wolves came again. Quartus and I had buttressed the sheepfold, yet the wolves still caught two lambs one night and another a few nights later. That spring, after Quartus took the almonds and the onions to market, the master purchased another donkey and another cart.

"Our farm is thriving," Quartus told me. "And you are part of that success. I think the master realizes that now."

In the fall, as the days grew shorter and the leaves on the almond trees began to turn crisp and brown, Quartus returned from the master's house. "We will go to the village. And we will take two carts." He looked at me sternly. I knew he was thinking of the boys who had taunted me. "It is the autumn market. It falls on the day after the first full moon of the autumn. It is the biggest market day of the year. The master wishes that both carts be filled."

For the next three days we gathered the produce we would take to the market. Each night I looked up and watched as the cheese-colored moon swelled toward fullness. The night before we were to go to the village, a clear dry sky invited the moonlight to fill the valley. I was filled with equal parts anticipation and dread.

"Malchus, wake up." It was well before daybreak when Quartus jostled me. We made the final preparations by moonlight, and I hitched the donkeys to the carts.

"Put the saddle and bridle on the mare," Quartus said. "The master will ride ahead of us."

The mare seemed reluctant to be put to work this early and would not cooperate when I first brought the bridle, but I soon soothed her and cinched the saddle. Quartus walked her up to the house. Lamps were lit inside, and I could see the silhouette of the lady as she moved through the house, preparing the items her husband would need for his trip.

The master came out, laid a saddlebag on the mare, and mounted. The lady followed him out and said good-bye. The master spoke briefly to Quartus before he tapped the mare and started down the path past me toward the village. The lady stood in the doorway. I watched her as she watched me.

I did not understand it then, but I do now. Of course she paid too much for me. Her longing for a son paired mine for a mother but I was a slave, not a son—yet she also was a slave, a slave to her husband. Her master and mine were the same. Our mutual master was never cruel, yet both of us belonged entirely to him, and we both understood that.

Quartus and I threw a few more bundles of wool on the carts. I tightened the cords on both carts and followed him as he led the cart in front. After an hour or so we stopped to eat duck eggs, pickled olives, and flatbread. "We will do our business quickly," he said, "and be back at our hut before dark." I knew by the way he spoke that he was preparing me to be careful while we were in the village.

The master was waiting for us when we arrived. I tethered the donkeys near the master's mare, under the poplar tree I remembered from the previous year. Dozens of wagons and many more horses and donkeys were tethered in the same area. Men and boys unloaded their carts and carried baskets of goods into the village. The master gave Quartus instructions as to where to distribute the items on the cart. The metalsmith and the leathersmith were to receive most of the items, the master having made the barter arrangements already. Quartus chose a route that took us behind the shops and away from the village square. That route required a few extra steps, but I knew his purpose. I made several trips to these shops and returned to one of the carts with the metalwork and leatherwork that had been agreed upon. Before the sun had reached its peak, our carts were empty of what we brought, and the metal and leather we had traded for filled only a part of one of the carts.

"We will depart soon," Quartus said firmly. "But the master needs his saddle repaired. Take it to the leather shop, but be quick about it. I must stay with the cart. In this crowd there are surely thieves."

I hoisted the saddle on my shoulder and began walking, but I did not follow the route we had taken earlier. I went instead on the street that led to the square. The place was full of more people than I had ever seen in all my life. I kept a watch for the boys I had seen the previous year but did not see them.

I passed by the wine shop and stopped to look inside. A great number of men were congregated there, and I saw my master's back as he sat at the largest table. Three other men, all landowners like the master, sat at the table with him, while a dozen more men stood around.

I knew the master was an important man, and I took some satisfaction in his status—that even though I was a slave, I was a slave in a respected household. But despite my pride in my master, I knew I should not linger at the doorway of the wine shop. He would not take kindly to my loitering.

The leathersmith greeted me as I entered. He took the saddle and turned it over to see the place where the stitching had come loose. He nodded as he saw the problem and took the saddle to his bench to repair it. The shop was filled with stacks of leather, some cut into various widths and lengths, dozens of knives and other metal tools on the walls and on the benches. I wandered around the shop, inspecting the tools of this man's trade as he threaded an awl and replaced the flawed stitching. The job took only a few minutes, and soon I had the saddle on my shoulder, and I was back in the street.

The wine shop was empty—which I thought odd. Up the street a crowd had gathered in the city center. I was curious and I picked up my pace to make my way toward the gathering. Everyone in the village, it seemed, had assembled there with a great deal of jostling and conversation. I stood on my tiptoes to try to see what was creating such interest, but I could not see anything, so I threaded my way under the elbows of the crowd to see what had created such interest among the villagers.

As I emerged on the inside of the circle, my body went cold.

The slaver.

Hardly five paces away he stood. A boy whose hair was the color of mine, and perhaps a couple of years older, was tied to the post, the same post on which I had been tied three years earlier. The sounds and images returned—my mothers' screams . . . the leather bag . . . the beatings . . . the trek through the hills . . . the cord around my neck.

"A strong boy!" the slaver said in his hoarse voice, trying to make himself heard to the crowd. With the end of his rope he lightly slapped the boy's legs and arms to verify his claim. "From the north," the slaver shouted, pointing up toward the higher mountains beyond the village. Then he took the boy's hair and raised his head for all to see his face. If there had been any defiance in the boy when he was taken from his village, it was gone now. Nothing but terror and fear remained.

I trembled. My legs went numb.

The slaver circled around the crowd, his cord in his hand, searching for a face that showed interest. He came in my direction. I put my head down. He went by me—and then turned back.

I kept my head down. His feet came in front of me. He took my hair and raised my head. My hands went unconsciously to my neck. His face brightened. "I remember this one." He smiled as he looked around. "I remember this one! This little yellow-hair gave me some trouble. I had to use my cord on this one."

He released my hair and took a cord from his waist. He made the motions of winding it around my neck—and then throwing the cord over a branch and pretending to pull me into the air. He pointed at me and then played out the scene, acting as if he were a twitching boy, tongue askew, eyes rolling, legs shuddering, and gasping for air.

The memory returned—my hanging suspended in the air, the cord choking the life out of me.

The men laughed. He pointed at me again and repeated his performance, thrashing wildly this time, contorting his face as if he were strangling and bawling with great exaggeration. Many of the crowd had come directly from the wine shop, wine gourds still in their hands. Their drunkenness gave them greater appreciation of the performance. The laughter became louder. Some pointed at me as they laughed. The slaver nodded to acknowledge their laughter. He pointed at me again and then thrust his hips obscenely, mimicking the high-pitched screams of a woman. The men laughed even louder. He said something which I did not understand, but the crowd laughed again. A coarse man, reeking of sour wine, leaned down to me and shouted in my ear, "He says your mother screamed when he took her."

The laughter rose again. A sickness swelled inside me. A quiver ran through my bowels. My knees lost their strength. I felt like I was tethered to the post again.

A hand caught my collar. Quartus' thin arm was stronger than I imagined. With his good arm, he pulled me away. With his other, with difficulty, he picked up the saddle which I had dropped. The crowd, still laughing, made an opening as we left.

He put me in the wagon where I sat numb while he hitched the donkeys, tying a rope from the first cart to the second donkey. Then quickly he saddled the mare, leaving it for the master.

"You must forget this," he said as he took the reins and tapped the donkey to put the cart in motion. I said nothing. "You must forget this," he repeated. I said nothing. I wanted to cry, but something deep inside me instructed me otherwise. I had made a promise to never again let the slaver make me cry.

As we edged out of the village, the sun was sitting, throwing purple and pink against the undersides of the hovering clouds. I kept my head down and Quartus threw his cloak over me. Moments later the master came up behind us on his mare and he trotted alongside us for a moment, saying nothing, and then he tapped the mare's neck and went ahead.

Quartus made soup when we returned to the hut, but I could not eat it.

The screams came back that night. To them was now added laughter.

"I have breakfast for you," Quartus said as he stood over my bed. The sun was well above the horizon. Never had I slept this late before, yet I wanted to sleep more. Sleep had given me some respite, but now the humiliation all came back—the obscene gestures of the slaver, the crowd's coarse laughter, my inability to respond.

"After you eat, feed the ducks," Quartus said.

I did not reply. I did not speak all that day or the next. Quartus allowed me my silence. He carried on his regular conversation as if everything were normal, perhaps for my sake. After that, Quartus and I never spoke of the incident.

For many days the image of the slaver mimicking those screams, and the crowd laughing, haunted me. And the screams returned in the night. I would awake in my bed, screaming, as Quartus restrained me.

As time passed, the sense of humiliation began to subside, and the nightmares became less frequent. I worked in rhythm with the farm— planting, weeding, harvesting. The seasons passed along predictably, and Quartus and I fulfilled our duties. Sometimes in the evenings, as we sat on our stools outside the hut, our fire dwindling, my mind would go back to the events in the village and the slaver. But at those times Quartus sensed my mood and would comment about the day's work to distract me.

"You are now the taller one," Quartus said one morning as we pulled weeds from around the onions. "I suppose it is true what they say about the north—taller trees, taller mountains, taller men."

I said nothing at the time, but that night Quartus and I talked about the north. "The Romans say the men from the north are yellow-haired savages. Fierce fighters they say, but not well organized. About the time you were born, however, the northerners gave the Romans the greatest defeat they had ever faced. Fifteen thousand Roman soldiers died in one battle. But the emperor sent his general Germanicus to subdue the northerners. He was successful. The alliances that the tribes had formed have not held up. The Romans have been able to defeat them."

Quartus' report again put me in mind of my origins. Was my village made up of "yellow-haired savages"? I wondered.

The figs ripened, and I took great effort to pluck every one of every cluster. "What is it to me," Quartus admonished me as he stood below, "if you fall and break your neck? It will not be because you did not hear my warning. Just be careful not to fall on me. The master needs at least one slave to feed his animals." The fig trees were the tallest trees on the estate, some of them six men high, and I often extended myself on a high wobbly branch. It would waver back and forth as I reached for the sticky fruits to put in the bag slung over my shoulder, but I enjoyed being high in the tree and the challenge of gathering the highest cluster. And there was a view to be gained from that elevation. In midsummer the fields had begun to burn brown in places, but green ribbons—beeches and poplars lining the streams—curved through the valley. The orchards and vineyards of the adjoining estates formed straight lines and squares and rectangles to contradict the curves of the streams. I would sometimes watch as great towering clouds, white and gray and black, swelled up on the horizon, and I wondered what world lay under those clouds.

"You can come down, Malchus." Quartus broke my reverie. "No fig in the grove has escaped you."

I looked below me, hesitant to leave my perch. The olive trees trembled in a late afternoon breeze, their silver undersides sparkling as the wind moved down the valley as if an invisible god had waved his hand along the terrain.

"We must get these figs in the baskets. *I* will take them to the village tomorrow." I took his sense. He would go alone to the village.

With the last light of the day, we filled the cart with figs and covered the baskets with straw to keep the bees away. "Never have we had a full cart of figs," Quartus said. "The master will be pleased."

If the master was pleased, he did not say so. He came to see Quartus off the next morning but said nothing to either of us.

The grapes turned purple, and we cut them and put them in baskets, and again Quartus went to the village alone to deliver them to the market. During those late summer days, I would often look up from the vineyard and see the lady standing outside the house looking down in our direction, her black hair covering her shoulders, her skirt blowing in the afternoon breeze.

Shortly after the grape harvest, the master was summoned to Rome. A few other landowners, four of them, joined him for the journey. They seemed somber as they departed.

"Germanicus is dead," Quartus told me as the riders departed. "I heard the news in the village. There is suspicion that he was poisoned. He had become too popular among the people, it is said, and his enemies had him killed. That is the rumor. The senate has called for the landowners to come to Rome."

The master was gone ten days. Part of each day I spent with the lady at the house. She had a wax tablet and stylus, and she taught me letters, sometimes standing over me guiding my hand as her black hair fell down along my cheeks. She let me keep the tablet when her husband returned, and I kept it beside my cot, practicing those letters over and over. She sometimes sang when I was in the house. I cannot remember the words of her songs, but they were plaintive songs, sung naturally by one who knew heartache.

Sometimes even now, I will catch the lilt of her song when a certain melancholy note on the kithara is strummed, and I will remember her. Her singing will always live in my memory.

Chapter 5

The Bow

We cut the barley under the olive trees, now nearly white from the summer's heat, tying the stalks into bundles to dry. That night as we ate our dinner beside our hut, Quartus looked up at the roof of our hut. "The rains will come soon. We should replace our roof. If we fail to do so, we will sleep in wet beds this winter. Now that the olives are gathered, we can make that our task."

So we did. The next two days we cut and stripped young pines at the edge of the forest. They would replace the beams in our hut that had gone rotten. We gathered baskets and baskets of thatch that we stacked near the hut. When Quartus finally decided we had enough materials, he said, "Tomorrow—if the weather is favorable—we will tear off the old roof and replace it.

The next morning the sky was clear. "Let us begin," Quartus said. I climbed to the top of our hut and began pulling the old thatch off and throwing it down. Each piece threw out a small explosion of dust as it hit the ground. Quartus started a fire with some dead olive branches and he dropped the thatch onto the flames where it smoldered, raising thick gray smoke. Bugs tried to escape the inferno, but Quartus swept them back into the fire.

I continued ripping the thatch from the roof. Working my way to the outer edge of the stable area of our hut, I found a curved limb with notches on each end. "What is this?"

Quartus looked up. "Hmm—my old bow. I had forgotten about it. Before I hurt my arm I used it to kill rabbits. Look again. There may be a quiver with a few arrows in it."

I scraped through the loose thatch and found a moldy leather quiver. The shafts of the arrows were rotten, and the arrow points were covered with rust.

"Bring those down," Quartus said. "You should learn the use of that bow."

Quartus used his cloak to wipe the accumulated dust from the bow. He held it up and looked at it carefully. "Eight years—could it have been that long?—since this bow has been strung. I cannot claim I was a good archer, even before my injury. But a few rabbits came to the master's table. You have stronger arms. You will do better than I. But for now we need to get a roof over our heads before dark."

I worked especially hard that day, and we completed the new roof after sunset. As Quartus prepared our dinner, I brought the bow near the fire to inspect it.

"I fashioned it myself," Quartus said. "I made it from a pine bough from the edge of the woods." He nodded toward the woods to indicate the direction. "You would not want to go to battle with it," he chuckled. "But it was good enough for killing rabbits."

He took the bow and flexed it gently over his thigh. "Still has some bend in it. We will need to make a string—and find some reeds for arrows." He pulled an arrow point off its crumbling shaft. "These arrow points can be cleaned up."

After we had eaten, Quartus showed me how to use a flat-edged rock to clean the rust from the arrow points. Using the fire as my light, I worked on the points well after Quartus had gone to bed. The next morning he was surprised to see a row of six sharp arrow points lying beside the ashes of last night's fire.

"Some reeds grow in the pool of water that gathers in the bend of the stream near the place where the wild animals get their water." Quartus told me. "You know the place. Look for the straightest reeds you can find. Bring those back and we will see what we can do. I will work on a string while you are gone."

Within two hours I was back at the hut with an armload of reeds. For the next several days I used my time fashioning arrows. Quartus showed me how to cut the notch in the thick end of the reed, how to bind the arrow points to the tip, and how to attach the feathers. We had no shortage of feathers with all the ducks around our hut. "The feathers make the arrows go straight," Quartus explained.

I looked at him oddly as if he had made an incantation of magic.

"Do not ask me to explain it."

While I worked on the arrows, Quartus twined a string from goat-hair, using a wooden spindle he had made. I was impatient, but he seemed in no hurry, spinning the threads into a tight string, measuring ever so often to see if it came to the length he desired. Eventually it was finished to his satisfaction. He tied a loop in one end and slipped it over the notch in the bow. Then bending the bow to create tension, he marked the other end of the string and tied another loop.

Finished, he held it up. "Let us see if you can shoot an arrow."

I tried to remain patient as he demonstrated how to notch the arrow on the string and how to place my fingers on the string to pull it back. Eventually he stepped back and allowed me to try one arrow. I released the string. I screamed in pain and dropped the bow. The arrow had gone only about twenty paces, and the string had scraped my left wrist, causing a red whelp.

Quartus bent over in laughter. When he finally composed himself, he told me as I rubbed my wrist, "Ah, we forgot one piece of the equipment—a guard for your wrist." As I sat sulking, thinking this effort was a failure, Quartus took some lambskin, and with his knife he fashioned a wrist guard, which he tied around the inside of my wrist.

The rest of that day I spent shooting the arrows. I had no particular target. I simply shot the arrows into the field and then retrieved them. As the day wore on, I was able to shoot the arrows much farther than when I began. Darkness finally made me stop. My fingers were burning, and I still had a sore place on my wrist, but I was fascinated by this new object.

For the next several weeks, as the days shortened and the air cooled, I did my chores more quickly so I could use the last glimmer of light to shoot the arrows. Quartus bound some flax stalks into a tight bundle to serve as a target, and soon I found I could place the arrows in a tight pattern in the middle of the target.

Then, one afternoon as the early winter wind was dropping into our valley, I walked down to the edge of the onion field and within just a few minutes, I had two plump rabbits on the end of my arrows. Walking quickly back to our hut, I proudly held up the two rabbits for Quartus to see. He smiled and took the two animals up to the master's house.

I had become a bowman.

I practiced shooting the bow at every opportunity and I spent much of my time improving my arrows. I learned how to smooth the shafts of the arrows and how to fletch the duck feathers to improve the accuracy and power of my shooting. I added a great number of rabbits—and an occasional grouse—to my master's table and then in the first spring after I had obtained the bow, I emerged from the forest with a doe around my shoulder.

The master said nothing to me about the deer, but that evening Quartus told me, "The master has instructed me to obtain more arrow points from the metalsmith."

I smiled at this news.

A week later Quartus and the master made the trip to the market, but I stayed behind. That evening, when they returned, Quartus showed me the bag. Inside were two dozen new arrow points. I took them eagerly and began attaching them to the shafts I had prepared earlier. I worked by firelight until Quartus chided me and made me go to bed.

The bow and the arrows became my obsession. When daylight allowed, I practiced shooting. In the evening I sharpened the points, smoothed the shafts, and fletched the feathers, often working by firelight until the last embers faded.

Every day at daybreak, I took my bow and my arrows to the edges of the fields. I learned how to move quietly and how to sit without moving. I learned the habits of the animals as I lived among them, sitting patiently in the shadows as I waited for my prey.

"Your shoulders show your efforts with the bow," Quartus said one evening. It was true. My shoulders and my chest had strengthened as a result of my shooting. "Your muscles could draw a stronger bow. We should look for a new one."

Quartus and I searched the woods until we found a pine branch with a natural curve. I climbed the tree and chopped it from the trunk, while Quartus sat in the pine needles below and offered advice, "Cut underneath the branch first. Then chop from the top." In a few minutes it fell to the forest floor, and I scrambled down the trunk. We stripped it and dragged it back to the hut, where for the next three days we worked on fashioning the new bow. Quartus knew this craft and I watched him carefully. This was a skill I wanted. The next time a bow was fashioned, I would need to know how to do it. When it was finally ready and Quartus let me string it, I pulled it back with great satisfaction. Yes, this bow would have greater power.

I became a hunter.

Almost every day I was in the field or in the woods. Although the master never spoke to me directly, he seemed pleased with my role of keeping fresh game on his table. And when there was a surplus, which was not unusual, the master allowed Quartus and me to share in the bounty.

"You eat like three men," Quartus said to me one evening as I sucked the last bit of meat from a joint of a deer I had killed that morning. "And you are growing rapidly."

The woods became my home. Every hill that surrounded the estate became familiar to me as I sought prey. Often as I sat with my back against a tree, waiting, I had time to think. I often thought about my odd status—a slave who had the freedom to hunt in the woods. And often my thoughts would go back to my origin—where I came from and what had happened to my family. Even more often my thoughts would go to the village—and the humiliation I endured there. A tension would course through my body. Quartus had told me I must forget that incident, but I could not. It was burned into my memory, just as the memory of the slaver hoisting me in the air with his cord.

That summer Quartus showed me how to rob a beehive I had discovered in an opening of a tall chestnut tree. Using one of our olive-gathering ladders, I smoked the bees and dropped the honeycomb to Quartus who gathered it in a basket at the base of the tree. I yelped with every bee sting I endured, which gave Quartus great delight, but when I climbed down, Quartus scooped some of the drippings into his mouth and screamed as one of the insects stung his tongue. My laughter was hearty, and I realized I had not laughed in many weeks. But Quartus' tongue swelled so that he could hardly talk for the rest of the day. I ate all the honey cakes the lady left for us the next day, chewing them slowly as Quartus watched.

Quartus prevented me from making any trips to the village that year, but each time he returned I looked at him, and without saying a word, he knew the question I was asking him: *Did you see the slaver?*

He would shake his head and dismiss my unspoken inquiry. But one evening when he returned, I could tell by his face that he had seen the slaver. He tried to avoid me, but I persisted. "Did you see the slaver?" I asked him directly.

"You must forget the slaver," he answered.

I took his forearm in my hand, and he winced. I had grown stronger. I released the pressure. "I'm sorry."

"One boy," he finally admitted. "He had one boy—a strong boy. He was sold quickly to a planter who resides two days' journey from here."

He looked at me directly as if to say: *How has this information helped you?*

I had the answer to my question, but to what purpose? The information was of no value to me. If the slaver had had two dozen boys and sold them all, what would that mean to me? But still I wanted to know. I could not help myself. What I learned served only to make me angrier, and what purpose could there be to that? But somehow I knew—something in me sensed it—I would see the slaver again.

Every day I went to the woods. Sometimes I tracked my prey, but mostly I learned their habits and how to wait patiently without movement, sometimes enduring hordes of gnats in my ears and nose, until the animal came within range. I learned how to silently nock the arrow and silently draw and release it toward the target. Not all my arrows found their target, but most did, and I improved my skill with every season.

I grew taller. My shoulders strengthened. I outgrew the bow Quartus had fashioned a year earlier. "You need a new bow," he said. In the stream that runs down the edge of our valley I found a pliant aspen limb. I cut it and carried it back to the hut. Over the next few days I worked it into a bow. Quartus sometimes made a comment or a recommendation, but I was determined to master this craft myself. As the bow came into shape, I threaded goat-hair into a string, a tedious task, but the new string gave my arrows greater range and greater power. And I had a limitless supply of duck feathers, ideal for fletching. I learned how to trim and curve them so that the arrows stayed true in flight. I scratched my name, as the lady had taught me, into the bow handle.

"Will you soon attack the Persians?" Quartus teased me as he saw the dozens of arrows I stacked against our hut. I said nothing and went back to sharpening my points.

My master seemed pleased, in his own way, at the game I brought to him, and he made sure that Quartus and I had our share. Late one afternoon in midsummer when the fields were full of bees, and the grapes were turning purple and leaving the thick aroma of their sweetness in the air, I came from the forest with a doe over my neck. The master happened to be at the back of the house. He nodded his approval as I laid the doe on the porch and then bowed to him.

When I raised my head the master had an odd look on his face. At first I did not understand the concern I saw. Then I realized—I was the taller of the two. I had not stood close to him for a few months, and we were both surprised at the difference of stature. He made a motion of dismissal to me, and I went back to Quartus, still thinking about the master's reaction.

A few weeks later, as the first dry leaves began to slip from the tree limbs and drift to the earth, I sat in the fork of a solid oak that leaned over a meager stream whose faint gurgle helped conceal any noise I might make. Shade flowers, like small white stars, grew among the rocks. I had planned this day for two weeks. I waited for a prey that I had watched all summer—a big sow, whose eight piglets were now weaned. I knew her habits and I knew this place, her favorite wallowing spot. When I heard her grunts in the brush, I readied an arrow. As she neared the stream, she sniffed suspiciously, her pink nose twitching as she tested the air. Her ears quickened as she heard the hiss of the arrow. Her squeal filled the forest when it hit her neck. She bolted, kicking leaves and dirt, but the second arrow was in her ribs before she could reach the thick brush. She fell on her side and her legs twitched briefly before she went still.

I hoisted the carcass in the air with a rope over the oak limbs to keep her from scavengers, and then went quickly back to the farm to bring the donkey. Even for me this was a prey too heavy to carry.

When Quartus and I returned with the sow, the master was waiting for us, and he nodded to me in acknowledgement.

The master called for a celebration. He summoned some of the other estate owners and their families to join in the feast, and they ate outside near a roaring fire, laughing and drinking wine. Quartus and I ate our own plentiful portions at our hut, just close enough to hear the laughter of the group. As the dinner party went inside, we were summoned to put out the fire. The lady was the last to go inside, and before she did—looking first to be sure her husband did not see—she kissed my cheek.

As we pulled the logs from the fire's core, Quartus said, "You have great favor with the master. There has been no pork on his table in many years."

I nodded but took the acknowledgement with little joy.

I should have been more satisfied. No slave in the empire had a better life, I told myself. But I was a slave, and the discontent of that awareness continued to tug at my soul. I would never be able to alter my position. I knew that. Yet something in me rebelled against my slavery. It was a disquiet I could not dismiss.

Chapter 6
The Wolves

"The snow is early this year," Quartus remarked as he handed me newly cut pine limbs to fortify the sheep enclosure. I nodded as I pushed one of the limbs into a gap. It was midday, but the sun hid behind the thin clouds, its rays too feeble to give us warmth. Quartus' breath hung in the cold air. The valley was ankle deep with snow, and across the valley tree limbs drooped under the white weight.

"They will come again," he went on, looking at the woods. "Just like last winter . . . they will come again."

I tightened the branches with some aspen strips but said nothing. Quartus was right. Over the past two days I had seen their tracks in the woods and at its edge. For three nights, while Quartus slept, I had heard their calls, as if they were warning us. Yes, they would come again.

"We must keep vigil," he went on. "We will need to bring more wood for the fire."

I nodded in agreement, but I had a different plan that would not require a fire. I would protect the sheep. And I would do it alone.

I will not be satisfied with keeping the wolves away. I will rid our valley of them. After tonight they will not come again to steal the lambs away from the sheepfold. After tonight, those wolves that remain will need to find other prey.

I looked down at the sheep. They feasted on chopped barley we had thrown to them, oblivious to anything other than the meal they were consuming. Somehow, looking at the innocent sheep made me hate the wolves even more.

Tonight will be the night. Somehow I sensed it.

A thousand, thousand stars dotted the clear cold sky when I slipped away from the hut. Quartus, as always, slept deeply and had not heard me put on my clothes and take the bow and the quiver from the pegs on the wall. As I walked down the incline toward the sheepfold, a three-quarter moon slipped above the trees across the valley, throwing cold clear light on the snow-covered field. That light would be helpful.

I settled myself against the stacked stones in front of the sheepfold with my back against the stones, and looked across the narrow valley from which the wolves would have to come. I pulled my blanket across my shoulders—my muscles would need to be warm when it was time to draw the bow. With the bow across my lap I pulled my woolen cap tightly against my head but kept my ears uncovered. An icy wind, like probing fingers, filtered through the trees, seeking a gap in my cloak. My ears stung in the cold, but I did not cover them. The cap made me think of my mistress. It had been more than a month since I had seen her, at least closely. A small wisp of smoke from the chimney rose up and disappeared in the vast, cold sky. The lady was warm and secure.

But this was not a time to think about the mistress. I scanned the tree line across the valley. Nothing. I put my hands inside my cloak to keep my fingers warm and nimble.

The crusted snow sparkled as the moon rose higher, but there was no sound anywhere on the earth, and there was no movement at the edge of the woods. My feet grew numb. I stood to let my legs gain some relief. The world was without color—white moon, white snow, black sky, black shadows. The sheep stirred in the fold as I moved around. But the fathomless shadows of the trees lay fixed and unmoving across the flat snow. The moon threw a spidery shadow on our hut as it filtered through the bare pepper trees.

Across the field a pine branch cracked under the weight of the snow. Then the world went quiet again.

The sheep sensed the wolves before I did.

They stirred, shuffling their hooves, bleating some complaints. Slowly I stood and looked at the white and black world. Were there wolves in the shadows? I wasn't sure—but then I heard their snuffling and growling across the crusty snow. I squinted. Dark shadows across the white snow. I tried to count them. Seven, eight, maybe nine in the pack—they moved erratically across the snow, coming closer, not in a direct path, dispersing and then congregating again. The snow crunched under their paws. The sheep's fearful bleats grew louder. I notched an arrow. Four more were propped on the stones beside me. Another eight were in the quiver. I stood . . . slowly. I braced myself. The wolves were now close enough that I could make them out individually. The pack leader was in front, moving back and forth, his nose close to the snow. The others, including the matriarch, suspicious and wary, followed behind him, all sniffing the air.

They came closer. Their sniffing became clearer. Their shapes became more distinct. I kept my eyes on the big male in front. He looked like the same one I had seen in the pen two winters earlier. *Did he remember me?* He was now close enough that I could distinguish his sniffing from the others. He paused, raised his head. Behind him the pack whimpered. They had caught my scent. Growls, like deep thunder from a distant mountain, replaced the sniffing. The deepest growl formed in the belly of the leader. He paced back and forth as if to gain courage. The others joined him. The sheep were now in panic, running back and forth against the walls of their enclosure.

The big wolf dropped his head. Cautiously, tentatively he took a step toward me. He bared his teeth as he growled. Just behind him his queen held the same posture, head low, teeth bared. The other wolves whimpered and growled nervously as they moved back and forth behind their two leaders.

The leader's growl became louder, his warning more insistent. He was now close enough that I could see his eyes—and his eyes were on me. His body was coiled, every muscle in tension. He took another step. With my thumb and finger I slowly pulled back the string. The growl grew louder. He snapped his teeth as he came even closer. I pulled the string to my cheek and released the arrow. The sounds were clear in the cold air—a twang, a hiss, and a soft thud. The arrowpoint caught the wolf in his neck. He screamed in surprise. He fell in the snow, yelping in agony. He tried to regain his feet, but fell again, yelping even louder. His queen whined and paused to look at her mate. That was her mistake. My second arrow caught her in the ribs and the point went through her. She took two steps and fell also, her screams joining those of her mate. The other wolves, now confused, began moving away slowly—one of them too slowly, for my next arrow caught him in the hip as he started to run. He yelped as the point caught him, but he did not fall.

The sheep were now in full panic, bleating and running back and forth, trying to escape the fold. Down the hill, torches came my way. The master arrived first, then Quartus. Holding their torches over their heads, they stood over the two wolves, their mouths open in the snow, their red blood staining the field. "Quartus," I said, "help me drag these away. The sheep will not rest until their scent is gone."

We tied cords around their hind legs and began dragging them up the hill toward our hut, a job made easier by the snow on the ground. As we went back down the slope we saw the master's torch at the edge of the field. He stood over the third wolf, now dead, a final blow dispatched by the master, the body outlined in blood.

"Three. You killed three," Quartus said.

The master said nothing.

I cinched some string to the legs of this wolf, smaller than the leader and the queen, and started up the hill, throwing the carcass on the two others. Quartus had remained with the sheep, trying to calm them, but the master followed me and stood over the three dead wolves with his torch, looking at them carefully. Their eyes were open and their tongues hung out of their mouths over their big teeth. And then the master looked at me. The torchlight illuminated his face. I cannot be sure what I saw in his eyes.

What was in the master's face? Was it respect? Respect that I had killed three wolves? Was it fear? Fear that a boy in his charge, a boy almost a man, could kill three wolves? Or was it both?

We dressed the skins and cured them. The master gave the smallest one to me. He kept two for him and the lady, to grace their bed. But I gave mine to Quartus. It gave his older bones the warmth needed at night.

The wolves did not return that winter.

Chapter 7

Return to the Village

Did I have a premonition? Perhaps.

Two years had passed since I had seen the slaver. But today as Quartus and I jostled along in the cart on our way to the village, I was especially quiet. Would I see him this autumn market day? That was the question that kept me quiet.

"Have you nothing to say today?" Quartus asked.

I shook my head. I had spent the morning loading onions onto the cart, saying little, and I still had nothing to say.

The carts jostled along. Bay bushes and arbutus overgrew the edges of the cart path at places and tugged at the wheels. At the places where the path opened, cyclamen and iris found sustenance around the rock edges, splattering their pink and purple through the meadows. Mustard bushes, waist high and higher, put out butter-yellow blossoms on their fragile stalks.

Would this be the day I would see him again? For some reason I thought this was the day.

The familiar clatter and clanging of the metalsmith's hammers filled the air as I approached the shop. The fire from his forge warmed my face as I entered. "Onions for arrow points—that's the bargain," the metalsmith told me cheerfully as I brought the first of several baskets to his shop. He took a rag from his belt and wiped the sweat from his face. "Here they are. Fresh and shiny. I hope they find their targets." He opened the bag and poured them on the table.

I nodded my head in appreciation as I examined the new pieces. Ten triangles of polished metal, more valuable to me than pieces of jewelry, lay on the table. I looked at the metalsmith, asking with my eyes if I could touch them.

"Take them. They are yours. At least they will be," he said with a laugh, "when you bring me the rest of my onions!"

I ran my thumb over the edge of the blades. "Very sharp." I smiled. "I will do my best to make sure these points find their target."

"If what your master says about you is true, that will not be a problem," the metalsmith answered. "He says you are the best archer ever known in this area."

The report intrigued me. The master had never complimented my skill.

"And I can see," the metalsmith added, "how your shoulders make you able to drive an arrow through a sow-pig. What is your age, Malchus? Already you are half a head taller than any man in the village."

"According to the lady, I am in my seventeenth year. I . . ."

A commotion stirred in the street.

I stepped out of the shop, one of the arrow points still in my hand.

The slaver.

His most recent raid had been successful. Two boys, brothers for certain, were tethered behind his horse. His two minions grinned at the crowd as they slapped the boys on their legs with switches.

The slaver seemed pleased with himself. He sat proudly astride his horse—a little heavier in his saddle, having eaten well, but the skin on his face sagged. I could see the folds in his jowls. The slaver had aged.

The crowd, as always, was fascinated by this spectacle as they followed the procession. Village boys jeered at the boys tethered behind the horse. Others followed as the slaver and his troupe headed toward the town center.

Villagers gathered to gain the best view of the procession. The metalsmith's hammer stopped, and the sound of the horse's hooves filled the void. The slaver came nearer. I could make out yellow and purple that had collected under his eyes. In a few seconds he would be beside me. How would I respond? The humiliation of our last encounter came back to me. The laughter of the crowd came back to me. The same men who had laughed before were now around me again.

But I was different.

Maybe I was not a man—but neither was I a boy—not the boy who had cringed before the slaver.

A hundred times I had asked myself how I would react when this moment came. I surprised myself by feeling confident.

The horse and the slaver came closer.

There was some movement on the opposite side of the street as the crowd jostled about. It was Quartus. He was trying to get through the crowd—to get to me. I turned my eyes away from him. The horse and the rider were too near. He would not have time to cross the street. And this time I did not want his help.

A sense of defiance swelled up inside me. I stepped into the street—in the path of the slaver's horse. The slaver did not notice me at first. He was waving to the crowd and pointing to his captives, but then he turned and saw me. He seemed confused.

I fixed my eyes on his. I raised my head so that he could see the scar around my neck. I wanted him to know who I was.

The scar on my neck identified me, but I was not the little boy he had brought to the village years ago. The slaver pulled the reins on his horse. He stopped. He nodded his recognition of me. A thin, evil smile came across his face. He pulled his knife from its sheath and made a mock threat toward me, a growl coming from this throat. I did not move. If he expected I would shrink away, he was disappointed. I was now a match for the slaver. I looked into his eyes. Somehow I knew our fates were tied together.

Uncertainty came over the slaver's face. He looked around him. Dozens of men were watching this drama in the street, their faces tight with anticipation. He looked back at me. I held his stare. My face and my eyes dared him to come down from his horse. He shook his head slightly and then slapped his horse's flank and went around me—the two boys in tow. The men in the crowd moaned. They had hoped for a fight.

Quartus came running across the street. "I cannot stay here," I told him. "I will start back along the road. When your business is finished, you will find me along the road."

I walked back in the direction of our cart, thinking about those boys, wondering if they were indeed brothers, wondering if they could still hear their mother's screams.

Quartus said nothing when he brought the cart alongside me and I climbed up beside him. We made our way back to the estate without words. He knew the questions in my heart, but he had no answers for those questions. Neither did I.

The confrontation in the village stayed on my mind. Many hours I sat beside our hut sharpening arrow points until they could be no sharper, my mind working through the confrontation in the village. I had demonstrated courage, but nothing had changed. I found no satisfaction in the demonstration of my courage. The slaver was still at his work—stealing children from their homes and selling them to those with money to buy. Quartus counseled me to turn my thoughts elsewhere. He said my contemplations brought me no benefit. His advice was sound, but even as I got into the rhythms of my responsibilities, the slaver was never far from my mind.

I was now a hunter. That was my role. The master liked wild game on his table—and I took readily to the role of providing it. Most days, before dawn, leaving Quartus snoring on his cot, I fed the ducks, then set my bow and quiver over my shoulders and took to the woods. The key was to find the right spot and wait with patience.

Patience, I told myself. Patience is the important thing. Wait for the opportunity, I told myself. Then make your arrows fly true. What I advised myself about the particular quarry of that day also held a greater meaning. Patience was the important thing.

As the summer passed, Helios's trek across the sky shortened, and the evenings came earlier to our valley. We took the grapes from the vines, pressed them and put the mash in casks to ferment. The limbs on the olive trees, weighed down with their heavy green fruits, waved ponderously in the afternoon breezes as we watched for signs of purple among the green. The barley ears yellowed, and we gathered them in stacks high as my chest. We threshed the grain under thin gray skies when the pale sun gave us no heat. When the olives were speckled black, we gathered them in huge baskets. The upper limbs would no longer bear my weight, but I shook the limbs to make them release their fruits as Quartus gathered them below. The woods were full of game, and the master shared what I killed, so Quartus and I ate well that season. We ate our dinners beside our hut until the air turned cold, and we moved inside with our cloaks over our shoulders as the hard, cold wind slid down the mountain and whistled through the chinks of the hut.

The snow came early that winter, as did the wolves, but I had prepared. Two of them took my arrows in their ribs, and the pack moved to other valleys. We lost no lambs that winter.

Chapter 8
The Slaver Returns

The rains were heavy that spring, making muddy gullies around our hut and in the fields. The first seeds were washed away, so Quartus and I had to recast the barley seed under the olive trees. "It will be better in the end," Quartus said. "It's more work for us now, but the rains will make the crops greater." Eight lambs were born that spring. Quartus took great delight in helping deliver them, as they burst into the world, slick and bloody.

Quartus was right about the rain. The plums, the almonds, and the early figs were plentiful that season. We took them to market, along with the two wolf hides Quartus had cleaned and tanned. I returned with a bagful of arrow points, which I set to the shafts I had gathered. In that season I went to the woods often and found spots along the stream where I interrupted the croaking frogs as I sought a place among the myrtles that concealed me. When I settled into place the frogs found their voices again, subduing the gurgling of the stream. Game was plentiful that spring and I brought several deer to the master's house and one young boar, still tender.

The master made a trip to Rome, and I spent the days with the lady at the house. She watched carefully as I wrote letters on the wax tablet and sometimes correcting my mistakes. She had woven a blanket for me. I ate honey-cakes and she rubbed balm on my neck and held her mirror so I could see that the scar was diminishing.

When the weather warmed, we sheared the sheep and bundled the wool into bales, enough to fill one cart. In the other cart we loaded cabbages and beans. That night lightning flashed in the sky beyond the village, and deep thunder shook the ground. Some rain fell, but not much—as though the sky had used up its energy with the bluster of light and noise. With the morning dew sparkling on the grass, we started toward the village.

I was quiet in the cart that morning—so quiet that Quartus commented on it. The little rain we had was adequate to muddy the cart ruts and slow our progress. My thoughts took the tempo of the cart—slow and methodical.

The clanging of metalsmith's hammer grew more distinct as I approached his shop. Before I could enter, some men shouted, and I turned as they began to gather at the street. I heard hoof beats.

The slaver had returned.

He rode while his two minions walked beside him. His face had altered. His brow was lined, and his eyes had sunk deeper. Only a year had passed, but he seemed to have added more age than a year. He was less comfortable in his saddle. He winced when the horse took an awkward step. His hair was thinner, and the yellow-gray folds under his eyes had deepened. His jowls were thicker. The horse's motion pained him. Three raw scratches ran from his ear nearly to his chin.

Some woman fought you. Some woman did not give up easily. Some mother did not readily relinquish her offspring.

The slaver's last raid had not been easy. The pain of that last confrontation was borne in his face. The confidence, the arrogance, the swagger seemed diminished.

While I looked at the slaver—all others had their eyes on what was tethered to the horse, trailing behind.

Two sisters, younger than I, nearly naked, just beginning to come into womanhood, hysterical in their grief and fear, clutched to each other in shame and fear as they looked out at the leering crowd.

My arms and shoulders quivered. My teeth went tight.

Whatever it is inside a man that prepares him to fight; whatever it is that makes a man willing to meet an enemy in battle, whatever it is that gives recognition to evil—whatever that is—it ran through my body. The muscles in my back, my shoulders, my arms, my legs, quivered with tension. With the strength I felt, I could have killed both man and horse with my hands.

I was in my eighteenth summer, according to the lady. Even so, no man in the village could bring the crown of his head to my chin, and the years with the bow had strengthened my shoulders. Not yet a man, but no man in the village matched my strength. Perhaps just a boy, yet in any crowd of men I stood out.

At this moment that was my intent. I wanted to stand out. I wanted to be seen.

I wanted the slaver to see me. That intention came suddenly as I saw the terror in the girls' faces. I wanted the slaver to see my stature. I wanted him to know I no longer feared him, he could no longer dangle me in the air, he could no longer kick my ribs, and he could never make me cry.

I stepped onto the muddy street. As I had done the previous year, I raised my chin. I wanted him to see the scar.

A murmur ran through the crowd.

He nodded to the crowd as he approached. His head turned in my direction. He saw me. His expression changed. There was recognition—then confusion.

Was it fear I saw in his eyes?

The slaver tapped the reins on his horse's neck, turning it to the other side of the street. He kept his head faced forward, but he looked at me through the sides of his eyes. He seemed unsettled. He went by, but he turned in his saddle for one more look. I raised my chin even higher. *He feared me. I was sure of it.*

The girls were already sold when I came from the metal-shop, my bag full of new arrow points and bridle bits the master had ordered. A landowner a few miles to the south took both the girls. "What will his fat wife say, I wonder?" one of the drunks asked. "And where will *she* sleep tonight?" another bellowed. Coarse laughter and coarse jokes followed.

The crowd began to disperse. Some headed to the wine shop. I followed and stood at the open door. Along with his minions, the slaver sat at a table with his back to the door, celebrating their fortune. They had done well. The slaver emptied his cup and called for another, wiping his face with his arm. As he received the new cup of wine, he saw me. He squinted his eyes, took deep breaths and adjusted his stool. The wine and the company of his companions gave him new courage. He half-turned toward me and glared with yellow eyes. He stood, almost stumbling, and put his hands around his neck as though he were strangling. His mimic confused his friends at first, but he pointed at me and said something to them I could not hear, but knew what he said. A great drunken laugh came from the table. He placed his knife on the table, took a long drink from his newly filled cup, and looked at me defiantly, spitting a stream of wine on the floor as if he dared me to come into the wine shop. He thrust his hips toward me in the obscene manner I had seen years before. He emitted a great, high-pitched scream. His companions laughed in drunken approval. I held the slaver's eyes with mine and did not move.

The slaver made one more defiant look at me and then returned to his stool, turning his back to the window as he downed another gourd cup of wine. I stayed there in the doorway for some moments. The slaver emptied his cup again and looked back warily over at his shoulder to the door where I stood. I saw again in his face what I had seen in the street. Fear. I was sure of it . . . *I saw fear in his face.*

I returned late from the village. Quartus asked no questions. He did not have to. He could sense I had seen the slaver. A thumbnail moon rose early as Quartus, and I shared a silent meal together. The sparks from the fire rose up pretentiously as if they would join the stars that dotted the infinite sky. There was much on my mind, but nothing I could say to Quartus. I worked grouse-bones around in my mouth, sucking all the meat from the joints, but my mind was on the two girls . . . and the slaver.

Quartus was already in bed when a breeze came up from the valley, chilling my shoulders and interrupting my contemplation. The draping fronds of the pepper tree waved silently in the breeze. The fire turned gray and cold. An owl hooted from the fig trees edging the meadow as I slipped into the hut and pulled my blanket over me.

I knew what I must do.

Chapter 9

The Reckoning

I awoke and my mind knew its purpose.

I rose from my bed and pulled back the fronds at my window. The new day was barely a promise in the eastern sky as a pale, yellow-white light crept up against a flat band of low, unmoving clouds just above the horizon, painting the clouds the color of the bellies of day-old ducklings.

Quartus's steady breathing filled the stillness of the hut. He slept longer these days, rarely waking until the full ball of the sun had slipped over the hills. By that time I would be far across the edge of the hills, and about my purpose. My absence would not trouble him. "Probably tracking a deer," he would tell the lady, but he would surely scold me for not telling him my plans.

I stepped quietly onto the dirt floor and slipped on my clothes and cinched my belt. Then pausing to assure myself that Quartus's breathing was undisturbed, I took my bow and quiver from their pegs and stepped into the early morning air. I took one additional item— the leather cord—the one that the lady had removed from my neck years before. I tucked it in my belt and stood for a moment. The horse whinnied as if he were ready to be fed. A nightjar issued its tremulous notes from the grapevines, but otherwise the world was quiet. The dawn-star, like a yellow jewel, had found its place above the horizon, but the other stars had abandoned the sky.

I moved slowly at first, lest I disturb the ducks, and walked quietly through the grove of fig trees, which had put out their first hard buds. I slipped through the grapevines, just beginning to throw out their sticky-sweet aroma of summer. Then I walked more purposefully, and my legs found unusual energy as I moved quickly up the gentle slopes that cradled the house and the fields. As I crested the hills above the farm, the clouds were gaining their hue, mimicking the vivid colors of the oleander blossoms around me. I followed the path through scrubby oaks down to the stream that split the two hills. There I paused for some water and ate the crust of bread and the duck egg I had saved from last night's dinner. As I sat, a young doe—her ears twitching—came to drink hardly twenty yards away. On another day she would have become dinner on my master's table, but on this day my arrows had other purposes. When I refilled my water skin, her ears caught the sound, and she bolted through the brush.

The mountain bees were already at their work in the meadow beyond the stream, and they took offense at me as I waded through the ankle-deep grass, still wet with dew. Slender aspens fringed the meadow, and above them myrtle and scrub oak led me toward the peak. On other days I would have moved carefully and quietly lest I disturb my quarry, but today I gave no regard to the noise I made underfoot.

The route became more arduous nearer the higher elevation. There was no path—at least not one that men used. But it was not terrain unfamiliar to me, I had killed a few deer on this slope and now used their switchback paths for my ascent. There were easier paths to my destination, but they would have put me in the vicinity of farmhouses, and I could not risk detection.

I scrambled through rocks and gnarled pines, using their branches on some occasions to steady myself as I ascended. As I reached the top, I paused to catch my breath as the sun won its struggle against the hills and slipped unimpeded into the sky. My lungs took in the keen sweet air of the top of the hill. Across the way I could see the edge of the village, nestled against the hills, and the small figures of men in the fields near the village were beginning their morning chores. The road I sought was out of view, but I had scouted the site when hunting, and I had no doubt I could find it again. At this height there were no good paths, so I purposed not to tarry. My destination, if I had gauged it properly, was still an hour away. If I missed the opportunity, it could be another year before it came again, if ever.

When I reached the site, it was just as I had remembered. It would serve my purpose. Great gray boulders, big as barns, were strewn along the hillside. I recalled the stories I had heard of the Greek gods who battled on the hills and threw boulders like pebbles.

I heard many such stories from Quartus, and when I was younger they filled me with dread as I went into the forest. In those days I watched for these gods, for I thought they may still visit the domain of mortals—but I never saw them. The gods, I decided, must now have better things to do than throw boulders around.

The road was wide and bordered on both sides by huge pines. Little grew under these tall straight trees. The season's pine needles, still copper-red, covered the forest floor and softened the sound of my sandals as I walked. A giant pine, the girth of two men's arms, rose from the edge of the road. In eons past, it had arrested a falling boulder the size of a nobleman's bed and held it against its trunk. Taking my arrows from my quiver, I laid them in a row on the flat table of the boulder. I leaned my bow against the tree and kept my knife in its sheath. I sat on the gray boulder and took a drink from my waterskin. I looked up through the branches of the giant pine to gauge the angle of the sky. It was still three hours until the sun was at its highest. The birds, quieted by my arrival, returned to their chirping.

I heard them before I saw them.

The slaver would have been better served by guards who were more alert, but these two sensed no danger. The place I had chosen was open—not a likely place for ambush. One minion walked in front of the slaver and his horse, the other behind, but all seemed to be enjoying some story as they approached the giant pine. They were close enough that we could have easily called to each other.

The slaver was the first to notice me. His guards were snickering over some obscene joke. Seeing me, he pulled the reins of his horse.

He put up his hand to quiet the others and turned his head at an angle as if trying to make sense of what he saw. I could see the confusion on his face as I sat on the boulder by the road's edge, my hands empty. I waited for them to come nearer. The front guard saw me. He shouted and his companion came to the fore. Both held their knives at the ready. The horse snorted and reared slightly as it sensed conflict. The slaver grimaced as the steed pitched. The gray under his eyes and the red in his nose betrayed the amount of wine he had consumed over the previous days.

I stood. The slaver looked in all directions to see if others accompanied me. He was confused. He looked around again and satisfied himself that I was alone. His confusion turned to irritation. He motioned for his two men to advance. He prodded his horse. The two men, still looking from side to side in fear of an ambush, moved forward also.

I slid down from the rock and took the bow from where it leaned against the tree. I nocked an arrow. Quickly I drew the string. The hissing arrow went straight through the first man's neck. Before his knees hit the ground a second arrow pierced the chest of the other, protruding out his back. The slaver's horse reared on his hind legs, and I sent a third arrow into its chest. The horse fell, kicking wildly in its agony, dropping on its side. The slaver struggled to free himself from the writhing horse. He scrambled on unsteady legs to gain his feet. He stood and cursed as he pulled his blade. I stepped toward him. He looked around him. The other two men were gurgling on the blood in their throats, and the horse kicked in agony. I nocked another arrow and the slaver flinched as it went whistling by his hip into the neck of the horse, shortening its suffering. He looked at the horse and back at me. The confusion in his face turned to defiance. He knew me. "Ah, yes," he seemed to say, as though he expected me.

We were alone in the forest. I set my bow aside. My blade was still in its sheath.

The forest went quiet—the slaver's companions and his horse were out of their agony. No birds moved in the trees, and no wind disturbed the leaves in the canopy above.

It seemed as if the whole world stopped for a few seconds—as if fate, or something greater than me, had appointed this place for this effort.

I held his eyes in mine. I felt strangely calm. No emotion came to my face, for there was none in my heart. I had a purpose, and I was about it.

The slaver's eyes flicked back and forth around him. His thick hands coupled his knife-handle. I stepped closer. He readied himself, one foot slightly in front of the other, his knife pointed at my head. He had known other fights. In youth and in strength he was no match for me, but he had been a fighter and I had no doubt that other men had felt his blade in their bellies.

I took the cord from my belt and held it for him to see. He saw it and he recognized it. I am certain he knew why I brought it. He looked around. He worked his tongue around his teeth. He sought an escape. He thought better of it. He had not lived this long without making good decisions. He could not outrun me. His only chance, he knew, was to fight me. He had won other fights. Perhaps he could win this one. He braced himself and pointed the blade at me.

I refolded the cord and threw it on the boulder.

"I will slit your miserable, scarred throat!" he yelled, waving his knife. It was a vain threat, and his words were quickly absorbed into the heavy leaves around us.

I did not honor his words with a response. I took my blade from my waist and felt the weight of it in my hand. My mind was strangely calm, and my motions were deliberate and orderly. We stood ten paces apart, and I held the slaver's eyes in mine. He looked around him. He was slightly crouched, body tense, holding his knife with both hands, still pointed at me. Behind him his horse and his companions were still, puddles of blood around each.

His eyes came back to me. His nostrils flared, and a loud curse came up his throat and spilled out into the forest as he ran toward me.

He lunged. I stepped aside. My counter-stroke caught his forearm, and I heard the crunch of the blade on his forearm, breaking the bone. The knife fell from his useless arm as his scream filled the forest. Before that sound reached the treetops, my second stroke came from below, into his belly, and split him open. He fell to his knees, his guts and his blood spilling out onto the pine needles. The fight was over. I slipped the leather cord around his neck and dragged him to the pine, where I lashed the cord around it.

Had I been bent on revenge I would have strung him up by the neck to dangle a fitting and painful death. Instead I lashed his neck around the tree to give him a more merciful end. My first purpose was removal. I wanted this man removed from the world. Revenge was a portion of my motive—but not my first purpose. From behind the tree I tightened the cord, pulling his head snugly against the tree. I stepped in front of him and took my blade in both hands. No arrogance remained in his face, only terror. His life was spilling out of him onto the forest floor. His eyes were wide as I ended his misery. He saw clearly the blade as it took his head from his shoulders.

The next morning there were three heads on poles on the road that led into our village. No more slavers came that season.

When I returned to the hut, the moon was up, and the owls were hooting in the olive groves. I hung my bow on its notch on the wall and placed the half-full quiver beside it. Quartus noticed I had no quarry and started to ask a question, but perhaps sensing something in my face, said nothing. He gave me a bowl of soup and left me to my thoughts.

Chapter 10

Removal

A month passed before they came.

It took longer than I had expected. Such arrangements take time, I suppose. I was sitting in the dappled shade of the pepper trees, sharpening my arrow points when they arrived—two men riding mules and leading a third. The sun was halfway to the top of the heavens, the time of day when animals find shade for the day. I was alone at the hut, Quartus having been given an assignment by the master that required him to leave at dawn. The feeding of the animals had fallen to me in his absence, but those chores were now accomplished, so I sat sharpening my points and re-fletching arrow shafts

Sheathed on the hips of the two riders were the short swords of the Roman type. Former soldiers was my guess. The Romans allowed their old soldiers to keep their swords. They rode toward the main house casually in the manner of men who are expected.

I put down my sharpening rock. I would not need arrow points again. I now made sense of the odd instructions Quartus had been given the night before: "The master wants me to gather laurel berries tomorrow," Quartus had said, shaking his head, as he took a bag from a peg.

"It will be a week, at least," I said, "until they are ripe."

"I said the same," he answered. "But he would not hear it. It will take me half the morning to get to the bushes and just as long to return. And I will have an empty bag when I return—but he is the master and I am the slave."

Now I understood.

It was better that Quartus was gone. He did not need to see this event. Better that he was in the hills looking for berries on the laurel trees.

I stood and watched. The master came to the door to greet the men. After a short conversation he pointed in my direction. They looked toward me. It was better for everyone that Quartus was not here to see what was happening. I determined to play the part of the man. I began walking up the slope toward the house. They looked at me oddly as I came close. Their hands went to their short swords. I stopped and looked at the master. He said nothing but he held my gaze. Inside the house the mistress was wailing and beating against a locked door. I give my master credit for staying in the door—for seeing me off in person. A lesser man would not have witnessed what he had commissioned. He played the part of a man. I did the same.

Resistance would have proved nothing. I extended my arms to the ex-soldiers, looking directly at the master all the time. One tied my hands firmly with leather cords but left enough slack that I could move my arms. The other kept his hand on the handle of his blade just in case. Each of them eyed me carefully. Men who have been to war know it is important to assess the situation. I stood taller than either of them, and my shoulders were broader. One of the men handed my master a coin purse. That gave me some relief. I had been sold—for a reasonable price if the apparent weight of the purse was an indication. I had value. Someone had paid for me. That was some reassurance that I would not have my throat cut and my body thrown in a ditch.

A few years earlier, sitting in the fig tree, with the master below me . . . evaluating me, I asked: Do I have value? What am I worth? The answer to that question was in the little purse that the soldier had handed the master. Whatever the total of those coins . . . that was what I was worth.

The master held the purse in his hand as he looked at me. A lesser man would have slipped the bag in his pocket, but he did not. He showed no embarrassment. His expression was constant—with neither compassion nor contempt. I was a commodity to him, nothing more.

What am I worth? How many coins are in that bag? How does it compare with what the lady paid ten years before?

The lady's wailing grew louder. Her cries came in stuttered, jerking sobs as she relentlessly beat against the locked door. The master held his eyes on mine. He took no pleasure from this transaction, but neither did he have mercy for his wife, whose sobs filled both our ears. I did not speak, nor did he. I bore him no ill will. His concern was adequate reason to rid me from his household. A slave who has killed a free man was a danger. A man who heads a household could not afford to have such a man near—particularly one whose size and strength outmatched his. It was a necessary precaution. He could do nothing else.

The mistress kept wailing, and her screams pierced my heart.

The older soldier tugged at the tether, and I nodded to my master—no longer my master. He nodded in return. I mounted the mule and rode behind one of the soldiers and in front of the other. I did not look back as we rode away. But the wailing of my mistress stayed in my ears longer than the air held the sound.

I called myself a man again. What would Quartus say of that? Yet still I am grateful he did not see me led away in cords. If he had been there, I think he would have acknowledged that I was truly a man, even if I could count only eighteen years.

Down the road I turned and looked for the last time on the estate. I held no animosity toward the master. I had been afforded more than most who had been on the slave block.

As Quartus had told me repeatedly, I was near death when the lady rescued me. I had no assurances about the future, but there was some reason to be grateful. My actions brought about my circumstances, but I had no regrets. The slaver and his evil needed to be removed. I had done what needed to be done. And with that assurance I started this new journey.

"No ill will, I hope," the soldier in front said. "Just doing a job."

I said nothing. As with the master, I held no resentment toward these men.

"Old soldiers must find work as they can," said the one in the rear. "The Roman pension is not much."

The one in front stopped us all, turned back to me, and said, "They told us in the village we should be careful that you do not get your hands on a bow. Otherwise we might end up with our heads on a pole." Both men smiled, but I said nothing.

Chapter 11

Rome

"Four days, perhaps five." Draco, the younger of the two, said.

The other Roman was Cadmus. He looked at me on my mount. "It may take longer than usual. The mule is not accustomed to a load your size. But Rome can wait. We will arrive when we arrive."

The lady had, on several occasions, talked of going to Rome. "Perhaps my husband will take us with him when he goes to Rome," she had said more than once. The lady may never make that trip, but the city was now my destination, and I wondered what the future it held for me.

We headed south, the three of us in single file, each wobbling on our mules as they found their pace. One kept a few paces in front of me and the other an equal distance behind. Although I was a slave and a prisoner, their treatment of me was reasonable. The cords were never removed, but they checked them regularly to make sure they were not cutting my wrists. I received an equal share of the food along the way.

How different from the previous time I was on a journey with my hands tied.

Our route took us through the village, and I could hear the hammer of the metalsmith as we passed his shop. Not being a market day, only a few people came to gawk at me. I looked to the posts in the middle of the open square—where the lady had rescued me from death. I had little time to think of these things as we passed quickly out of the village. Going south, we passed a few mud-and-wattle huts with goats grazing under olive trees. I had never been south of the village before, and I took in the sights with interest. The trees thinned and the fields opened. The clomp of the mules' hooves found a rhythm on the hard-caked road. Scrubby heather grew over the ditches beside the road. Blackbirds, sipping the water, flew away as the mules came near.

Cadmus and Draco talked freely between themselves as we rode. Mostly they talked about their years as soldiers. My status as a slave seemed of little importance to them. They were not slave traders. They were simply fulfilling an assignment to earn a living. I was the commodity. Their minds seemed to have little inclination to question the status of any of us. And if they treated me with appropriate courtesy, there was no sympathy in their demeanor. In their minds it seemed that each of us had a role—a role that was predetermined and not to be questioned.

The first night we found a site to camp under some birches beside a small stream, adequate to provide water for the mules and for the pot that boiled our beans. The moon was tardy that night and the sky dark, but speckled with stars when we finished our meal. The sound of the stream gurgling around pebbles mixed with the occasional crackling of the fire as the two Romans poured wine from a goatskin, giving me an equal portion. Cadmus put more sticks on the flame.

Around a fire, late in the evening, after the flame has served its purpose and men have fed from the pot it heated, men will stare at the flame and say things they will not say elsewhere. I have often seen it. Embers of a fire loosen a man's thoughts and bring those thoughts to his tongue. When a man shares a common flame with other men, he will say things he would say at no other time. Things that touch at the heart, things held in reserve, woman-like things, will spill out of his soul as he shares a fire with others. A man who has told a ribald joke in the afternoon will take a more somber tone around the flame.

Around such a fire, men will gather and stare at the flame and ask themselves questions for which they have no answers. Whether the fare was meager or sumptuous, it is at these times, when the embers rise up to chase the stars—as if they would become stars themselves—when men's eyes are fixed on the fire's core . . . it is then, when only the crackle of the flame disturbs the quiet of the night, that a man will say things to other men, without fear of reproach, that would remain unsaid at other times.

Unbidden memories will come to a man's mind at those times. I have seen strong men, hands folded across their knees, gazing into the core of a fire, the flame throwing flickering shadows across their brooding faces, speak of a dead parent, or a lost brother, or a wife now departed from this life. Does a fellowship around a fire remind men of eternity? Is a man's finitude exposed by a flame? These are questions for which I have no answers.

"When I was in the north," Cadmus said after a long silence, "there were times I wished to be a slave rather than a soldier. It is an option for poor men—men such as those in my family. Linus, my cousin, surrendered to slavery rather than become a soldier. He said he had no wish to be killed by barbarians. And yes, when I was with the army in the north, I often wished I had done the same as Linus. Every day I spent in those forests in the north with Germanicus's army, I envied Linus. He was a house servant for a nobleman in Rome. He slept in a bed at night. He ate full meals every day. And he was safe. He did not have to worry about fighting wild barbarians with sharp axes—their long hair flying behind them as they attacked us. Better a live slave than a dead soldier, that's what I told myself."

He looked at me with a wry smile. "Some of them looked a little like you, Malchus—nearly your size. Straw-colored hair, blue eyes." He nodded as some old memory apparently came back to him. "They were smart. I will give them that. They knew better than to fight us from the front. They always came at us from the side or the back, or at night when we did not expect it."

Draco nodded in agreement. He had also fought in the north.

Cadmus fixed his eyes on the fire. "We marched on a muddy road, double file, a column in each rut. It was cold, past sunset, and the trees were filled with snow. The limbs hung heavy over the road. My feet were numb, and my body ached. We were seeking a secure place for the night, but the heavy woods seemed to go on forever. We marched for hours. I believe I had fallen asleep while I was walking."

He took a long drink from his wineskin and was quiet for a moment. "I was near the back of the column. And then came the scream. That's what woke me from my walking slumber. Maybe thirty of them. Or forty. All screaming. Hidden hardly the length of two spears away from our column, they attacked. The man in front of me fell with his head split open. The barbarian turned toward me—his axe held above his head, the red blood on the blade."

Cadmus paused and unbuttoned his shirt. He smiled as he pulled it open. "See how close the barbarian came." A purple-and-red scar ran from under his chin across his chest. "Over in just a few seconds. The barbarians attacked and then ran into the woods—still screaming. We dared not follow them. I looked around me. Like the man in front of me, the man behind me was dead too—eleven in all, and about that same number hurt badly."

Cadmus took another long drink from his skin. "We stripped the dead of their weapons and their clothes and left their bodies on the side of the road. As we marched out, the snow had begun to cover their corpses."

He smiled again. "On that night I envied my cousin his warm bed." He stared into the fire. "Sometimes at night I can still hear the screams of those barbarians."

The two Romans went quiet. They stared into the fire. After a while, saying nothing, they drew their blankets around them and went to sleep. My last thoughts were of the estate . . . and the lady.

The nightmares returned. I smelled the smoke, and I heard the screams. If I thought that ridding myself of the slaver would rid me of the screams, I was wrong. All I had achieved was to make another woman scream. Would these new screams now become part of my dreams?

The next day, as we continued our journey, both men talked constantly.

I asked few questions of my captors, but they were quick with information about Rome.

"Our emperor, it seems—" Cadmus mused as we trudged through some open fields where peasants were gathering barley, "—has now . . . how shall I say this?" He and Draco shared a knowing smile. "Our emperor has become unpredictable." Draco nodded heartily in agreement as he tried to suppress a laugh.

Cadmus saw the confusion in my face.

"Not that you will ever be in the company of Tiberius, mind you, nevertheless his . . . unpredictability could still affect you. I will explain. When Tiberius came to power, maybe eight years ago, the people of Rome welcomed him—none more so than those of us in the army. Tiberius was a great general, perhaps the only one better was Germanicus, our general, but Germanicus paid the price for his greatness."

"What do you mean?" I asked.

"Well, Germanicus had become a hero—and rightfully so—in the eyes of the Romans. Everywhere he went his armies were victorious and his reputation swelled. There was much talk of his becoming the next emperor."

"Then what?"

"Germanicus died—suddenly. Isn't that odd?" He looked at me. "Thirty-five years old. A man among men—strong as a bull, I tell you. I saw him in the saddle two days before he died. I tell you there are men who are made for sitting in a saddle—who can inspire soldiers just by the way they hold the reins. He looked like more than a general. He looked like a king. That was the problem. No one who ever looked at Germanicus in the saddle—straight back, strong shoulders—could ever look on that pot-bellied Tiberius with admiration. Maybe Germanicus should not have been so successful in his campaigns. In the end, that may have been what condemned him. When his victories outmatched Tiberius's victories—and the accolades from the citizens poured in—it was too much for Tiberius. He had to get rid of him."

Cadmus paused for a moment. "Not that any of this can be proven of course. But we all know what happened."

Cadmus took a long draught from his canteen and offered me a drink.

He continued. "I lost heart that day—the day Germanicus died. Most of us did. I never felt good about soldiering again. What was the purpose? To enlarge Rome? To build a bigger empire? For whom? Tiberius? More often now in Rome you hear someone whisper, 'Tiberius in Tiberium,' that is, throw him in the river. But you have to be careful to whom you say that. He has spies throughout the city."

Cadmus turned toward me, and an odd smile came on his face. "Tomorrow we will arrive in the great city. Draco and I will lead you to the slave market." The rueful smile became more pronounced. That will be a different procession than the one five years ago, will it not, Draco?" Draco nodded in agreement.

They laughed, shaking their heads as they recalled some event I knew nothing of.

"Excuse us, Malchus," Cadmus said as he regained composure. "Our joke is not at your expense. You see, five years ago, when Draco and I entered Rome, it was part of a triumph."

Cadmus assumed the posture of a man about to tell a long story. "A triumph does not happen often, but when it does, it is a significant event." Draco nodded enthusiastically. "A triumph is provided for a general if he achieves a significant victory. I think he is supposed to kill so many enemies, capture so many prisoners, gain so much land. I'm not sure exactly what is required, or even if those numbers are all that important. But six years earlier the Roman army had been humiliated in the north. Three entire legions—fifteen thousand Roman soldiers!—were killed in those northern forests. The notion that we Romans could not be defeated was shattered. Of course our armies had suffered some small setbacks over the years, but this was a massacre. And that event festered in the minds of Romans for all of those six years."

Cadmus moved slightly closer to me. "Well, Germanicus got the assignment to set things right. And when we were marching north, I did not feel good about this effort. We had eight legions, but we had also heard about those wild-eyed northerners and their fierce tactics. We were going to face off against Arminius, their leader. Arminius—they called him that because his eyes were the color of the armenium stone. He pointed at me. "Eyes like yours."

He adjusted his stool again. "Arminius was able to pick off a good number of our troops in his ambushes. But eventually—after more than a year, and with the eight legions Germanicus had at his command—we were able to put Arminius to flight. We never caught Arminius, but we captured his wife, Thusnelda—pregnant to the point of popping."

A smile came on Cadmus's face as he recalled the event. "And this was the amazing part. Germanicus set aside a tent for

Thusnelda—right next to the command tent—treated her like a queen. I guess she was a queen of some sort."

Cadmus took another long breath. "When the reports came to Rome that we had conquered Arminius's armies and given the Romans some revenge for the defeats seven years earlier, Tiberius granted Germanicus a triumph. Draco and I were there, marching as proud as anyone. But of course, we were in the back!" he laughed.

"The procession started at the Triumphal Gate—I will show it to you tomorrow when we come to the city. The politicians were in front—of course—and then the musicians, a few dozen bulls who would be sacrificed, several carts of war booty—mostly weapons we captured—and then the captured prisoners, walking in their chains. They were a somber group, I can tell you. And then came a few dozen prisoners who were not in chains—all women and all with the red or yellow hair that fascinates Roman women so much. And then behind them, just in front of Germanicus' chariot was Thusnelda herself, a striking woman with her straw-colored hair, all festooned in the northern style, a fortune in jewelry on her arms and neck. And right beside her, toddling along, clutching his mother's arm, was little Thumelicus, hardly two years old, yellow hair glowing in the sun. The Roman ladies swooned at this sight." He shook his head and smiled.

"And just behind them, came Germanicus himself, riding in a gilded chariot. The triumphator wore a purple tunic, worked with gold thread. He held a laurel branch in his right hand and an ivory scepter in his left. At his side, by custom, was a slave holding a golden crown over Germanicus' head, appointed to whisper into his ear and remind him that he too was mortal."

Cadmus went solemn for a moment. "Unfortunately, that prophecy became true too soon."

"But there was no one whispering in *our* ears, was there Draco?" He laughed.

"No. No one whispered in our ears," he replied with a smile.

Cadmus turned back to me. "The soldiers came last. But do not think we were marching in formation. No. We were dancing and singing—all bawdy songs, of course. The crowds still lined the streets and the music and the aroma of the incense still filled the air. We sang lustily—the way soldiers sing when they want to forget the horrors of their battles and remind themselves they are still alive—even though many of our comrades' bodies lay in the cold mud of the north. The crowd handed us skins of wine, which we guzzled quickly, spilling as much as we drank. The procession made its way to the Temple of Jupiter, where the bulls were sacrificed, and then eventually through the Forum, where Tiberius viewed the procession from his elevated throne. By the time we had arrived at the Forum, the emperor had already dismissed himself, so we did not get to see the man."

He turned to Draco. "But that was his loss, eh, Draco! He did not get to see us either!"

"That was his loss," Draco concurred, laughing. Cadmus went quiet again as he reflected on that day. "Tomorrow will be different. We will enter the city, but there will be no music, no dancers, no incense, no cheering crowds, no feast. Only the three of us, and we will go unnoticed by the citizens of Rome as we deliver you to the quaestor at the slave market, where Draco and I will receive payment for our services. Rome always pays."

The city came to my nose before it came to my eyes.

Cadmus laughed when he saw the expression on my face. "Ah, yes. The aroma of Rome. When the wind comes up from the south, it fills your nose. You will get used to it. When you have been here a week you will notice the odor no more."

I had no confidence in that assurance, but in a few moments we came over the crest of a hill, and in my first view of the city, I forgot the stench in my nostrils.

Rome, the great city. The late afternoon sun warmed the stone buildings in a soft light and threw shadows across the city that outlined the thousands of red-roofed structures that spread out before us. The Tiberium, the river that defined the city, curled below us, and on each side of its banks stood more structures than I could imagine. Near the middle of this spectacle, one edifice in particular, the largest building on the landscape, caught my eye.

"The hippodrome," Cadmus said as I stared at the oblong building. The rounded curves seemed out of place among all the squares and rectangles of the rest of the buildings. "That's the place we hope you can avoid. And next to it—all those large buildings on the hill—that is the imperial palace—another place you should avoid. Nothing good happens in either of those places."

"We should camp here," Draco said. "There is no purpose in arriving in the city as the sun goes down."

A gold sky, tinged with pink, greeted us the next morning. Cadmus, until now the talkative one, had nothing to say. We ate our raisins and bread as the sky turned a brighter yellow and the ball of sun emerged from the hills. Cadmus ignored me as he gathered his camp items and secured them to his mule. In a few hours I would be delivered to the slave market. There was little reason for conversation.

I did not know there were this many people in the world. The streets teemed with people, and the red tile roofs extended as far as I could see. Draco and Cadmus pointed out some of the landmarks,

Capitoline Hill with the Temple of Jupiter on it, the Circus Maximus, and the aqueduct, like a snake with its back broken, crossing through the city—but I heard little of what they said. The mass of people in Rome was a greater fascination than the buildings in it.

Both men grew quieter as we came nearer our destination. We came to the area of the Forum. The shops around it, as I was to learn later, were where the wealthy citizens could find their luxuries. Behind the Basilica Julia we entered the Saepta Julia, an expansive open court a hundred paces in both directions.

The slave market.

The scope of it surprised me. Several dozen Roman soldiers, apparently chosen for their size, stood at the ready around the open palisade. A line of perhaps twenty slaves, some pale like me, some with darker skin, and a few with black skin, each accompanied by two escorts, waited their turn to be processed. The line led to an elevated dais where a few Romans officials sat. Ten posts were positioned near the stone wall behind them. This was the place where the slaves would be exhibited when the sale began. As each slave was processed, the escorts were handed a small bag of coins, and two Roman soldiers took the slave away. Cadmus stood beside me, saying nothing, but averting his eyes.

I broke the silence. "This is not to your charge. You have done your duty. A man must do what he can."

Draco nodded.

When I came to the dais, Cadmus handed the document to a soldier, who passed it up to the quaestor. He looked down at me. "A big one," he said to a man sitting on a bench beside him. quill and parchment on a small table. "Notify Eligius." The man made a notation on his parchment.

A look of concern came across Cadmus's face when he heard the name Eligius, but before I had a chance to ask him why, a soldier pulled me away through a wide door. As I turned back, Cadmus and Draco were out of sight. There would be no good-bye.

I was led to some nearby stairs, and the soldier motioned for me to go down. The smell of human waste and human sweat poured up like bubbles from a boiling pot. My eyes began to adjust to the dark interior. A few small windows well above the floor allowed a little light to the damp place. Along a long, curved, descending hallway in the dim light, stood dozens of men on both sides, each one chained to rings about waist high. The chains afforded some movement but not enough that one slave could reach another. A few looked up at me but most kept their heads down. We descended a little farther until we came to a few empty slots along the wall. Two small blankets of rough wool were folded and lying under the remaining metal rings in the wall. The soldier motioned for me to kneel. I did as he instructed, and he connected a chain to my ankles and then to a ring in the wall.

The soldiers left. I looked at my chains. The clink of chains and coughing were the only sounds in the corridor.

"Do not test the chains," a voice came from the prisoner nearest me. "Not even a man your size can break the Roman chains."

I nodded.

"Three days until the day of sale—according to the soldiers—and after that, who knows?" He sighed. "But anything will be better than this."

He was a young man himself, perhaps a few years older than I, lean and muscular. He seemed eager to talk and I let him go on.

"I had my own horse," he said with some pride. "In Mauritania—that's across the Great Sea. Where I'm from. Where the Romans caught me." He laughed. "I had been stealing their provisions for more than a year. I was called 'the cheetah.' I had great speed. I found it easy to sneak into their camps and steal their weapons and their food. However—" He shook his head. "I shared my spoils with my friends. That was a mistake. The Romans have ways of making men talk. My friends betrayed me. The Romans came to my tent and found what I had stolen from them. I expected them to kill me, but instead they sold me to a trader—two months ago."

He began to repeat himself, and I had the sense that he was not really talking to me as much as he was recounting his situation to himself.

"I may become a gladiator. That's what the soldiers on the ship said I was suited for. It is dangerous of course. But they said if I could prove myself in my first battles—and could win the favor of the crowds for my courage—then the managers would make sure I fought only weaker opponents after that. The soldiers said some of the gladiators are given their freedom and live in their own houses. Can you imagine that? Yes, I will become a gladiator."

He twisted nervously, clinking the chains around his legs. "You also should become a gladiator. You are made for it. But of course we should never fight each other."

Chapter 12
The Slave Hall

"Awake slaves!"

A Roman soldier called to us. His torch spread light into the hallway. A soldier unlocked my chain. He then unlocked the chain of "the cheetah" and the chains of two others. Had I lost track of the days? I did not think the slave sale was scheduled until the following day.

"A special sale," the soldier explained, seeing the question on my face. "Roman dignitaries and the gladiator schools get first choice. You and your friend beside you have been selected. Only four for sale today."

The two of us and the two others were led down the corridor to a bathing area. We were stripped and sponged by slaves. They rubbed lotion over our bodies, and then we were led outside—still naked—to the dais I had seen earlier. Slaves were busy arranging cushions on the stone benches facing the dais. Above the benches cloth awnings had been strung to shield against the sun.

We were chained to posts in the center of the dais. A soldier came with placards attached to leather cords and placed them over our necks. Something in Latin was written on them.

"What does it say?" I asked the soldier.

"What does it matter to you?" he laughed. "You will know soon enough." He laughed again, walking away.

The potential purchasers began filing in, taking a preliminary look at us as they found their seats. A few came who did not wear the Roman toga. I would learn later they were slaves themselves, not eligible to wear the toga, but with the responsibility for supervising the *familia*, all the other slaves in the household. And to them had been delegated the responsibility for purchasing additional slaves. A man entered—different than the others. He seemed neither citizen nor slave. He wore leather trousers and a leather jerkin. His large arms, flecked with scars, were bare. "That is Eligius," the cheetah whispered. "He is the head of one of the gladiator schools." None greeted Eligius and he did not take a seat. He stood at the side of the seating area, arms crossed, leaning against a pillar.

A well-dressed servant arrived and positioned some brightly covered cushions at the back of the seating area. A moment later a lady in fine clothing, attended by the same servant, took that position. The men acknowledged her with special deference, but they soon went back to their conversations.

The quaestor stepped onto the stage, his secretary beside him carrying a stack of parchments. The quaestor nodded to another soldier, who blew a short blast on his horn, and the quaestor announced: "The market is now open!"

The soldier who had blown the horn stepped up to the dais and approached me first. In a loud voice he read the card around my neck. "Malchus the Cherusci. Captured in Gaul ten years ago. No skills. No defects."

The soldier then proceeded to read the information about the other three slaves, but I did not hear what he said.

Ten years. Ten years had elapsed since I was taken from among my people somewhere in the north. Ten years I was in the house of the master and the lady. Ten years I had gathered the produce of the estate. Ten years—and my status was summarized by "No skills. No defects."

There was movement in the benches. The purchasers were coming to the dais for a closer inspection. The two slaves who were there to represent their masters were first on the dais and went about their work quickly. One said to the other as they looked at me: "This is one for the gladiators—not my household. There would be trouble in the household with this one," he laughed. "The women would never be satisfied with their husbands with this one nearby." They both laughed again, nodded to each other and moved on. Eligius was watching me, still leaning against a pillar, in no particular hurry to come on the stage.

Eligius came up the stairs, the weight of his body creaking the wooden steps and came directly to me. "Did you gain these shoulders by swinging a blade?" he asked.

"I hunted with a bow."

He smiled. "If the rumors are true, you have skill with a bow."

He looked at me for affirmation, but I said nothing. The story of the slavers had preceded me.

"Strong shoulders—however they have been attained—can serve a man well in the arena. A man who can shoot a bow can learn to swing an axe or heft a spear. You have a future in the arena."

As we spoke, the servant of the lady in fine clothing came on the stage. He walked around me, looking me over carefully. He nodded at the lady, and she returned his nod. He descended the stairs, and the lady handed him a piece of parchment, which he brought to the quaestor.

The quaestor took a moment to look at the document, then handed it to the secretary for him to read. The two of them huddled for a moment, then the quaestor raised his hands to gain everyone's attention.

"The emperor Tiberius Claudius Nero," he announced in a loud voice, "has conferred a writ of privilege to the esteemed Claudia Procula, wife of Pontius Pilate, newly appointed prefect of Judea, to grant one slave of her choice at the largess of the emperor." He nodded to the lady who returned the recognition.

"Am I to understand, esteemed lady," he asked her, "that you, in accordance to this writ of privilege, have chosen Malchus the Cherusci as the slave of your choice?"

"I have, sir," she responded in a strong voice.

The quaestor turned to the soldiers on the stage. "Prepare the slave Malchus the Cherusci for delivery to the house of Pontius Pilate."

At that moment Claudia spoke in the ear of her slave. The slave then motioned to ask permission to return to the stage. He and the quaestor spoke briefly, and the quaestor amended his announcement: "At the request of the lady Claudia Procula, the slave Malchus is to be delivered to the house of Manaen the Jew."

My eyes, at that moment, caught the eyes of this woman who had purchased me. In her face was the evidence of something that spoke of pain or tragedy—and for a moment she looked directly into my eyes, before lowering her head and stepping away to depart.

I never expected to see Claudia Procula again, but neither of us had any sense of how our fates were bound together.

A soldier unlocked the chain securing me to the post. As I was led away, the cheetah nodded to me in such a way as to wish me good fortune. I returned the nod.

What is a Jew? The quaestor said I was to be delivered to the house of Manaen the Jew. I had never heard the term.

Chapter 13

The House of Manaen

The soldier removing my chain saw my confusion and offered some explanation: "Odd people, the Jews. Not many of them in Rome. Keep to themselves mostly. Have their own god. Will *not* worship the Roman gods. We tried for a long time to get them to worship the gods, but we have given up. Now we let them worship their own god—as long as they pay their taxes and don't cause any trouble." He leaned in near me as if he were telling a secret. "To be honest, I don't think the emperor cares if any of us worship the gods—as long as we pay our taxes and don't cause any trouble." He laughed. "That is the new Roman way—pay your taxes and stay out of trouble. Worship whatever god you want. Here is your robe. Get dressed and we will go to the Jewish quarter."

We made our way from the slave market through the streets of Rome and soon came to the *Pons Cestius,* one of the bridges over the Tiber. I looked over the side to see small boats going in both directions on the river.

"The Jews stay on the west side of the river," the soldier told me. "They keep to themselves. And the Romans like it that way as well."

We turned right as we crossed the bridge, and the streets immediately narrowed. We walked only a few minutes before we entered an open gate set in a wall that seemed to enclose a section of the city. Every street seemed a warren of shops, doors and windows open, men going about their trades. As soon as I entered the walled area, I felt as if I had stepped into a different city—even a different country. None wore the Roman toga. Dark robes covered the men who moved briskly through the streets. Those on the street as well as those working in their small shops looked at us and then turned away. And there was something different in the way they looked at us—

something in the expression of their faces that I could not immediately gauge. After we had walked a few minutes and seen the expressions, it came to me. *Contempt.* A certain squint of the eyes, a constriction of the mouth, an upturned nose. For some reason the Jews held both the soldier and me in contempt.

Before I could consider this more, we came to another wall with a heavy metal gate and behind it a courtyard.

A servant boy, who seemed to be waiting for us, opened the gate and took us across a stone walkway to massive cedar doors decorated with hammered bronze set in ornamented limestone. From this spot near the doors, I could not tell the true dimensions of the house, but it was extremely large—far bigger than what the master and the lady lived in. The Roman soldier looked around as well, obviously impressed at this huge edifice, which seemed out of place among the cramped streets of this Jewish quarter. The boy motioned for us to step inside an open courtyard within the house. This area alone was larger than most of the houses I had so far seen in Rome. The floors were laid in intricate patterns—like a honeycomb—of black, gray, and white marble. The walls ran up to the height of five men. The color of the walls put me in the mind of the sky at the estate, just before the sun slipped over the hills. My mind went back to the estate and the fields and Quartus and the lady and my bow.

I had been confident I was doing the right thing when I left early that morning with my bow strung over my shoulder and quiver full of arrows—that day I met the slaver on the path. Did I think I would conquer all the evil in the world that day? Would it have been better if I had stayed at the estate? Many questions, few answers.

"A moment please," the servant boy said. "I will call Manaen." He dismissed himself, and I looked up at the open sky. Around the opening was a series of squares framed by limestone, each painted the color of the sky with gold medallions in each square. When I moved to get a better view, my chains struck together and echoed off the chamber walls.

"Welcome," a strong voice said. The one who spoke entered the atrium from the outer courtyard. Like the others in the Jewish quarter, he was dressed differently than the Romans. His brown cloak was embroidered neatly with green and purple thread, which as he came closer, I made out as a rendering of vines and grapes.

The Roman soldier bowed slightly. "Sir, our orders are to deliver the slave Malchus the Cherusci to the custody of Manaen the Jew. Will you attest that you are authorized to accept this delivery?"

"I will so attest," the man said. "I am Manaen—and I am certainly a Jew," he seemed to say with some amusement. "But you could as easily refer to me as 'Manaen the Roman,' for I have been a citizen of the empire for several years."

He was not a tall man, but his shoulders were square, and his posture erect. His beard and hair were neatly trimmed and oiled. About him he carried an attitude of confidence—and I did not sense the contempt I had seen in the faces of those outside. I thought him to be a man in his thirties, but when he came closer, I saw gray scattered in his beard.

The soldier ceremoniously handed him a parchment. Manaen stepped to a nearby table, signed the document, and handed it back to the soldier.

"You may remove his chains."

The soldier hesitated. "Sir, are you sure?"

"Yes. We will accept Malchus into our household on the request of the lady Claudia Procula and her husband, Pontius Pilate."

Pontius Pilate. For the second time I heard that name. I would hear it often in the coming years. This man, whom at that time I did not know, I would come to know well. And we would share a destiny.

How could I have known that my destiny would be caught up in his and that his name would become known all over the world?

In a moment I stood in the hallway with no chains on my legs or my hands. My arms had grown accustomed to the chains and now felt oddly light.

The soldiers left. The deal was done. My fate had turned.

"Verus," Manaen said to the boy. "Bring water to Malchus. He must be thirsty after walking from the slave market. Malchus, please have a seat and let me explain why you are here in our household. You must have many questions."

The oddity of having no chains was now matched by the oddity of being treated with courtesy. I could not imagine that from a master.

He motioned to a cushioned stool, one of five arranged together, all with vibrant colors. I sat down. He took the one opposite me, looked at me directly, and spoke. "The first thing is that you will be treated well while you are in my custody. I do not know how you have been treated previously, and I cannot guarantee how you will be treated in the future. However, while you are with me, you will be treated well."

Verus returned with a tray, clay cups, and a pitcher. He poured two cups. Manaen handed one to me.

"I have had your chains removed because I trust you will not try to run away. It would not be wise. The Romans almost always find those who run away—especially someone like you. Your stature and the color of your hair would betray you wherever you went. There is no place you could hide. The Romans would deal with you severely when they found you. All to say, it would be to your great benefit if you were to stay here." He looked at me directly. "I cannot make you a free man, Malchus. Please understand that. If it were within my capability, I would pronounce you free today. But that is not a power I hold. However, as long as you are in my custody, you will be well treated, and I will always tell you the truth. The first thing I will tell you is this: It will not go well for you if you try to escape the Romans. You are obviously a strong man, Malchus. But the strength of Rome cannot be countered. Many have tried, but few have succeeded. Do you understand?"

I nodded.

"Please. Drink your water."

I brought the cup to my lips and was surprised how cool it was. I had heard that there were those who kept ice from the mountains in their homes to cool their food.

"You are destined for Jerusalem." Manaen looked at me for a moment. "The name of that city has no meaning for you. That is understandable. Jerusalem is the capital of Judea, where the Jews live, which are my people. That land is across the Great Sea. We, the Jews, do not live only in Judea, of course. Besides Rome, others of us live in a hundred different places around the world. But Jerusalem is our true home. All of us who live elsewhere are sojourners, and we long for Jerusalem." He paused for a moment to take a sip of water and began again, looking in the distance as he spoke. "There is much to tell you about us—and it is difficult to know where to begin. We are an odd race, to which all will attest. We ourselves do not deny it. At the core of our oddity is the conviction that God has chosen us— chosen us for a purpose. God told the patriarch of our people that he would bless him and his offspring, and subsequently all the nations of the earth would find a blessing through our nation. That, I suppose, is both a humbling and haughty ambition." He went quiet for a moment, looking out the window, perhaps reflecting on his own statement.

I took another drink as he continued.

"Malchus, your destiny is to be delivered to the household of Joseph Caiaphas, who is currently the high priest of the temple in Jerusalem. You are to be a gift to the household from Pontius Pilate. He has just been appointed prefect, the Roman governor, for

Jerusalem and the area around it. He will not assume that post for a few months, but when he does, he will try to build favor with the priestly family by lavishing gifts on them. You are one of those gifts. However, before you are sent to Jerusalem, you must be prepared. You must learn about the Jews—and you must learn about the Romans. That is why you are here in my house. Pontius Pilate and his wife, Claudia Procula, have entrusted your preparation to me. There is much for me to teach you—more than I can possibly hope to accomplish in a few months—but I will do my best. I trust you will also do your best. It will be to your great benefit to learn all you can before you are to go to Jerusalem. It can be a dangerous place. Success cannot be guaranteed, but the more you prepare, the greater the opportunity for success. Do you have any questions?"

I put my cup on the table. "If the Jews are from Jerusalem, why are they in Rome?"

"A good question. I cannot answer for all the Jews in Rome, for we are a few thousand, and each has his own story, but I will answer for myself." He repeated the question to himself. "Why am I a resident of Rome rather than Jerusalem?" He smiled as he pondered the thought. "I will answer that another day. But know that I sometimes ask the same question myself. But there have been enough discussions for today. Verus will show you to your lodging. Tomorrow we will talk more."

Verus led me out. "Manaen is a good man," Verus volunteered as we walked. I nodded and looked at the boy. He was perhaps fourteen or fifteen, only a few years younger than I but slightly built. "He is the best man among the Jews," he went on. "He is well respected by the Romans also."

We walked along a marble path beside a long, narrow pool of water, which led to the back of the villa. I had never seen or imagined such a place to live. Between the pool and the outer walls, clusters of lush trees and bushes shielded portions of the garden from the sun.

Stone benches and tables were situated in several places along the walls, ornamented with bright mosaic stones in intricate patterns.

At the back of the courtyard, he led me into a one-story building connected to the outer wall. The inside was fairly spacious, and two raised cots were situated in the corners. On one was a stack of clothing, and several sets of sandals sat on the floor nearby.

"Manaen said for you to pick a robe you prefer. And if none of them is large enough, he will have a robe made for you."

I nodded, still overwhelmed.

"Manaen is a good man," Verus repeated.

Verus was amused when I inspected the cot before we went to sleep. It consisted of a wooden frame crisscrossed with wide leather strips and overlaid with a mattress of goose down. I had never seen such a thing. I poked at it and rubbed it and turned it over to examine it before I stretched out on it. It seemed to have been made from a cloud, and I was asleep in moments.

When I awoke, Verus was bringing a tray of food. Apples, pears, and pickled olives along with soft cheese and fresh bread filled the tray. As he set the tray on the table, I asked, "Verus, are you a slave?"

"Manaen holds no slaves." He motioned for me to eat. "He is a descendant of the Essenes in Judea. Essenes hold no slaves. None of the ones you will see in his service are slaves. We work for wages—and in my case I am provided food and housing. I was an orphan when Manaen took me in. All the others—the gardeners, the cooks, the household servants—all are Jews employed by Manaen. He holds no slaves." He looked at me as if he wished he could say something that would explain his sympathy with my status as a slave. But instead, he informed me that Manaen asked to speak with me after my breakfast. "I will take you to meet him," he said.

The sun had not yet climbed above the level of the enclosing walls, but its light had filled the garden. We walked under a brightly painted ceiling, the roof supported by columns, which was mirrored by an identical walkway on the opposite side. Intricate tiles, with intersecting designs, formed the walkway beneath us. Low hedges framed the long, narrow pool to our side. I picked up the aroma of citrus blossoms, and orange fruits brightened the corners of the courtyard. Likewise, olive trees, with their gray-blue undersides decorated the edges, and for a moment my mind went back to the olive trees at the estate. Other trees, which I did not know, and flowering shrubs—pink and purple and white, filled up the space around the pool.

Verus led me to a corner of the garden near the great house, where Manaen was waiting. A large fig tree, with branches that ran up over the high wall, was situated in the corner, and below in both corners were matching grape arbors, their black vines putting out small green clusters. He sat at a round marble table with a mosaic of a grapevine and grapes in the center, the same art I had seen on the hem of his robe.

"Join me, Malchus." He motioned to one of the marble benches around the table. Manaen poured water from a silver jug into two silver cups and set one of the cups before me.

The cup was cold to my hand. For the second time I drank from a chilled cup. Manaen noticed my surprise but said nothing. I sipped the cool water carefully and let it run slowly over my tongue. Manaen took his water in one draught, and then took his cup in both hands, twirling it back and forth as he seemed to gather his thoughts.

"I did not sleep well last night." He smiled. "Our discussion yesterday was brief, but afterwards I realized how much responsibility I have in preparing you to go to Jerusalem. And it has forced me to think about the priorities. I have asked myself, 'What are the essential things Malchus must learn about the Jews?' That has made me think through the things that make my people distinctive. What are the things Malchus must know if he is to be successful when he arrives in Jerusalem? That is the question. Look above you." He turned his head upward. "You see the fig tree towering over us and the grapevines around us. These plants are important. They have meaning to Jews." He leaned forward on his bench, his hands before him. "What you must realize, Malchus, about us Jews—and this is more important than what we eat and what we don't eat. It is more important than our sacrifices and worship. It is more important than our festivals and religious observances." He paused. "While all those things are important to us, if you are to understand the Jews, you must understand we Jews live in constant dissatisfaction and in constant expectancy. Those things—dissatisfaction and expectancy—are the things which define the spirit of the Jews."

He leaned back to let me take this in.

"With what are we dissatisfied? We are dissatisfied with our forefathers because they failed to keep the obligations God had placed on them. We are dissatisfied with ourselves because we are a subjugated people. We are dissatisfied with the Romans, who do not respect our ways. But—" He leaned forward again "—we also live in expectancy. We do not think that things as they are now are things as they should be. We are certain God will send someone to make things right—to make things as they should be. He will be the one who brings peace and security. And more than one of our prophets has indicated that when this time comes, every man will sit with his neighbor under his own fig tree and his own grape vine. So the tree above us and the vines around us are reminders of our expectancy." He leaned back again. "We will talk more about that another time. Today we must begin something else."

We ascended the staircase, my eyes drawn to the geometric mosaics in the wall. When we reached the top of the staircase, we walked down an open hallway and came to a room at the corner of the house. Manaen lifted a bronze latch on a heavy wooden door and opened it. "This is where you will take your lessons."

The room was expansive and surrounded by stacks of dark wooden shelves. In the middle of the room sat a long stone table and at one end sat a small, white-bearded old man with a scroll open before him on the table.

"This is Gavriel. He will be your tutor."

The old man nodded to us in acknowledgment and went back to his scroll.

On the shelves, all around, lay scrolls. Hundreds of scrolls. I walked over and rubbed the wooden knob on one of them. The aroma of ink and papyrus and vellum and wood permeated the room.

"Our library." Manaen said. "Herod started it, and I have added to it. Herod's hope was that his sons would read and perhaps become wise. But his sons took no interest in reading—and they certainly did not become wise. Their interests were in the parties the living Romans held, not in what the dead Romans wrote—or what the Greeks or Jews wrote, for that matter."

I walked along the scrolls, laid in neat stacks on the shelves, touching the smooth handles.

"Can you read?" Manaen asked.

"I know all the letters. The lady at my master's house gave me some instruction."

"It is a start," Manaen answered. "We are not certain how much time we have. Pilate is eager to go to Judea, but he waits for his final orders. However, Gavriel is a capable tutor. He will bring you along. And I will provide some assistance as well. Your classes start now. Have a seat, Malchus. I turn you over to Gavriel."

And so my instruction began. At the beginning Gavriel was appalled at my limitations, but I was a ready learner, and over the next few weeks I listened carefully and made progress.

"Gavriel has paid you a compliment," Manaen said one evening. "And a compliment from Gavriel is not easy to obtain. But he says you are a ready learner, and you are eager to learn."

What Gavriel said was true. I was fascinated by the writings. Every morning I reported to the library, and Gavriel would have me read a section of the scrolls and drill me with endless questions—making sure I had absorbed the material. I learned the history of the Romans and read the works of the Greek scholars. He gave emphasis to the Torah, the writings of the Jews.

Once when Manaen looked in the library and I was poring over a passage from the Torah, he smiled and said to Gavriel, "Why do you require Malchus to know the Torah? Annas and Caiaphas pay little attention to it." He laughed. It was a joke I did not understand at the time, but I would come to understand later.

Gavriel taught me enough Aramaic, the common language in Judea, to be competent. My spoken Greek improved, and most of my reading was in that language. Gavriel was appalled at my Latin, but I knew only what was spoken at the estate. He drilled me constantly on enunciation and I improved. I had been about my studies for a few weeks and had fallen into a rhythm—the mornings and early afternoons were given to my sessions with Gavriel, and in the afternoons, I did additional reading and practicing. Then often, but without a given schedule, Manaen would sit with me in the library or under the fig tree and supplement my instruction with information about Rome or Judea.

As I took my lessons one morning, I saw Manaen go out the gate. He returned late in the afternoon.

"I have just returned from the house of Pontius Pilate," he said as he came to the library. I put the scroll down. "I have seen the man before," he went on, "but this is the first time I have spoken with him. He requested this meeting. He, like Gavriel and I, would like for you to be prepared when you arrive in Judea. However, the preparation he is requiring is different than we are providing—he would like for you to undergo military training."

Manaen saw the surprise on my face. "It is not an unreasonable idea," he said. "You see, the high priests in Jerusalem have their own security troops—temple guards who carry their own weapons. Only a few dozen comprise the group—enough to keep the peace around the temple, but not enough to be a threat to the Roman forces. And they are constrained to stay in the temple precinct unless permitted by the Romans to carry out an assignment. Pilate, I suppose, has heard of your stature—perhaps from his wife—and has surmised that you would be more useful in the temple guard than in carrying cups and bowls to and from the kitchen. He is, after all, a military man, and he thinks like a soldier. All to say, he wants me to send you to him for some training with the sword. His intent is not to make you into a Roman soldier—that would require most of a year. He intends only to equip you to handle the sword of the temple guard. If you are a quick learner, he expects a month or two will suffice."

I looked out the window. I had become so comfortable around Manaen and Gavriel and the limitless scrolls that I had forgotten about going to Judea—as a slave.

Chapter 14

Roman Training

Manaen and I left the palace early in the morning and made our way to the bridge leading to the city. Small boats passed under us, going in each direction, the southbound ones laden with grains and vegetables, and those going north filled with metal items, leatherwork, and other items from the shops of the city.

"Our walk is not a short one," Manaen said as we crossed the bridge. "The *Castra Praetoria* is on the opposite side of the city, but there is much to show you along the way."

I moved aside to allow a boy pushing a vegetable cart to pass by. There was more traffic on this side of the bridge—people, animals, and carts—and all seemed to be in a hurry. We began walking single file, Manaen in the front, to better negotiate the crowd.

"The walking will be easier soon," Manaen said, turning back to me. "The streets are wider when we get closer to the Forum." I nodded and turned sideways to allow an old man leading a donkey to come by. The street became steeper but soon widened, and we came out of the congested alleys into an open area where we could see the city's center.

"That is the Palatine Hill," Manaen informed me. "That's where Romulus, according to the legend, founded the original city. You have read the story."

The huge Coliseum rose up on our left. We were close enough to this great oval building that I could hear the faint click and clack of wooden weapons and the shouts of men as they went about their training. I thought of the cheetah and wondered if he was among them.

"Some Roman soldiers will resent you," Manaen said as we approached the barracks. Some lost uncles and fathers in the north.

They will think it was *your* uncle or *your* father who killed them. Be wary. The officers will seek to protect you, but they cannot watch everything."

"Is it new?" I asked as we approached the Castra Praetoria.

"It *is* new. Hardly more than a year old. It was Sejanus's idea. He had these barracks built to house the Praetorian Guard, which he commands. The idea is without precedent in Rome. Previously the soldiers were billeted miles away from the city—and many of the senators are not pleased with this change. Previous emperors kept the pretense of a republican government. Part of that pretense was that the army had no political function and should be kept away from the seat of power. But Sejanus convinced Tiberius into bringing these elite soldiers into the city." As we kept walking Manaen leaned toward me. "If you listen to the talk on the street, the citizens think Sejanus, not Tiberius, makes the decisions these days. Tiberius, according to all the talk, has grown weary of the demands of ruling Rome and has passed the responsibility to Sejanus."

"Will Sejanus become the emperor when Tiberius dies?"

A wry smile came to Manaen's face, and he looked around him as if to see if anyone could hear our talk. He stopped. Two men passed by, and he waited until they had moved along to continue. "Malchus, you have asked the question that is on every Roman's mind, but never gets to his tongue. I will provide as much of an answer as I can, but I recommend that you put these questions out of your mind while you are at the Castra Praetoria."

He waited for my affirmation.

"I understand."

"To your question, Sejanus is from the equestrian class. He has no lineage from the imperial families. There is no precedent for anyone from the equestrian class to become emperor. It would seem—on the face of things—there is no way for him to ascend to the throne. But Sejanus is ambitious. All in Rome know that. And as prefect of the

Praetorian Guard, he now has more than one thousand soldiers, some of the best in the army, close by and at his personal disposal. And he has the ear of the emperor—who apparently is disinterested in ruling the empire."

The area around the fort was flat and open, and I could see clusters of soldiers going about their training.

"What the future holds," Manaen went on, "is difficult to predict. It has been five years since Germanicus's death, but his memory still holds the hearts of the people of Rome. There are as many rumors as there are citizens in Rome, but most of those rumors connect both Tiberius and Sejanus, in some way, to Germanicus's death."

A slight smile came to Manaen's face.

"What has come to your mind?"

"It has never occurred to me until this moment that we Jews have a similar experience in our history. We had a king—this was about a thousand years ago. He was named Saul. A young man named David became his most successful general. And the people of Israel fell in love with this handsome young man who brought glory to their nation. Saul realized his Israelites loved David more than himself, so he decided to have David killed."

"I read the story. Saul was not successful."

Manaen smiled again. "He was not. Saul's own son befriended David and helped him avoid being murdered. Eventually David became king, and God made him a promise that another king would rise from his line, a king whose kingdom will endure forever."

"Is this the one you have told me about, the one that you anticipate?"

"It is indeed, Malchus."

"I would like to hear more."

"You will, but first you must learn how to wield a Roman sword."

We came to the gates. A young officer approached us. "I am Marius, centurion of the cavalry for the Italian Cohort. "Are you Manaen the Jew?"

"I am," Manaen answered.

"And you must be Malchus the Cherusci."

No contempt was contained in his voice. I was glad he had acknowledged me. It gave me a sense of value—in addition to the value that Manaen affirmed in me. Marius looked to be in his early twenties, with a muscular leanness about him, an easy confidence, and a greater maturity than his age. His face and jaw had clean lines; his eyes were intelligent and expressive. I sensed this was a man I would like to know better.

A man without a friend is a man who might as well be dead. Enemies come easily, but friends, true friends, are rare. I could not know at this time how valuable this man's friendship would become.

"Malchus..." Marius turned the name over one more time, thinking about it. "A king..." but he let the thought go. "I have orders to ensure you are provided training in personal warfare. Six weeks have been allotted to provide this training. You will not be taught battle tactics. You will learn the skills of personal combat only." He paused for a moment as if to reflect on the unusual nature of this arrangement. "I will not provide this training. That will be the duties of others. I am responsible only that you receive this training. I am a cavalry officer, not a foot soldier. The camp commander has assigned me this duty because there is some possibility I will also go to Judea."

He had been speaking to both of us, then turned to Manaen. He made a polite bow of his head. "If I am assigned to the land of the Jews, it would benefit me to learn more about the people of that nation. Would it please Manaen the Jew to instruct me in the ways of his people?"

"You are welcome at my house—the house of the Herods—at any time. I would be honored to host you and tell you about my people."

"Very good. May I suggest you give me one month with Malchus, and then we will afford ourselves of your hospitality. At that time I can provide a report of the progress we have made, and you can tell me about the land where I may be sent. If that is agreeable with you, then I will show Malchus to his quarters."

Manaen bowed.

Marius turned to me. "I have decided it would be unwise to place you in the barracks with the other men. There is a storeroom adjacent to my quarters. I have put a cot there. It will be better for you than the barracks. A few among the troops harbor resentment toward those from the north."

He smiled. "Yet you cannot be hidden. You are taller than all but one man in the fort. Every time you enter the courtyard or go to the training fields you will be noticed. I will do all I can to protect you, but you should be wary. Do you understand?"

"I understand."

Manaen took his leave with the confirmation that we would meet again in a month.

One enemy and one friend. That would be the outcome of my weeks among the Roman soldiers. Of the enemy, I know little, except that he was left with a useless arm after our struggle. I regret the injury. Of the friend, he remains my friend today.

"The Spear," was what his soldiers called him. The first time I saw Pontius Pilate was the first day of my training. He stood with his hands on his hips, watching the exercises. A thick head, closely shaved, sat on a thick neck. Red cheeks, rasped clean by the barber in the pre-dawn, looked raw in the morning sun. His small ears seemed pinned to the sides of his head. Thick forearms matched his thick neck. They were arms capable of handling the short sword fitted against his hip. His nose was short and blunt, his lips thin and tight in a face without emotion. As he passed near me, I saw his gray, alert eyes. They were the eyes of a soldier—eyes that made assessments with every movement.

Often would I see those vigilant gray eyes in the coming years. I would have many opportunities to watch those eyes as they watched others. The eyes of Pontius Pilate were the eyes of a soldier—and I would get to know this soldier better.

Much of my training dealt with the short sword, the key weapon of the Roman soldier. I learned the skills needed for close-contact combat—how to feint and parry, how to repulse a charge, and most importantly, how to deliver a death thrust.

"Bring your sword *under* the ribs, not *through* the ribs," our trainer shouted, demonstrating the skill with a wooden sword.

I was matched once with Brasus, the only one my size. Indeed, he was slightly taller and many pounds heavier. His black hair, matted on his arms and shoulders, gained him his name in the barracks— "Brasus the Bear." We clattered our wooden swords against each for a few moments, neither of us gaining an advantage. He grew frustrated and tried to wrap me up in his massive arms, but I ducked under his grasp, and he fell into the dust. The other trainees, I realized, had quit their contests to watch ours, and they laughed. I offered my arm to help him, but he swung the wooden sword at me. I pulled away to avoid an injury. He came to his feet shouting curses, but the trainers interrupted. I hoped the altercation was over, but I was wrong.

Six weeks I spent training with the Roman soldiers. I learned much. The skill I learned with the sword would serve me well when I came to Jerusalem. The rigors of the daily exercises suited me. Except for one man among the troops, I had little of the antagonism that Marius was concerned about. That antagonism would eventually lead to confrontation. I did not seek it, but it became inevitable. It is a story for others to tell, not me. Did Brasus deserve his fate? Some say so. Those that say so can tell the story.

Much of the training for Roman soldiers dealt with battle tactics and words of command—training for which I was exempt, but I watched with great interest. The trainees were spread apart across the great field in groups of eight for this beginners' training.

Marius came beside me one afternoon as I observed. He pointed to the field. "This is the reason Rome rules the world."

I looked at him for elaboration.

"Listen," he said.

I heard "*Depone dextra!*" from the trainer of the group nearest us, and the eight trainees executed a right turn. "*Depone senestra!*" the trainer shouted as all but one turned left. The offender suffered three lashes of the trainer's cane for his failure.

"Obedience," Marius said. "Quick obedience. And organization. Those are the qualities that have made Rome great. It is not superior skills with the sword, or the spear, or the bow, or even skill with the horses, that have brought Rome success. It is obedience and organization. A Roman soldier also knows he will be fed, and he knows he will be paid. Those he fights against have no such assurances. That is the reason Rome prevails."

The fight with Brasus was not something I sought. Sejanus was there that day, sitting beside Pilate, to watch the contests of the soldiers. Yes, in the contest of spears, I threw farther than Brasus. The cheers of the soldiers offended him. When he first challenged me for a fight, I declined. But there are some things a man cannot say about another man's mother and believe it will go without remedy. The fight was short, and I took no pleasure in the outcome.

Only a few days after the fight with Brasus, Marius told me, "I have been instructed to go tomorrow afternoon to the house of Pontius Pilate—for a discussion, I am sure, concerning our plans for Judea. You will accompany me. You cannot stay in the barracks alone."

The next day, after training, and after we had afforded ourselves of the baths, Marius put on his dress uniform, and we made our way through the streets to the house of Pontius Pilate. "His house is better than most of his status—thanks to his marriage to Claudia Procula," Marius told me as we arrived. "But if he is successful in Judea, he will certainly return to Rome, able to purchase a villa—perhaps more than one. His predecessor, Valerius Gratus, lived meagerly in Rome before he took the preceptorship in Judea. Now he will return to a large villa on the edge of the city and an ornate apartment in the center of the city. Judea, according to the gossip on the street, is a difficult, but profitable assignment."

A servant admitted us, and we stood inside the courtyard for a moment as he alerted his master. In a moment he returned and indicated that Marius should follow.

"Wait here," Marius told me. "This audience will probably not be long."

A small fountain, inlaid with yellow and blue enamel, trickled in the center of the courtyard. Lily pads grew in the pool. Above the sound of the water, I could hear the voices of Pilate and Marius in a nearby room—but I could not make out their words. Two other voices, female voices, came from another section of the house. The voices came nearer. Then Claudia Procula, accompanied by another woman—not quite a woman, yet not a girl—entered the courtyard, still talking with each other.

When I saw this young woman, something in my spirit erupted. What is the heart's greatest pain? Is it not the yearning for something that cannot be obtained? When I first saw her, two realizations—each at the same moment—came to me: She was the greatest desire I had ever known, and I could never have her. This dual realization came without warning, without forethought. I had not sought her. Neither was she part of my imagination. Neither did I think such a woman could exist, yet at the moment I saw her, something deep inside me was stirred—a longing for that which could never find fulfillment. It was ecstasy, it was grief. A man may have a premonition of his destiny, but that was not what I sensed at the moment. My sense was that whatever destiny I might seek—and whether it would include this woman—could never be achieved—because I was a slave.

I saw her first in profile, her fine nose slightly tilted. Her hair, like mingled copper and bronze, was pinned above her neck with ivory combs. In color and gloss her cheeks and forehead matched the ivory. Her sleeved tunic was linen, bordered with golden thread. An ivory clasp held the deep blue fabric that cinched her narrow waist. The tunic extended to the floor and covered all but her feet and carried the rhythms of her graceful walk as her sandals whisked across the floor.

The lines of her lips were clean and composed. Her mouth betrayed no servility. Her bearing was erect, and her eyes were alert as if they held an unspoken secret. It was the bearing of a princess, not a slave.

Claudia noticed me and stopped the conversation. It was an awkward moment. She looked at me, but my eyes were on the young woman at her side—who looked at me with some curiosity before turning away.

Claudia's discomfort was apparent. She looked at me as if she would speak, then caught herself. She took the arm of her young attendant, who looked at me one more time as Claudia led her out of the atrium. I was left alone again, but my heart was stirred.

How long I stood there in a stupor, I cannot say, but Marius returned and broke my reverie.

"We may go," he said, and the servant showed us out the gate.

"'The Spear', as the men call him, is impatient," Marius told me as we began walking. "He wants to get to Judea. Only two weeks remain for safe travel. Once the autumn winds start blowing from the north, the Great Sea cannot be crossed. Pilate wants to leave immediately. He has asked Sejanus to approve his travel, but Sejanus will not do so until he has authorization from the emperor—and the emperor, it seems, has forgotten Rome. He is content to stay in Capri and let Rome take care of itself. However, in the middle of all this uncertainty, I have this news—I have received my orders for posting. It is as I wished. I am also going to Judea."

"This is good news," I said.

"When Pilate goes to Judea—and takes you with him—I also will accompany you. Pilate wishes me to take charge of the cavalry in Judea. I will have the title of centurion. I will command fifty men, sixty at the most. All are horsemen and will be stationed at several garrisons in Judea. My duties require me to make sure that messages are transferred promptly between those garrisons."

"I am glad to have this news," I said.

"As am I. But I command no one right now, and I have few duties until Tiberius gives the order, and no one in Rome can guess when Tiberius will give that order. So, we will wait."

Our wait was longer than we expected. A year and a half I would be in Rome. But Marius and I waited on Pilate and Pilate waited on Sejanus and Sejanus waited on Tiberius, who waited on something— but no one in Rome knew what Tiberias waited on.

Tiberius's indifference would prove a boon for me. Pilate would not receive the timely authorization he sought—not before the winter winds poured down from the northern mountains over the Great Sea, closing the sea lanes, and I would gain the benefit of staying longer with Manaen. There in the library under the supervision of Gavriel, I would have the opportunity to pore through the scrolls. The world was a larger place than I had supposed. The world of the Greeks and their literature was opened to me. I read Herodotus and Socrates and Plato and Euripides and Sophocles and Homer and Cicero and oth- ers. I also read the books of the Jews. I learned their history—how their patriarch Abraham came to the land and how his family pros- pered, how his great-grandson was sold into slavery, and how he prospered in slavery. It was a good story, but I took little consolation in it. Joseph was a Jew who was a slave. I was soon to be a slave to the Jews.

The days shortened. The air cooled and the winds from the mountains in the north winds that kept the ships in harbor—also spilled down to Rome. Frost formed on the outside of the windows in the library, but the room was warmed by heated water pipes in the floor. Nonetheless, Gavriel wore a heavy robe each day as we went about our studies. Marius was a frequent visitor that winter. After dinner, the three of us—Manaen, Marius and I—had long discussions about my reading, but the topic sometimes went to politics as well. "Tiberius lingers in Capri," Marius said. "He gives no indication about his return to Rome."

"What of Sejanus?" Manaen asked. "Does he correspond with the emperor?"

"Yes—" Marius replied, "—to some degree. Messengers go back and forth between the two. Sejanus has become more powerful—and more ambitious. He now has a statue of himself near the forum, and his birthday has been proclaimed a national holiday. He is hated by many, but no one speaks against him openly. Some of his enemies have had suspicious deaths, and other enemies have gone silent—but he is hesitant to make significant decisions without the emperor's approval."

"Does Sejanus aspire to become emperor?" Manaen asked. "That is the question on the streets."

Marius shrugged. "Tiberius has no heir, and he is aging. Sejanus is ambitious and his control of the Praetorian Guard intimidates his enemies. Yet he is equestrian—not of noble stock. For him to become emperor would have no precedent—yet those who might oppose him would do so at great peril."

"And what of Pontius Pilate? How is he enduring this postponement?"

"Not well. I know more of this from Claudia Procula, than from Pilate. I am occasionally summoned to the house of Pilate, and often she and her slave girl will sit with me in the atrium.

Slave girl? She is a slave girl? Memories have emotions attached to them. They exist not only in a man's mind. They are twinned in his heart. The emotions I sensed at that moment were opposite to each other—one was alertness, a bright remembrance of her countenance and her beauty . . . and the other was despair, the realization I would probably never see her again.

"I should hardly call her a slave girl," Manaen said. "She is more like a younger sister to Claudia. She has been her attendant since Claudia was in her teenage years. Her name is Sabrina. The girl was captured as a child on one of the islands in north Britannia and brought to Rome. But to answer your question, we all know Pilate is impatient, but for the moment, all he can do is wait on Tiberius in the hope that once the sea lanes are open, he will receive authorization to go."

Sabrina. I now had a name to attach to my longing. I often wished I did not have the name. It made the longing even more painful. Sometimes, in my quiet reverie, I would hear the name slip unbidden from my lips as I thought of her . . . Sabrina.

Chapter 15

The Delay

"There is no word from Tiberius."

Marius spoke as he sat in the garden with Manaen and me. The orange trees had put out their fruit, the size of a man's thumb. A few of the dried blossoms lay on the marble at our feet. "The feast of Vinalia has ended. It is the middle of April. The sea-lanes are opening. Both Sejanus and Pilate expected to have some word from the emperor by now."

"Is it too much to hope—" Manaen started. "—I'm hesitant to voice this question, but is it too much to hope that Pilate may never receive his commission to transfer to Judea and that Malchus might stay here in Rome—in my custody?"

"I can give no answer to your question," Marius replied. "Tiberias is unpredictable. Once, in the forum he said, 'Let them hate me, as long as they respect my conduct.' And although he is well-hated by many, there is no conduct to judge him by. Though he has effectively left the rule of Rome to Sejanus, Sejanus knows his limits. He is afraid to authorize Pilate's transfer to Judea until Tiberius approves it."

The roses in the courtyard bloomed—clusters of them in several shades of pink and red and their petals fell in profusion on the marble walkways. The oranges grew to full size, bending the branches with their weight. Verus gathered them and squeezed the juice from them to cool our throats in the summer heat. Days and weeks passed. I became accustomed to the weekly Sabbath, when the streets were hushed, and the Jews stayed in their apartments waiting for the sunset and the Sabbath meal.

Late one afternoon as Manaen, Marius and I sat in the courtyard, a breeze stirred and brown and yellow myrtle leaves drifted down around us, some finding the pool around the fountain, others swirling around the polished marble walkway at our feet. Marius looked up at the branches. "The season is late. The *Mare Clausum*, the closing of the sea, is upon us. I fear we will not go to Judea this year."

Indeed, no word came from Tiberius, and Pilate's plan to go to Judea would wait another season.

It was better news than I could have hoped for. I spent another winter in the library, the gray clouds suffusing the light through the high windows as I worked through the volumes, a wool blanket pulled around me for comfort. The scrolls seemed inexhaustible. Gavriel guided me through them, making recommendations and, when I finished a volume, asking me questions to make certain I comprehended what I read. Marius continued to come to the house. We took our dinners indoors beside the fire. As the days lengthened, the crocuses in the garden below were the first to recognize spring's imminence, courageously spattering the garden with their purple blossoms. The irises soon answered the crocus's purple with their own purple, and then as if summoned by a horn, the garden came out of its lethargy with a dozen colors, and the tangy scent of the orange blossoms filled the library.

The news of the death of 'the cheetah' bothered me more than I expected. He died in training and never made it to the arena. From all accounts he had irritated an experienced gladiator, who claimed the injury to be an accident. He did not mean for the point of his sword to slice the neck of the young Mauritanian, he said. Whatever the truth, the cheetah was dead—along with his hopes of achieving glory in the Coliseum. It could have been me.

I was grateful to Claudia Procula for rescuing me from the arena. She was the second woman to rescue me.

Pilate has his orders," Marius stood in the doorway of the library. Manaen stood beside him. Both had stern faces. "Tiberius sent the authorization. Sejanus has passed it along to Pilate. He plans to leave within two weeks. I have just come from his house."

It was not news I welcomed.

What determines a man's destiny? Is it his own decisions? Or is it the decisions of others? Or perhaps, as some believe, is a man's destiny in the hands of God in heaven?

Ten days later Marius returned to give me instructions. "I leave tomorrow for Ostia, the port. I will accompany Pilate. He wants to make sure everything is in order. He has waited a long time for this voyage. Last night Sejanus commissioned him as the new prefect of Judea. He gave him a medallion from Tiberius. On it is inscribed *Amicus Caesaris.*"

"Friend of Caesar," I translated.

"Yes," Marius continued. "Pilate took it as a great honor to be acknowledged as a friend of the emperor. As for you, you will come to Ostia two days later. On the following day we will sail for Caesarea."

Two days later Manaen and I stood on the bridge at the quay along the Tiber. In the good-byes earlier that day to Gavriel and Verus, I had expected tears from Verus, but I was surprised to see Gavriel wipe his eyes. I now had chains on my arms again. Two Roman soldiers stood with us as we awaited the boat that would take us downriver to Ostia, the port.

How can a man be given a sword and walk freely one day and be in chains another?

"I must commend you to the care of Almighty God," Manaen said. "I hope to go to Jerusalem soon—but the time is not now. Marius waits for you in Ostia and assures me he will do all he can to help you."

I thanked Manaen for his care. We embraced and he turned away.

I am sometimes asked about Rome. In truth, I know little of Rome. I was insulated from the city while at the barracks and while in the Jewish quarter. Of the great intrigues of the great city I was well removed. The complaints of the city's citizens were not spoken in my presence. What was whispered in the streets I did not hear. The discussions of the debates at the Forum did not reach my ears. Though the great city lay near me, it may as well have been across the Great Sea

Yet I held the world of the Greeks and the Jews in my hands, opened up to me in the scrolls of the library.

Chapter 16

To Caesarea

The two soldiers and I walked down the stone steps that led to the quay.

Two soldiers brought me to Rome and now two soldiers take me from the city.

From the bridges I had watched the movements of these boats, but this was the first time I had been near them. Barrels of wheat, the product of Egypt, were being unloaded from several boats. Great bales of cotton, also from Egypt, stood in high stacks along the quay. Foremen shouted instructions to bare-shouldered slaves—their skin of a dozen different hues—who transferred the barrels and bales from boats to carts to be delivered to the city. That wheat would soon become the bread that would sustain the citizens of Rome and the cotton would soon be rendered into white togas for those same citizens. We were on our way to Ostia, the port, to board the boat that would take us to Caesarea.

We stood beside a great stack of barrels to get the shade. "Large boats cannot come up the Tiber," one of the soldiers explained. "The merchandise has to be transferred to these smaller ones and brought up to Rome. At Ostia this afternoon, you will see the real ships that cross the sea with cargo. But you will not board one of those ships. You will take a bireme—a war ship, better for a quick crossing." We boarded an open boat, manned by two boatmen who poled us out into the river.

We caught the current and began the trip to the coast. The reeds on the bank swayed in a slight breeze. Some were bent by the weight of blackbirds perched on the stalks. Swallows darted around us, snatching insects invisible to our eyes. A heron, disturbed by our intrusion, squawked and flew downriver. Dragonflies sparkled in the sun, flitting around the reeds. On the opposite bank, mules pulled the laden boats upriver, struggling against the current.

When we came to Ostia, the sun was low on the horizon, and Marius was waiting on the dock. Behind him were the great red brick warehouses that stored the grain and other goods in transit to and from the teeming dock. Men of all hues were about the work of loading and unloading cargo. The great grain ships the soldier spoke of tipped back and forth in the waves.

"Welcome," Marius shouted as our little boat docked. He gave me his hand to help me onto the dock. The two soldiers signed me over to Marius.

"That is our boat." He pointed to a craft that was small in comparison to the cargo ships.

It rose and fell slightly with each wave. Fifteen oars protruded through rectangular windows on the side of the ship. Through those windows I made out the images of men inside.

"Are they slaves?" I asked.

"Oh no. Slaves and criminals row the war ships, but Rome would not trust high-ranking passengers to slave-rowers. These are free men working for wages—good wages. Most rowers get a drachma a day. The men on this ship get more—two drachmas each day for most. Only the strongest backs get this duty. Thirty strong men pull these oars for important passengers or valuable cargo like gold bullion or coins or such. But there is no gold bullion or coins on this boat—only a prefect of Rome and those who attend him. These are free men, capable rowers, and unless the wind is our adversary, with that square sail and those sixty strong arms, we will be in Caesarea in fewer than twelve days."

At the side of the boat I saw Pilate—watching provisions being loaded onto the bireme. He stood in the posture I came to acquaint with him—feet slightly spread, hands on his hips, neck and head erect.

"Yes, that is the new prefect," Marius said. "He plans to leave at first light, and is making sure all provisions are aboard. The rowers, however, are angry. Pilate will not allow them to spend the evening ashore. He is eager to get to Judea and will not risk losing a rower to a drunken brawl."

Our conversation was interrupted by movement above us. A litter with purple curtains, carried by four Nubians, was deposited at the edge of the quay. The purple curtain parted slightly, and I saw the face of Claudia Procula peer out.

Pilate saw her too. Their goodbyes, no doubt, had been said earlier that day and perhaps Claudia had hoped to go unnoticed as she watched her husband sail away, but she was noticed—by all on the ship. For a moment all activity on the vessel was arrested. Those onboard all looked at the litter. It was an awkward moment. Pontius Pilate, the soldier of Rome, the prefect of Judea, the commander of three thousand Roman soldiers, did not want to appear sentimental before his men, but—as I would come to better appreciate later—he held a genuine affection for his wife and could not ignore her. All movement, save for the swifts and swallows around us, was suspended. The ship's captain, seeing Claudia, barked orders to the men to distract them. Pilate, however, at the prow of the boat, stood erect for a few moments looking at his wife—his hands clasped behind his back, the motion of the boat swaying his body slightly. Each of them looked at each other for several moments until Claudia closed the curtain. But just before she did, I saw another person in the litter. Sabrina. For a moment, she leaned forward and put her head just above Claudia's shoulders and the late afternoon sunlight caught her face. Her copper-bronze hair framed her face. A dozen emotions ran through me—but grief prevailed. My mind told me I would never see this face again. She seemed to be searching for something. I wanted to believe it was me. Then her eyes caught mine. We looked at each other for a few seconds. Then the Nubians hoisted the litter and she moved away from the curtain.

The memory of that gaze would torture me for months.

As the litter bearers walked away, Claudia poked her head out of the curtain again to look, her eyes on the ship and her husband. I looked with gratitude at this woman who had rescued me less than a year earlier.

Claudia Procula had intersected my life in Rome and changed its direction. Neither of us knew our lives would again intersect, but those days in Jerusalem changed everything.

Marius motioned for me to follow him to the front of the boat. "For the time being you will need to stay below decks. I'm sorry. Once we lift anchor in the morning and get to sea, you can come above."

He lifted a hatch and motioned for me to go below. When he closed the hatch above me, I was, for the moment, encased in darkness. As my eyes adjusted to the dim light of some chink-holes between the planks, I could see metal rings on the wall and on the floor. I counted them and determined this cabin provided space for eight slaves packed shoulder to shoulder. I was the only slave in the hold and was not chained, and for that I was grateful.

I slept fitfully. I tried to attribute it to the hard floor and motion of the ship and the creaking of the timbers, but some of it—I am sure— was related to the face I saw through the purple curtains of Claudia's litter.

As the first dim light seeped through the chink-hole in the inner part of the boat, I heard the urgent movement of men's feet on the wooden floor and the sound of an equally urgent voice—the booming voice of the boatswain. The boat was coming alive. The rigging of the mainsail rattled against the mast in the breeze, as if the boat itself were impatient. The voyage across the Great Sea would soon begin. I put my eyes to the chink-holes in time to see the ropes lifted from the piers on the harbor, and then the voice of the boatswain, with a voice that resonated like thunder, called his rowers to attention. The drummer found his cadence and, as if a great god from the sky had reached down and pushed our boat, the vessel lurched forward. I lost my balance as sixty strong arms pulled on thirty oars, pushing our vessel into the great sea.

The boatswain's voice called for silence among his rowers. His voice, deep and big, became the only voice as he organized the rowers. The rasp of the oars in the oar-locks and the commands of the boatswain formed a rhythm as our ship entered the Great Sea.

We were bound for Judea.

Marius handed my breakfast down to me. "In an hour," he said, "I will open the hold."

By the time he let me onto the deck, Ostia was behind us, already out of sight. "There is no place here," Marius said with a wry smile, "that would allow a slave to escape. I think you do not swim as well as you throw the spear." Our sails swelled, having caught a favorable breeze. The rowers racked their oars, and we moved gently across the top of the water. I stood near the rail, taking in the salt-tanged aroma of the open sea, trying to find the line between the blue of the sea and the blue of the sky. Others have told of their exhilaration at being in the open sea, and I felt it this day. For a few moments, at least, my mind was not occupied with concerns with what awaited me in Caesarea.

Blue. The whole world was blue. The sky above me and the sea beneath me contested against each other over which was bluer. In all directions the world was blue. No coast or island or cloud impugned this blue. Only our puny craft, a tiny brown and white stain on an otherwise perfect blue world, intruded on the blueness.

We were ten days crossing the Great Sea. On each of those days Pilate often stood watching the prow of the ship cutting through the water, occasionally looking back at the square sail to see how much wind it had caught. I had full liberty on the boat, and I likewise watched the water and the sky, but I stayed nearer the back of the boat. A slave should never be in the proximity of a Roman officer— especially one who is to be Prefect of Judea.

Yet, on a few occasions our eyes met, and in his face there was something different than in most men's faces—something, if not respect, at least something better than contempt. I could not call it respect—yet it bordered on it. He had been there in the barracks' stands when the contests were held. He saw me throw the spear. He saw me contend against Brasus in the wrestling pit. And although— in the ten-day journey—he spoke to me only once, yet sometimes I would see in his face some recognition, some remembrance as if he were saying to me, "I was at the training ground that day. I saw you throw the spear. I saw you subdue Brasus." Perhaps I have imagined all that, but I think not.

As he stood in the prow, he carried a noticeable impatience in his bearing. On the fifth day of the voyage, when the winds were light, and the rowers had to bear the greater responsibility, his impatience became even more apparent as he looked at the flaccid sails and scanned the horizon for some evidence of wind.

Marius noticed Pilate's impatience and whispered to me, "I think he might like to take a turn himself with the rowers."

On the ninth day of the voyage I stood at the rail, watching the sea. It was late afternoon. The sun was behind us, as was the wind. The square sail swelled as we caught a good breeze. Whitecapped waves flecked the blue water. Those waves slapped against the hull as the boat rose and fell in rhythm. Above us two curious seagulls dipped and darted around the boat, squawking. A glittering silver spray was thrown up from the prow as the ship rose and fell.

I became aware of someone beside me. I turned to see Pilate along the rail, near enough that I could see the sea breeze blow the fine hair on his forearm. I made a movement to dismiss myself, but Pilate put up his hand to let me know it was not necessary. I remained.

"Sejanus was impressed," Pilate said after some time, still looking at the sea, not turning in my direction.

I said nothing.

"It was quite a contest," he added after a moment. "No one thought Brasus could be bested in throwing the spear. And certainly no one thought he could be bested in wrestling."

He went quiet for a moment. "Sejanus thought you should be brought into the Praetorian Guard. He thought your skill and strength could serve Rome. 'Why give him to the Jews?' he asked."

He went quiet again. The gulls above us squawked as Pilate thought.

"But . . ." He looked at me, then after a time said, "Malchus." But he was not addressing me. He was just turning my name over. I turned to look at him. "Malchus," he repeated, his mouth in a thin, ironic smile. "Malchus, the name of a king. Are you a king, Malchus?" he asked, still looking at the sea.

The dinner bell rang, signaling that Pilate's meal was ready. He raised his hand to say it was not necessary for me to reply. He stepped away and went below.

Are you a king? He would ask that question again— to another one. It would be the question that would define him forever.

"Land in sight!" the boatswain called.

I went to the rail. I saw no land, only an odd sparkling reflection on the horizon. Pilate came up from his cabin. The sun was behind us, throwing a sail-shadow on the water below us, but also throwing its rays across the water to what seemed like a great mirror, which brought the light back to us.

"Caesarea," one of the deckhands said. "Seen it a dozen times, I have. At this time of day, when the sky is clear, it looks like a thousand mirrors on the shore. Old crazy Herod built it. Made it all out of white marble, he did. Made a harbor where there wasn't one. Crazy as he was, he knew how to get a job done."

As the sun behind us dropped below the sea, it cast soft pinks and purples onto the clouds above us, which reflected down to the city of Caesarea, those soft colors pinks and purples moved across the white buildings as if the stones were alive.

"Herod's city," the captain said to me as I looked at the shoreline. "The man had a way with stones."

Chapter 17

Ironies

Ironies atop ironies. I would learn more about Herod and his stones. He built many edifices, all magnificent buildings, one of which is now his resting place.

King Herod's body is now interred inside his mountain fortress just outside the city of Jerusalem. His tomb is set on the side of the mountain that faces toward the city—as if he were still watching. Herodium, as the mountain is called, was the fortress Herod built to ensure his security—a place to which, if danger came, he could retreat quickly. But a man, no matter how great, cannot watch from a tomb. For Herod, watchfulness is no longer needed. He is now insulated from any dangers. No enemy, no insurgent, no conspirator can any longer threaten Herod the Great. The security he sought he has now found—in the side of the mountain overlooking Bethlehem. His dead eyes, which were blind to many things, are now fully blind—and covered with layers of dirt.

Of all the ironies, this one prevails: The body of Herod, the human king, the one who conspired to kill the divine king, now decays inside the earth of the hill he constructed—while the body of the divine king has broken free from the earth.

If a traveler were to pass through the valleys between Bethlehem and the Herodum, the mountain of Herod, that traveler's eyes would be naturally drawn to that artificial hill, built by the effort of a thousand slaves, each of whom carried, I suppose, ten thousand baskets of earth. I have been told it is higher than the city of Jerusalem. If that traveler had been granted access to climb the switchback road to the top, he would have seen bronze, silver, and gold in abundance, mosaics, frescoes, and gilded columns, with ample stores of water, grain, and oil.

That traveler would not have naturally looked to the other side of the valley—to a cave where a true king entered the world. Is not the world turned inside out? One king—the human king—sought grandeur and safety at the top of a mountain; another king—an authentic king, a heavenly king—sought no grandeur, sought no safety, but made himself vulnerable to the world he entered. He was born, not on a mountain, and not even on the earth's surface—but below it. One king sought the highest point, the other the lowest. One king surrounded himself with an army; the other with a few shepherds. Gold and silver surrounded one king; the other had straw and barnyard animals around him.

In these events, all our natural ideas about the nature of a kingdom are undermined.

Herod told the magi—those men from the east that sought the new king—that once they had found the king they sought, that they should return and inform him so that he also could "come and worship him". Such irony—King Herod built a mountain that looked down on the cave where the new king was born. He had a place of observation—but he could not see.

Who am I to chastise Herod? I also heard reports about that king—a true king. Neither did I believe the reports. Neither did I seek to worship him. Neither was I willing to follow him—until he confronted me. To the ironies I have mentioned, I must add this one: I, the slave, did not immediately recognize the freedom available to me and I did not seek the true king—he sought me.

More like Herod was I than like the magi. The wise men from the east made an effort to seek him out. I heard reports of a birth, reports of healings, reports of teaching. But those reports did not prompt me to investigate this one who was born miraculously, with the power to heal, who taught with the authority of God. Unlike the magi I was not alert to the seeking of truth. Consumed with my own duties, my own responsibilities, my own concerns, I remained dull in my spirit.

And although I did not seek him—yet he sought me. Before I came to him, he came to me.

PART II

Chapter 18

Jerusalem

I heard the quarrel.

The words were not clear, but the exclamations carried over the boat. Pilate and the captain faced each other in the prow. Pilate's voice was high-pitched, and he waved his arms in exasperation. A seagull squawked overhead, as if mocking the argument. Caesarea was in view, the last rays of the day's sun reflecting off the marble city, throwing reflected light, undiminished in its strength, back at us—as if there were two suns in the sky. The men's voices carried over the sound of the waves slapping against the anchored boat.

"'The Spear' is anxious to get ashore," Marius told me, smiling. He and I had moved to the stern of the boat to avoid intruding on the argument. "But the captain will not dock his boat as daylight is fading, even though Pilate has demanded he do so. The captain knows his domain. He knows the prefect of Palestine is not the prefect of this boat. As soon as Pilate gets ashore, he can give orders to anyone he wishes, but until then, while he is on this vessel, the captain makes the decisions."

The voices eventually quieted. The two men stood looking at each other for some moments. Pilate, realizing he could not prevail, left the prow and went below to his quarters. A little later Marius and I shared dinner together and then went to our beds. I slept poorly that night, even with the rhythm of the waves rocking the anchored boat. *What will I find in this new land? What does the future hold? What is my destiny?*

At first light we lifted anchor and with sails down, the rowers pushed us toward shore. Pilate stood in the prow looking landward. The captain steered us deftly into the turquoise narrows of the harbor. Stone colossi guarded the entrance, and a few dozen masts, their tips pointing to the sky, rocked lazily in the placid waters behind the jetties. Herod's palace, set on the rock promontory, reached audaciously to the edge of the sea, where the waves threw themselves at its base. Boys played in the waves among the rocks, diving into water the color of lapis and amethyst, colors so rich it seemed they would surely stain their skin.

To our right and just above us sat the white marble palace, the porches extending almost to the water's edge. It seemed a residence for an emperor rather than a prefect, especially a prefect of a minor colony, but it was to be Pilate's new home. He remained at the prow, spread-legged for balance, watching everything.

We docked, and a cheer went up from the rowers as they withdrew their oars from the water.

There was a ceremony, as there must be. The cohort stationed at Caesarea stood at attention as Pilate came ashore. Speeches were made, brief ones, but I could not hear what was said for the sound of the waves behind me. Pilate was led up marble steps to his new residence.

Marius leaned over to me. "Notice there are no Jews at this event. They will not come to him. He will have to come to them."

Four days only we stayed in Caesarea. Marius gave me freedom, and I was billeted with the troops. I quickly grew accustomed to the salt air and the breezes that freshened each afternoon. Herod had done what no man had done before—built a harbor where there was none.

This small city was much different from the empire's congested and dirty capital. Caesarea was clean and white and orderly, and the breeze did not carry the pungency of Rome, but the clear, crisp aroma of the Great Sea.

"Enjoy the sea," Marius told me. "There is no sea in Jerusalem." We sat in the arena of the hippodrome, which ran along the edge of the beach, watching the chariots at practice. A few dozen gulls searched the water just beyond the hippodrome where the waves lapped the shore. Farther down the beach a fisherman hurled his net near some rocks. Marius took two oranges from his pocket and gave me one. He peeled the skin as he continued. "Only a couple of meager streams in Jerusalem, I am told—hardly enough for drinking water. Rome at least has the Tiber, sluggish as it is. Jerusalem has no river at all. But for some reason they think it is a special place, a holy place. It sounded odd to me, but Manaen said that Abraham, the patriarch of the Jews, was passing through that area, and his god told him to sacrifice his son there.

"I learned this story from Manaen," I said. "Abraham was about to do the act when an angel stopped him. The angel gave him a goat to sacrifice instead. Yes, it is an odd story."

"I suppose so," Marius responded. "But it explains why the Jews think so much of the place. And then, a few hundred years after Abraham, David, the new king of the Jews, made Jerusalem his capital. Later the Babylonians razed the place and took most of the Jews off into slavery. Then the Persians defeated the Babylonians and let the Jews come back to their homeland. Then the Greeks under Alexander took over. And now we Romans are in charge. But they hate us—we know that—and they say, in private, of course, that a great military leader will rise up from among them and with God's help, he will kill all the Romans and everyone else who oppresses them."

"Manaen told me this as well."

Marius wiped the juice of the orange from his mouth. "I'm sure he also told you the high priests likewise hate Romans, but . . . it is hatred is tempered by reality. If, in fact, we Romans were thrown out of Judea, what would that leave them? Their revenue—a great revenue—would be cut off. And who would protect them from the nations around them? They scorn us—but they need us."

I took my meals with Marius and his cavalrymen. These men, I could tell, were grateful to meet their new commander. He promised he would be straightforward with them and told them of his expectations.

"This is Malchus," he told the cavalry-men. "I wish he could be part of our ranks, for he would be a great asset to our cohort, but that is not to be."

"One of the sailors," a cavalry-man said, looking at me, "told us you defeated Brasus in a wrestling match. Is that true? We saw Brasus when we were in Rome."

"Ah!" said another. "It was said his mother mated with a bear to produce Brasus!"

"I will tell you what happened," Marius said. "It was Pontius Pilate's birthday, and the men held special games in his honor. Sejanus was in attendance. It was a festive event. The soldiers were chanting, 'the Spear, the Spear' to Pilate, their commander. Pilate smiled—a rare thing. Sejanus, sitting beside him, slapped him on the back. There was a contest to throw the spears. Brasus, the giant, had always won that contest, but the soldiers insisted Malchus compete–"

I dismissed myself and went out of the barracks down toward the beach, where I stood with the waves coming in on my feet, looking back over the sea, back toward Rome.

I had no need to hear the story again. It was a story I knew. I threw a spear farther than another man. He was offended. He chal-

lenged me to a match. I did not wish for the fight, but the insult could not go unanswered. It was a story which I did not need to hear again.

"Pilate has summoned me," Marius said as we shared breakfast on the third day in Caesarea. "You must accompany me. You are still in my charge."

As we were admitted through the outer gates, I could hear the horsemen in the hippodrome, adjacent to the palace, coaxing their steeds through their early morning paces. We passed through a colonnaded courtyard, escorted by four soldiers. The curving trunks of the palm trees extended above the tops of the walls, and their fronds rippled in the morning breeze. We walked through a second courtyard, somewhat smaller, where sparkling mosaics of glass and stone decorated the floor. Finally, we came to the palace itself, thrust to the very edge of the sea. A double door, cedar studded with heavy bronze, admitted us into the official chamber. Pilate, attended by a secretary and two soldiers, sat in his curule chair with his back to the sea, great open windows behind him. Behind them a wide, curving porch overlooked the sea. Crimson curtains, as tall as three men, fluttered in the morning breeze. Outside, the waves, as if angry at Herod's impertinence, threw themselves against the concrete harbor. A hundred or more could have been accommodated in the chamber, but only six of us occupied it. Velvet chairs—purple, red, and yellow—ringed the room. Low tables of ebony inlaid with ivory filled the corners alongside great bronze pots, chest high. To the existing decorations Pilate had added his own—Roman standards. At least twenty lined the walls. The gold-plated images of Tiberius alternated with those of Sejanus. The plates, the size of a man's hand, were affixed near the top of a stiff wooden shaft, the height of a short man.

Red ribbons, the same red as the soldiers' tunics, draped from the standards' shafts and fluttered in the breeze. I stood at the door as Marius was admitted to Pilate's presence. Pilate leaned to one side of his chair to look around Marius and take a brief look at me, a question on his face. Marius reminded him that I was still in his charge and would soon be delivered to the Jews. As Pilate and Marius conferred, I examined the intricate mosaic on the floor. No men or animals were rendered. Herod, in sensitivity to the Jews, had instructed his artisans to avoid rendering anything that could have been considered an idol. A better measure of that sensitivity to the Jews would have been helpful to Pilate for what lay ahead.

Some years later, Paul would more than once stand in this chamber. Not Pilate, but another prefect would sit in judgement in a similar curule chair. The images of Tiberius and of Sejanus would no longer decorate the walls, but little else would have changed. I was not there when Paul stood before his accusers, but I would hear Luke's account of it. It was here in these marbled chambers, with its high windows, velvet chairs and crimson curtains, with the sea-breeze filling the hall, that Paul would address the great-grandson of the man who built this city and this palace and say with stunning boldness: "I say nothing except what the prophets said—that the Messiah must suffer and that, by being the first to rise from the dead, he would proclaim light both to our people and to the Gentiles."

And it would be on this very floor that Paul would confound both the Jews and the Romans, when he would say, "I appeal to Rome," setting in motion his trip to the seat of the empire. But those events were in the future . . .

The meeting was brief. Pilate gave Marius orders which I could not hear. Marius saluted and dismissed himself. "Pilate knows his priorities," Marius said as we left the palace. "He is eager to get to Jerusalem. We leave at first light."

The sky that morning seemed ill-suited for the enterprise on the ground. Cream and pink clouds, gentle and soft, held against a still sky, slowly swelling as they coaxed a reluctant sun to come above the horizon. On the ground, however, the colors and the activity were harsher. The cohort wore their long capes—the color of blood. The iron and brass of their polished armor sparkled in reflection of the morning cook-fires. The voices of the commanders—sharp and harsh—gave directions to their troops. A few donkeys complained about their loads, and horses whinnied as they were saddled.

An impressive Roman retinue departed from Caesarea that morning. The standard-bearer led the way. Two paces behind came the first rank, a dozen—four abreast and three columns—of the most experienced soldiers. They marched in full battle array, red shields worked with gold trim in their left hand, spears over their right shoulder, all at the same angle. Behind them came the second rank, another sixty soldiers, six abreast. Pontius Pilate followed on his horse, a white stallion bedecked with the same red-and-gold decorations as the soldiers. Marius and I rode behind Pilate, along with three other centurions. Then came more marching men and behind them dozens of mules and their attendants carrying baggage. "We're traveling lighter than usual," Marius had told me the day before. "No tents or a kitchen. Our camps are set up and waiting for us. That will allow us to make twenty miles each day. We will be in Jerusalem in three days."

Sunlight filled our faces as we departed that morning, making our way over the sandy hills behind Caesarea. The guards in the watchtowers saluted us as we departed. Broom-brushes covered the hills, and bees attended to the white flowers on the drooping tendrils. We turned south, crossing a gully edged with dusty oleanders, the sun now on our left cheeks.

Glad to have activity, the troops were in good spirits, and we made good time. Boys from the villages and some of the older men came out to watch us pass, but the women and young men stayed away. The soldiers looked for fruit on the hawthorn trees along the road, but the little apples had all been plucked. We heard a shepherd piping to his flock. Above us, in the open sky, a hawk tipped its wings, banking in a circle.

"Mount Gerizim," Marius said to me, pointing to a hill in the distance. "We are now in the land of the Samaritans. That is their holy mountain. The Jews will not pass through here—even though it is the shortest route between Jerusalem and Caesarea. According to the Jews, the Samaritans are unclean. So the Jews add a day or two to their journey just to go around this territory. He shook his head. "Strange people, these Jews."

We camped at Antipatris, a Roman way-station set in the open plain, shaded by a grove of poplars. Situated about halfway between Jerusalem and Caesarea, Antipatris sat alongside a winding stream in the flat plain between the Judean hills and the higher hills of Galilee. It was the ideal outpost and stopover for Romans traveling between the two key cities of Judea.

The soldiers ate well that night. They were issued wine and sang lusty camp songs around a blazing fire. Pilate however, stood at the edge of the camp looking southward—toward Jerusalem.

"Antipatris will be my posting," Marius told me. "It is best situated to carry messages throughout the country. Caesarea and the sea would have been my choice if I had one."

The next morning Marius was cinching the belly-strap on his horse when I found him. "Tonight we will be in the valley that runs below

Jerusalem," he told me. Through the next day our progress was steady. By midday, when the shadows of our steeds were underneath us, Marius pointed to a hill ahead. "Jerusalem. The city is on that hill. We will camp at the base tonight and make the ascent tomorrow."

The horses and mules found good grass along the stream where we camped; the soldiers stripped and bathed in a pool, shoulder deep, where the water spilled around gray boulders, worn smooth by lifetimes of the water's current. The sun fell early in the valley. I looked at the hill we would ascend in the morning. I could not see the city itself, but above the city, I could see the light of a fire that raised its orange glow against hovering, gray clouds. "The fire of their temple," Marius said. "It burns all the time—day and night." Manaen had told me that the Jews kept a perpetual fire burning at their temple. I would come to know that fire intimately during the next few years.

The ascent was as steep as Marius had warned. Tattered clouds, like shreds of wool left from the shearing, hung motionless against a pale blue sky. The gravel road switched back and forth, and dust filled our faces and stuck to the sweat on our bodies. Our track steadily rose and the hills around us were strewn with white boulders. Poppies, like living blood-drops, waved in a breeze we could not feel. Farmers stood behind fig and olive trees as we passed. Goats and sheep sought clumps of grass alongside the white rocks and paid us no attention. A shepherd, both hands on his staff, stood motionless. What had looked like an hour's journey from the base of the hill took half a day. We arrived at Jaffa Gate at the time when our shadows matched our height. A portion of the Jerusalem cohort, fewer than one hundred soldiers, stood at attention as we arrived. The heralds sounded their horns, and the gates of Jerusalem opened to us. If I had expected a city on the scale of Rome, I was disappointed. If I had expected the orderliness and cleanliness of Caesarea, I was profoundly disappointed.

Is this the great city of the Jews? Is this the city Manaen told me about? Is this the city the Jews revere?

The ranks went two abreast to make their way through the narrow streets. The biting odor of salted fish subdued the other aromas of the marketplace. The severed heads of lambs and goats hung beside their skinned carcasses. Baskets of fruit intruded on the street, forcing the soldiers at times to go single file. Old women waved palm fronds over the baskets to drive away the flies. Goat hair awnings with red-and-black stripes hung across the street, offering shade. Above, a few of the city's citizens looked out from their rooftops at the scene below, their faces contorted in hatred.

The Assyrians, the Babylonians, the Persians, the Greeks and now the Romans. All have had a turn at ruling these people—and for a thousand years the Jews have looked on each of them with contempt—all the while waiting for their Deliverer, the one who will rid them of their oppressors.

Our route took us straight through the city and around the walls of the temple. I, like all those who had never before seen the temple, marveled at the height of the walls and the size of the stones at the base, some as large as a house.

"Old Herod had a way with stones, didn't he?" Marius said.

Our procession skirted around the great walls until we reached the barracks. Herod had named it the Antonia Fortress after Mark Antony, his benefactor at the time. Four towers defined the rectangular structure—one taller than the other three. The building abutted the outside wall of the temple.

We entered the courtyard of the fortress. The Roman cohort, all red and gold, stood at attention, holding their spears erect. Pilate was escorted to a platform built for the occasion. Marius and I stood near the water clock, which sat on a stone pedestal.

"Quirinius brought several of the clocks here," Marius said. "He thought it would be helpful for the priests, but they said, 'Who but God can measure time?'"

A trumpet sounded. The imperial flags—more red and gold—fluttered in the swirling breeze. Pilate began his speech. Neither Pilate nor the soldiers who listened seemed inspired. Pilate, as always, was a man eager to get ceremony out of the way so he could get to his task. The most important thing on his mind, I would find, was meeting the high priest. We heard "glory of Rome" and "honor of the emperor" several times as the speech wound down. After one last exhortation to his troops, a trumpet was sounded, and the troops came to attention as Pilate left the courtyard. The troops marched out with precision.

"Stay with me," Marius told me as he gave the reins of his horse to his steward. "I want to see the temple. You should see it too."

"I thought only Jews—"

"Follow me," Marius said. He led me up a series of staircases to the tallest tower. I followed him up the stone stairway, the hob-nails in his sandals clattering in my face. We emerged onto a walkway open to the sky. More than a dozen soldiers, spaced apart, stood guard on the walkway. They snapped to attention, bringing their spears erect. Marius gave them "at rest" and led me to the wall. The Judean landscape spread before us. The gorge below us met another gorge and merged, running away to the south. Small cultivated fields in squares and rectangles, like green patches on tawny rugs, dotted the hills. Flocks of sheep moved slowly across the hills, providing the only movement.

"That, I believe, is the Herodium, where Herod is buried," he said, pointing to an odd hill with a flat top. "He wanted a place of safety. I guess he got it. He's safe enough now, inside the hill."

I squinted, trying to make out the details of the distant valley, beyond Herod's mountain. The bottom of the valley was light blue, as if milk had been poured into ink.

"The Sea of Asphalt," Marius told me. "No fish in it. Nothing alive at all... strange place. Beyond that, where the hills rise up again, is Moab."

He motioned for me to come to the opposite parapet. I came to the edge and looked down. The temple and the courtyards lay before us. Marius looked at me to see my reaction. It seemed to be a city unto itself. Clusters of men were gathered in the colonnades that ringed the platform. Closer to us, practically underneath us, was the temple itself. As tall as twenty men, the white marble caught and dispersed the afternoon light. Four bronze columns in front of the huge gold-plated doors rose to the height of the temple. The bronze candlestick was the size of an oxcart. The buildings in Rome had been magnificent, but this building seemed even more so, perhaps because of its size compared to the city. Rome had dozens of impressive buildings over a large area. But this building seemed out of place in Jerusalem. It dominated everything else. Jerusalem may not have matched Caesarea for orderliness or Rome for scale, but neither of those cities had anything like this edifice.

"This is what Herod gave the Jews," Marius said, smiling. "It was his effort to buy their favor. And this," he continued with a larger smile, sweeping his arms at the Antonia Fortress," is what he gave the Romans. For the Jews he provided a place of worship. For the Romans he provided a place for us to *watch* them worship."

He peered down at the hundreds of Jews milling around the temple grounds. "The Jews hate this tower. Who can blame them? We are here watching them, making sure they do not misbehave. They resent the fact that we control their land and watch their worship. Herod himself was never able to mollify the Jews. How can Pilate expect to do better?"

I pondered the question.

"Tomorrow, my friend," Marius went on, "you will be delivered to Caiaphas the high priest, but in truth you will be subject to Annas, his father-in-law. Annas holds power in Jerusalem. What will happen I cannot predict." He paused for a moment, stumbling for his words. "After you are transferred to the priests, I will be little help to you."

"You have been a good friend. Do not be concerned for me. We shall see each other again." I reached for his arm and grasped it in the Roman manner. "Let us make that our objective."

Marius grasped my hand firmly in agreement.

The official ceremonies began the next afternoon. This was to be the first meeting between the new Roman governor and the high priestly family, and Pilate was determined, it seemed, to make a good impression. The soldiers had been up well before dawn to prepare themselves. A dozen barbers, working quickly, shaved each soldier. Each man dressed in his finest uniform, re-polished the brass that had been polished the evening before, and sharpened swords and spear points already sharp.

"Marius sends his apologies." It was one of his aides who spoke. He held a set of leg shackles and a set of arm shackles. I was not surprised. For this ceremony, my status would need to be evident. "I understand," I assured the aide, offering my hands. He placed them on my wrists and then my ankles. I shook the chains. On board the boat I had worn chains briefly, but before that it had been nearly two years—when Claudia Procula found me in the slave market in Rome.

The chains scraped against my arms and legs, but they chafed at my spirit as well.

Six hundred Roman soldiers, the entire complement from the Fortress of Antonia, lined the way to Herod's Palace. They stood single file, shields in their left hands, spears in their right, pointed straight upward. Through this imposing line the high priest, his temple guard, and the other Jewish representatives would have to proceed in order to reach Pontius Pilate in the palace. If the intent was intimidation, I thought it effective. The power of Rome was well displayed. Anyone who walked through this phalanx, including Annas and his attendants, would be reminded of that power. And I knew, as did all the Jews, this contingency of soldiers was a meager fraction of what Pilate could summon from Syria if needed. I, walking in my chains, was part of a small caravan of items being delivered to the Herodian Palace. Four donkeys, laden with double saddle bags, and guarded by a dozen of the cohort's best troops, comprised the rest of the caravan. The contents of the bags—and I—were to be offered as Pilate's gifts to the priests. I wondered if Claudia Procula had chosen the items in the bags, as she had chosen me.

The donkeys were unloaded at the foot of the stairs that led up into the palace. The donkeys brayed—whether in complaint of having carried the load, or gratitude at having been relieved of the load, I was not sure. A half-dozen slaves, watched by twice as many soldiers, took the bags on their shoulders, and we walked up the wide marble staircase, flanked by more Roman soldiers. Some of these I recognized. These were from the cohort in Caesarea. We had marched together only three days before. They avoided my eyes.

Entering the palace put me in mind of Manaen's mansion in Rome, but on a grander scale. Ten of them could have been placed on this site. King Herod had commissioned both edifices, so the similarities were not surprising.

The Augustan wing of the palace was Pilate's choice for the ceremony. The other wing, the Agrippa, was of equal size and could have as easily been chosen. Each was capable of hosting three hundred guests. Colored marble columns ran up to high ceilings painted with vermillion, the beams gilded. Chairs and tables ringed the huge room, some inlaid with silver, some with ivory, some with gold, and some with jewels, magnificent in their own right, but out of scale in the cavernous room. Herod could never have imagined his palace would become the temporary residence for a Roman procurator. Herod planned that one of his sons would succeed him as king. But those in Rome had other ideas, and now Pontius Pilate, more accustomed to field tents than mansions, was the occupant of Herod's grand palace. Not even Tiberius, when seated on his throne in Rome, occupied accommodations as extravagant as the new prefect fresh from Rome.

Three towers decorated the exterior of the palace, each with a name. Herod named the tallest tower Phasael after his elder brother. Another he named Hippicus after his Judean friend who died fighting alongside him when both were young, And the third, the most heavily decorated, he named Mariamne—after his Hasmonean wife whom he murdered.

We walked up the steps, my leg chains scraping against the marble with every step. I tried to minimize the sound, but it was difficult. As we entered the great hallway, I was led to a corner in the back of the massive room. Beside me were the other items designated as gifts to the high priest. Pilate's curule chair, the symbol of Roman authority, the same one on which he had used a few days earlier in Caesarea, sat on a small dais near the middle of the room. To his right and at an angle to the chair, was another dais slightly lower than Pilate's. On it were two chairs, both composed of ebony and worked with gold that formed images of grape clusters. These chairs, I assumed, were designated for Caiaphas and Annas. Behind those two chairs were a series of shorter chairs for the others in the high priestly family, and behind those, a series of benches designated for the members of the Great Sanhedrin, the Jewish legislators.

I was chained to a ring in the wall, and the four soldiers took their positions around me and the grand chest beside me. Dozens of servants were moving through the huge room, making the final preparations. The sun-patches under the windows were settled in place, stretching across the floor.

About an hour later a handful of Roman dignitaries from Caesarea who attended on Pilate entered the hall and took their seats to the left of Pilate's chair. Behind them came two dozen of Pilate's most impressive soldiers, the tallest and most muscular—a centurion leading them. The centurion reviewed his men and put them at ease.

A few moments later trumpets at the doorway sounded, and the Jewish delegation began to enter. Members of the temple guard, twelve only, not the full complement, came first. They carried ceremonial spears, not sharpened ones, and the sheaths for their short-swords were empty. Rome allowed its subjugated people to maintain small forces, but it would not allow weapons in the vicinity of its representatives. As a matter of policy, the temple guard was required to surrender its weapons before coming into the proximity of the prefect. The Jews were accustomed to this procedure. They suffered greater humiliations than this from the Romans, and were accustomed to the slight.

Next came the members of the Sanhedrin, the seventy-one Jewish sages who made policies and administered justice—to the extent Rome allowed—for the Jewish people. They entered single file, eldest to youngest in procession. The first few members shuffled into the auditorium slowly, pushing their walking canes in front of them, each step a labor, but each man seemed determined to fulfill his role. The first one stopped momentarily to cough, halting all behind him. His hacking went on for some moments, vibrating his frail body and bouncing raspy echoes through the chamber. After a while he composed himself and was assisted to his seat.

Eventually all the Sanhedrin members were seated. More trumpets sounded. The five sons of Annas, all designated "chief priests," entered. They were seated in special chairs slightly behind the two prominent chairs. I did not know these brothers at the time, but I would come to know them well—Eleazar, Jonathan, Theophilus, Matthias, and Ananus.

At the back of the hallway, in the arched doorway stood Pilate, surrounded by his retinue, peering out, watching the procession. He wore the Roman toga. I had never seen him in a toga before. I should not have been surprised. He was now a politician, not a soldier. His torso waved back and forth, moving his weight from foot to foot. This posture of impatience, common to Pilate, I had come to recognize.

Another fanfare from the trumpets and Annas and Caiaphas entered together.

In later years I would count myself an authority on the way men walked—an expertise gained from years in the great temple. But even this day—before I had that experience in the temple—to me and for anyone else watching, we knew—Annas was a man who walked with authority.

The twin points of his beard were sharply barbered, some black still showing among the gray, framing a mouth formed into a perpetual frown. He wore the sleeveless blue robe reserved for the high priest, and the tiny silver bells on the hem made a flat sound as he walked. Blue, purple, and scarlet tassels, in the shape of pomegranates swayed as he walked. The cone-shaped turban on his head gave him height that God had not provided. A scarlet sash around his waist fell straight down from his thin frame.

But it was his countenance, not his dress, that drew attention. Contempt radiated from his face. All could see it. For Rome, for Romans, for this palace, for these proceedings, for everything, Annas held contempt. If ever there was a man who could pronounce curses with his eyes, it was Annas. The hall was hushed as he entered. Slowly and purposefully he walked, his sandals scooting across the agate and lapis stones of the mosaic, the sound matching the flat chime of the tiny bells on the hem of his robe. Joseph Caiaphas, his son-in-law, younger and taller by half a head, walked behind Annas. He tried to match his pace to his father-in-law's, but he was clumsy and out of step.

I often recalled this first impression of Annas and Caiaphas and how the procession into Herod's modeled the workings of the high priestly family. Here was Annas, who no longer held an official position—yet no one doubted he held authority among the Jews, authority over Caiaphas, over the Sanhedrin, over the high priests, over the other priests, over the scribes, over the temple, and over the temple sacrifices. And as Pilate would learn, Annas made every effort to impose his authority over Rome.

I wonder if ever two men hated each other more—yet needed each other as much.

From an arched door Pilate watched the man who would be most important to the success of his governorship. Those in the military will say that you cannot know too much about your enemies—or your allies. In which category Pilate assigned Annas, I cannot be sure— perhaps both—but Pilate watched with special interest, rocking back and forth, side to side, as he watched.

Pilate had allowed both Caiaphas and Annas to enter together—a mark of shrewd statesmanship. Perhaps it ran contrary to his military instincts, but perhaps it showed he was willing to listen to advice.

Valerius Gratus, his predecessor, may have advised him to show deference to Annas. Twin chairs awaited Annas and Caiaphas. When Annas came to his chair, he paused for a moment, taking one last scornful look at his surroundings before taking his seat, as if were wearisome to do so. Caiaphas then took his seat and had hardly adjusted his robe, when another trumpet fanfare sounded. All rose to await the entry of the representative of Rome—Pontius Pilate, the new prefect of Judea. Other governors in similar circumstances had often made the local rulers wait for an hour or longer before the grand entry—an effort to humiliate the local rulers and make them aware of who held real power.

That was not Pilate's manner. Astute enough to know that the Jews were an odd people, he knew it would not serve his purpose to alienate Annas. His predecessor, no doubt, had advised him that cooperation, not intimidation, would be essential for the success of his administration.

All stood—except Annas. The eyes of all the men in the room went to him. *Would Annas defy protocol? Would he remain seated?* Pilate approached, moving briskly across the marble and mosaic floor. The Jewish delegation kept their eyes on Annas. As Pilate neared the dais, Annas took a breath and slowly stood, as if a great imposition had been thrust on him. The four guards accompanying Pilate had trouble keeping in step. The toga, although crisp and clean, the pure white accentuated by the purple trim—the *augusticlavia*—that denoted his elevated position, seemed to tug at his arms and legs as he walked. A gold chain hung around his neck. Affixed to it was the bronze medallion with the inscription *Amicus Caesaris,* "Friend of Caesar," the device given him at his commissioning. His eyes moved around the room as he came to the center of the great hall. He looked at Annas and Caiaphas. With Caiaphas he made eye contact, but Annas was looking away, as if these proceedings were an interruption.

Pilate stepped on the dais, turned to look at his audience, then took his seat on the curule chair, extending his arms to allow the Jewish delegation to take their seats.

A short fanfare blared from the trumpets, and Pilate's secretary stepped on the dais and unrolled a heavily decorated scroll. His voice was strong and filled the great hall. "Tiberius Claudius Nero, Emperor of Rome, to the citizens of Jud—"

The old Sanhedrist began coughing again. His hacking echoed off the walls. It seemed as if six ghosts in the wall had joined the old man in his barking, forming a chorus of coughers. The secretary raised his voice, but the old man matched him with deeper coughing, his body jerking with each spasm. Other members of the Sanhedrin leaned out of their rows, their pointed turbans protruding at odd angles, to see their afflicted colleague. The coughing subsided for a moment, then picked up again with new intensity. It endured intermittently through the reading of Tiberius' proclamation. What little could be heard of it had to do with all the benefits that accrue to the Jewish nation from their benefactors the Romans—and an appeal to those in Judea to recognize those benefits as extended through the mercy and graciousness of Rome.

Whether from disgust at the coughing spasms behind him, or from the condescending words of the emperor—or both—Annas' face, always composed in a frown, grew further contorted.

Eventually the reading and the coughing subsided, and Pilate stood from his curule and addressed the audience, "To the high priests of Judea, to the members of the great council of the Sanhedrin, to the men of Judea," he began.

As the words "men of Judea" bounced through the walls of Herod's great hall, I recalled reading the story the Greeks retold about Echo—a story I had read in the library at the house of Manaen. My mind did not stay on the story, but on the library and my time with

Manaen. I could not know how severely my life's direction would change.

Annas seemed especially indifferent to this speech, and perhaps his cynicism was not unwarranted. Pilate's speech, with some variety, had, without doubt, been read in a hundred different outposts of the Roman-ruled world. Annas may have heard a very similar speech eleven years earlier when Valerius Gratus had assumed the role of prefect in Judea. Annas glared at Pilate as if to say, *I outlasted the previous prefect—and I will outlast you.*

The speech Pilate gave, like the one given to his troops earlier, was not lengthy. When he concluded he motioned to the soldiers who brought the gifts designated for the high priest. First was a silver tray, with a matching jug and cups, worked in the theme of a grapevine. Then came a bolt of silk from the lands of the East with vivid red flowers against a green background. A Persian rug, intricately done, the size of a small room, was unfurled. Other items, many of them bronze and silver were placed in front of the Jews. To all of this Annas seemed indifferent, although his sons craned their necks to see. When all other items had been offered, my chain to the wall was loosened. I was last to be presented. I was led across the room to the high priests and a soldier gave the key to my chains to Caiaphas.

Another one, better than I, would later stand before these same three men—Annas, Caiaphas and Pilate. He would endure their scrutiny better than I. Forced to come, I came reluctantly with hatred and resentment in my heart. He, however, would come willingly—and with incomprehensible grace.

Pilate made some comments. I was watching Annas, who was watching no one. "From the north" and "Cherusci" and "strong man" were fragments I heard. Annas made an almost imperceptible nod of his head. The temple guards caught the message. Four went to the door and waited. The Roman soldiers took me to them and there was a brief conference between them. The Romans then escorted me out of the hall. We went down the marble stairs outside where I had entered a few hours before, the four temple guards following behind. "The Jews will not have you until your ear is pegged," one of the soldiers said. They led me back toward the fortress, through the warren of shops we had passed earlier. We came to the place where the fortress corners with the temple wall. It is there, I was to learn, where the lambs are washed before they are sacrificed. A thick post, old and weathered, was set near the wall. The Romans took me there and removed my tunic leaving me bare-shouldered. They lashed me to the post, snugging the bull-hide strips tightly. I did not oppose them. I knew the Jews marked their slaves. I was prepared for it.

One of the temple guards went inside an ante-room built into the temple wall. After a moment, he and a doddering old priest appeared who seemed to have been awakened from a nap. He had never been tall, but his age had now bent him at the waist. He carried a small leather satchel—even older than himself. The old priest walked slowly and intentionally as if every step was an accomplishment. The old man came near me. Deliberately, with quivering fingers, he put his satchel on a wooden table and unfolded it. From it he took a hammer and a metal punch—the length of a man's hand with a small triangle formed on the end. With the hammer in his right hand and the punch in the left, he looked at me. Realizing he could not reach my ear he shrugged his shoulders and looked at the guards. One of them soon produced a bench and assisted the old priest as he stepped on it. The other guard took a heavy board of wood from the table, well-marked with chisel points, and placed it behind my right ear. He then pushed my head firmly against the board. "Be very still," he told me firmly. The old priest pressed the metal triangle against my earlobe, braced himself, and with a strike of the hammer, cut a wedge in the lobe. The pain shocked, but I kept my teeth clamped.

The priest took a dusty, blood-stained cloth from his satchel and pressed it against my ear to slow the bleeding. He looked carefully at the wedge in my earlobe, squinting his eyes, as if to evaluate his work. Satisfied, he dabbed my ear one more time, and with the guard's help stepped down from the bench.

The old man closed his satchel, and as the Romans were about to untie me, one of the Jewish guards went over to him and said something out of my hearing. The old man nodded, and looked at me. He re-opened his satchel. The guards then grabbed my trousers and pulled them off. It surprised me. I was naked, and I did not understand why. The guards brought more rope and tightened it across my abdomen and my upper legs. "This time," the guard said, "you need to be *very* still."

I looked over to the old priest. He was whetting a knife on a piece of coarse leather.

As the old priest stepped toward me, one of the Romans smirked, "You are already a slave, and soon you will be a Jew."

The old priest brought the knife near. I went still in fear.

The priest went quickly to his work. My body contorted with the pain, my arms and chest bursting against the cords that bound me. A scream rose up inside me, but I held it behind my teeth.

It was over quickly, and a small pool of blood began to form in the dust between my feet.

I was untied and the old priest, with neither malice nor compassion, wiped his blade with the same bloody cloth that had been applied to my ear and then gave it to me to hold against my groin.

The Romans loosened the bull-hide ropes, and I slumped onto the dusty ground, waves of pain washing through me.

"On your feet, big man," the Roman said. "We are giving you to the Jews. They will grant you a day of recovery. Enjoy it. On the next day you will be sawing stones."

The Jews hold that an uncircumcised man may not enter the temple or touch the things of the temple. I now met the standard. I now carried in my flesh the "sign of the covenant," as the Jews call it. I had now three marks imposed on my body—none of them to which I had consented: The scar from the slaver's rope, the ear mark of a slave, and finally . . . the mark of a Jew.

Chapter 19

The Quarry

I was led to an ante-room just outside the temple wall. Several straw mats, stained with the blood of those who had preceded me, lay on the dirt floor. A priest brought cold beans and bread and sour wine, but I could not eat. I fell into a delirious sleep—full of the old dreams. Eventually I awoke to the sound of trumpets—a sound that later would become familiar to me—as the priests acknowledged the new day and the Levites opened the gates of the temple.

Shortly after, Marius arrived. "This was not Pilate's plan," he said as he embraced me. His face was contorted in pain as he looked at me. "This was not Pilate's plan." He shook his head. "He did not offer you as a quarry worker. Pilate offered you as a temple guard. But Annas is stubborn. He wants the new prefect to know that he does not heed his advice. But I will not forget you. I will not rest until I find a way to free you from the quarry."

I nodded but said nothing.

"I am not supposed to be here," Marius said. "I cannot stay. I have to return to Antipatris. . . But I will not forget you." He embraced me one more time and then left.

Later that day I was again provided beans and bread, and then in the late afternoon two temple guards appeared.

"You are to go to the quarry," one said. "It is usually a one-hour walk, but you will walk slowly today. Today it will require two hours. Put on your tunic."

With chains on my hands, we headed north out of the city along the Cardo through the same warren of noisy, congested shops I had passed earlier. Some of the citizens of the city looked briefly at me, but if I expected to see pity in those faces—I would have been disappointed. We left the city through the Jaffa Gate and continued up steep hills then down in a valley and back up again. As we came to the top of the ridge, I looked down and saw the quarry, a great gash in the earth, with many dozens of men, perhaps hundreds, at labor.

"Let's go down," the guard said.

The sun had set when we came to the quarry, and the workers were eating their evening meal, scraping the last bit of beans from their bowls with their bread. Some of them looked at me, but then looked away.

We came to a large tent, one of several that flanked the outer edge of the quarry. Fine dust covered the tents and the ground. There I was transferred to the care of a foreman who called out to one of the quarry workers, "Cyrene, take the new man to your tent."

A black man, more gray than black because of the white dust, responded.

"Follow me," he said.

Two rows of straw mats, perhaps twenty on each side, with an aisle between, ran the length of the tent.

"This is your mat," the man said. "It is next to mine."

He was a man near my size, and I looked at him carefully. *Did I see some faint sense of compassion?*

"Thank you," I said.

"I am Cyrene." He smiled. "My name and my country are the same. Once I had another name, but it is lost."

"I am Malchus."

We had in common—Cyrene and I—not only that we were slaves to the Jews, but also that our names had been left behind in the lands of our origins. We would find more commonality, but neither of us could know it on this day.

"You must be careful," he said to me. "The stones have no mercy, the Jews less. This mat belonged to a Cappadocian, a big man—

almost as big as you—but a stone crushed his hand. He was given no medicine. A man with one arm is useless in the quarry. The poison festered in his arm and went through his body. It took only one week for him to die."

I looked at the mat. It still bore the impression of the man who had slept there until a few nights earlier.

I slept a troubled sleep that night on the mat with the imprint of the Cappadocian I never knew. A month earlier I had slept on a soft bed in a magnificent house, surrounded by a thousand books and by people who meant me well. Was I destined to die in the quarry like the Cappadocian who had slept here before me?

"Do not consider escape," Cyrene told me the next morning as we came to the quarry. I looked up at the top of the hill where a few trees grew above the sharp straight lines where the limestone had been cut. "Others have tried—perhaps a few succeeded. But for you and for me there is no hope. Where would I hide that my black skin would not betray me? And where would you hide that your yellow hair would go unnoticed? And do not forget—you now have a wedge in your ear."

He motioned for me to follow him. We came to a large stone table covered with dust. Beside it was a long thin saw with a wooden handle on each end.

"The temple work is completed," Cyrene said. "A few artisans with chisels work on the stones for the temple, but only a few. The stones we cut now are for the new road that runs below the temple." He handed me a small square of cloth. "Take this. I cut it from the tunic of the Cappadocian. Hold it as you grip the saw. Your hands are not yet ready for this work. Your palms will grow thick—but until they do, use the cloth to cushion them. Now, take the handle of the saw."

I did as he said, wrapping the cloth around the handle.

"Hold it lightly and follow my rhythm," he said. "You have shoulders for this work, but the stone responds to persistence, not strength." He pushed the saw blade toward me. "Receive the blade and then return it. Yes, that's it. Receive and return."

A thin vapor of dust rose up from the groove we were cutting. "Receive and return," Cyrene continued to say, "Receive and return," reminding me of the boatswain calling the rhythm to the rowers on the boat only days ago.

The rhythm of the saw and the rhythm of the quarry became the rhythm of my life. All day Cyrene and I pushed and pulled the saw, and at night, exhausted, we slept among our fellow slaves, many coughing through the night as their lungs tried to expel the dust of the day. The steep, sheer banks of stone that rose up around us—the height of twenty men—comprised our world. Each day a segment of that stone wall was cut away, crashing to the ground, increasing the size of the gash in the ground. But it did not make our world any larger. The sky remained inaccessible.

"It is a curse to be a big man," Cyrene said one day. "As the need for stones has lessened, smaller men have gone to farms or to households. Only those of us with broad backs remain with the stones." I learned that at one time, ten thousand men and a thousand oxen worked the quarry. Now only a few hundred men and perhaps a hundred oxen were on the site.

"I do not know," Cyrene answered when I asked him what would happen to us when the road was completed. "Perhaps there will be another road, or another building. The work will outlast us, I fear. But we must not lose hope. Perhaps we will be sent to a farm, to a place where there are trees with fruit, and where a man can see the whole sky, not just that part above him."

A man who says he has no regrets or a man who does not question his decisions is not honest with himself. Many hours, as I pushed and pulled the saw, my mind would go back to the estate and my life in the hut with Quartus. "What if I had not killed the slaver?" I often asked myself. What if I had endured my shame and allowed the slaver to go free? What if I were still at the estate, hunting game with my bow and picking olives and almonds from the trees? What if I could sit in the lady's house when the master was away and have her rub salve on my neck? For these questions I had no answers, but they churned in my deepest soul.

"Today we will take the stones to the city," Cyrene told me. "You must be careful. This is how the Cappadocian lost his hand."

I had lost count of the days, but perhaps it had been a month since I had arrived. Some brown leaves from the trees above us had blown into our pit, settling on top of the dust, indicating that summer was passing.

Very carefully we loaded the stones onto wooden rollers, which were hitched to oxen, and some twenty of us followed the teams out of the pit and down the hill toward the city.

"Do not think of it," Cyrene said to me as we walked. Somehow he knew my mind and the fleeting thought that went through it. A man who is desperate will sometimes think desperate thoughts. "There is no escape," he said firmly.

The temple guards kept the road open before us, pushing the vegetable carts and donkeys to the side to let us pass. Bystanders came to see the procession—the stones, the oxen . . . and the slaves. One could find any kind of expression in their faces as they looked at us—disgust, fear, and occasionally a note of sympathy.

The great temple complex stood before us, looking nearly as big as the city itself, its high walls thrust up, protecting the temple itself from our view. Only a few weeks ago Marius had shown me the temple from above. Now I could see only the walls.

We followed the oxen, the carts creaking under the burden of the stones they carried. But the stones they carried were small in comparison to the ones we saw on the wall.

"These were cut before you were born," Cyrene said. "Old Herod started this project forty years ago. The slaves who laid these stones are now dead." He pointed down the hill. "When the road is finished, it will run down toward the Kidron Valley to the Pool of Siloam."

"How—" I started to ask as I stared at the huge stones of the temple wall.

"I was not here. I do not know."

A contingent of Roman soldiers stood along the roadway. "This is a Roman project," Cyrene explained. "The Jews don't even think of building roads like this. Valerius Gratus, the previous prefect, started it. I suppose the new prefect will continue it."

A week later we returned to the site with fresh slabs of stone. A group of Romans stood on the hill looking at the road.

Pilate. Standing among them was Pilate. I recognized his posture. He had again come from Caesarea to Jerusalem and stood with the same impatience I had seen in Rome at the training field, the same impatience he showed on the prow of the boat, hands on his hips, moving his weight from foot to foot. *Why was Pilate in Jerusalem?* I stood for a moment, looking at him. I thought once he saw me, but I am not certain. If he recognized me, did he wonder why I was unloading stones rather than fulfilling the duties for which he had me trained? I could not know, but the Roman prefect had more important things to think about than the role of one slave.

That evening as we returned to the pit, Cyrene told me, "This week we will stay at the quarry. It is the Jews' Feast of Booths."

I nodded. Manaen, of course, had told me about this event—when the Jews celebrate the time their ancestors spent in the wilderness after escaping from the Egyptians.

The Jews were slaves to the Egyptians who put them at hard labor, but they appealed to their god, who freed them. Now, I was a slave to the Jews, who put me at hard labor. But I had no god to whom I could appeal.

Pilate had come for the feast. But he would not stay outdoors with the Jews. His home would be the Antonia Fortress among his fellow soldiers.

I would witness several more feasts in Jerusalem, including Passovers—the most important feast. Pilate likewise would attend these celebrations. But neither Pilate, nor I, nor the priests, nor the Jews, nor the Romans, nor anyone else, could predict the future Passover that would change everything, one that would offer release for all. In it I would have a role. But for this one I would be deep in the quarry, impervious to the celebration above.

The week of the feast ended, and we went back to work. The cutting of stones was endless. Most days, from early light to darkness, were consumed with cutting stones. Once a week or so we delivered the stones to the road as it moved nearer and nearer to the pool at the bottom of the hill.

A note came from Marius. He had bribed one of the quarry guards to deliver it. He had sent a message to Manaen asking him to use his influence to have me released—but he admitted it was unlikely Manaen would be able to send a message back to Jerusalem until spring. "Do not lose hope," the message said. "I will not forget you, and I will not rest until you are freed from the quarry." I read the message one more time and then chewed it slowly and swallowed it.

Once, when the cool rains of the winter came, a Syrian slave slipped on the pavement and the stone fell on his chest, crushing his ribs. He was carried off—to where I do not know—but that night, his mat was empty and the men in our tent ate their beans silently.

Winter passed, and our road progressed down the hill, approaching the Pool of Siloam, where the Gihon Spring provides water for much of Jerusalem. Across the Kidron Valley beside it, I could look over to the olive trees banked against the hill, their tiny yellow flowers—beyond number—waving in the breeze.

I could not know it, but in that grove, I would later have an appointment. Among those trees, I would find my destiny.

As the season changed, and as we had cut enough stones to complete the road, we spent each day on the road site, carefully laying the stones at the angles the Roman engineers directed. Sometimes the young girls bringing water from the pool would look at me and giggle among themselves.

We were given another respite when Passover came, and I got another note from Marius, expressing hope that Manaen's letter would arrive soon.

When the road was completed, we were given a new task— erecting the columns along each side. "These columns will provide some shade for the citizens when they are finished," Cyrene said with a wry smile.

I took his meaning. "But none for us," I answered. I looked at the sky. It was still the earliest part of the summer, but the sun pushed down on our backs as if the sunlight itself had weight.

Eventually the columns were in place, and the work was left to those with skill with chisels to complete the road. At the quarry, our work went on as usual, but without purpose. Cyrene and I, along with the others with saws, went about our work of cutting stones—but the stones were stacked at the edge of the quarry and the oxen went idle. There was no place to take the stones we had cut.

Where my mind was when the foreman came to me, I do not know. I had learned to disassociate my mind from my arms as I cut the stones. Perhaps, in my mind, I was back at the estate, sitting among the roots of an oak tree, my bow at my side, listening to the gurgle of the stream as I waited for my quarry.

"Come to the gate," he said, breaking me from my thoughts. For a moment I was not sure I had heard what he said.

"Come to the gate," he repeated.

I looked at Cyrene. He had the same question on his face as I am sure was on mine. I released the handle of the saw and followed the foreman.

"Malchus!" I heard my name called as I approached the gate. It was Marius!

He embraced me, and as he released me, I saw the dust from my body had attached itself to his Roman uniform.

"There is much I would like to say," Marius said. "But these guards are not pleased I am here, and I cannot stay because I have no authority at this site. I have just arrived from Caesarea and brought a letter from Manaen. This morning I delivered his letter to that friend of Manaen's, Nicodemus bar-Mattiat, a member of the Jewish council. The letter seeks your release from the quarry. I do not know how long the appeal will take or even if it will succeed, but I had to see you."

"I cannot leave," I said, "without Cyrene." I turned to look back at the gray-black man standing beside the stone table, his hand still on the saw handle.

"But the letter requests only your release, not another's"

"I cannot leave him. He has kept me alive for this year."

"I will do what I can." Marius looked at my friend. "His name is Cyrene?"

I nodded.

"I must go now. The guards are growing impatient."

We clasped hands again, and I tried to rub the dust from his uniform. "I am grateful that you and Menahem have not forgotten me."

"Take courage. Manaen still has some influence here in Judea."

I went back to the saw. Cyrene looked at me intently, but he asked me no questions and I offered no explanations.

Five days later Marius returned with a parchment. A group of temple guards called Cyrene and me, then escorted us, leading us up the hill away from the city. An hour later we entered a large villa.

Orderly orchards—almonds, apricots, lemons and pomegranates—covered the rolling hills around the villa. Servants met us at the gate and led us to a room where we bathed in warm water. Fresh clothing was laid out. Cyrene and I said nothing to each other. The servants led us to a richly furnished room with dozens of cushions and pillows. We were given fruit and wine in silver pieces. I took an apricot cautiously. I had eaten little more than beans and bread for a year. I felt the juice trickle out of the edge of my mouth. Cyrene watched me, uncertain what he should do. One of the servants motioned for him to take the fruit. He, like me, took an apricot and he closed his eyes as he put his teeth into the fruit.

A moment later we heard footsteps and stood as Marius entered. "Malchus!" he called as he embraced me again. He turned to Cyrene. "Thank you for keeping my friend alive." He turned back to the doorway. "This is our host, Nicodemus bar-Mattiat."

Cyrene dropped to his knees as the man approached.

"Please, please," the man said, taking Cyrene by the shoulders and raising him up. "In this household, we bow to no one except God in heaven."

I looked carefully at this man as he raised Cyrene from his knees. If kindness and weariness can be found in equal measures in a man's countenance, I saw it in Nicodemus bar-Mattiat. I would come to know this man better and better appreciate his kindness, but even at this first meeting, it showed on his face.

"Please," Nicodemus said. "Take your leisure here in my household. All are welcome here." He smiled at Marius. "Even a soldier of Rome who has news for all of us."

"There is more to tell than I can offer," Marius started. "But here are the main things to tell you: Both of you are released from the quarry." He turned to Cyrene: "You are now the responsibility of Nicodemus. This is your home."

Cyrene's eyes widened. Nicodemus spoke: "You will be well treated here, Cyrene. You will have work in the orchards—but you will have food and clothing and a comfortable place to sleep."

"How can this be?" Cyrene asked incredulously. "I have heard of such things, but—"

Nicodemus shrugged his shoulders. "Who can account for the mind of Annas? I make ten requests to Annas—he grants me one. This one he granted, but while you are here, it is not enough that you are called only by the name of your origin. Since you have said, 'I have heard of such things,' I would like to call you Simon. The meaning of the name in our language is 'I have heard.'"

Cyrene, now Simon, nodded. "I will be Simon."

Marius continued: "Manaen's letter apparently carried some influence, Malchus. You will serve as the protector for Caiaphas."

"There was an incident—" Nicodemus said.

"Only a week ago," Marius added. "A Zelote—perhaps a deranged one—tried to stab Caiaphas as he came to the temple."

"I don't understand," I said.

"The Zelotes," Marius explained, "are committed to driving Romans out of Judea. They oppose any whom they consider cooperative with Rome—including the high priests."

"However," Nicodemus added, "their political ideas are often merely excuses for their crimes. Some of them, no doubt, have our nation in mind—but many of the brigands who make our roads unsafe, call themselves Zelotes, when the only thing they are zealous about is robbing wayfarers."

Marius picked up the conversation. "To Manaen's appeal I added an additional element. I recommended that you, Malchus, serve as the personal guard for Caiaphas as he performs his duties at the temple. At first the old—" Marius caught himself. "At first, Annas was reluctant to agree, but Caiaphas was apparently shaken by the attempt to kill him, so he implored his father-in-law to make the agreement."

"I am to be the protector of Joseph Caiaphas?" I asked.

"That will be part of your duty," Marius answered. A wry smile came to his face. "But there is one provision in the agreement." He looked at Nicodemus and Cyrene. "You are to have residence in the temple, not in the house of Annas and Caiaphas—they do not want you near the women of the household." He smiled again. "Caiaphas comes to the temple regularly only one day each week. On that day you will escort him from the house to the temple and then escort him back home."

"Will I have duty only one day a week?" I asked.

"No. I have requested that you assist the temple guards as they keep watch over the temple. Annas has agreed to this, with the provision that your assignment is at the site where the animals are sold for sacrifice."

"Annas sometimes surprises us. We did not expect he would make this agreement," Nicodemus said.

Marius nodded. "Yes, but as you know, Annas fears a disturbance at the temple that would require Roman soldiers to intervene. It has not happened yet, but if it did . . ."

"If it did," Nicodemus assisted, "it would interfere with his enterprise—the selling of the animals and the changing of the coins."

"Although he would say the real purpose would be to prevent the profaning of the temple," Marius added.

"Yes," Nicodemus concurred. "The high priest, or I should say the former high priest, is a difficult man to deal with, but he has the capacity to make decisions, even difficult decisions, if they advance his own purpose."

And so I came to the temple, the great temple, the grandest edifice of all—the place where the Jews say history began, the place where the patriarch Abraham offered his son as a sacrifice, the place where the smoke of sacrificed animals continually rises to the sky and their blood runs continually through the sluices to the ground, where a thousand priests occupy themselves with these sacrifices; where bulls and goats and sheep and doves without number are offered in atonement; where the sacrifices of Adam, of Noah, of Abraham, of Isaac, of Jacob, of Moses, and of David are recounted; where the temple of Solomon, in its great glory was built—and its story told—housing the ark of the covenant; where the remnant from Babylon returned and reconstructed the former temple, where Herod, nearly four hundred years later would build an edifice commensurate with the scope of the dreams of the Jews and where, supposedly, in their sacrifices, they anticipated the Redeemer, the Messiah, the Deliverer, the one who was to come to them—but where, in fact, their relentless activity rendered them senseless to his coming.

To that place—to the temple—I came.

Chapter 20

The Temple

"The Court of the Gentiles—" Zuriel, the captain of the temple guard, waved his arm over the vast expanse. We had just emerged from the underground tunnel that ran from the street level to the temple mount.

I squinted my eyes as they adjusted to the bright light of the sun overhead and the reflection from the limestone and marble that surrounded me. I shielded my eyes. I had seen the temple area from the Roman parapets earlier, but I was again stunned by the great scope of the site. Slowly taking in the scene, my eyes were drawn to the double colonnades of marble columns that formed cloisters around the edges of the expanse. Across the way was the temple itself—its marble, gold, and bronze glistening in the sun. Protruding above the corner of the temple walls rose the Antonia Fortress, where I had stood some months earlier. "I had forgotten," I told Zuriel, "the magnitude of the court."

"A common reaction. All who come for the first time are surprised. Here, let us stand in the shade." Zuriel pointed to the colonnades behind us. Clusters of men sat on the benches under the decorated boards, engaged in conversation.

"Mostly they are here to hear the news of the day and spread the gossip of the day," Zuriel said. "On the Sabbath there will be thousands on this mount. These benches will be full when the rabbis come to teach their disciples."

I looked at Zuriel more closely. He had the trim look and the bearing of a soldier. His black beard, speckled with some gray, was neatly trimmed, accenting a lean face. A black leather skullcap fitted tightly over the brown scarf tied neatly over his head. His cape was clasped at the neck and laid back on his shoulders, keeping his hands free. Over his woolen robe, a bronze chainmail vest fit his torso. A leather belt held a leather scabbard that held a short sword. In his right hand he held a staff, taller than himself. He saw me looking at the staff.

"The best weapon of the temple guards," he said, smiling. "The sword we rarely need, but the staff we use often. Arguments are plentiful at the temple. Arguing is a way of life for Jews, even here at the temple. When those arguments become too loud, a poke in the ribs, or sometimes a rap on the head is enough to put things in order. That is much of what we do—but we have our swords," he put his hand on the scabbard, "just in case."

Who can describe the temple? I cannot—though I was a resident for four years. The immensity of the edifice and its stones is matched only by the immensity of the activity in the edifice. A thousand men or more—priests, Levites, and scribes—daily go about the great business of the temple. Each of those men has a purposeful task and with some exceptions, each goes about his task purposefully. Unless a man walks on the pavements and looks upon its magnificent stones—and feels himself diminished by the scale of the place—he cannot understand it.

"Two hundred forty men are under my command," Zuriel said as he took me across the Court of the Gentiles, A thread of gray smoke from the altar lifted up to an equally gray sky, smoke and cloud becoming the same, intermingling gray with gray. "Twenty-four stations with ten men at each station." He pointed to the men, obvious in their blue-black robes, short-swords at their hips and the tall staff in their right hands. "Half of those men are well-trained and are permanent. The other half are priests who serve for a few months or perhaps a year. The temporary ones are helpful. They provide additional eyes for watchfulness, but we do not depend on them if there is trouble. To them I provide a sword, but I do not assign them duties that might require them to need one. They serve to watch the worshippers—and to report anything they think is unusual. They are also responsible for inspecting the priests."

"Inspect the priests?" I asked.

"The priests, just like the animals they offer, must be free of diseases and broken bones, so we must verify their worthiness. But their primary role is to be watchful—to watch those who come and go at the temple."

There are men whom our instincts tell us to trust and others our instincts tell us to distrust. Zuriel fell in the first category. I trusted him immediately. That trust was never betrayed, and he taught me much those first few weeks. I was only beginning to learn of all the tensions and factions in Judea. Every man in Judea, and especially Jerusalem needed someone he could trust. I found that man in Zuriel.

From the Nicanor Gate we walked down the steps to the Court of Prayer and then through the Court of Israel, where the low partitions separated it from the Court of the Gentiles. There we came to "the booths of the house of Annas," small tents of black-and-tan goat hair where the money-changers exchanged the foreign coins with their offensive images for the prescribed shekels approved by the Sanhedrin. Two men sat at each booth. One controlled the chest of coins. The other kept the ledger.

"Two booths only are open now," Zuriel said. "During Passover it will be ten times that number, and the lines will be long. Annas would open more booths if he had more men he could trust."

We walked toward the corner of the court. A dozen cattle and perhaps thirty sheep were penned there, but several hundred doves—a more common sacrifice at this commemoration—were stacked in baskets next to the booths and awnings of the sellers. As the birds were purchased, they were pulled from their baskets, their legs were strung, and they thrashed upside down as they were handed to the purchaser.

"When Passover comes," Zuriel told me, "for every cow and every sheep you see now, there will be ten."

"I am told," I responded without betraying Manaen's name, "that Annas has turned the Court of the Gentiles into a stockyard."

"It was not always so." He looked around him. "Before I say more, you should look over to the portico behind me. There you will see two of Annas's sons. Other sons may be nearby as well. Always be aware of them. And be careful what you say when they are near— as I am being careful of what I am saying now." He looked around again. "Soon after Annas secured the high priesthood, he had the sacrificial animals moved from outside the walls to the Court of the Gentiles. The Pharisees objected, but they had no recourse. Some in the Sanhedrin said it made the system more efficient, and no one can argue with that, but—"

He paused for a moment.

"But?"

"We Jews," he began, "are required to be a blessing to all nations. That is the requirement God made of our father Abraham."

I recalled a conversation with Manaen while I was still in Rome. He had said the same.

"The Court of the Gentiles has become a stockyard," Zuriel continued. "But that was not its original purpose." His face took that pained expression that was common to him when he reported on activities in Judea. "You see," he went on, "we Jews hold that we are God's covenant people—that he has set us apart for a purpose, and that purpose is to be a blessing to the nations of the world. The design of the temple has that in mind. The Court of the Gentiles is the place where the people of the nations can approach the things of God. But Annas has turned it into a marketplace—a stockyard. A place designed for exposing the people of the nations to the covenant of

God has become a place that exposes them to the stench of animals." He looked around again. His forehead was furrowed. "But the odor of the animal droppings is not as offensive as the haggling and cheating that takes place here." Zuriel looked at me with a rueful smile. "Great amounts of money flow to Annas and his sons from the sale of animals and the changing of money."

Behind us, at one of the money-changers' booths, we heard raised voices. Zuriel moved in that direction, and I followed. "Attend to me!" a young man shouted. Two of the temple guards came quickly.

Zuriel stopped. "My men are capable."

The young man, now restrained by the two guards, shouted, "His wealth does not make him a better man!" He pointed to a man dressed in fine clothes at the front of the line who was exchanging his coins. Zuriel turned and whispered to me, "Annas instructs those in his booths to serve the wealthy first. Most of the peasants, accustomed to being slighted by the rich, are indifferent to this treatment but some, like this one, will protest. But my guards are capable. We can go."

As we left, he nodded to the two sons of Annas standing among the columns. "I want them to know," he said with a smile, "that I know they are watching me—as I watch their booths."

Several supplicants, most with doves in their hands, going toward the temple, met us as we walked toward the Court of the Gentiles.

Watchfulness. Men in authority must always be watchful. They must always keep watch. Why is that so? That question came often to my mind. Only one violated this rule of watchfulness. Only one was not fearful of losing his authority. Only one—the one who had real authority—was not concerned that he would lose it to others. That one, with genuine authority, who confronted me with his authority— had no need to set watchmen on his walls. His kingdom was one that could not be challenged—and needed no one to set guard around it. But those whose authority is feeble, who build earthly kingdoms, must always be watchful lest their kingdom be wrested away—so they keep watch. The temple itself, a symbol of a kingdom, required much watching. Annas watched it from a distance, relying on his spies to tell him all that takes place there and the Romans watched from above, in their Antonia Fortress, so offensive to the Jews.

Chapter 21
The Duty

One can tell a lot about a man by the way he walks.

The way a man walks offers a window into his soul. The way a man walks tells what he thinks of himself and . . .what he thinks others think of him. This is true wherever a man walks, but it was especially true at the great Temple of Jerusalem.

Four years I served there. Four years I watched men walk in the courtyards of the temple. For four years my duty was to keep order at the temple. Some in Judea attempted to disrupt the temple and its services. I was there to make sure they did not. I watched men to determine their motives, to find one with evil purposes in his heart to thwart their malignant ambitions. To know a man's motives, to know what is in his heart, is not an easy task—but the great temple made that task easier. A man's motives came closer to the surface when he approached the shadow of those imposing walls. Gauging a man's intent was made easier by those giant stones and the reflection from the great golden doors seemed to pass through a man, exposing his heart.

For four years I kept order. Tens and tens of thousands came and went during my duty at the temple, pressing their sandals on those sacred stones as they made their sacrifices, as I watched them.

I watched them carefully. I had a duty. I kept order at the temple. That was my duty. That was my responsibility—but eventually I failed.

Smoke and blood—the temple was a place of smoke and blood. A man's sins—a nation's sins, Israel's sins—are not easily accounted for. Enough smoke to fill the sky and enough blood to fill a river was necessary—so it seemed—to absolve Israel of its sins. The nation's sins must have been profound—that they required the work of so many men and the death of so many animals—to confer atonement. Hundreds of priests worked perpetually to attend to the business of atoning for the nation's sins. Untold animals, their blood thrown on the base of the altar and their carcasses burned on top of it, were required for this atonement. It is no simple thing to account for a nation's sin. But that was the role of the temple—and for the achieving of that role, there had to be order. Order was essential. And to have order at the temple there must be watchfulness, diligence, and a quick response to disorder.

The maintaining of order was my role. The Jews expected it. The Romans expected it. The two nations agreed on little, but both expected the regular and uninterrupted functioning of the temple. Two hundred forty good, alert men helped with the task, but the temple itself was my best ally. It had a profound effect on those who came into its proximity. Those who came were changed in some unexplainable way. Why those rocks had this power, I cannot say. Perhaps their massiveness diminished people in their own minds, as if they saw the frailty of their own bodies in comparison. Or perhaps when they saw how much effort was required to purge a nation's sin, they became aware of their own sin. Or as some said, God himself inhabited the site. Whatever the reason, in those years I stood sentinel in the temple, I saw it with every visitor.

A good man became better when he came to the temple—but the opposite was also true. Worship and reverence inhabited the hearts of most that came. Those men expressed their humility before their god and it showed in their faces and in their posture—but for others, it was the evil in their hearts that found better expression.

That great edifice, thrust toward heaven on the cleft rocks of the hill called Zion, somehow seemed to expose a man to judgement of the heavens. There, in the courtyards, one could not see the world around, for the walls obscured the view; there one could see only the temple and the heavens; and there, the brilliant light, thrown back from the polished white stones and the golden door, went right through a man, exposing his soul. I saw it every day . . .

A humble man, arriving at the temple, had a certain way of walking—as if his steps were an affront to the stones beneath his sandals. The *amharetzin*, the common folk, the people of the land, walked in that manner. They brought their sacrifices, for that was their obligation—but their intimidation showed in their step. Ill at ease, with careful, tentative steps they made their way around the great open spaces of the temple—bewildered by the sounds and activity around them. They, in their deepest hearts, yearned to have the pilgrimage over, to have their obligation satisfied—so they could go back to their small villages, sleep in their own beds and find comfort in the routine of their simple lives.

Old men, men who knew the temple before Annas moved the booths and animals to the Court of the Gentiles, have told me that a man at the temple—in those days— was even more readily exposed to his sin. But now, they say, the bleating of the sheep and goats and the haggling of the coin-changers distract a man from his accountability to God.

Members of the Sanhedrin came regularly to the temple. Some of them walked as a man limping, their heavy black robes, like curtains, pulling at their fat legs. They beat their breasts, looking up into heaven, crying out "Deliver us, Lord!" But in truth they had nothing to be delivered from—and when they were assured that all in the courtyard had witnessed their piety, they returned to their litter-carriers to be taken home.

Hundreds of priests resided at the temple. They had grown accustomed to the great stones and had lost any sense of awe. Their walk had a pace different from the supplicants. They scurried about, focused on their responsibilities. Whether their task was menial, like hauling wood, or essential, like offering the sacrifices, most went about their tasks with indifference.

The money-changers and animal-sellers, to whom I was required to give particular attention, were likewise indifferent to the temple, inured to its beauty and its purpose. These had their own way of walking—like thieves, with wary eyes, hunched over, suspicious of all movement. They slept under awnings around the Court of the Gentiles. They kept close watch on their booths while I kept close watch on them. The traditionalists said it was an affront to bring the animals into the courts, an affront to have the money exchanged in the shadow of the temple itself. But Annas and his sons prevailed. The convenience he offered gave him and his sons more income. Great income and great contention—those were the products of the booths, but contention has the possibility of leading to disorder. My responsibility was to quell the disputes, to mediate the contention, to make sure there was no disorder. Doing so made certain the booths functioned profitably.

It was there among the booths where I had the greatest responsibility and where I had my greatest failure. Amid the animals and the booths I would be tested—and found wanting. In the eyes of those who gave me my duty, I failed. That failure to protect those at the 'booths of the sons of Annas' was well-noted. For that failure, and my inability to provide an excuse, I would endure the wrath of Annas and his sons. I could offer no defense for my failure. I had been powerless. Although I had a sword in my hand, and he, a mere cord in his—even so I was rendered helpless. My arms found no strength and my heart no will to oppose the one who came to disrupt the 'booths of the sons of Annas'.

Four years I would watch the booths amid the sheep's bleating and the odor of their excrement. Others watched too. Some of the temple guards had stations nearby, and one or more of the sons of Annas was always lingering in the shadows of the porticoes, watching, making sure the animals were being sold and the coins being exchanged.

Rancor and anger were the regular by-products of the exchange of the coins and the sale of the sacrifices. There were few days when I was not called to quell some dispute. Resentment and ill-will seemed to breed in the stones under the booths—and the men who administered those booths took the character of the site. They were impatient and contentious men. And they were nervous, for they were watched carefully by the sons of Annas. If their countenance and their language were indicators, they were filled with curses to the overflowing—cursing their fellow sellers, cursing the animals, cursing their customers—and if no one was nearby, cursing under their breath because that had become their habit. When they closed their stalls in the late afternoon and clutched their money bag under their arm and hobbled away, watching behind them to be certain they were not followed, they seemed to be men accursed.

Others walked differently at the temple. Old men, sometimes on the arms of their sons or grandsons, came to the temple with mincing steps, stopping often to rest, moving their heads slowly from side to side, taking in the sights around them. These were men making their last trip to the temple. They knew it. I could see it in their eyes.

Joseph Caiaphas, the appointed high priest, was my master and had a different pace from any other. At the temple he trod slowly and deliberately, at least in public. His pace was slow like the village folk, but not humble. It was measured, precise, intentional. Caiaphas walked as a person on display—as if everyone were watching him—which was often the case. The laws of the Jews required the high priest, while at the temple, to be accompanied by three others—one on each side and one behind, and on most occasions I was the one behind. He did not like this duty of walking through the temple, but Annas, his father-in-law, who had procured the position for him, required it. And Joseph Caiaphas, the high priest in title, feared the wrath of his father-in-law. When Caiaphas took his course around the temple, I followed behind as the blue-trimmed fringe of his cloak brushed along the smooth stones, moving rhythmically with every step. Chin raised, eyes moving from side to side, he sought from those around what he thought he deserved—deference, obedience, and respect.

But the pace of Caiaphas was not his own. He merely tried to model the steps of his father-in-law. The deportment of Annas was his ambition, but it did not come naturally.

Of all those who trod the stones at the temple, Annas had the most distinctive pace. In those days he rarely came to the temple. He depended on his sons and his spies to keep him informed of the temple activities. But when he came his presence changed the mood at the site, and no one who watched him doubted that the temple was under his control. Every step for Annas seemed an accusation. When he came to the temple, he wore the high priest's robe, twined blue linen with tassels of blue, purple and scarlet, fashioned like pomegranates. His face was pinched and tight, the lines around his eyes like knife-cuts. His dry, parched skin was the color of the desiccated hills that run down to Jericho. To some he seemed like a lizard from those hills—one that tested the air with its tongue. Annas, likewise, with his twin-pointed beard, braided and oiled, with his onyx eyes, tested those around him. "Are there any," he seemed to say, "who will counter my authority?"

There were none.

Many would curse him in private, but no man dared match the gaze of Annas, much less counter him, in public. It was not wise for a man to counter Annas openly. Caiaphas made men nervous, but Annas made them afraid. Dark eyes, deep-set behind a tangle of eyebrows, sought a motive in the face of all others—and no one who felt his glare would think he could conceal a secret from Annas. Children, by instinct, ran to their mother's apron when the eyes of Annas fell on them. Roman soldiers, who by report, fought bravely against the wild barbarians in Brittany or Gaul, found themselves dropping their eyes to avert the gaze of Annas.

Annas walked in a way meant to cast fear. Yes, one can tell a lot about a man by the way he walks.

The first time I saw the Nazarene was in the temple . . . and he was in full stride.

Chapter 22
The House of Annas

Jerusalem, as I was to learn, was a city of resentments, of antagonisms, of conflicts. The greater conflicts were evident: the Jews resented the Romans; the Romans despised the Jews; the Sadducees despised the Pharisees, and the Pharisees had the same opinion of the Sadducees; the Herodians hated the Romans and the high priests; the high priests were wary of everyone; the Zelotes hated all who cooperated with Rome. And the Essenes, weary of the multiple resentments, had removed themselves to the desert.

Affinities in Jerusalem, I learned, were more likely developed along shared resentments than shared ambitions.

Into this poisonous, seething atmosphere, the citizens of Jerusalem heard a rumor—a rumor of a teacher in the Galilee who advised them to "love their enemies" and to "do good to those who abuse you." To those weary of the venality of Jerusalem, it was a refreshing and intriguing admonition. But many, like the sons of Annas, the admonition was received with derision.

To the northwest of the temple, the land drops off and rises back up again at the corner of the old city wall. That is the site of the house of Annas. It sits a little lower than Herod's palace, but the site offers an advantage: one has to look in only one direction to watch for trouble. Sitting on the higher edge of the Upper City with a broad view of Jerusalem, it is the place where Annas, his five sons, and his son-in-law looked across the city to the temple. Annas had chosen this site well. The great porch of the house afforded a wide view of the city, and although he and his family were too far removed from the temple to hear the activity there, if there were any unusual gatherings—they would know.

I had become an agent of Annas and his place of watchfulness, serving at the temple as additional eyes, assisting Annas' efforts to maintain his power, helping him watch for those who might attempt to subvert his authority.

They often gathered on the wide porch and looked over the city to the temple. Annas, especially, as I would learn, often sat on that porch, his eyes trained on the temple. Although his vantage point was not close enough or high enough to see the booths where the coins were exchanged, and the sacrificial animals sold—still he watched with interest. From this promontory, banked up above the steep hills of the Valley of Hinnom, and well protected in the back by strong city walls, he sat with a blanket across his lap watching the lingering smoke of the sacrifices lifted into the sky and dissipating over the Mount of Olives. Herod's palace, with its three ostentatious towers, was nearby and obscured the view to the immediate left of the porch, but there was little to observe there. None of the Herods were resident in Jerusalem any longer, and the great palace had little use those days. Other than when the Roman prefect came from Caesarea to make a state visit, the great halls and the dozens of bedrooms were vacant. There was no better place in Jerusalem than the house of Annas to keep a watch on the city, and it was to this place that Zuriel took me. "Joseph Caiaphas never intended to be the high priest," he told me as we left the temple. "but the office was imposed on him. Valerius Gratus, exasperated with Annas and his sons, instructed Annas that neither he nor his sons could continue in office. So what did Annas do? Appointed his son-in-law as high priest!" He laughed.

"The priests are critical of Caiaphas," Zuriel continued. "But of course, they make their comments out of Annas's hearing."

"Why is it," I asked, "the priests are critical of Caiaphas?"

"They say he does not take the ceremonies seriously. They say he has little interest in the sacrifices or the laws."

"Are the accusations true?"

Zuriel looked at me with a little smile on his face. "That is something you will be able to determine for yourself—very soon. It is time for you to meet Joseph Caiaphas."

We left the temple complex through the tunnel and out the Huldah Gates, where we walked down the steep road I had helped construct only months before. I looked at the stones on which we were walking. Unconsciously I wiped my arms. The dust was gone from my arms, but the memory of the stone-dust that covered my body came back to me.

"There are other routes." Zuriel said. "Some are quicker and less steep, but they require traveling through tighter streets, through the shops, places where a crazed man might hide, and Caiaphas is not concerned about the steepness. He rides in a litter."

As we approached the Pool of Siloam, through which the water of the Gihon Spring flowed, a number of Jews were performing their ritual bathing for purification before entering the temple. We turned sharply right and sharply uphill along the edge of the city's wall, and a few moments later we came to the house of Annas. We entered the gate.

There is something in the heart of a man that bristles at his slavery that tells him he was not born for servitude. I speak as if I speak for all slaves. I should not. But I often felt it—that sense that told me I was no less than those around me. The afternoon I was shown to Joseph Caiaphas and his father-in-law and his brothers-in-law, I felt it strongly as they, from the balcony of their house, looked down on me as Zuriel presented me to them.

Contempt poured off Annas' porch as though it were oozing mud. Annas himself sat in his chair, almost indifferent to the introduction. His five sons milled around the porch, sometimes looking at me, sometimes talking among themselves. One of them said something to the others and they laughed. The joke was likely about me. Among those on the porch, only Joseph Caiaphas looked at me without contempt. He was taller than his brothers-in-law, but his flesh held loosely to his frame as if intended for an even taller man. He was, I learned, given to his wine. The residue of that wine had collected in double bags under his eyes, and the weight of that wine had gathered in his belly, which swelled out under his robe.

I realized that Zuriel was speaking, "—will provide protection for the high priest as he performs his duties."

The session was brief. For that I was grateful. Zuriel made the arrangements that I would come to the house on the Sabbath and accompany Caiaphas to the temple to conduct the weekly service.

"It is required," Zuriel told me as we departed, "that the high priest, when walking, be accompanied by three guards, one to each side and one behind. You should take the rear position. It provides the better view. Keep your hand on your blade as you walk—and stay alert. There are those in Judea, and especially Galilee, who wish the high priest dead. They are not great in number, but one crazed man with a short sword can do great damage."

During that summer I fell into the daily pattern of the temple. Well before daylight the designated priests—those determined by the casting of lots—cleaned the altar. With shovels and prongs they removed the ashes of the day before, moving aside any unburned portion of the previous day's sacrifice and gathering the wood to be burned that day. A second lot was cast, and the priest designated by that lot then went to the pinnacle of the temple, where if the sun had risen, would say, "The sun shineth already." The officiating priest would respond, "Is the sky lit up as far as Hebron?" If confirmed, the officiating priest would have the lamb brought forward. Water from a golden bowl was offered to the lamb. In the dim light the priest brought a torch near the lamb to examine it one last time. Any blemish would make it unacceptable. It was an unnecessary ceremony because the lamb had been kept in readiness for four days and examined multiple times by multiple priests, including a thorough examination the prior evening.

Then the priest would declare, "I find no fault in it."

'I find no fault . . .!' That evaluation would later be repeated—by a different examiner referring to another Lamb, for so the Baptizer called him. That examiner, from the porch of Herod's palace, on the eve of Passover, would say those same words when making his evaluation. The 'lamb of God,' the Baptizer called him, had endured previous examinations. But no amount of scrutiny—by any number of men—had discovered a fault, and neither did his final examiner, who would repeat, 'I find no fault in him'.

The lamb's legs were tied, and it was placed on the altar. The priest ordered the temple gates to be opened. As those great gates swung on their hinges, three trumpet blasts—crisp, loud and penetrating—sounded by three dozen silver trumpets on the edge of the temple wall, woke the city. All Jerusalem knew this moment. The morning sacrifice was about to be offered. The priest hearing the trumpets, gripped his knife, and with a quick upward motion slit the throat of the lamb as another priest caught the blood in a golden bowl. The blood was splattered on the altar in the prescribed manner.

The priests in unison repeated the *shema:* "Hear, O Israel: The Lord our God, the Lord is one. You shall love the Lord your God with all your heart and with all your soul and all your might. And these words that I command you today shall be on your heart. . . ."

A new day had started in Jerusalem.

The slumbering city came awake, but activity in the Court of the Gentiles had started more hours earlier. There, slaves had cleaned the refuse from the penned animals and shoveled it into baskets to be taken by donkey to Dung Gate and emptied at the bottom of the valley. Other slaves fed and watered the animals—sheep and goats penned in the corner and doves in their baskets. The money-changers yawned as they positioned the wooden poles and goat-hair awnings of their tables, then positioned scales and weights in anticipation of the supplicants who would soon arrive.

Indeed, some had gathered outside the Huldah Gates, waiting to hear the blast of the temple trumpets that would signal the opening of the gates.

An hour or two later, after their breakfasts had been consumed, the teachers and their students would arrive, settling into whatever section of the porticoes was their traditional gathering place. Older men arrived mid-morning to visit with friends and catch up on the news. As the sun hung overhead, men returned to their houses for their mid-day meal and their naps, some of them returning for the afternoon. As the sun fell below the temple walls, the booth-keepers began closing their booths for the day.

To my duties was added the responsibility of transporting coins to the house of Annas. On the afternoon before the Sabbath, I gathered all the coins collected by the booths, and with the assistance of four temple guards, we took the chest of coins to the house of Annas.

"Annas spends the Sabbath counting his coins," was a common joke heard in Jerusalem in those days.

It was the custom that Caiaphas met us as we arrived, he on the lower porch and Annas seated above on the high porch. The sons of Annas, not Caiaphas, would take the chest of coins. At the windows above, the women of the household, both the Jewish women and the slave-girls, peeked out the shuttered windows, looking at me and sometimes I could hear them giggle.

And so the summer went. Only one incident interrupted the rhythm of the days and weeks of those first months at the temple. A deranged man with wild eyes and spittle on his face made his way to the penned sheep, pulled a knife from his robe and slit the throats of two lambs, shouting "I am the priest of the Most High!" before I subdued him. The temple guards came quickly. They tied the man's arms and feet and put a rope through his teeth to stifle his shouts. He was given over to the sons of Annas and we heard no more of him.

"Annas has his own ways," Zuriel told me a few days later when I asked about the man.

The summer season was passing. As the afternoon fell in the west and the evening air cooled, the congregants at the temple began wearing woolen shawls on their shoulders. The air became thinner and each morning as the great gates were opened, a man looking toward the rising sun across the Kidron Valley, could see the orderly rows of olive trees against the hill that rise up opposite the valley. A series of stacked-stone fences formed knee-high striations across the hill. An olive-press, composed of the same stones, sat in the lower portion, ready to crush the olives when the time came. The olive trees were perfectly still in the early morning, but there was movement around them. Women and children arranged ladders and baskets under the trees. It was time for the olive harvest. My mind drifted as I watched. . .

Is it time to pick the olives at the estate? Have half the olives now turned black? That was the rule Quartus employed. Two olive harvests had passed since I left. Is Quartus able to pick the topmost olives of the trees at the estate? Has the master bought another slave who can shake the olives from those branches? Someone who can pick the uppermost figs? Someone who can put meat on his table? Someone who can kill the wolves who try to steal the lambs? And has the lady's sorrow subsided? These questions served no purpose, yet I was unable to dismiss them.

The pilgrims began to arrive for *Shauvot,* bringing their baskets of grain for the sacrifices.

"During *Shavuot* you must be careful where you walk," Zuriel laughed. "For there are nearly as many donkeys in the city for this festival as there are people."

A few days before the festival, as I stood near the booths at the temple, I heard my name called.

"Sit with us, Malchus."

The bright afternoon sunlight kept me, at first, from seeing who had spoken. The voice came from the shaded portion of the portico. I shielded my eyes and stepped into the shade afforded by the colonnades and saw two men sitting in one of the alcoves. Nicodemus was one of them. He motioned for me to come nearer. "Surely your duties can be put aside for a few moments—and you can sit with two old men in the shade. Here, we have brought water. Come, have a drink."

I loosened my belt and put my sword beside me as I sat down. "This is Joseph. He is called the Arimathean." Nicodemus handed me a cup and filled it from his waterskin. I thanked him and drank it all. "Simon sends his greetings."

"Please return those greetings. I remain indebted to Simon. And to you."

"Joseph and I have a custom. We meet here prior to the gathering of the Sanhedrin—and we often meet here at other times."

"It is said you are unlikely friends," I said.

Both smiled. "Malchus," Joseph answered, looking directly at me, "What has been said about you is indeed true. You are an honest man. Others, both Sadducees and Pharisees criticize us, but none are bold enough to say something to our faces."

"Yes," Nicodemus added. "We know what those in the Sanhedrin say about us—'The Sadducee who is not a Sadducee—'" he nodded to Joseph "—and 'the Pharisee who is not a Pharisee,'" pointing to himself.

"And who are we to deny their accusations?" Joseph said, his voice trailing off. "For both of us have found we cannot be defined by the party whose name we carry. Am I a Sadducee only? Is Nicodemus a Pharisee only? Have we no other identity?"

Nicodemus smiled. "One of our fellow Sanhedrists suggested that Joseph and I initiate a new group, neither Pharisee nor Sadducee, but 'the party of the pessimists,' as he called it."

Joseph smiled. "Yes, our brothers consider us pessimists. Yet *we* think we are the most hopeful of all in Jerusalem. We have hope for the future of our nation, yet..." he paused, seeking words for his thoughts.

"Yet," Nicodemus filled in, "our hope is not founded on the edifice where we now sit."

"I don't understand," I replied.

Joseph pointed across the courtyard to the temple. "Look there. And look around. The temple is magnificent, is it not? We Jews glory in the magnificence of our temple. Look at the golden doors. Look at the great stones. Look at the marble beneath our feet. Look at these tall columns above us. We are told that nothing, even in Rome, compares with our temple. Yet is it in the splendor of stones we should exult? Should we find our nation's glory in gold and silver and bronze?" He pointed again to the temple. "If you were to enter the Holy of Holies, you would find it empty. The Ark of the Covenant is not there as it was in the time of Solomon. The Book of the Covenant is not there. Aaron's rod is not there—none of the items that constituted the real glory of the first temple are now enclosed. And who built this temple? An Idumean! And who guarantees its security? The Romans! Yet we in Israel, especially those of us in the Sanhedrin, speak of the glory of this place. One of our prophets told us that God would one day 'fill this house with glory.' Has that prophecy been fulfilled? Has this house been filled with glory? My friend and I question that."

Nicodemus spread his arms in exasperation toward the sheep and cattle and goats and birds. "Does this look like glory to you?" Yet, as my friend asks, Is this what the prophets told us to expect? Or—should we have a greater expectation? Is what we see around us the fulfillment of the prophecies? Or should we anticipate more? Is there something—or someone—greater that we should look for? Those are the questions we ask ourselves."

Nicodemus filled my cup again. "The friendship between Joseph and me is a source of irritation to both parties. The Sadducees don't approve and the Pharisees don't approve."

"And sometimes," Joseph added with a mischievous smile, "we enjoy their disapproval."

Nicodemus took a drink from his cup and looked into the distance. "Ours is a land of contentiousness." He sighed. "Pharisees against Sadducees, Jews against the Romans, the Herodians against all but themselves, the insurrectionists likewise opposed to all, the common people against the rulers, the slaves against their masters—the contention is endless." He looked at Joseph. "It is important that a man have a friend when he lives in such a land."

Joseph took his friend's wrist, but said nothing.

"This festival is called 'the season of our joy,'" Nicodemus said. "And truly it should be, for this is the time when our people have gathered in their crops, and they are grateful for our Lord's provision. Our people will sing and dance, and the musicians will play their instruments. But it is forced merriment. Our hearts can never be truly festive until our Messiah comes."

"And so," Joseph said, patting his friend on the knee, "we sit and grumble to ourselves, because we are too old to dance."

Both laughed.

"It is good to see you smile, Malchus." Joseph said. "Smiling, it seems, does not come naturally to you. If your countenance remains dour, you may also be assigned as a member of the party of the pessimists."

"I would be glad to join this party," I replied. "I like the members, but I must now return to my duties. Thank you for the water and for the conversation. I wish you well."

Two days prior to the beginning of the festival, Zuriel informed me, "It is required of the high priest that he spend the first night in his quarters at the temple. I will accompany you to bring Caiaphas here at mid-afternoon tomorrow."

When we arrived at the house of Annas, we were directed to the kitchen to wait. A young servant girl pulled back the curtain. "Please have some soup while you wait."

Another man was in the kitchen. "I am Shaul," he said. My master is upstairs with Annas. Join me. The lentil soup is hot, and the bread is fresh."

Zuriel and I took seats near Shaul. As the servant girl put my bowl in front of me, she leaned over me and let her hair fall on my head as she brushed her breasts across my shoulder.

As she left, Zuriel leaned over and whispered, "Be careful of that one. She talks much. And she—"

The servant girl returned. "I am Chaya," she said, bringing water and looking directly at me. "What is your name?"

"I am Malchus."

"Ah yes," she said. "I know of you. You are Malchus the tall one, the yellow-hair. You are the protector of Caiaphas. I have seen you in the courtyard, and now I see you closely."

Zuriel and Shaul sipped their soup, keeping their eyes down. Chaya waited to see if I would respond. I said nothing.

"This house," she said, "is always full of coming and going. Always there is someone who must talk with Annas the high priest. Shaul's master has brought news, no doubt. What news, Shaul, does your master bring?"

"News that seems to have your master Annas worried."

"Annas is always worried," she said. "There is nothing new in that. What news do you bring that could add to his worries?"

"My master and I have been in the Galilee, along with some others of the Sadducees. Annas sent us there because a rabbi in the Galilee has him concerned."

"Why," Zuriel asked, "would a Galilean rabbi concern Annas?"

"They call him 'the miracle-worker,'" Shaul answered. "He has healed a number of sick people." He wiped the last of his soup with his bread. "He has a following—a few thousand. We saw them. We were surprised—and not all of them were from the Galilee. They had come from all over, as far away as Tyre and Sidon."

"Tyre and Sidon!" Zuriel exclaimed.

"Yes, some even from Idumea. The crowds grew larger each day." He gave his empty bowl to Chaya. She pressed her leg against my back as she took the bowl.

"My worry," Shaul continued, "is for the Galilean. Those who worry Annas do not usually live long.

I must tell you what happened on the hill above the Gennareset." His eyes brightened as he started his story. "My master and two scribes were the ones Annas sent. When we arrived at the hills just before Capernaum, we saw the crowd. When we got near, I pushed through the crowd and said, 'Stand aside. A member of the Great Council approaches.' My master adjusted his turban before he started through the crowd. He held his blue linen robe with both hands, lest the hem catch the ground. The scribes came behind him and I behind them. My master kept his head aloof. He would not look at the common people as they let him through."

A smile came to Shaul's face as he recalled the event. "I wish you could have seen it yourself. The rabbi's disciples formed a ring around the rabbi to protect him from the crush of the crowd. As my master approached, they seemed confused, but the rabbi made a motion to them to allow us to come to the front. My master's face turned to a sneer when he saw these disciples—some were fishermen; one was a Zelote and one was a tax collector!"

He held his bowl out to Chaya asking if there was more soup, but she shrugged and shook her head.

He grunted his disappointment, but went on. "There's more to tell." He began to speak at a more measured pace. "What did I expect to see when I saw this rabbi? I do not know, but whatever I expected—"

Shaul struggled to finish his thought. He squinted his eyes as if visualizing the incident. "He had a *presence* about him. How do I explain that? The *amharetzin,* the common people, say of him, 'He speaks with authority.' That is true, but more than speaking with authority, he *carried* authority. How do I explain that? I cannot. How can a carpenter's son from a poor village in the Galilee walk and talk with the authority of God? Or so it seems. I have no answer to that."

He paused as if working out something in his mind. "I can tell you this. If my master expected deference from this carpenter's son toward a nobleman, from an *amharetzin* to a member of the Great Council, he did not receive it." The smile came back to his face. "It was an odd moment, very awkward, when my master came near the rabbi. Jesus bar-Joseph did not speak. He looked directly at my master. His countenance, with neither condemnation nor contempt, seemed to say, 'You have come for a reason. What is that reason?'"

Shaul paused again. "The crowd was quiet. Even the lake was placid. The two scribes shuffled their feet nervously. My master eventually found his voice, making the inquiry he had been assigned: 'Why,' he asked, 'do your disciples break the traditions of the elders? For they do not wash their hands when they eat.' There was a stirring in the crowd as the question was passed along. Jesus bar-Joseph looked intently at my master and spoke: 'And why do you break the commandment of God for the sake of your tradition? You hypocrites!' he said. Then he quoted Isaiah the prophet, *'This people honor me with their lips, but their hearts are far from me. In vain do they worship me, teaching as doctrines the commandments of men.'"*

Shaul took the last drink from his cup and put it on the table. "That is the report my master is providing to Annas—that he was called a hypocrite by the Galilean rabbi. Annas can add that to his worries."

Chapter 23

Joseph Caiaphas

Zuriel hammered his fist on the heavy wood door of the Chamber of Wood. "It is time, sire! It is time."

Zuriel looked at me with exasperation. "The early morning does not suit Caiaphas's temperament," he said. "But we must wake him. He has duties."

More than an hour remained before the sun would find its way over the hills of Moab and throw its light on the temple, but the high priest was required to be ready at the moment of sunrise. I held a torch in my hand to provide light as the two of us stood outside the Chamber of Wood, the apartment where Caiaphas slept.

I had accompanied Caiaphas the previous afternoon, walking beside his litter with two other guards, as we escorted him to the temple. The Pharisees complained about the ostentatious use of the litter, but those complaints were ignored.

"Damned pilgrims," he had said, poking his head out of the curtains, cursing those who had set up their pallets alongside the route, impeding the litter carriers. "Kick them in their ribs and get them out of the way."

Zuriel took the handle of his sword and hammered on the door. It seemed like a noise that could have awakened all in the temple. He put his ear to the door. "He is stirring."

In a moment Caiaphas cracked the door and looked out. His eyes had the look of one who drank wine until late into the night.

"It is time, sire," Zuriel said. "You must collect the vestments."

Caiaphas blinked his eyes as if he were trying to make sense of what Zuriel said, but eventually nodded and closed the door.

"He fears only Annas," Zuriel said, his voice a whisper, "but he fears him greatly. He will do his duty. These duties do not come naturally to him. He was not trained as a priest and never expected to be the high priest. When Valerius Gratus forbade any of Annas's sons to be high priest, and Annas maneuvered around him, Gratus fumed for days. But in the end, he knew he had been outwitted. He had the authority of Rome behind him, but it served no purpose to go against the Sanhedrin. So the appointment of Caiaphas was tolerated."

A few moments later Caiaphas came out of the apartment. He said nothing as Zuriel and I led the way out of the temple walls and around to the fortress Antonia.

We left the temple mount, just as the dewy forms of the trees emerged on the Mount of Olives across the Kidron Valley. The trees were just beginning to take form in the early light—gray against gray below the outline of the mount. Like orderly, hulking soldiers in formation, they waited for their morning orders, their leaves motionless. Nothing stirred around them. The only sounds were of a few donkeys who resumed the unresolved arguments of the evening before. In the opposite sky a thin silver-white moon, perfectly curved, held its place among a hundred stars, reluctant to relinquish their place to the imminent sun.

The Mount of Olives—this peaceful, quiet place where gray, ghost-like trees awaited the morning to lift the mist—how could I have guessed this place would soon become a place of violence?

The three of us approached the gate of the fortress. The Syrian guards at the fortress were surly, as they often were at this hour, but they opened the gate, and the commander of the legate stood waiting. A soldier beside him held a bundle in his arms.

Zuriel stepped aside and let Caiaphas approach the commander. Caiaphas spoke his rote lines without enthusiasm, moving his head about in an effort to bring himself out of his slumber. "I, Joseph

Caiaphas, high priest of the people of Israel, will today perform the duties of my office at the Feast of Weeks."

The fortress commander responded crisply, "As commander of the Syrian legate under the authority of Pontius Pilate, the duly-appointed prefect of Rome who rules Judea under the authority of Tiberius Claudius Nero, the emperor of Rome, having been given the responsibility for the safekeeping of the holy articles of the Jews, I hereby transfer the vestments of the high priest of Jerusalem to Joseph Caiaphas, the high priest, with the understanding that these vestments will be returned to me at the end of this festival period so that they may be secured for safekeeping."

He took the bundle from the soldier beside him and handed it to Caiaphas. The commander, unlike some other Roman officers I would hear of, took no delight in the indignity of transferring the vestments to the high priest and did not protract the ceremony.

"Damn Herod," Caiaphas said, as we walked away. "He was the one who took the vestments from the priests and gave them to the Romans. It was all part of his plan to bring the priests under his authority. When he died, the Romans kept them."

As we went around the fortress toward the Northern Gate, a dozen sheep were penned by the gate next to the Pool of Israel. Those sheep would be washed in the pool and prepared for sacrifices in the coming days. Sheep that would be sacrificed this morning had been prepared the night before, and they were now waiting at the place of sacrifice. I looked across the pool toward the eastern sky, which had gained some yellow as it framed the round hills of the Mount of Olives.

Zuriel also saw the tinge of color in the sky. "We should hurry," he said. "It would not be appropriate for the high priest to arrive late for the opening ceremony of the Feast of Weeks. And it would not go well with Caiaphas if he had to answer to Annas why he was late for the opening sacrifice." We rushed across the pavement, crossed the Court of Gentiles, and entered the Court of Israel. Caiaphas handed

Zuriel the bundle with the vestments and hurried to the priests' chambers next to the temple. Two priests were waiting. They took the bundle from Zuriel and quickly unwrapped it. Caiaphas removed his outer robe, and the priests slipped over his head the solid white high priest's robe with its embroidered sleeves. The little golden bells at the hem made a dull tinkling sound. The priests took the breast piece with its twelve stones and slipped it over Caiaphas's head. Next was the gold plate inscribed with the words "Holiness unto Jehovah," which they bound around his forehead. They were about to place the tall miter on his head, but he grabbed it and started toward the door.

Zuriel and I followed and emerged in front of the temple itself. A few dozen priests, white-clad with red sashes, were at their stations near the altar. The trumpeters and the lyre players were tuning their instruments, and the Levite choir was humming softly to gain their voices after the night's sleep. Now that the high priest was in place, everything was in order to begin the ceremonies. I looked around. The marble and polished limestone of the temple rose above us. In less than an hour the sun would throw its light directly against those white stones and the great gold-plated doors they encased, doors taller than ten men. But at this moment, as Caiaphas climbed up the altar, the light was subdued. Reaching the platform, he placed his miter on his head, adjusted it, took a deep breath, and waited.

The instrumentalists and the choir members ceased their tunings, took their prescribed positions, and looked toward the tower where the appointed priest stood. The only movement and the only noise at that moment was that of the lamb who tugged at its tethers and bleated its complaint. For four days it had been held in the chambers of Beth-Moked, the designated chamber, under the scrutiny of the priests, awaiting its fate.

The priests, as was their daily custom, had earlier cast lots to see who among them would ascend the tower at the southwest corner of the temple to the Place of Trumpeting to watch for the sunrise. His silhouette and those of the three trumpeters with their silver trumpets, four gray outlines against a sky that was gaining its hue, stood on the highest spot of the temple, its height exceeded only by the offensive Roman tower on the opposite corner of the temple compound. I wondered if the selected priest had a strong voice. The lot for this duty did not always fall on one with a strong voice, and more than once this morning sacrifice, so I had heard, had not gone smoothly because the priests at the place of sacrifice could not hear their brother on the tower.

We waited. Caiaphas adjusted the miter on his head but otherwise, no one moved. A soft yellow light bouncing off the low clouds fell into the place of sacrifice. The white of the lamb and the white of the robes of the priests, softened to the color of cream, assuming the hue of the early morning sky.

After a moment we heard the priest call from the place of trumpeting. His voice was clear. "*Barkai!* Behold! The morning shineth already."

Caiaphas, having trouble getting his miter properly seated, seemed to have not noticed that the priest on the tower had begun the ceremonies. The president of the priests, who stood nearest Caiaphas, leaned forward to look at him.

"Is the sky lit up as far as Hebron?" he mumbled. His voice did not carry to the priest on the tower, but that was unimportant because the response was the rote liturgy.

The priest on the tower scanned the horizon. "Behold. The sky is lit up as far as Hebron."

At that word the lamb was brought forth and led to a golden bowl to drink. Water had been withheld from it to make certain it would be thirsty. The lamb lapped the water in the bowl, looking up with its brown eyes as if trying to understand the ceremony. When it finished its drink, four priests carrying torches came forward to make the final ceremonial inspection. It had been declared without blemish four days earlier, but this final examination fulfilled the ritual requirement that the sacrifice be "a lamb without blemish".

The lamb bleated a small complaint as its feet were secured and fastened to the rings on the altar. Then its head was likewise fastened by a ring. The great doors to the temple began to move on their hinges—the indication that the sacrifice was about to take place. The trumpeters sounded three blasts from their silver trumpets. Jerusalem was now alerted. The officiating priest, irritation filling his face, looked at Caiaphas, waiting for his response. Remembering his responsibility, Caiaphas raised his hands in the manner of the high priest's blessing. He made some motion to Caiaphas, who lowered his arms slightly. According to custom, the high priest was to raise his hands no higher than the golden plate on the front of his miter.

The third blast of the trumpets was still reverberating from the walls as the officiating priest moved quickly. Holding the head of the lamb securely, he drew the knife across its throat. A scarlet cleft appeared in the white wool, and the lamb knew its death, but there was no sound from its mouth. The legs kicked in protest, and the rank aroma of warm blood filled the area. The priest's assistant caught the blood in a golden bowl, but some splattered on his white robe. The lamb's body twitched for a few moments, then went still. The priest sprinkled some of the blood on the corners of the altar and poured the remainder on the base.

The cymbals clanged, the trumpets sounded, and the lyres joined in. Then the Levites picked up their song, "The earth is the Lord's. . ." they sang.

Caiaphas lowered his arms and again tried to get the miter to fit his head.

And thus, the daily sacrifice was completed. But because this was the first day of the Feast of Weeks, more ceremony would follow. Two priests, each carrying a lamb, proceeded toward the altar. Behind them came two more priests, each carrying a silver tray with a loaf of bread. This bread had been prepared the previous night in a special ceremony, its ingredients coming from the "first fruits" of the field. A few moments later, the two lambs were dispatched in the same way as the first. But these two would have a different purpose: they would be roasted and "waved" before the Lord along with the two loaves. Later in the day, the priests would consume the meat and the bread in a ceremonial meal, but it was meager portions for the great number of priests. However, more provision would soon be available. Outside the gates of the temple a throng of pilgrims were gathering with their bundles of first fruits. For the remainder of the week the pilgrims would be bringing their baskets, and their offerings would more than supplement the priests' diet.

Caiaphas waited at the altar for the first supplicant, an aged man assisted by his two sons. One of the sons held the arm of the old man, helping him slowly make his way toward Caiaphas, while the other son helped him hold the basket on his shoulder. I wondered how many times this old man had celebrated the Feast of Weeks—and if this would be his last. The old man stopped for a moment to catch his breath. A barely audible groan came from the impatient Caiaphas. The old man gathered himself, adjusted the basket on his shoulder, and started again. He handed the basket to Caiaphas, who waved it above his head and placed it against the altar. It would be the first of a few thousand baskets placed there during the coming week.

Caiaphas turned back to the old man and forced a smile. Zuriel handed Caiaphas the piece of parchment that had the appropriate passage written on it, but when Caiaphas started reading, the old man knew it by heart, and his gravelly, reverent voice overshadowed that of Caiaphas:

"A wandering Aramean was my father. And he went down into Egypt and sojourned there, few in number, and there he became a nation, great, mighty and populous. And the Egyptians treated us harshly and humiliated us and laid on us hard labor. Then we cried to the Lord, the God of our fathers, and the Lord heard our voice and saw our affliction, our toil, and our oppression. And the Lord brought us out of Egypt with a mighty hand and an outstretched arm, with great deeds of terror, with signs and wonders. And he brought us into this place and gave us this land, a land flowing with milk and honey. And behold, now I bring the first of the fruit of the ground, which you, O Lord, have given me."

In the end, Caiaphas quit reading and allowed the old man to finish the passage alone, which he did with his eyes closed, his bony fists tightened in devotion as he rocked back and forth until he finished. He stood there with his eyes closed for some seconds in some private meditation, and then with his sons' assistance, the old man moved toward one of the low platforms near the altar, where with some difficulty, he prostrated himself on the cold stones. His two sons lay on either side of him, and the three of them gave thanks to their God, who had given them the land and the fruits it yielded.

When they completed their supplication, the two sons assisted their father to his feet. All three bowed to Caiaphas and then moved slowly away from the altar. At this point Caiaphas had fulfilled his duty. The other priests could now take over. The eastern gate was opened, and the throngs began to arrive with their baskets.

Caiaphas stepped briskly beside the altar and the bronze laver. Zuriel and I followed. We went through the Court of Stones, where the scribes were settling into their seats after the morning sacrifice. Several rows of stone seats and stone tables filled the room. Shelves of ink bottles and great baskets of papyrus rolls lined the edges of the room. Here, these scribal assistants would spend the rest of the daylight hours making copies of their holy scriptures. This was a job for young men. It required the keen eyes and steady hands of youth. However, if a young apprentice could prove himself here, and if he could garner enough of the accumulated wisdom of his predecessors, he had the opportunity to be appointed as a scribe, and therefore gain the required respect of all the Jews.

Asriel, one of the chief scribes, known as a "well-plastered cistern," one, for whom "not a drop of the law escapes," whose ingenuity and cleverness was well known in Jerusalem, looked up as we entered. He was as well known for his contempt for the house of Annas, Caiaphas in particular, as he was for his knowledge of the Jewish law. That contempt was evident on his face as we made our way through the benches toward the stairs at the back of the room. Caiaphas ignored him, although he could not have failed to see him, and moved quickly toward the stairs.

But Asriel spoke just as Caiaphas had dipped his head under the stone arch that led out of the room. "Master Joseph Caiaphas, *high priest*." He pronounced the title in such a way to make his disdain evident. "Recognizing your office and the essential role it plays as the intermediary between our God in heaven and those of us who are common people, I ask you if it is not correct that you are enjoined by our law, while conducting your ministrations at the holy temple, that you are required to be escorted by three others, one at each side and one behind? It appears you are accompanied by only two—the captain of the guard and this slave."

The room went still for a moment. The scribal assistants were required to pay no attention to any conversation around them lest they be distracted from their responsibilities and allow an error in their copying. Although they kept their eyes down, their ears were tuned to the conversation. For many in the room, it was their ambition to become as respected and feared as Asriel. He was one of the final authorities on the interpretation of the law in Jerusalem. He, by reputation, stood above the rude, ignorant and profane common folks. His great learning set him apart, made him an authority and gave him status. Yes, the apprentice at the desk held the hope that he too could one day move among the people, with them giving way to him—one who was an authority on the law—one to whom the less educated looked for answers, hanging on his utterances, one to whom respect and admiration were given . . . and one who confounded others by the scope of his knowledge, his wit and his cleverness. And no one more than Asriel had a better reputation for intimidating and provoking his adversaries. Few in the Sanhedrin dared contend against him on any issue. He would provide long, convoluted responses to issues, quoting respected teachers of the law in the course of the argument, mentioning illustrations related to the application of the law to the issue at hand, so that at the end of his discourse, most had lost track of the argument—and even of the original question. Even the high priest was not immune to his interrogation, at least not Caiaphas. But though Asriel might provoke Caiaphas, he would not risk the wrath of Annas.

The room remained still. The hands of the apprentices went about their transcriptions very slowly. The sun had lifted above the Mount of Olives and over the temple walls and flooded into the great open windows, throwing bright glowing light on the benches and the floor of the room. Caiaphas had both hands on the miter to remove it as he stepped under the archway leading out of the Hall of Stones to the stairway leading above. He slowly took his hands from the miter, turned toward Asriel, and forced a thin smile. "Your advice, Asriel, as always is profound. And of course, I am grateful for it." With that he nodded and began to turn away.

"And," Asriel continued, "would it not be more appropriate if these three required attendants be chosen from among the scribes, men who could advise you on matters of our law? Surely they would be better attendants—" he looked at me "—than a common slave?"

Caiaphas again forced a smile of acknowledgment, dipping his head slightly, but said nothing and turned away and up the stairs.

A servant opened the heavy oak doors leading to the high priest's chambers, the Chamber of Wood, the only structure in the temple composed of wood. The original intention for the chamber was that it be occupied for only one week of the year, the week prior to the Day of Atonement, and only by the high priest. Constructed of wood and devoid of ornamentation, its purpose was to remind the high priest to be humble and to make sure he had no distractions as he spent a week preparing himself to be the representative of all the Jews on the Day of Atonement, when he would enter the Holy of Holies and entreat their god to accept the sacrifice for the sins of the people over the previous year.

The structure of the room was basic. It had no decorations on the wall and only a few high windows to admit some light. But the stringent rules the previous high priests had observed before Annas came to the position had been relaxed. Annas may have contented himself with a pallet on the floor and a jug of water, which was the original provision for the room. However, when Eleazar assumed the position of high priest—replacing his father and prior to the ban on Annas's sons—he had a couch and cushions placed in the room. Now Caiaphas had had a serving table and serving pieces installed. He made no pretense of fasting as the previous priests had observed, and instead of one jug of water, an amphora filled with wine sat in its holder. Likewise, although the room had originally been designated for use one week each year, now Caiaphas used it every time he came to the temple as a place to escape the frenzy of temple activities, and he did not mind if others joined him there.

One could often hear the scribes, such as Asriel, joined by the Pharisees, complain about this abrogation of the law. But nothing came of those complaints. The Sadducees held power in the Sanhedrin, Annas ruled the temple, and the Romans had no interest in any of it. So it remained one of a thousand topics the scribes and the Pharisees would grumble about in relation to the Sadducees—but were powerless to change.

Caiaphas dropped the miter on one of the many cushions that outlined the room, relieved to be rid of it. He rubbed his head with his fingertips as if to remove any residue of the miter. "A curse on Asriel." He took a honey-cake from a silver tray and pushed it in his mouth. "He hates us—but then, perhaps we hate him even more. Annas will not allow his name to be spoken in the house. And if he hears it in the city, he spits upon the street." Caiaphas looked through a bowl of pears, selected one, and bit into it. The juice ran down his chin onto his white robe. Dissatisfied with it, he tossed the remainder into the corner. He took a cup of the wine and sipped it, working it on his lips to determine its quality. Wiping his mouth with his sleeve, he resumed his tirade. "Asriel has a reputation for being knowledgeable of the law. Ha! What did that knowledge get him when the house of Boethius and the house of Annas were contending for the office of high priest? He chose the wrong party, didn't he? If he had such wisdom, why did he contend against Annas and cast his lot with the house of Boethus?"

Zuriel and I said nothing. These were not questions meant to be answered.

"Yes." Caiaphas went on, too agitated to sit, "Asriel considers the house of Annas to be pretenders to the priesthood. A curse on him! Let him wallow in his supposed wisdom. What has his wisdom brought him?" Does he have any of the temple revenue?" A smile came to his face at his thought, and he looked at me as if to verify his point. "If Asriel is so wise, and if he has the ear of God, as he would like us to think, then he should have aligned himself with Annas." Caiaphas nodded as if he were working this all out for himself. "Annas says God comes to the aid of those who seize their opportunities." He took a sip of the wine and worked it around in his mouth. "Did Herod come to power because he studied the law?" Caiaphas laughed at the preposterousness of the thought. "Do the Romans control all the lands of the Great Sea and the lands of the north because they are reverent? They who worship gods that fornicate with each other and murder each other? No! Annas has it right. God honors those who have the courage to seize the opportunity."

Zuriel looked at me. We both knew how Annas had "seized the opportunity." He had offered greater bribes to Quirinius, the former governor, than the others who sought the high priesthood. I had heard the stories. Herod had appointed his brother-in-law, Joazar, brother of the second Mariamne—given that name by Herod when he regretted murdering his first wife, Mariamne—as the high priest. But after Aristobulus's failure at ruling Judea, and the Romans' decision to govern directly, they made known they were seeking new candidates for the office of high priest. Annas's family had some wealth, most of it derived from their date farms near Antioch. Nevertheless, other Jewish families were wealthier and could have offered more. But Annas made Quirinius an intriguing offer: if Annas were appointed high priest, a portion of the temple proceeds would be allocated to Quirinius himself, or so they say on the streets of Jerusalem, and I had no reason to doubt it. The revenue passing through the temple had been enormous for many years. Herod used great portions of it to finance his many building projects, so Quirinius would have understood the value of the offer. And although he agreed to the arrangement, it was said of him that he often regretted it, such was the contentious nature of his relationship with Annas. However, when Quirinius returned to Rome, he was an extremely wealthy man.

Two cups of mulled wine and another honey cake helped dissipate Caiaphas's anger. "I must sleep," he said as he stretched out on the couch, muttering some additional complaints under his breath. Zuriel and I dismissed ourselves and walked down the stairs. Asriel had left the Hall of Stones, but one of the other senior scribes, left in charge of the hall, looked at me with the same contempt as Asriel. In his eyes I could see all the resentment of the scribes toward the Sadducees, and particularly the house of Annas. And even though I was a slave in the household, that was no protection from the contempt of the scribes.

The apprentices were now seriously at their work, bent over their stone desks, sitting on their stone benches, meticulously transcribing. Vats of specially formulated inks sat against the wall. Above them a series of wooden shelves, which ran up to the ceiling, were filled with stacks of specially prepared vellum and papyrus. On the opposite wall a stone shelf held clay pots filled with dozens of quills. These were the essential tools of the scribes, and all were ceremonially prepared for their holy assignment. As each of these young scribes went about his work, he pronounced each word aloud to himself before he wrote it, which, when compounded by the three dozen or so scribes at work, created a strange murmur in the room. Occasionally a scribe would stop to clean his quill, having come upon the word "Lord" in the text. That was the requirement of their rules. Less often, but regularly, the scribe, having come to the covenant name of their god—a name they would not pronounce aloud for its holiness—would dismiss himself from the room in order to bathe himself before rendering that holy name in ink.

As I left the room of the scribes and came outside, I could see there was now a throng of supplicants at the altar, offering their first-fruit baskets. A dozen or so priests accepted them and waved them in the air before placing them at the base of the altar. After the offerings had sat there for a few minutes, other priests carried them to a storehouse underground.

The week after the Feast of the Booths, at mid-day, I saw Nicodemus and Joseph in their customary place along the porticoes. I joined them, and as we exchanged greetings, a small commotion developed in one of the groups. A young man who stood among his seated fellow students was being reprimanded by the scribe teaching the group.

"That is Stephen bar-Jonas," Nicodemus said, shaking his head. "We call him 'the irrepressible one.'"

"But the rabbis and the scribes call him 'the impertinent one,'" Joseph added. "He frustrates the teachers because he knows the Law and Prophets as well as they. But he asks many questions—questions that are difficult to answer."

"What questions?" I asked.

"He asks, 'Why did our forefathers fail to obey God?' and 'Why did our forefathers persecute the prophets?' And sometimes he asks, 'What is the appropriate way that the high priest is to be ordained?'"

Nicodemus added, "Which is a dangerous question and probably does not go unreported. The questions Stephen asks are not unlike the questions we and many others have. But we do not raise those questions as openly as Stephen does."

"Perhaps that is to our shame," Joseph said. "We should be more irrepressible and more impertinent."

The two men looked at each other and then went silent. I dismissed myself and returned to the booths.

The sun came later each morning and cool winds poured over the edges of the temple walls, rippling the goat-hair awnings of the booths, as the supplicants pulled their robes closer to their bodies. As the air chilled, fewer came to the temple. During the coldest season, only the hardiest teachers and the hardiest pupils continued their lessons, huddled in the corners of the Royal Portico, where there was less wind. My duties were fewer in those days, and I had time to resume my readings. Nicodemus provided me scrolls, and Cyrene, now Simon, brought them to me at the temple.

"Nicodemus treats me well," Simon told me as I pored over the volumes. "Sometimes I forget I was once a slave in the quarry."

I held a copy of *The Odyssey.* I had read twice in Rome, but I could read it ten times more and never grow weary of it. A few plays by Sophocles were included as well as some of the writings of Plato and Socrates.

"Nicodemus says you must not tell from where you received these scrolls," Simon said. "He said he endures enough criticism from his fellow Pharisees already. They do not approve of his reading the Greeks."

I nodded.

Through the winter Simon came the day before each weekly Sabbath and replenished the scrolls. "Nicodemus instructs me to inform you that you have almost exhausted his library. He has little else to offer. The only volumes he could offer you now would be the writings of the Pharisees themselves—which he says are tedious beyond endurance."

"Please tell Nicodemus I am grateful for his provision."

Marius came once that winter. "I have managed a few weeks posting at Wadi Qelt," he smiled. "The weather is better there in the valley. The winds have turned cold in Antipatris." We spent two evenings together at the Antonia Fortress, reminiscing about our time in Rome.

From the Roman soldiers in the fortress we heard consistent complaints about their training regimen. "The Spear," one of the officers told us, "thinks we will soon be attacked by the Persians, by the Parthians, by the Gauls, by the Goths, and by the Huns—all at the same time. Every week he sends a new training schedule. We expected new rigors and every new commander must assert himself, but my men have grown weary with this training. I have told them it is worse in Caesarea. I go there regularly. Pilate personally drills that cohort. They will have no relief from their training for months. Pilate will make the rotation after the Passover. That is the custom."

The rains that winter were meager. "It is now three years," Zuriel told me, "since we have had good rains. The cisterns in the city are less than half full. It will be a difficult summer." We stood near the booths, at the edge of the Royal Portico. It was late afternoon, the time at which the priest would begin preparing the evening sacrifice and the servants of Annas were shuttering the booths. A uniformly gray sky hung above us.

Nearby, a Pharisee lectured a group of boys who leaned in to each other for warmth. More than one of them looked around absently. Their faces betrayed their hope that the lecture would soon conclude. "Nehemiah," the Pharisee droned, "taught us to separate ourselves. We have knowledge and understanding and cannot profane ourselves. We are the ones chosen by God to—" He droned on, fascinated with the topic. His cold students paid little attention to the lecture.

Zuriel looked at the dark, unyielding sky. "She hides from us tonight. I am speaking of the moon. If she appears, we would see she has reached her fullness, looking like a golden plate on a king's table. Then over the following nights, she will recede, slowly, and eventually hide her face like a bashful girl. And then, slowly again, she will reveal herself to us. When her face is full the next time, it will be Passover."

Jerusalem was a city filled with tension. Every day it sulked and seethed with apprehension and nervousness. Every day a thousand intrigues brewed in its houses and streets. But what was true on an ordinary day was true ten times over at Passover. At Passover it was a palpable tension one could feel in his bones. Passover reminded the Jews of their deliverance from an oppressive nation that held them captive. The parallel to their current situation was not lost on the Jews—or the Romans. When the Jews looked at their Roman over-lords at Passover, the wish behind their eyes was that these soldiers of Tiberius would find themselves alongside the soldiers of Pharaoh of Egypt, lifeless, heaped over by a flood, at the bottom of the sea.

Zuriel continued. "Passover is unlike any other event. Jerusalem is changed during Passover. The Jews come from all over Israel, from all over the world. Look around you." He waved his arm across the open space of the courts. "The crowds will be so great that it will hardly be possible to walk through these courts. Every house in the city will have twice its normal residents inside, and the hills around us will be filled with tents. They all come to 'eat the Passover,' as we say, and some come for that purpose, to fulfill their obligations. But not all are sincere. Some come for the festivities. There will be musicians and jugglers and acrobats. Many will come to sell their wares—jewelry, leather-works, and clothing. The city will become a bazaar." He stopped again. "These I have mentioned will be of no concern to us. But some will come for other purposes—to steal. We must make certain they do their stealing outside these walls."

The Pharisee concluded his lecture, and the boys gathered their scrolls, bowed to their teacher, and ran quickly to the tunnel that led out of the temple.

"And there are others," Zuriel went on, "others for whom we must be especially watchful—the Zelotes. They are the ones we must watch for. There are those who wish for war with the Romans. 'God will protect us and we will prevail,' they say. Their hope is to ignite a war by provoking the Romans. During Passover we, the temple guards will be alert, but the Romans in the fortress will be equally alert. Look across the way. How many Romans are on the wall?"

"I see eight."

"Where you now see eight, at Passover you will see eighty. Forty will stand side by side from corner to corner and another forty will stand behind them. Below them, out of sight, another eighty will stand ready. If an altercation occurs, they will pour into the temple—"

"Which could start the war you mentioned."

"It is a foolish hope, but it is the hope of these Zelotes. In a war God will protect us, they say. In the war we will prevail, they say. In the war our nation will be restored to us. These are the ones we must watch for, the ones who hold such ideas in their hearts." Zuriel paused for a moment. "Malchus, you will not be able to see the knife that man has hidden in his robe. But his face will betray his intent. You must learn to observe the expression of that man, how his eyes move side to side, how he keeps his lips tight, how he walks. His countenance and his steps will expose the evil in his heart—and the knife in his robe. You must watch carefully."

Chapter 24

The Standards

"Blasphemy. It is blasphemy." The horror in the old priest's face was evident in the torchlight. Zuriel and I, along with others of the temple guard, stood outside the Fortress Antonia in the pre-dawn.

Zuriel moved closer to the wall to see what troubled the old priest. I had no need to move closer. I recognized the offensive items. I had seen them before—Roman standards.

"They came during the night," the old priest said. "The Romans came during the night—from Caesarea. I heard their hammers. When I arrived, this is what I saw—blasphemy."

Gold-plated disks of the images of Tiberius and Sejanus, attached to ribboned poles, sparkled in the torchlight. They were identical to the ones Pilate had affixed to the interior walls of the palace in Caesarea. One image of each man was secured to each side of the fortress entrance.

"Annas must be alerted," Zuriel said.

As he spoke, the three blasts from the silver trumpets sounded above our heads. A new day in Jerusalem was beginning. Zuriel and I set off quickly through the nearly empty streets toward the house of Annas.

"The cohort from Caesarea was expected," Zuriel said as we walked. "But we did not expect them in the night—and we did not expect them to put the Roman standards on the walls. The new prefect, I'm afraid, does not know how to deal with Jews."

We stepped through the gate, and Zuriel announced our presence.

"Come inside, Malchus," I hear a woman's voice say. Chaya, the servant girl, stood in the doorway—a sultry expression on her face. "I have soup and wine . . . and no one is in the kitchen."

Caiaphas came to the rail of the porch at that moment. Annas took his seat just behind him. "What news do you bring, Zuriel?" Caiaphas asked.

"The Roman cohort from Caesarea arrived last night at the Fortress Antonia. They have placed their insignias on each side of the gate."

Caiaphas turned to Annas, but we could not hear their words. Caiaphas turned back to us, "Should we understand that these insignias bear an image, the image of the Roman emperor?"

"There are two insignias. One bears the image of the emperor. The other bears the image of his consul."

Caiaphas turned back to Annas. They spoke briefly and then Caiaphas asked, "Did the Roman prefect accompany the cohort? Is he in the city?"

"Sire, I do not know if the prefect accompanied the cohort. I will make every effort to find out."

Once again Caiaphas conferred with Annas and then said, "Return to the temple. We will send further instructions."

The shouts were loud as we arrived at the fortress: "Blasphemy! Blasphemy!" A group of Jews, mostly priests, were gathered outside the fortress. The temple guards held them away from the gate. About twenty Roman soldiers had lined up around the gate, standing at the ready. The sun was now above the Mount of Olives and threw its light directly on the offending golden plates. Tiberius and Senajus, each man in profile, were radiant in the early morning light. "Blasphemy! Blasphemy!" The Jews continued their chant, spitting in the direction of the soldiers, but the temple guards, using their staffs like an interlocking fence, held them back.

A rock came from the crowd and bounced off the wall only a hands-breadth from a Roman's face, throwing dust on his helmet. "Swords!" their commander shouted, and twenty blades came quickly from their scabbards, the steel blades whining against steel sheaths as they emerged. The metallic sound silenced all other sounds, and the crowd went quiet.

Zuriel broke through the crowd of Jews with a ferocity I did not expect. Knocking two men aside he tackled the one who had thrown the rock, throwing the man's face on the stone pavement. He stood on the man's neck, holding his face to the ground.

"You must disperse!" Zuriel shouted, his voice deep and booming. "You must disperse! This gathering serves no purpose! Take your complaint to the Sanhedrin!"

The priests and the other Jews looked at each other.

"Disperse, I say! By the authority of the temple guard, I command you to leave this place!" He took the man who had thrown the rock and raised him up by the collar. One side of his face was covered with blood.

I looked at Zuriel as he looked at the crowd. If at war, this was a man you would want at your side.

The Jews began slowly to walk away.

The Roman commander gave the signal for his troops to sheathe their swords. He nodded to Zuriel as if to say, "well done."

Pilate had not accompanied the Italian Cohort to Jerusalem. It was better he was not in the city. As a precaution Zuriel stationed guards around the fortress gate, and we returned to the temple. I remembered that once at the estate I had disrupted a beehive. The scene at the temple seemed the same. There was buzzing everywhere—"insignias . . . blasphemy . . . Romans . . . sacrilege . . .!" Several men pulled at Zuriel's robe to stop him to ask him questions, but he shrugged them off. He and I went to each of the guard stations where he admonished the guards to be wary. "Do not let these discussions become unruly," he told them.

A messenger came. "Joseph Caiaphas, the high priest, summons you to his house," he told me. I dismissed myself from Zuriel and started toward the house of Annas.

The city and the shops seemed oddly normal as I passed through, as the merchants went about their business. For those who sold fish or apples or grapes or bread or other things—it mattered not at all if a Roman emperor's image, the size of a man's hand, had been placed on a wall they could not see. But for others it was a great matter. A great number of priests and many members of the Sanhedrin were gathered on the upper porch with Annas and Caiaphas. Other Jews stood below. The word "blasphemy" seemed to be on all their lips. When Caiaphas saw me, he came down the stairs.

"Some of these priests—" he told me, "—are determined to go to Caesarea. They wish to bring their grievance against the prefect. We think the prefect should be warned. You will go ahead of these priests and give him notice. We will write a letter to Pilate. It will be delivered to you before dawn. You will give it to him in person."

Caiaphas nodded to me that I was dismissed. I turned away in a daze.

The letter for Pilate arrived as promised, along with a mule for my transport. A slow cold rain, more mist than rain, filled the air as I departed the city. I rode alone, well-provisioned and with two wool blankets for warmth. Others were leaving toward the same destination, Caesarea. The priests and Jews seemed to have had no consideration for the weather—and most were walking. Only a few rode donkeys.

My route would take me almost due north through Samaria, stopping one night at Antipatris, the Roman way-station. The conscientious Jews who refused to associate with Samaritans would take the longer route down the Jordan valley, across the river above Jericho, up through Perea, then re-crossing the river again just below Lake Gennareset. I would arrive in Caesarea two or three days before the earliest of them.

At Antipatris I was received and sheltered for the night. Marius was not there. He had gone to Caesarea. Those in command seemed unaware of the events in Jerusalem, and I was glad I did not have to answer any questions. Two of Marius's cavalrymen were at Antipatris, and one dispatched with a fast horse to Caesarea to notify Marius I was coming. The other rode with me, at my mule's pace, to offer protection against any brigands in the hills.

The faint aroma of the sea came to my nose in mid-afternoon, bringing the memories of my sea voyage and the few days in Caesarea the previous year. When I reached the Roman watchtowers edging the city and felt the sea-breeze on my face, a rider approached me. It was Marius.

"That is a poor mount, my friend." He dismounted and embraced me. "We have a dozen good horses in the fortress in Jerusalem I could have loaned you."

"Tell it to the Jews. Annas was in a hurry, and he seeks only one favor from the Romans, and it is not the borrowing of a horse."

We came over the sandy hillocks above Caesarea just as the sun fell below the sea's horizon, throwing orange and yellow streaks into a blue, cloudless sky.

Over a meal of lamb and lentils, cheese, olives, stacks of bread, and good wine, we shared the news.

"It is a Roman building. It is full of Romans," Marius said. "The gates are out of the way. No Jews pass that way with regularity. And even a man with good vision must stand near to make out the images on the plates." He poured more wine. "Although it is difficult to understand why the Jews are so upset, still we remember, do we not, what Manaen told us?"

I washed my fingers in the water bowl as I finished the last of the lamb. "The Jews are odd people. I'm not sure Pilate realizes how odd they are. Perhaps he is about to learn."

"I will accompany you in the morning when you deliver the message."

When we arrived at Pilate's palace, the morning sun was trying to find some openings in the heavy clouds that hovered over the sea. The sea was dark but quiet. Languid waves, almost silent, swelled over the rocks where fishermen threw their nets.

One year had passed since I was here. One year ago I arrived at these shores. One year ago I passed through these courtyards. One year ago I stood in the great hall overlooking the sea. One year ago I had no premonition of what lay ahead—the months at the quarry and the duty at the temple.

The memory of a year ago came clearly to me as we passed through the courtyards with their intricate mosaics and were admitted into the great room where Pilate sat in his chair facing the sea. He was attended by his barber who held a razor in his hand and a towel across his arm. Another towel was draped over Pilate's neck and a tray of the barber's tools lay on a table beside him. Pilate's secretary sat nearby, at his table, his writing utensils at hand. The waves underneath the porch slid through the pilings underneath us as they spilled water onto the sand.

"Sire," the guard announced, his voice reverberating through the hall. "Marius of the equestrian cohort and Malchus, the servant of Joseph Caiaphas the high priest, request an audience with the prefect."

"Come," he said, without turning his head, but he motioned us closer. "Ah, the Cherusci," he said, looking at me. "*Malchus . . . the king,*" A little smile came to his face. "The *king* of the Cheruscis." His smile widened a little bit. "You have returned. So soon you have come to a trusted position with the Jews. Perhaps my wife has some special perception. She selected you, after all." His smile turned to a sneer. "The Jews no longer have a king. You, Malchus, have the name of a king. Why shouldn't you become their king?"

I ignored the insult. "I have brought a message from Joseph Caiaphas, my *master*."

His face curled and his lips pursed. He looked at the scroll as if it were something rotten. "I will read your message," he said dismissively. "After I have had my shave. When I read it, I will know—as well as you—that the message is not from Caiaphas, but from his father-in-law."

The barber sharpened his razor on the leather strap hanging from his waist. Pilate nodded to him, and he began to scrape the hair from Pilate's cheek, using short, deft movements, turning Pilate's cheek raw-red with each stroke. He washed the razor in the bowl of water on the table.

"Romans shave every day," Pilate said, keeping his head still. "Jews, they never shave. How different we are."

As we waited, I looked beyond the railing to the open sea. The breeze was freshening, and salty air filled my lungs. Gulls, hoping for an easy meal, floated over the water, complaining to the fishermen who cast their nets into the shallows.

I turned back to Pilate. A small dot of blood had formed on his upper lip and the barber put down his razor, dabbed the spot with his towel and then opened a little pot from the tray and took some salve on a wooden stick and applied it to the abrasion. Satisfied, after a moment, that the bleeding had stopped, he replaced the pot and the stick and again stroked the razor against the leather strap.

The barber examined Pilate's face from both sides. Pilate took the towel from the barber and wiped his face. The barber gathered up his razors and tweezers and combs and other paraphernalia into a leather bag, bowed and left.

Two slaves brought chairs for Marius and me.

"I will not make you stand," Pilate said. "I am a reasonable man."

He looked at me with an odd smile. "I heard they turned you into a Jew." His smile intensified. "These Jews—they don't cut their beards, but they use their knives in other ways." He chuckled at his own joke. "Yes, we are different—Jews and Romans, are we not?"

I said nothing and reached for the cylinder in my cloak. The secretary took it and waited for a response from Pilate.

Pilate's expression turned to a hard glare. "I know its contents before I read it. Annas thinks he can resist Rome. Rome cannot be resisted. Rome always prevails."

He walked to the rail and looked at the sea as if he were looking in the direction of Rome. "Would it surprise you to know that my grandfather fought against the Romans?" He did not wait for an answer. "My grandfather and the other Samnites thought they could break away from Rome. It was a futile effort, and it was crushed." Pilate's voice trailed away for a moment. "And the Cherusci and their allies, your cousins, they also tried to resist Rome. You claim you do not know your origins, but I still remember those yellow-haired savages in the forests. They could well be your cousins. Yes, they had a small victory against Rome, just like my ancestors the Samnites. But Rome learns from its defeats. We went back to Teutenberg." His eyes squinted as he recalled the memories. "And we recovered the standards."

He looked at Marius. "You understand this, don't you, Marius? It was not enough to merely gain revenge. It was necessary that we recover the standards. *The standards* represent Rome. For a Roman, especially a Roman soldier, the standards must be honored. He pointed to the images of Tiberius and Sejanus on the wall. Bitterness entered his voice. "Rome has honor. The standards represent that honor. And that honor must be recognized." Pilate clenched his teeth. "It *will* be recognized."

For a moment there was no sound but the shushing of the waves beneath us and the sharp calls of the seagulls.

Pilate took a deep breath as he came out of his reverie. "Yes, Rome prevailed." He looked directly at me. "Rome prevailed against *my* people, and Rome prevailed against *your* people. It will now prevail against *the Jews*, whatever their protests."

He reached for the cylinder, opened it and unrolled the scroll inside. It made a whisking sound that carried through the open hall. Marius and I waited. Pilate read some of the words clearly and mumbled other portions, tossing his head back and forth slightly as he digested the contents: ". . . offensive to loyal subjects of Caesar . . . no precedent in Jerusalem . . . holy temple . . ."

Pilate pursed his lips as he finished reading. Very deliberately he re-rolled the scroll and replaced it in the cylinder. He cocked his arm as if he were about to throw the scroll into the water below but then turned and smiled at me and Marius.

"It is as I expected," Pilate said. "Annas asks that I remove the standards from the Antonia Fortress. He says it is an affront to the holy temple and to all the Jews. He says the Jews are loyal subjects of Caesar."

Pilate's face went red. He threw the cylinder across the marble floor where it clanged and skidded across the porch, coming to rest at the base of the balustrade.

"Caesar will be honored," he said, composing himself. "Caesar will be honored," he repeated. *I* will honor Caesar. And the Jews will honor Caesar." He turned back to Marius and me. "If the Jews indeed are loyal subjects as Annas says they are, then why will they not honor Caesar?"

We remained standing beside our chairs.

"You say that the Jews are on their way to Caesarea. How many are coming?"

"I saw only thirty, perhaps forty," I answered. "But others may follow."

"When should I expect them?"

"Their journey will require four days, possibly five. It was two days ago when I departed Jerusalem."

Pilate stood at the balustrade, looking over the rail to the gray horizon.

"Yes, of course, the Jews could be here already if they followed the direct route—but they will not pass through Samaria, lest they become polluted by their impure cousins. Instead they will go two days out of their way to arrive here—and what will they find? Equally impure Romans! Yes, these are strange people, these Jews. My predecessor warned me about them and their superstitions—but be sure of this...they *will* honor Caesar." He raised his voice as he repeated himself. "They *will* honor Caesar! All other subjects of Rome honor Caesar! The Jews will do the same!"

Pilate went quiet, still looking over the sea, his head and shoulders wet as the moisture gathered on his skin. He braced himself on the marble rail. After a moment, without turning back to us, he said quietly. "You are dismissed."

The first Jews arrived in Caesarea three days later. They were a pathetic sight, sitting on their donkeys, soaked by the daily rains. Those walking began arriving the next few days. Each day, and throughout the day, more Jews from Jerusalem—and from Hebron and other villages, including a good number from the Galilee—poured into the city.

"The Jews have not yet requested an audience with Pilate," Marius said to me. "It has been three days since the first arrived."

"They will wait until their numbers are greater," I suggested.

Another day passed. The Jews found some protection from the weather around the edge of the hippodrome, where they prayed and talked and slept. A few more of their brethren arrived. There were now several hundred of them encamped not far from the palace.

On the sixth morning after I had arrived in Caesarea, the third morning after the first Jews arrived, Marius shook my shoulder to wake me. "The Jews are gathering. I will be at Pilate's palace. Come quickly."

It was an odd scene. The gray morning light was just filtering into Pilate's courtyard on the side of the palace away from the sea. It was filled with dark, swaying figures. Hundreds of Jews in their black robes, their chanting voices creating a trembling, cumulative hum as their individual prayers melded into those of those around them. There were more Jews than I had expected. The courtyard was full. An equal number stood in the street. Most were Pharisees. On their foreheads they wore their phylacteries, the leather cubes bound by string around their heads. Those heads bobbed back and forth. In their hands they held prayer books as they chanted.

Marius came to my side.

"Is Pilate aware—?" I started.

"Yes. I just came from his bedside. He peered out his window at the scene in the courtyard but said nothing. I asked if I should disperse them, but he said no, that these were harmless Jews. These were not the ones who carried daggers in their cloaks," he said. "Let them moan and pray until they become weary."

The Jews rocked back and forth as the cool morning air distilled their incantations into white clouds of breath that quickly disappeared. The gurgle of the fountains mixed with the murmur of the invocations.

About mid-morning one of the scribes came to the courtyard and stood just below the balcony that extended to the courtyard. He spoke to an empty balcony. "Sire!" he called out to an absent prefect. "We have come from Jerusalem with a grievance."

The other Jews went about their swaying and chanting without pause. "We are loyal subjects of Rome. We pay our taxes and do our duties."

Pilate did not appear on the balcony, but I saw a curtain pulled back slowly at one of the windows to the right.

The scribe went on with his appeal. "The laws of our ancestors have been offended, and we seek redress. We petition the governor to remove the graven images from the walls at the holy temple of Jerusalem."

The curtain in the window fell straight again. The scribe stood in silence looking at the empty balcony. The scribe stood there for some minutes before he left the courtyard.

I found a seat in one of the many alcoves of the courtyard, a place where I could see most of the area. A few of the older Jews had fallen asleep, their limp black figures prominent in the sea of hundreds of others swaying back and forth.

Marius brought bread and olives and cheese, and we shared the food together in the alcove amid the ongoing drone of the supplicants' prayers. "Pilate goes about his business," he told me. "But he is aware of the Jews in the courtyard. Whether he will hear them or not, I do not know."

Later in the afternoon the scribe returned to the courtyard and repeated his appeal to the empty balcony. His words were the same as the morning: "...a grievance... loyal subjects... pay our taxes... laws of our ancestors have been offended..." Behind him the black-clad Jews, prayer books in their hands, went about their rhythmic chants. After his final words, "We petition the governor to remove the graven images from the walls at the holy temple of Jerusalem," he stood quietly again for some minutes before leaving the courtyard. Then as the sun was setting, he appeared again and delivered the same appeal to the same empty balcony.

Many of the Jews slept in the courtyard, the older ones in the alcoves where the marble shielded them from the greatest cold, the others huddled under their cloaks and blankets under the open sky.

The next morning the previous day's scene repeated itself. The dark-clad Jews went about their swaying prayers and the scribe delivered the identical appeal to the empty balcony.

"Pilate is irritable this morning," Marius said as he brought bread and figs. "'Do these Jews,' he asked, 'think they alone, of all Rome's subjects have special status—that they do not have to honor the emperor?'"

Marius threw a fig stem to the side as he chewed the fruit. "I did not answer him, of course. He did seek an answer, but the truth is, as he should know, the Jews *do* have special status. They are the only nation in the empire who are not conscripted into the Roman army. And Jerusalem is the only city in the empire where the statues of the emperor and of the Roman gods are not displayed. The old king Herod negotiated those arrangements. He explained the particular stubbornness of the Jews in relation to their religion. He asked the emperor and the senate if instead of having a statue of the emperor, the Jews could rather offer a daily sacrifice for the emperor on the temple altar. The rulers in Rome had the good sense to realize that—if they wanted the taxes from Judea, which is the primary goal of the rulers in Rome—they should allow the Jews these concessions."

"Why," I asked, "do you think Pilate has violated these accommodations?"

He tore some bread and handed me a piece. "Perhaps he did not adequately consider the nature of the Jews. I'm not sure. However, I am sure he did not expect this response." He took a drink from the wine-skin and offered it to me. "And after all, he placed the standards on the Antonia—a building that houses the Roman garrison. It is a Roman building. He did not place the standards on the temple walls. If his intent was to offend the Jews, he would have placed the standards on the walls of the temple."

He chewed his bread as he collected his thoughts. "Pilate's job is difficult," he went on. "He must keep the Jews mollified. And there are a dozen strains among them who are all at odds with each other. And he must keep those with authority over him in Rome satisfied. And he cannot be certain who in Rome truly has authority—is it Tiberius or is it Sejanus? And all the while, he must keep the taxes flowing back to Rome."

Marius thought for a moment, turning over something in his mind. "Don't you find it interesting that Pilate not only displayed the image of Tiberius, but also Sejanus?" He offered me the last of the bread. "Tiberius dawdles on the island of Capri, while Sejanus, who has been appointed Warden of the City, handles the affairs of Rome—an interesting situation for the empire. And Pilate, who does not know to whom he owes the greater allegiance, has put both their faces on the Antonia Fortress."

At that moment two Roman guards came to the balcony and stood at each side, their spears at their side, standing at rest. Some of the Jews looked up and then went back to their prayers, while others seemed unaware of the soldiers.

A moment later the two soldiers on the balcony snapped to attention, and Pilate stepped through the open curtains. In most circumstances an ovation from the audience would have greeted a Roman governor, but Pilate did not expect it from this crowd, and they did not offer it. A few who were leaders stepped closer to the balcony, but most kept to their prayers.

Pilate surveyed the scene for some time and then turned his attention to the scribe below him. "Is the high priest among these assembled? Has he requested an audience with the representative of Rome?"

"Sire—"

"If the high priest is not among you, this is not a lawful assembly." Pilate's voice went sharp. "And it tests the patience of Rome. If the high priest has reason to speak to the governor, let him come here himself."

"Sire, we are loyal subjects of Rome," the scribe responded. "Please hear our grievance. The tradition of our ancestors does not allow us to display the image of a man. This has been our custom for many generations."

"The images are placed on a *Roman* building. The Antonia Fortress is not in your temple."

"What you say is true, Sire. Yet it touches our temple—and it is in our holy city."

Pilate released an exasperated sigh. "Do you wish to dishonor the emperor?"

"Sire, each morning at the altar of sacrifice we offer a bull in honor of the emperor."

Pilate paused for a moment. His fingers strummed nervously on the rail of the balustrade as the hum of the Jews' prayers continued to fill the courtyard.

"Sire," the scribe implored, taking advantage of the quiet, "will you remove the images from the wall of the fortress? That is our request."

"No." Pilate's jaw clenched, and his eyes narrowed. He stood looking over the crowd below him. "No! Rome and Caesar will receive the honor they are due."

The scribe bowed to Pilate. "Perhaps the governor will change his mind. To that end we will continue our prayers." He bowed again and stepped away.

Pilate's shoulders quivered—a seething quiver—before he turned back through the curtains to his palace.

The next day the Jews made their appeal yet again, but Pilate refused to hear them. If Pilate had as his wish that the Jews would grow weary and go home, he would have been disappointed. Their numbers grew slightly.

The following day the Jews continued with their prayers, and with the identical appeal. Pilate did not respond.

We learned that one of the old Pharisees had died during the night, but his body was removed and prepared for burial, and the Jews went about their praying and their petition the next day again as they had the previous days.

"Pilate has become irritated," Marius told me. "And he has called his commander for a conference."

"What does this mean?" I asked.

"I do not know, but I have concerns."

On the afternoon of the tenth day of the Jews' appeal, Pilate's secretary came to the balcony. "The prefect of Rome will hear your petition," he shouted. The volume of the humming prayers in the courtyard lessened. Some of those swaying became still. "Gather in the stadium tomorrow morning. The prefect will meet you there."

"Has Pilate changed his mind?" I asked Marius as we shared our evening meal.

"I do not know. It is odd, is it not?" he responded. "If he had changed his mind, he could have simply said so."

A messenger from the palace arrived. "The prefect Pontius Pilate summons Marius to the palace."

Marius stood and brushed the crumbs from his face. "We will soon know what 'The Spear' has in mind.

Marius returned much later than I had expected, and his face showed distress.

"You carry bad news, I fear," I said.

He sat on a stool, took a deep breath and wiped his hands across his face. "Do you count me as a friend, Malchus? Do I have your trust?"

"I am a guest of your house. And no one in Judea has proven more trustworthy than you. But—"

"Is your sword there?" He pointed to the shelf where my scabbard lay.

I nodded.

"May I see it?"

I nodded again.

He went to the corner and took the belt and scabbard. "I would like to hold this for you—in trust—for a day."

I stood to face him. "What—"

"I have stationed four men to watch this house and instructed them that you are not to leave. I will bolt the door behind me as I go."

I grabbed his right arm, which held my sword. We stood face to face.

"Here is my sword," he said, reaching with his left arm to the blade that hung on his belt. "If you do not trust me, then take my own weapon and slit my throat."

I shook my head and loosened my grip. "But what—"

"I can tell you nothing now—and in truth I know little. But tomorrow I will return. When I do your sword will be restored to you."

We looked at each briefly, I dropped my hand from his arm, and he went out the door. I heard the bolt go tight as he departed.

It was an uneasy sleep for me that night. At times I was certain I heard the dull clink of hobnailed boots in nearby streets, but the noise could have come from a troubled dream.

Two guards accompanied Marius's cook when she brought my breakfast. As I ate I wondered if Pilate would soon be addressing the Jews in the stadium. My mind was filled with questions. *Why has Marius imprisoned me here? What news or orders did he receive at Pilate's palace? Has Pilate changed his mind? Will he remove the standards? If not, what will happen?*

My questions persisted through the morning. The cooks brought fruit and cool water. I sipped the water, but I had no appetite. I paced back and forth, wondering what was taking place at the stadium. I thought of breaking down the door that held me in the room, but there were four competent soldiers outside that door. *Yes, I trust Marius. But why did he not want me to go to the stadium?*

"Unbolt the door," I heard Marius's command outside the door.

I had fallen asleep on the cot. It was mid-day. I heard the bolt slide, and Marius stepped in, my belt and scabbard in his hand.

"Pilate relented!" he said exuberantly, as he handed the belt to me. Joy and relief were in his face. "The standards will be removed. Pilate has ordered it." He embraced me. "Malchus, forgive me for making you a prisoner, but it was best for you and for me."

"Tell me."

"I will tell you all, but I will tell you as we consume our meal. Come downstairs."

The rain that had persisted for several days had ceased, and the sun filled a nearly cloudless sky, so we sat in comfort in the middle of his walled courtyard as the table was filled with choice foods. Marius poured us each a cup of wine.

"A massacre was avoided."

"Massacre?"

He nodded, working the wine around his teeth before swallowing. "When I arrived at the palace, all the tribunes were there. It was a somber session. Pilate laid out his plan. He ordered the entire cohort to be stationed under the stadium platform. We were required to be there three hours before dawn—and to remain quiet. 'Be prepared,' he said, 'to respond to my summons.'"

"'Your summons, Sire?' one of the tribunes asked, 'How should we respond to your summons?'

'With your blades in their scabbards at first. Enter quickly. Surround the Jews. We will ask them to respond to logic. If they will not respond to logic, then they will respond to authority—the authority of Rome. At my command bring your blades from their scabbards. And likewise at my command, be ready to use them.

Inform those under your command. Dismissed!' Pilate said. When he dismissed me, I came and took your sword. I expected a massacre. I could not allow you to be there because Annas would have held you responsible."

I nodded my understanding. "But why did Pilate relent? What changed his mind?"

"The Jews assembled at dawn in the stadium. The entire cohort was hidden. Pilate came soon after. I attended him. He did not make the Jews wait. He did not want some coughing soldier to betray his surprise. His chair, the curule, was brought out, and he took his seat. Only a few older Jews were praying. Most stood facing Pilate as he sat. I stood beside him. The men served as the barrier between the Jews and Pilate. The Jews looked uncomfortable in the great arena, where they stood in the ruts of the chariots that raced around the oval. The scribe who had made the previous appeals came before Pilate and bowed. He waited to see if Pilate would speak first, but Pilate said nothing.

'Sire,' the scribe started, 'we are loyal subjects to the emperor in Rome. However, our God does not allow us to make any graven image. Our father Moses delivered that command to us many generations ago and we must adhere to that command. Recently the images of the emperor have been placed on the walls of our temple–'

'They are not on the walls of your temple!' Pilate shouted angrily. The buzz of the praying went quiet.

'Sire, please remove the images from our holy city.'

'No.'

'The images offend the customs of our nation and the customs of our ancestors. It is the request of our nation that you please remove them.'

'No!'

'The images of men have never been known in our city. Your predecessors did not place any images in our city. Please do not insist on placing these images.'

Pilate's fingers drummed on the polished wood of the chair. 'I will have the emperor honored.'

'Each morning we honor the emperor with our sacrifice. Please remove the images.'

'Your appeal is denied. I will not remove the standards.' The fingers in both his hands had gone white against the ebony arm of the chair. The Jews began to murmur and talk among themselves. Pilate stood, throwing his white toga from his shoulder, 'I order you to disperse!' The soldiers heard this signal and they poured into the arena, surrounding the surprised Jews, who looked around at six hundred soldiers in full array, their hands on the handles of their swords. 'Disperse and return to your homes!' The Jews went quiet and looked at each other and at the soldiers around them. There was stillness in the arena for a few seconds."

Marius paused. "A surprising thing happened. One of the older Jews knelt down and prostrated himself on the ground. The others looked at him, then at each other, and gradually, one-by-one, dropped to their knees. It sounded like a basket of leaves being emptied, All of them, other than the scribe who stood before Pilate's podium, put their heads on the dirt."

Marius took a very slow drink of his wine. The expression on his face was that of a man who had seen something that he could not adequately explain.

"'Draw swords,' Pilate shouted, his face red with anger, raising his right arm, and I heard the terrible rasping sound of six hundred swords being unsheathed filling the stadium." Marius paused again, shaking his head in bewilderment. "Then something happened that a man could not believe. The Jews, to a man, pulled back their robes to expose their white necks. At that moment the sun came over the rim of the stadium and flashed against the uplifted blades of the Roman soldiers. Flecks of light chased each other in the shadows around the area where the prefect stood. Out of the corner of my eye I looked at Pilate's face. Anger had been replaced by confusion. His upraised arm quivered and a little tremor passed through his face. He held his arm above his head. The soldiers watched for his signal. His arm quivered again. His jaw clenched. His shoulders trembled. The Jews kept their heads down, their necks exposed. As if being shaken by an invisible demon, Pilate's whole body trembled. His chest heaved as if he could not breathe—and then I saw it..." Marius looked at me. "I saw it. Pilate's eyes changed. Defeat. Defeat came into his eyes. He took a great breath. And then he shook his head. 'Centurion,' he said to me, his voice hardly a whisper, 'Have the soldiers sheath their weapons.' Never, Malchus, have I been so glad to give a military order. 'Sheathe your weapons,' I shouted, surprising myself with the strength of my voice. The metallic sound of the blades returning to the scabbards filled the air. Pilate's right arm, still quivering, was above his shoulder, but he slowly lowered it to his side. He stood for some time saying nothing, his shoulders fatigued, both arms limp beside him. 'Dismiss the troops,' he said eventually. It was the voice of a man who had just surrendered. I repeated the command and the cohort filed out of the arena."

A smile came to Marius's face as he recalled the events. "I glanced at Pilate. He had the appearance of a man who had eaten dry dirt in the arena. After a moment he said to me, 'Send a messenger to Jerusalem to remove the standards.'

I looked at the Jews in the arena. A few were on their knees or standing. Most were still prostrate. All were confused. Slowly they began to rise from the dirt and began brushing their hands, looking around them. They were alone. Many expected to be killed in that courtyard, so now they seemed confused. What should they do now? A few embraced. Some looked up at the balcony, but it was now empty. The Roman prefect with six hundred soldiers and six hundred swords had just been overcome by a smaller number of Jews—with no weapons at all."

What did Pilate learn from this incident? Did he learn something about Jewish obstinacy? That it was impossible to reason with them? He would later be placed in a position when he would have to contend with another group of Jews with a different appeal. Did this event—with the Jews in Caesarea—come to his remembrance at that confrontation? Did his acquiescence in Caesarea affect his fortitude in Jerusalem a few years later?

Marius and I had a spirited ride back to Jerusalem. He provided one of his best horses for me, and we made the return trip quickly. He personally supervised the removal of the standards. The news was soon in the streets. "The bare neck of a Jew is a better weapon than the sword of a Roman," men would joke among themselves. I gave the report to Annas and his sons and Caiaphas, which they received gladly. And I thought for a moment, I couldn't be sure, that a thin smile curled at the lips of Annas.

Annas, were you happy that your fellow Jews had been spared—or that the prefect had been humiliated? Pilate had made a serious misjudgment, I would realize later. He was fairly new with his authority, and he misjudged those over whom he had authority. His stated intent was to honor Tiberius and Sejanus, although his true intent may have been to ingratiate himself with those men. And he may have truly thought the fortress was only a Roman structure, and Roman images there would not have offended the Jews. But he learned a painful lesson, one that rankled him—but perhaps made him a better governor. To his credit, at the critical moment when the swords were held above the necks of the Jews, he relented. And all knew, as he knew, he relented not to show mercy to the Jews, but because the report of a massacre in Judea would have doomed his governorship. Tiberius may have been paying slight attention to the events of the scattered empire, and Sejanus may have been his benefactor, but Pilate knew that his responsibility was to keep the peace and to guarantee revenue. Everything else was secondary. In the end, when Pilate realized that fact, he ate the bitter dirt of defeat.

Chapter 25

Passover

Passover approached. Pilate came to Jerusalem, but his appearance was perfunctory. He stayed only two nights in the city and made no contact with the high priestly family, and he left before the final day of the celebration. Herod's palace had been made ready for him and his retinue, but he chose to stay at the fortress. Only three weeks had passed since his humiliation at Caesarea, and the wound was still fresh. For three weeks now, scorn and ridicule had been heaped on him in the city. Joking about the necks of the Jews as weapons was repeated endlessly. I often saw men imitating him by raising their right arms and then dejectedly dropping their arms and shoulders in resignation, pouting their lips. While Pilate was in the fortress, one of the Jews looked up at the Romans above and raised his right arm, laughing and mimicking the report from Caesarea.

For his jest, that man suffered a welt on his back that surely took a month to heal. I saw the blow. Zuriel struck the man with his staff with such force that the man's knees buckled, and he fell on the pavement. Zuriel surveyed the onlookers, who went silent. He said nothing. He did not need to.

Zuriel tried to prepare me for Passover, but no reports could have provided an adequate description. Thousands upon tens of thousands of Jews filled the city—and more tens of thousands camped on the hills around. The animal sellers and coin exchangers stayed busy. The inevitable arguments were quickly suppressed and did not affect the security of the temple. Outside the walls, merchants brought their rugs and awnings, silver-and-gold jewelry, leatherwork, sandals, and cooking utensils. They all competed with each other as they shouted out what they had for sale. The aroma of spiced meat cooked on charcoal filled the air. Cousins and uncles who had not seen each other for a year greeted and embraced each other. Children were fascinated by the jugglers tossing balls in the air.

By the week's end, the celebration—for most of the Jews—turned to its real purpose, the celebration of Moses' bringing the people out of slavery. Fathers and sons purchased the lamb or goat, took it to the priests to be sacrificed, then waited for the carcass that would provide for the "eating of the Passover." The blood of the sacrifice was splashed on the doorposts of the houses with hyssop clusters, in remembrance of the event in Egypt many generations earlier. Bitter herbs and wine complemented the evening meal as Passover was consummated and commemorated as it had been for two thousand years.

When Passover concluded and pilgrims departed, the cleanup of the city was left to its residents. Piles of over-ripe fruits and vegetables, lamb bones and goat bones and other items were left behind when the Passover pilgrims departed. Activity at the temple returned to its normal cycles; the priests with their pre-dawn patrol, their torches creating odd shadows on the walls . . . the city awakened by the temple trumpets . . . the slaying of the lamb . . . the opening of the gates . . . the sale of the sacrifices . . . the gathering of the rabbis and their pupils—all resumed. The daily schedule was punctuated by the sabbath, every seventh day of the week, during which the priests offered additional sacrifices and followed the stringent rules of avoiding any work. The city likewise returned to its regular rhythms. The sounds of the shopkeepers announcing their products joined with the clatter of carts and the wailing of babies filling the narrow streets of the city. Outside the city the pine trees threw their yellow dust all around while the tiny clusters of flowers on the olive trees were turning into hard green olives. Gardeners checked their vines for the small green grapes that gave promise of turning purple and larger months later.

A man's tolerance, I learned that summer, is related to the heat in the air. An unrelenting sun in a cloudless sky poured down most days on the temple, making tempers more volatile. Arguments between booth managers and supplicants were more common and more bitter. The rabbis quarreled with each other as they competed for shade for their students under the porticoes, and the priests themselves maligned each other as they went about their daily tasks. The marble pavement seemed to throw back more heat that it had absorbed, and the men who walked across the stones held their hands to their eyes to shield the blazing whiteness of the light. Little breeze could find its way over the temple walls to cool the stones. Annas had awnings erected to protect the animals, but many died, and the odor of their refuse held in the air.

Chapter 26

The Letter from Manaen

I saw a young man in the courtyard whose manner caught my attention. The way he walked seemed to lack intention, and I watched him carefully as he moved about the outer edge of the courtyard looking around, sometimes looking at me. The sun had inclined to the west, and the wall of the temple provided some slanting shadows. I continued observing the man. Eventually he moved in my direction, looking about as he came nearer. I gripped my sword as a precaution.

He did not look at me as he spoke, "I am the servant of Chuza, the steward of the house of Herod Antipas. Are you Malchus, friend of Manaen?"

"I am."

"You were described to me. You could be no other. I have brought a message from Manaen. May I give it to you?"

I looked around to make sure we were not watched. Annas and his sons had many eyes in their employ in the temple, some of which I knew, some I didn't.

"I will take the message," I said.

He took a scroll from his robe, and I slipped it inside my own robe. The young man nodded and departed.

The scroll seemed to burn like an ember against my stomach, I wanted desperately to read it, but I dared not. When the sacrifices were over and the booths closed, I made my way to my quarters. I bolted the door and lit all the lanterns, then opened the scroll. Its aroma brought back the smell of ink and papyrus from the library in the palace in Rome.

From Manaen in Rome to Malchus in Jerusalem.

May the God of Israel secure you in his wisdom and provision.

I send you greetings from Rome as does Gavriel and the rest of the household. Our hope is that you have found security in the house of Caiaphas. I am grateful to God that our appeal to Annas was heard. It is beyond my hope to expect that life in the house of Annas is peaceful, yet I am grateful you are no longer at the quarry. Joseph, the Arimathean, is a trusted friend. You may seek his counsel at any time.

It has now been eighteen months since you boarded the trireme at Ostia Antica for your journey to Caesarea. There is much to tell you about Rome, especially about the events now taking place.

It is late at night as I compose this letter. Gavriel and I have lit a dozen lamps here in the library. We are not able to sleep because of the noise in the palace. Antipas, my foster-brother, is conducting a dinner party. Yes, Antipas has returned to Rome. He has brought his wife Phasaelis and their entourage. Philip, his half-brother, has accepted Antipas's invitation to join him here in Rome, and he has brought his wife Herodias and their daughter Salome. Among those making the noise in the banquet hall below are a number of prominent Romans, including a few senators. Even here in the library we hear the drunken guffaws pouring out the open windows.

I received the guests and stayed for the dinner, but I excused myself before the entertainment began—which was what both Antipas and I preferred. I was not the only uncomfortable one at the dinner. Phasaelis was uneasy as well. She and Antipas have an unlikely alignment in marriage—one that neither of them sought, but Herod the Great desired to bind the house of Herod and the house of Aretas. It was a good political union—connecting the two strongest forces in the lands between Judea and Egypt . . . but the marriage itself has been difficult. Antipas, it is said, having gained a glimpse of his bride a few days before the wedding, protested to his father. But the protest brought Herod's anger, not his acquiescence.

So they were joined, but Phasaelis is ill-suited for palace life. She is Nabataen and a daughter of the desert. She grew up within the precincts of the fabled city of Selah, which the Romans now call Petra, a stronghold cut into the pink rocks in the region below the Sea of Asphalt. According to Joanna, she longs for those rocky hills below the mountains of Moab where she spent her childhood. Antipas, by all reports, ignores her and her unhappiness is well known. Tonight, when she entered the dining hall, someone snickered, "Her bitterness has turned to fat." The excessive kohl on her puffy eyes and full cheeks could mask her acrimony. She, like I, did not wish to attend this dinner, but she, unlike I, could not dismiss herself as early. She sat silently as her husband joked with the Roman dignitaries.

It was apparent, watching Antipas, that he had a purpose in hosting this dinner.

I relate this to you so that you may know the ambitions of Antipas. What is his purpose? —to become king of Judea, like his father. He is not content with his current position as tetrarch over Galilee and Petra. He wants more. At one time his father's will had given him Judea, but that will was altered shortly before Herod's death, and Judea was entrusted to his brother Archelaus, who, of course botched his opportunity, which led Augustus to appoint a Roman to rule over Judea.

How long he will stay I cannot predict, but he has his own purpose in this trip, and I believe he will stay until this purpose is reached, or, until he realizes it is unattainable.

However, I think he misreads the situation in Rome. Yes, Sejanus makes all decisions in the absence of Tiberius, but Sejanus and Pontius Pilate have a kinship—not a kinship in blood, but in the fact that both are of the equestrian rank, not nobles, and so have formed a bond as each is trying to rise in the leadership of Rome. All to say, Antipas's intent is the subversion of Pontius Pilate. Antipas hopes to build an alliance here that will support an appeal that he be appointed the ruler of Judea. This dinner party is the first part of that strategy.

Where his efforts will take him, I cannot predict. I have cautioned him to be careful in his dealings with the Romans, but my warnings go unheeded. Antipas, many years ago, began ignoring my advice, and he continues to do so. And although I believe his appeal to Sejanus will fail, politics in Rome is too unpredictable for me to think I could accurately predict the future.

The situation in Rome is unchanged since you were here. Tiberius is still at Capri, and many wonder if he will ever return, though few hope for it. If just a few of the stories of his lasciviousness in Capri are true, Rome would be better served if he never returns. However, Sejanus is not popular either. Sejanus has proven, as many of us expected, to be an efficient administrator, but his ambitions are evident, and his cruelty has earned him many enemies. There is much grumbling among the citizens of Rome. Older Romans wish that Germanicus was still alive—and of course, they blame Sejanus for his death. And there is concern that Sejanus will find a way to do away with the sons of Germanicus, for they are the most likely ones to inherit the throne from Tiberius if Sejanus is unable to persuade the emperor to appoint him as his successor.

I must conclude my letter. You and I, Malchus, dwell in two different cities of different cultures separated by the Great Sea. Yet each city seethes with intrigue as men seek power. Will power render us happy? I have read what the Preacher in our holy book has instructed us, that the seeking of power is vanity. He is correct of course, but few heed his wisdom.

When the time is appropriate, as I have told you before, I plan to come to Judea myself. I live in expectation that the Redeemer will come to redeem his own, and when that time comes, I hope I am in Jerusalem to see it.

I pray for your welfare.

I read the letter again—and then again once more before putting it away.

Chapter 27

The Day of Atonement

On the days before the Day of Atonement the olives on the hill opposite the Kidron were spotting purple and black under the waving leaves, and the barley heads around the twisted trunks were heavy, bending the stalks in graceful curves. Men with scythes would soon come to cut and gather the barley and take the bundles to the threshing floor.

"The Day of Atonement will bring pilgrims," Zuriel told me. "The city will be crowded, but there will be no jugglers or dancers."

He saw the question on my face.

"It is a more somber festival," he went on. "It is the day the high priest must make the atonement for the sins of the nation for the past year." A thin smile came to his face. "I was once asked by a Greek merchant—and I believe he was genuinely curious when he asked, 'If, each morning and each evening you make a sacrifice for your sins, why is it necessary that you must again make another sacrifice for your sins on the Day of Atonement? When will your god ever be satisfied?'"

"How did you answer?"

"'Speak to the rabbis,' I said. 'The captain of the temple guard cannot answer such a question.' Yet it was a very good question."

He stayed in his thoughts for a moment and then said, "The high priest, for the Day of Atonement, is required to spend one week at the temple. Joseph Caiaphas does not like this duty, but it is required of him by custom—and by his father-in-law. During this week you will need to provide his protection. You will have the help of my temple guard, of course, but the duty will fall on you."

"Something concerns you," I said. "I see it on your face."

He nodded his acknowledgement. "It is this, Malchus. Here at the temple, many of the temple priests take their roles seriously and make great effort to adhere to the traditions of our forefathers. However, they are very aware that the position of chief priest is an appointment of the Romans—purchased by Annas and extended to Caiaphas, his son-in-law. The temple priests resent the house of Annas. They resent his indifference to the traditions. They resent the wealth he has generated from the sacrifices, and they resent the presence of the animals and the booths in the court."

He paused for a moment to collect his thoughts. "I tell you this for this reason: The Day of Atonement requires the cooperation of the temple priests and the high priest—for an entire week. Joseph Caiaphas, your master, will have responsibilities for each day for a week. And because of his indifference to the traditions, problems could arise. Be alert."

The week before the Day of Atonement, I walked alongside Caiaphas's litter as we made our way to the temple. We arrived in time for him to lead the ceremony of the evening sacrifice. The high priest, by custom, wore a white robe and a white sash during this ceremony, so it was unnecessary for us to secure the priestly vestments from the Romans. Caiaphas performed his duties clumsily, and the irritation of the officiating priests was evident, as Caiaphas had to be prompted several times during the course of the ceremony.

The aspiring scribes had quit their labors as the evening sacrifice had begun, so Caiaphas did not have to endure their scorn as he went to the Chamber of Wood above their workshop. Trays of ducklings, roasted vegetables, fresh bread, apples, and grapes—and a pitcher of wine—sat on the table. I left Caiaphas to enjoy his evening meal.

At the morning sacrifice he was half asleep and did no better in his duties. When the services were concluded and we returned to his chambers, he threw his miter on the floor and fell asleep on the pillows, still wearing his white robe and white sash.

We repeated this routine all week. If he improved in his ability to perform the services, it was not acknowledged in the continually scornful countenances of the officiating priests.

On the fourth afternoon of the week, when I came to escort Caiaphas to the altar, he grumbled as he drew himself up from his pillows, chewing a grape. He stood with a pillow in each hand, looked at them absently and said, "Eleazar, who had this duty before me, was the first to put pillows in the chambers. Before him, there were no pillows. Nothing. Eleazar provided pillows for himself—goat hair, stuffed with straw. The scribes protested, of course, but Eleazar retained them. 'Why,' he asked, 'should the high priest sleep on the floor?' When I took the duty, I asked, 'If the high priest sleeps on pillows, why should those pillows be goat hair?' These are silk, stuffed with goose down. An improvement, don't you think?"

He tossed one of the pillows onto the others, wobbling slightly as he did. His wine was in his legs as well as in his tongue. He examined the other pillow carefully. He rubbed his palm across the smooth material. "Silk. They say this silk is made by worms. Do you believe that, Malchus?"

"I do not know, sire."

"It seems preposterous to me, but it is what the caravanners say." He looked at the brilliant colors—red and green and blue, rendering an elegant bouquet of flowers. "How could a worm make such a thing?" he asked almost reverently.

Suddenly he began laughing, then laughed louder, spewing grape skins on his robe. After a moment he controlled himself, wiping the skins from the robe. "Malchus," he said, trying to control his laughter, "hardly a hundred paces from here, we have a handful of rustic priests who spend their day in nothing else but *removing* worms from the wood for the altar. It occurred to me—" he lost control and began laughing again. "It occurred to me . . . instead of killing those worms, why couldn't our priests train them to make silk like their cousins in the East?" Caiaphas laughed again at his own cleverness. "Train them to make silk," Caiaphas repeated to himself, still laughing at his own joke.

Later, as Caiaphas napped on the silk pillows, I asked Zuriel about what Caiaphas said. "Follow me," Zuriel said. We walked toward the Place of Sacrifice. Nearby was the great hall where the wood was stored. In that room, great stacks of wood rose twice the height of a man's head.

"Look there," Zuriel said, pointing to some benches near the stacks of wood. There, as Caiaphas had said, some older priests were examining logs. "They are among the temporary priests. They come for a few months, a year at the most. Their duty is to find worms in the wood. A worm, according to the priests, would contaminate the sacrificial fire."

One priest, older than the others, sat a few paces away. Two stacks of smaller logs, hardly thicker than an average man's arms, lay on each side of his bench. The old man ran his hands over one of the logs and examined it as carefully as his aged eyes would allow. Satisfied that it did not contain a worm or insect that would render it ceremonially unfit for the sacrificial fire, he placed it in the other stack, and then took another log for inspection.

"Watch," Zuriel said.

A younger priest took a few of the short logs from those the old man had inspected. He carried them away and gave them to another priest, who then returned to the old man and placed the same logs in the pile for him to inspect.

I looked at Zuriel with confusion.

"The resident priests cannot trust this old man's eyes, but he must have a duty. It is a great honor for him and his village that he is serving at the temple. When he goes back to his village—where there are more goats than people—the villagers will be proud that one of their own served at the Temple of Jerusalem. And what did he do there? He looked for worms that did not exist."

The high priest, by tradition, was required to spend the day before the Day of Atonement rehearsing the next day's ceremonies. The officiating priests, as they gave this instruction, spoke to Caiaphas in the way a pedagogue might speak to a dull pupil, but Caiaphas ignored the slights. The day's ceremony would require him to bathe himself completely five times and wash his hands and feet ten times, and perform a great number of other rituals. According to the scribes, if any of these components were not followed meticulously, in both manner and sequence, the effect of the ceremony—that is, the forgiving of the sins of the people of Israel—would be invalidated. After Caiaphas had been shown the animals that would be sacrificed the next day—bulls, goats, and sheep, he returned to the Chamber of Wood, where by custom, the high priest was to spend the rest of the day in prayer. That evening a few, but not many, of the Sanhedrin would gather in a chamber, where the books of Moses would be read all night. Before Annas, it had been the custom for the high priest to attend this session, but he quit this practice soon after his ascension.

Annas himself attended the rites. Perhaps because of his scrutiny, Caiaphas performed his duties that day with few hesitations. A few hours after the daily sacrifice was completed, the courtyard began to fill. Twice ten thousand gathered for the upcoming ceremony. The several hundred priests and scribes, along with the members of the Sanhedrin, stood just near the temple steps while the great throng of people filled the courtyards behind them. The trumpeters blared as the ritual began. A bull, some rams, and some sheep were sacrificed while many of the priests threw themselves prostrate on the pavement and on the steps, lamenting the sins of Israel: "Ah, Jehovah, I have sinned. I have committed iniquity. I have transgressed thy laws. Before you my house and my nation are guilty. I entreat thee—atone for my sins, for the sins of my house and for the sins of my nation."

Two goats, virtually identical, were led into the courtyard where Caiaphas stood. A golden urn was brought to him. He put both hands in and brought out two lots—one said "for Jehovah" and the other "for Azazel." He placed one lot on the head of each goat. Some of the people thought it to be a good augury if the high priest's right hand had selected the lot "for Jehovah." However, that lot was in Caiaphas' left hand, and a low groan went through the crowd.

Another priest came forward carrying two skeins of scarlet cloth, and Caiaphas tied one around the neck of each goat. The goat designated for immediate sacrifice was defiant, and two more priests came to help subdue him, while Caiaphas tied the cloth around his neck. The other goat, "the scapegoat," designated according to the words of Moses to be sent to "a land not inhabited," was turned around to face the crowd. The people of Israel were to see the one who would carry their sins away.

The officiating priest had to prompt Caiaphas to perform the next part of the ceremony, the laying of both hands on the goat's head and confessing the nation's sins, before it was led away. Hundreds of priests fell on the pavement, moaning their confessions as the goat was led from the temple. It would follow a several days' journey into the wilderness, attended by priests, where it would be thrown from a cliff to its death.

As the goat was led away, one of the scribes behind me muttered, "Better that the goat stay here and the high priest taken to the cliff."

At the officiating priest's prompt, Caiaphas moved to the final part of the day's ceremony—his entry into the Holy of Holies. Another bullock was presented first. Six priests held it to the altar as Caiaphas slit its throat, the scarlet cleft in its neck matching the scarlet of the priests' sash, as the warm rank odor of blood filled the air. The blood was collected in a golden bowl and a priest stirred it so it would not thicken. This blood, along with incense and ashes from the altar, he would take into the sanctuary. The crowd went silent as Caiaphas entered the sanctuary. He was compelled to perform his duty quickly, lest the nation worry that he had been stricken down by God for unworthiness. This part of his responsibility Caiaphas performed well, and he emerged from the sanctuary promptly, walking backwards, as prescribed, into the open court.

I watched and wondered, How much blood is enough? How many animals are required? How many ceremonies must be performed? How far should the scapegoat go? What is required for a nation's sin to be requited?

Chapter 28

The Baptizer

Two weeks after The Day of Atonement, the morning sacrifice had been completed, and the trumpeters, after having announced the new day, put away their silver trumpets. A cool wind, predicting the coming winter, angled across the temple, blowing the smoke from the Place of Sacrifice across the Kidron Valley where it disappeared in the open sky.

"You son of the devil!" an old man shouted at the booth attendant. "You have cheated me!" A lifeless dove lay on the counter. I knew this attendant, Zoreb, and I knew his practice. He often kept a sick bird under the counter and exchanged it for a healthy one as he put it in the supplicant's bag. Ordinarily Zoreb got away with his scheme, but this elderly worshiper from Ashkelon was not timid. He smacked his walking stick on the booth next to the carcass of the dead bird, its limp wings shivering with each blow of the stick as if it still had life in it.

"You son of the devil! I will have a healthy dove for my sacrifice!" He smacked his stick again emphatically. I admired the old man's insistence. I looked at Zoreb firmly. He took my meaning. He cursed under his breath and squinted in protest as he pulled a healthy bird from the cages and stuffed it in the old man's bag. The old man looked sternly at the attendant, pointed his walking stick at him as a warning, and then nodded his appreciation to me as he turned away. I returned the gesture.

A messenger came. "Malchus, your master Joseph Caiaphas requests your presence at the house of Annas."

We left the temple through the Huldah Gates, worked our way up the steep stairs below the Place of Trumpeting, and followed the line of the new road toward the house of Annas. Fruit and vegetable sellers had set up their booths under the arches of the aqueduct, and the servants of the houses of the city were haggling with the sellers to gain the best price.

When I arrived, Annas, his five sons, and Caiaphas were gathered on the porch. Caiaphas motioned for me to come up. No plants grew on this wide stone porch that overlooked the city. A single table, crafted of simple wood, and a few chairs were the only furniture. It was as austere as the man who lived there. Annas was seated, and the others stood around him, saying nothing. All were still except Ananus, the youngest son, who paced back and forth impatiently. I sensed that he and I held one thing in common: neither of us wanted to be here at this moment. Caiaphas greeted me by name, but the others said nothing.

There are times in a slave's life when he is reminded he is a slave. At the temple I had authority—but it was not my authority, it was imputed authority, given to me by these men assembled here. They had summoned me to a task yet to be stated. If a donkey could have performed the task, he would have been summoned rather than me.

Caiaphas turned to Annas, who gave a nod, as if to give him permission to begin. "We will send a delegation to the Jordan River," he said to me, "to the place where the Baptizer is preaching." He looked again to Annas for approval. "It is our opinion that he is harmless—and likely a little deranged—but it is prudent that we know about this message he is preaching and who is following him. You and those Zuriel chooses from the temple guard will provide protection. Some members of the Sanhedrin will join you." He turned back to Annas.

The old man spoke. "Three Pharisees and three Sadducees."

No words were wasted when Annas spoke. It was said of him in the streets of Jerusalem, "Annas spends words like a miserly man spends coins."

"Why not send all the Pharisees?" Eleazer asked his brothers. "For a few days we would be free of their complaints." The brothers smiled at each other.

Annas frowned. "Ananus will go also." He looked sternly at his youngest son. Ananus's face showed surprise. The boy, nineteen years old, had paid little attention to the discussion until his name was called. He began to say something in protest—but thought better of it. One did not counter the wishes of Annas. Annas dismissed us, but before I left, he motioned for me to stop and called Caiaphas to his side and whispered to him.

Caiaphas came to me and said, "Annas asks you to watch his youngest son closely on this journey."

I understood. Stories about Ananus circulated in Jerusalem—about his presence in the wine shops and among the prostitutes that occupied them.

When I returned to the temple, Zuriel provided the explanations I needed. "They call him 'the Baptizer,'" he started. "He preaches in the area where the river spills into the Sea of Asphalt. He has developed a following among the common people."

"Does Annas fear him?" I asked.

Zuriel considered the question with a thin smile on his face. "Annas did not come to his position without watchfulness. As you know, he has his spies all over Judea and Galilee, and he watches carefully any who might subvert his authority. But for this one, the Baptizer, John the son of Zechariah, he has special interest. There are stories told among the older priests about the birth of this one. Zechariah served as priest here in the temple in those days. He and his wife Elizabeth were childless, and although he and his wife prayed fervently for many years, they had no child, and both had become old.

Then one day Zechariah announced to his fellow priests that an angel had appeared to him and promised him a son—a son that should be set apart for the purposes of God—and in fact, Elizabeth, who was beyond childbearing age, did bear a son months later. That miracle is still recounted among the priests today. And now, thirty years later, this miracle child, the Baptizer, is preaching in the wilderness."

"But—"

"But you wonder why Annas should fear this preacher. It is because he does not submit to the authority of the priests, not even the high priest. He calls everyone to repentance, not just the common people, but also the Pharisees, the Sadducees, the scribes, the priests—even the Romans. He insists *everyone* should confess his sins and repent. But—here's the greater issue—he does not call on any of them to offer the temple sacrifices. *That* is what concerns Annas. Anyone who defies the authority of the priests, who does not pay the temple tax, who does not offer the sacrifices—concerns him."

I nodded.

"Also," Zuriel added, "Nicodemus asked to join the delegation. He will go with us."

"Why would Nicodemus wish to see this Baptizer?"

"For a different reason than Annas, to be sure. Nicodemus, as you know, is watchful in a different way than Annas. Nicodemus, like many others, thinks this is the time that the redeemer of Israel will appear. Is the Baptizer that one? Some say so. Nicodemus, I am sure, would like to observe and determine that for himself."

Two days were required to make the arrangements. Our plan had been to depart before first light on the third day—the six representatives, Ananus, the six guards, myself, and four slaves in charge of the donkeys and the baggage. The early departure was necessary to ensure we would arrive in Jericho before nightfall. We gathered near the Fortress of Antonia, where the men huddled against the wall for protection against the cool morning wind. Each member of my guard carried a torch, and I counted our number by that light. Only Ananus was missing.

Two of the Pharisees grumbled to each other, loudly enough to make themselves heard to all. "Annas has sent this youngest son only to keep him from the harlots, and now we wait for this insolent boy in the cold." In the flickering light of the torches, Nicodemus raised his hands to the two other Pharisees as if to ask them to say no more. He had pulled his hood over his head to protect from the morning chill, but his face showed in the torchlight. His beard, gone to the color of wood ash, framed an expression of composure, but with an equal portion of a settled weariness. It was the face of a man who had learned to distinguish between what was important and what was not, who had known hard disappointment, but who had not given up hope. The tardiness of the son of the high priest was not one of the things to be deemed important.

The sky lightened as we waited—just enough for us to see our breath when we spoke. I looked again at the face of Nicodemus. His eyes blinked steadily but he said nothing. He, I thought, could wait until nightfall if necessary.

Ananus finally came, riding a white mule. He offered no apology and did not greet us. His surliness was obvious to all, but we ignored it. I gave the word and we all climbed aboard our mounts—donkeys, mules, and horses—pulled our cloaks around us, and began our trek. We carried few provisions, only water and food for the day, for we had only to get to Jericho. Accommodations and food awaited us there.

We made our way out of the city and skirted along the Kidron, the Mount of Olives on our right as we ascended the hill. The trees had given their fruit more than a month earlier. Some of their leaves, green and silver, had dropped onto the barley-stubble underneath their branches. Stacks of branches stood at the ends of the rows in neat piles. The limbs that had gone dead during the year which would now—during the oncoming winter—be burned to warm the huts of the vinedressers.

The sun threw some gold on the underside of the few clouds toward the east—the direction we were headed. Reaching the top of the hill, the ball of the sun came up over the hills of Moab and warmed our faces. We stopped for a moment to look back at Jerusalem. The first rays of the sun reached the embossed gold at the top of Holy of Holies, sparkling like a divine ember in the gray of the temple and the surrounding city. The trumpets sounded, a peal familiar to all of us, but here atop the hill, it was barely audible. The priest on the wall at the Place of Trumpeting said words we could not hear, but we knew them by heart as he, by custom, confirmed the arrival of the new day: "Behold, the sun has risen as far as Hebron". At that word, as we all knew, the officiating priest slit the throat of the prescribed lamb, a lamb without blemish, and sprinkled its blood on the base of the altar at the Place of Sacrifice. The daily sacrifice for the sins of Israel had been accomplished. Now every resident of Jerusalem and Judea and every Jew dispersed to the nations of the world could be assured that the appointed priests had performed their appointed duties on this morning—as they did every morning—so that they all could be assured of the propitiation of their sins. All of us, save Ananus who had edged his mule farther down the trail, seemed captured by this moment of witnessing the ritual for the first time from this perspective, on top of Mount Scopus, looking down at the temple as the line of the sun caught the gold vines and gold grapes just above the great doors of the Nicanor gates, splattering light to all the courtyards.

There are moments of solemnity a man cannot explain, a melancholy pricking at one's heart that makes him question if men are made for this world—or for a world we cannot see. This was one of those moments. I sensed the others knew it too. I had no appreciation for the manners and customs and sacrifices of the Jews, but at that moment, something deeper inside me was touched for the briefest moment. If a moment constricted by its brevity can touch on eternity, I sensed it then. I had an inclination to pause, to stop, to stay and think, and maybe even pray, but that was not possible. The caravan was moving down the hills of Judea. We were on our way to confront the Baptizer.

We had hours of travel ahead of us and we were behind schedule. I gave the signal and we turned, reluctantly, away from Jerusalem in the direction of Jericho. No one spoke. We passed through Bethany, and the world opened up in a wide expanse—the great treeless hills of Moab lay straight across from us. Below us a thin haze muted the colors of the Sea of Asphalt, still shaded and surrounded by layers of sand-colored rocks as far as the eye could see. No breeze stirred. The cloudy water of the sea was as flat as molten lead, and just as lifeless. A few poplars, tall and pointed, like Roman spears, edged the road leading downward to Jericho.

Nicodemus and I rode beside each other, and sometimes, when our voices could not be heard by the others, we spoke of Manaen and his recent letter about Antipas and Rome.

Within an hour the hazy outline of the edge of the sea came into better view as we descended. The smooth water, lacking even a ripple, was milky blue. The sea was edged by white, where encrusted salt formed along its bank. A few scrubby acacias found sustenance in the gullies, but little else. Curious lizards crept out of the crevices near us, bobbing their heads, scurrying away as we came near. Little was said. Our shadows shortened. Dust rose from the hooves of our mounts and quickly settled again. The soft clop of the hooves was the only sound. The air warmed as we descended. We removed our outer robes. There was little conversation—except for Ananus. He had put aside his surliness, as if determined to make the best of his unwanted assignment. Turning around in his saddle, he said, "Tonight we will swim in Herod's pools. Fortunately for us, the old man's men will not be there to hold our heads under the water." He slapped his mule's flanks and rode ahead down the hill, throwing up dust behind him.

The account of Herod having his brother-in-law Aristobulus drowned at the winter palace was well known in Jerusalem. The murder had taken place twenty years earlier, but to the Pharisees—who wished for high priests from the Hasmoneans, the death of Aristobulus was still fresh in their minds.

The faces of the Pharisees went sour with scorn for Ananus's humor. In their minds Ananus's family held no legitimacy as the high priestly family, and they did not like his reminder of the murder of Aristobulus, the young brother-in-law of Herod and high priest—the legitimate high priest, in their minds—killed by Herod at the very palace where we were going.

We continued our descent. Above us, two vultures soared in an endless white sky. No one spoke. The only noise was the soft clatter of hooves on the hard ground. The haze over the valley held the sun's heat, and by mid-day as we continued to descend, we had forgotten about the chill of the early morning in Jerusalem. Beyond the milky-blue waters of the flat Sea of Asphalt, the hills of Moab rose up as if a mirror to reflect the image of the dry hills on which we descended. The trail switched back and forth, sometimes passing around dry hillocks that would have given wary travelers pause. Brigands still hid in these recesses, looking for victims. If any were hiding in the shadows, they would let us pass.

"Mount Nebo," Nicodemus said, pointing to the top of the hills beyond. "Moses, the one who brought our people out of Egypt, is buried somewhere on that mountain." I had heard that story from Manaen. Now I could mark the location of the story. Jericho, our destination, also figured in Israelite history with that story about city walls collapsing.

Later that afternoon, Ananus had ridden ahead of us again, then he trotted back. "I found the heretics." he said, pointing at the gray, layered hills between us and the flat sea. In a few moments we came to a place on the trail that gave us a view of the sea's shore as it rose into the Judean hills. "A curse on them," Ananus said, and he spat in their direction.

From our distance I could make out a few dozen white-robed men moving about among a number of small buildings. "Are they the Baptizer's men?" I asked Nicodemus.

"Essenes. An odd sect. Disaffected priests for the most part—and their followers." Nicodemus's face took the wearied look that I came to associate with him. "Who can blame them for their disaffection?" he said with a sigh, careful that no one else heard him. "They refuse to participate in the temple sacrifices. They will not pay the temple tax—which profoundly irritates the Sadducees and the high priests. But they are not a large movement, and the priests have found it better to leave them alone. They, like me, hope for a redeemer, but they have chosen to separate themselves into their own community." A smile of irony came to his face, an expression I came to recognize in him. "We Pharisees say we are the 'separate ones,' for that is what our name means, but these people are more separate than we are. And to their credit, they hold no slaves."

The trail turned north, and we put the Sea of Asphalt, and the Essenes, behind us. In front of us was a wide green ribbon running directly north as far as we could see. Two shoulders of dry hills sheltered each side of that green ribbon, and above those rolling hills, steeper hills rose. No boat could ply this meager river, but its waters gave life to the area around. In the bottom of this valley, the sun left our sight early, but the air held its warmth, and we were reminded why Herod had chosen this place for his winter palace. The chill of the upper hills, where Jerusalem sat, which we had felt earlier that morning, and which would linger in the city for three or four months, never approached the bottom of the valley. Jericho was famous for its date palms, which had been harvested weeks earlier. And the valley was filled with the graceful trees neatly arrayed, like rows of Roman soldiers.

Cypros, the watchtower Herod named after his mother, came into view. Now a garrison for Roman soldiers, it rose up on a prominent cliff with a view across the valley. A small cavalry contingent waited for us. The Romans had offered to send an escort for the entire journey, but I declined the offer, knowing the temple guard was adequate for the purpose. I signaled the group to stop.

The leader of the cavalry, wearing a centurion's uniform, looked familiar. He came nearer. "Greetings in the name of the Emperor Tiberius and Pontius Pilate, the Prefect of Judea." It was Marius.

I moved my horse ahead a few paces, out of earshot of the others.

"Is that you Malchus?" he said.

"Indeed it is. But I did not expect to see you in this place."

"Nor I you. But it is a welcome surprise. My responsibility is to provide your escort to the palace."

I looked at the twenty cavalry soldiers. Half of them formed in front of us and the other half behind, and we arrived at the palace in less than an hour.

"Herod's palace," Ananus shouted, pointing to the huge structure ahead of us. Great palm trees, taller and thinner than the date-producing varieties, sheltered an expansive compound of white stone that sat on both sides of the Wadi Qelt.

Immediately I was reminded of the palace in Rome where I had spent nearly two years. The stone here was of softer tones than that in Rome, but the lines were similar, and this palace was larger, much larger. In Rome Herod had limits, but here in Judea, his own kingdom, Herod had had no constraints.

"Stay and share our dinner," I said to Marius as we dismounted.

"I will stay, but not for your dinner. Before the dinner however, we will share some chilled wine under the potted palms near the heated baths."

"You know this place?"

"The privilege of the Roman army." He smiled. "The Herods no longer need it. I have often soaked in those hot waters, and I wish I could again today to wash away the dust that covers me. Another time perhaps. But this afternoon we will talk, and I will learn about all you have done in the last year." He dismounted. "Allow me to take care of my men and my mounts, then I will meet you."

Servants came and took our mounts; others brought us cool water and led us to the gates.

"Herod spent many of his winters here," Nicodemus told me, "and he continued to expand it over the years." We entered the reception hall, which had the familiar honeycomb patterns of the floor as I had seen in Rome. Nicodemus went on, "Herod, who spent his early life in a goat-hair tent, was astounded when he first visited Rome. He decided to bring the glory of Rome to his new empire in the desert. No one can deny that he succeeded. Some of us wish he had spent more energy on building our nation." A fountain, surrounded by abundant ferns in clay pots, trickled in the courtyard, and the sound bounced softly off the marble walls decorated with colorful frescoes in brilliant oranges, reds, blues, and greens representing the flora of the area.

"The Hasmoneans had a small palace here, but when Herod came to power, he tore it down and replaced it. Then, a few years later he added a second section on the other side of the wadi, joining the two by a bridge—and then afterwards he built the third section on both sides of the wadi, larger by far than the previous two combined."

We crossed the stone bridge over the Wadi Qelt, and through it flowed a silent, placid stream the height of a man's knees. Pink oleanders took advantage of the stream and grew in profusion along its banks. Dragonflies chased each other among the reeds, their wings sparkling like flying diamonds in the bright sun.

I made my way to the courtyard Marius had described. Water poured from the bronze heads of six leopards in the central fountain, spilling into a circular pool filled with water lilies. A runnel, decorated with floral ceramics, led the water out of the courtyard. When Marius arrived he pointed to the corner where, as he said, potted palms provided shade for the benches. Pomegranate trees, some with a few of their red fruits still hanging on the limbs, rose up between the palms.

Marius arrived and we sat together. "Tell me about your life in the temple. I want to hear all."

"I will tell you all, but not before I have heard a report from you. When last I saw you in Caesarea, Pilate had just relented."

"He sulked for days. When he finally left his palace, he took his anger out on his troops, drilling them without mercy—and woe to the soldier who was sloppy in his performance. Several endured his personal wrath, beaten on their backs with his cane." He paused, sipping his wine. "And then he had to suffer the indignity of attending Passover. Since then, some of his anger has subsided, but his demeanor is still severe. When he put the standards on the wall at the fortress, his ambition was to ingratiate himself to Sejanus, but instead that action made him seem inept. Was he laughed at in Rome? I do not doubt it. You have heard in Jerusalem 'The necks of the Jews are better weapons than the swords of Pilate.' Those same words, you can be sure, have run through the halls of the Senate."

A quarter-moon, like a silver scythe, rose over Moab. Dinner that night was subdued. Our group was weary and soon retired to their rooms. As it was my duty, I checked to make sure all those in my charge were safe. All except Ananus were accounted for, but I had assigned one of my guards specifically to Ananus and received assurance that the young man was swimming in Herod's famous pool.

The next morning—after a breakfast of olives, figs, dates, cheeses, and bread, we began to explore the palace. This was the Sabbath, the day had been set apart for rest, so we were required to stay in place. The following day we would make the short trip to the site on the river where the Baptizer was preaching. The Sadducees, along with Ananus, had discovered Herod's *caldarium,* the heated baths, and were soaking in those chambers. The two Pharisees had found a shaded area with benches and, as was their custom, were discussing Jewish law and the Sabbath. After some searching I found Nicodemus in a small alcove sheltered by potted myrtle trees, reading from a scroll. "Pharisee who is not a Pharisee," I said. "I am sorry that the Sadducee who is not a Sadducee is not here with you." His eyes lightened as he greeted me with the expression I came to know—part weariness, part graciousness, part wisdom.

"Ah, yes. Sincerely I wish Joseph were here with me." He pointed to the bench facing his. "Please join me. Yes, I am a Pharisee—or at least I am the representative of the Pharisees on the Sanhedrin."

The look on his face reminded me of Manaen—the expression of a man who has given much time to thinking about something and then formulating his ideas.

"Let me tell you about Pharisees. Our movement began with good intentions. We were called to be 'separate', for that is what our name means. We were to be separate from the nations around us. That had been our downfall in generations past. We Jews had been instructed to be a distinct people with a distinct purpose, but instead we adopted the idols and the worship of surrounding nations. I am sure Manaen made you aware of our people's history. We were judged for our unfaithfulness. We were exiled. But some, a remnant, remained faithful and we were allowed to return to the land that we were given. And so, this faithful remnant determined that we should follow the laws of God and never again succumb to the idolatry of the nations."

"I read this in the books in the library in Rome," I acknowledged.

"At one time, I was a conscientious Pharisee. Like my brothers over in the alcove, I spent endless hours in discussion about our law. I studied under the sages. I fasted twice a week. I tithed. I went about all the things that a Pharisee should do, but . . ." his voice trailed off. "Some concerns, over the years, began to creep into my mind. I asked myself: 'Do we worship our fidelity to the Scriptures rather than the one who called us to fidelity?' I began to wonder if we had not moved away from the main message of the Scriptures into a self-centered and self-righteous religion. It troubled me a great deal. Once I sat through a dozen lengthy sessions, in the shade of the Royal Portico at the temple in Jerusalem—over a period of a week—when the discussion was completely about whether or not spitting on the Sabbath should be allowed. The sages eventually determined that spitting in the dust causes a furrow to be raised, and that raising a furrow is an act of farming—and thus, spitting on the Sabbath was ruled to be a violation of the Law. That troubled me. And never in any of those sessions was there any discussion of the one prophesied to deliver us. That troubled me even more."

His face took a far-away look as if he were still working out his convictions.

"Let me recite for you. 'Behold, I will send you Elijah the prophet before the great and awesome day of the Lord comes.' That is from the prophet Malachi—some of the final words from our prophets. You see, we are promised many times that the Deliverer will come, but we are also told that Elijah, one of our greatest prophets, will precede him—will come and prepare the way for him."

He looked around him at the rugged hills that rose up around the palace. "Let me tell you why I have come on this journey. I have come because this is the land of Elijah. Look around you. This is the place to which Elijah escaped when he ran from Jezebel, the wicked wife of the king of Israel, and this is the place from which God took him up to heaven." Nicodemus stood from his bench and paced.

"When the first reports of the Baptizer came to Jerusalem, the question was raised, 'Could this be the forerunner? *Could this be Elijah?*' It was a legitimate question and deserved our attention. Is this the one that will fulfill the prophecy? Perhaps not, but it deserves our consideration. However, I wonder if my brothers have *any* questions in their mind. Their minds are made up, it appears. The Sadducees have little interest in the prophecies. However, they have great interest in any leader who might disrupt their authority, so their interest in the Baptizer is not related to the prophecies. When my brothers the Pharisees heard about the Baptizer, how he was attracting crowds with his preaching, and the question as to whether he might be the one that Malachi prophesied, they dismissed the idea immediately. 'He is not one of the *hasid*,' they said, one of the faithful ones. And 'he attracts the *amharetzin*,' the unrefined and illiterate. So because he is not one of us, one of the Pharisees, he could not possibly be the forerunner."

Nicodemus sat down on the bench again. "But how can we be sure? Why should we expect the forerunner to be traditional, to fit into our specific expectations? If Elijah preached along this river hundreds of years ago, why shouldn't we expect him to preach here again?"

I said nothing.

"I'm afraid, Malchus, the distinctions between the Sadducees and the Pharisees, which each party likes to deem as religious differences, may indeed be more political than religious. Each of us may say we want the Deliverer to come, but maybe we want him to come in order to validate our own way of thinking."

A breeze ran through the wadi, rustling the fronds of the tall palms above us.

After a moment, as if coming out of a reverie, he smiled. "Malchus, these are the ruminations of a weary man. I hope I have not burdened you."

"Not at all, Master Nicodemus." I stood to leave.

"Sometimes, Malchus, I wonder if we have misplaced our worship."

"I don't understand."

"Sometimes I wonder if in our effort to follow the Law of God, we Pharisees have begun to worship the Law and not the God who gave us our law. And sometimes it seems our brothers the Sadducees worship the temple of God and not the God of the temple. And then the Zealots—they seem to worship freedom more than anything else." His voice trailed off. "Forgive me. I have many questions in my mind. This is just one of them."

There seemed to be nothing more to say, so I dismissed myself.

The Jericho palace did not regularly receive guests in those days; however, our dinner was sumptuous, featuring a roasted antelope as well as lamb and poultry. The tables teemed with cabbage, lentils, figs, grapes, and pears—all of which were grown in the valley.

Some jugglers from Jericho came for entertainment, but they seemed out of practice, which was understandable. Twice they dropped a club, and Ananus laughed loudly each time. The lyre-player lost his place once, and when he did, Ananus put his fingers in his ears and grinned at the other dinner guests.

When the entertainment concluded, one of the Pharisees stood and said, "We should be prepared when we approach the Baptizer. My brother and I intend to ask him: Are we not the sons of Abraham? How is it that you call the sons of Abraham to repentance?"

"It is a good question my brother," one of the Sadducees said. "But the greater question is this: By whose authority are you preaching? The Sanhedrin has granted you no authority. How is it you compel these Jews to be baptized?"

"And why," the other Sadducee said, "is it you do not honor the temple and the sacrifices? That is a question to be asked."

Ananus, who had been nursing his wine cup and paying little attention to the conversation, suddenly jumped to his feet, a thighbone in one hand and his wine cup in the other. "Tomorrow—" He spilled wine on himself as he stood. "Tomorrow—" He interrupted himself and summoned the wine ladler to refill his cup. "Tomorrow I will make the Baptizer an offer." It seemed this idea had just come to his mind. He wiped his face with his sleeve, not bothering to use the water bowl, and smiled in a self-satisfied way. "Tomorrow I will ask the Baptizer if he will baptize *me*!" He took another swallow of his wine. "I will tell that goat herder in his camel-hair robe that *I* want to repent." He laughed. "Think of it. I will ask him to baptize the son of the high priest, one that someday—"

The Pharisees and the Sadducees looked at each other.

All of Annas's sons had ambitions, and Ananus caught himself before he said too much. "Ummm . . . Tomorrow I will throw a rope around the leg of this Baptizer and drag him up the hill to Jerusalem. I will—"

One of the Pharisees leaned over to the one next to him. "The wine has his tongue."

Ananus heard the comment. He threw the bone to the table and left the hall.

After dinner I followed Nicodemus outside, and we walked across the bridge to the large pools Herod had built in the final section of the palace. The light from the torches sparkled on the surface of the water as we stood at the edge. Palms leaned over the walls, and the light showed on the undersides of the fronds. Beyond the palm trees the sky was black. A few insects trilled their songs along the edge of the stream on the other side of the wall. A moth flew too close to the torches and fell on the stones, its wings scorched.

"This is where Aristobulus drowned," Nicodemus said as he pointed toward the water.

I looked at the water, trying to imagine the scene. "Why did Herod order that?"

"Herod had been king only a year. Call it jealousy. Call it fear. He saw Aristobulus as a rival to his throne."

"A seventeen-year-old?"

"To understand his fear, Malchus, you must understand Herod. Herod was not a Jew. He had an Idumean father and a Nabatean mother. His father had been compelled, by the Hasmoneans, to convert to Judaism. As a young man Herod aligned himself with the Romans and fought valiantly in a series of wars. His own brother died beside him in battle. The Romans, in appreciation, designated Herod as King of the Jews. At that point, he had Rome's authority, but he knew that authority would not be enough—he needed to be accepted by the Jews. For a hundred years we had been ruled by the Hasmoneans, the high priestly family. Herod knew that unless he could gain the trust and authority of the Hasmoneans, he had no chance of gaining the approval of the Jews."

Nicodemus turned to me. "We Jews have been called a stiff-necked people by our own prophets—and it is true. And our necks were stiffening when Herod, this Idumean from the desert, was appointed our king. No one in Israel regarded him as an authentic ruler. Our rulers and heroes were the Hasmoneans. So what was Herod to do? He contrived a plan—a plan to unify the family of Herod and the family of the Hasmoneans. The line of the king would merge with the line of the high priest. He divorced his wife Doris and sent her and their son Antipater away from Jerusalem. He then married Mariamne, from the Hasmonean line. And here is the odd thing, although this marriage was contracted on a political basis, by all accounts, Herod truly loved Mariamne."

"I have heard of his love for her."

"Those who saw her said she was an especially beautiful woman, with a regal bearing. I was told that whenever she entered a room, the room went quiet and that both men and women were captivated by her appearance."

The other two Pharisees walked near us, their hands clasped behind them. Pharisees were always evaluating things around them. That was their nature and their training. These two walked along the edge of the pool, but they turned back before they came to the dressing rooms and steam rooms. Such indulgences apparently were indecent, even for observation. Nicodemus nodded in acknowledgement to them, and they nodded back before strolling on to their accommodations for the evening.

Nicodemus picked up where he had left off: "Mariamne's brother, Aristobulus, was only seventeen when Herod appointed him as the high priest. Herod was reluctant to make that appointment, but the prominent Jews in the city wanted an authentic member of the Hasmonean family as high priest—and perhaps Mariamne pressured him, so Herod relented. Aristobulus's first opportunity to officiate came at the Day of Atonement."

He paused and turned to me. "According to all reports, Aristobulus was a tall, broad-shouldered, striking young man. 'The Hammer of God has returned,' someone in the crowd said as Aristobulus officiated. My uncle told me that the vestments on Aristobulus 'looked more like the breastplate of a warrior than the garb of a priest.' 'Is this the Anointed One?' was the question that ran through the city."

"This was dangerous talk, of course, but Aristobulus was unaware of any of it."

Nicodemus saw the confusion in my face.

"Let me explain. About two hundred years ago the Greek Antiochus destroyed our city, defiled our temple by sacrificing a pig on the altar—what we call the 'abomination of desolation'—and massacred thousands of our people. He closed our temple and forbade our worship. Our nation was in mourning. Eventually, one named Judas, a priest from the Hasmonean line, raised an army and defeated the Greeks. He was given the name of *Judas Maccabee*, Judas the Hammer. Judas Maccabee was neither a descendant of Aaron, which according to our tradition is necessary to be a high priest, nor was he a descendant of David, a requirement to become king—nevertheless he became both. He ruled as king and priest. Many saw him as the one who would redeem Israel. Eventually he and his sons defeated the Idumeans and the Nabateans, the two strongest nations in the south, forcing them to convert from their paganism to Judaism. Even today many Jews hold high regard for the Hasmoneans, or the Maccabees, as they came to be called, for their defeat of the nation's enemies. Yet there was an internal civil war going on as well. What you see now between the Sadducees and the Pharisees is harsh disagreement, but in those days it was a civil war. And of course, the Romans, coming up from Egypt, took advantage of our civil war and, with the help of the Idumeans and the Nabateans, subdued our nation."

An odd smile came on Nicodemus's face. "Do you see the irony, Malchus?"

He did not wait for my answer.

"The irony is this: Judas Maccabee, Judas the Hammer, conquered the Idumeans and forced them to become Jews. Is that possible? Can a nation or a man be forced to worship God? I think not. And the result was that Herod the Idumean—forced by Judas to become a Jew—would eventually eliminate the line of Judas. It started with Aristobulus, but it would not end until all the Hasmoneans, all the 'Hammers of God' were dead."

He nodded toward the pool. "Here was the beginning of the murders. Jerusalem was abuzz with the infatuation over Aristobulus. Mature women wept for joy when they saw him, and the young women swooned at his beauty. 'The Hammer of God has returned,' the people whispered. And those whispers, of course, found their way to the ears of Herod."

"A banquet was held here," Nicodemus waved his arm, "and all the royal family was here, including Alexandra, the mother of Mariamne and Aristobulus. That night, after the banquet, some of the young men in Herod's employ enticed him to join them in *this* pool. Once Aristobulus was in the water, they pulled him under and held him there until he drowned. They reported it as an accident. Alexandra, his mother, was inconsolable. Her screams, according to those who were here, filled the valley. She knew Herod was behind the murder, as did most of Israel, but Herod feigned grief and sponsored a great funeral for Aristobulus. He himself spoke eloquently of his brother-in-law at the funeral. He would later name his first son with Mariamne after Aristobulus, but the damage was done. The family of the Herods and the family of the Hasmoneans could never be united. As Herod realized this, he changed his plans. Rather than unification with the Hasmoneans, he planned elimination."

"Alexandra eventually was starved to death. Mariamne was executed, something Herod came to regret. And eventually their two sons were strangled to death when he accused them of plotting against him. With the deaths of the two sons of Mariamne, the line of the Maccabees was ended. The 'Hammers of God' would ring no more."

"Did that end the threats to Herod's throne?" I asked.

He thought about this for a moment before he answered. "It seemed so, at least for a few years. And then an odd thing . . ."

He seemed to turn something over in his mind, and I waited.

"You've seen Herod's palaces in Jerusalem and Caesarea, and this winter palace here. But he also built a palace in the Galilee and still one more across the valley in the hills of Moab, where he would go to soak in the warm waters that spring out of the rocks there. But oddly, he also built yet another palace just outside the village of Bethlehem—actually more fortress than palace, but luxurious just the same. Bethlehem, of course, is called the 'the city of David.' Herod intended to watch this village carefully because of Jews' hope that the successor of David, a new king come to redeem us, would perhaps come from the city of David.

"Shortly after Herod had murdered Mariamne and his two sons by her—Aristobulus and Alexandros—his health began to fail. He regretted killing Mariamne. He became deranged. He suffered from nightmares and screamed her name through the night. At that time a delegation from Persia arrived in Jerusalem. I remember their arrival. I was a boy at the time, studying under Rabban Jebediah. Among the boys there were reports of the magnificence of the caravan—gold-studded bridles on the camels and flowing silk on their riders. These *magi* had come to the temple and made some very interesting inquiries. It seems that they had seen some sign in the heavens that "the king of the Jews" had been born nearby. This, of course, was reported to Herod. He sent some members of his guard to Bethlehem to ask if there had been anything unusual in the village. The guards reported that there were some *amharetzin*, shepherds no less, who ranted about a vision of angels they had seen in the sky. These angels supposedly told the shepherds, 'A king is born.' The report was dismissed, but Herod summoned advisors. Jebediah, my teacher, along with others, was called to Herod's palace. Herod asked if the ancient prophets had had anything to say about this purported 'king of the Jews.' The prophecy of Isaiah was read aloud to him: 'And you, O Bethlehem, in the land of Judah, are by no means the least among the rulers of Judah; for from you will come a ruler who will shepherd my people Israel.'

According to those who were in Herod's hall that morning, he flinched in his seat when the word *ruler* was spoken. Others had threatened his throne, either intentionally or unintentionally, and all had been suppressed. Now it seemed his throne was threatened by a baby.

"Herod invited the magi to a dinner that evening, and many of us who were in Jebediah's class tried to gain a view of these magi, who had created such a sensation. I wish I could tell you I was able to see them, but Herod's soldiers kept us away. The next day the caravan left the city, and nothing was heard of them again. It was not until years later, when I myself became a member of the Sanhedrin that Jebediah confided in me the events in Herod's hall. He said he had not seen Herod in a few years and was surprised at how he had declined. His face had gone yellow, and the skin sagged around his eyes and jowls. His arms trembled under his robes, and he scratched his arms and legs incessantly. Jebediah had been warned to hold his breath when he greeted him. Herod's breath was putrid, and there seemed to be an even stronger odor emanating from his robes. A rumor went around that his genitals were rotting. According to Jebediah, the magi were very forthcoming in their conversation with Herod. The signs they had seen pointed them to Bethlehem. Herod, when he heard this, began scratching his arms even more vigorously. He reached under his robes to scratch his legs and Jebediah saw blood run down his leg. 'Make a diligent search for this one,' Herod told them. 'And when you have found him, come and inform me. I also would like to worship him.' These Persian magi must have sensed the insincerity of the monarch because the next day they were gone."

Nicodemus's expression turned from weariness to sadness. "I remember Jebediah's words well. 'The screams of the mothers in Bethlehem did not reach Jerusalem, but I hope they reached heaven— for Herod the King of Judea was determined that no rival, no King of the Jews that might have been born in the city of David, would survive. He had all the boys under two years put to the sword.'"

"All? Killed?"

He nodded.

"He killed the baby that the magi sought?"

Nicodemus took a deep breath. "There was a story—a story about a family that escaped to Egypt. But it may have been only a story. Is that enough to give a man hope?"

Nicodemus again took a deep breath. "Malchus, I am a man who is committed to having hope. God promised one would come to redeem us. I am committed to that promise. That is why I am tonight at the palace of Herod and why tomorrow I will go to see the Baptizer. The others want to embarrass and discredit him, but who are we to say that God cannot use a man of his choice to announce the Redeemer?"

The mournful sound of a dove in the trees just outside the walls seemed to complement Nicodemus's words.

"On the morrow," I said as I stood to leave.

"On the morrow," Nicodemus agreed.

Chapter 29

The Confrontation

Marius, along with one of his cavalrymen, joined us. "Aulus will show us the way. He knows the site." Ananus was late again, as we had come to expect. At least there was no chill in the air as we waited. Across the valley, over the hills of Moab, a few reticent clouds had slipped above yellow-brown hills, as if they were watching us. Two hours would be required to reach the site where the Baptizer was preaching. Ananus arrived. He walked cautiously, squinting his eyes, as if movement was painful. We could see he had been at his wine late into the night. Seeing us stare at him, he pulled his cloak over his forehead. Trying to mount his mule, he slipped off at his first attempt. He slapped the creature's flank. One of my guards came and held the animal's bridle. Another offered to assist Ananus, but he refused. At his second attempt he got seated.

At my signal we departed, headed north through the dry hills. Atop the first rise we saw where the Jordan River, like a giant green fan, spread out across the valley as it entered the Sea of Asphalt—as if the life-filled waters were reluctant to enter the sea where nothing lives. The green ribbon ran north, flanked by crusty brown hills, lower hills than those we descended, out of sight to the lake I had heard about but never seen, the Gennareset.

Several dozen peasants picked cabbages in the fields. They straightened from their labors for a moment to watch our strange delegation. We came to the ferry, paid our fee and along with our mounts were poled across the shallow water by young men with strong arms.

Ananus seemed to recover from his wine, at least enough to grumble. He said something to the Sadducees about "bringing this false prophet to the temple to show him the proper way to worship." None bothered to respond.

We continued our trek through the yellow-orange hills to where the Jordan River flattened into a half dozen shallow streams before trickling into the briny, dead water. The blackbirds whistled to each other in the broom bushes, and a hoopoe somewhere in the scrub called its name to us.

Aulus pointed to an area flanked by a few tall palms and thick undergrowth. "He will be around there. From here we go by foot."

We dismounted and began walking through a sandy trail between the tamarisks. Finches, disturbed by our presence, flitted away.

Footprints told us that many others had used this path recently. Marius and Aulus led the way while the temple guards and I came up the rear. The group had gone quiet and somber. The brushy tamarisks with their gray-green needles were hardly ten feet tall but they were thick, scratching our shoulders and obscuring our view. As we got closer I could hear the murmur of the stream and the voice of a man talking.

We emerged from the scrub growth to an open area by the river. Several dozen men stood at the edge of the water. They turned to look at us as we came near. From behind them came a deep and booming voice, "You brood of vipers!"

The strength and magnitude of the voice alarmed me, and my hand went instinctively to my sword.

"Who warned you to flee from the wrath to come?"

There stood a man with the posture and muscular leanness of a gladiator. Knee-deep in the water, he wore a camel hair mantle, hanging loosely on one shoulder, cinched with leather around a narrow waist. My sword was unnecessary. The Baptizer carried a staff, not a spear. He looked directly at us. "You brood of vipers!" he repeated, taking a step toward us. He paused for a moment, looking back and forth across our group, then stepped closer.

The Pharisees and the Sadducees looked at each other in uncertainty and clustered closer together. No one spoke. The brave questions they rehearsed the previous night failed to come to their lips.

The Baptizer continued his scrutiny. Each member of our delegation dropped his eyes as the eyes of the wild prophet caught him. I had the odd sensation that this man, whom we had come to evaluate, was rather evaluating *us*. He took another step in our direction, pointed a strong arm at us, and shouted even louder: "Again I ask you, who warned you to flee from the wrath to come?"

Whatever I may have expected to see when I saw the Baptizer, I did not expect this. I did not expect he would directly insult dignitaries from Jerusalem the moment they arrived. Both the Sadducees and the Pharisees were accustomed to deference. Ananus especially enjoyed the fear of the people that his father required. But this man seemed a man without fear, and it was apparent no deference would be shown to anyone this day.

"Do not say to me—" the Baptizer continued, stepping closer and gaining energy as he spoke, "—that you have Abraham as a father." The water dripped from his rough cloak and ran down his legs. He stepped to the riverbank and picked up a stone the size of his fist.

Ananus moved closer to me. The others huddled closer together. Of all our group only Nicodemus stood in his place, listening intently to the prophet's harangue.

The Baptizer's eyes moved back and forth across our silent group. "God can make sons of Abraham out of these rocks if he chooses." He threw the stone at our feet. Ananus jumped out of the way and a feeble yelp came from his throat. "Take him, Malchus!" Ananus screamed, moving behind me. I ignored him.

The Baptizer took another step toward us and again brought the gaze of his fiery eyes from man to man. Ananus pushed me in the back as if to make me confront the Baptizer. I made no move. We were in no peril. Six others from the temple guard accompanied us, all with swords and trained to use them.

In a man-to-man contest, the Baptizer would have been a worthy adversary. He brought to mind the best soldiers in Rome, men whose training had built and tightened every muscle of their frame. What months of training had done for the soldiers in Rome, harsh living in the Judean desert had done for John the son of Zechariah.

Ananus made another motion for me to put my temple guard into action. I continued to ignore him. I, like Nicodemus, was waiting for more words from the Baptizer. I was smiling and found myself wishing this sturdy prophet would throw another rock.

The prophet continued to examine us. No one spoke. No breeze stirred. No one moved. The flow of water and the finches flitting in tamarisks were the only movements in the whole world. Our huddled delegation was struck dumb.

The Sadducees and the Pharisees began murmuring among themselves. I sensed they were agreeing we should leave. But I wanted to hear what the Baptizer had to say.

I wanted to know this man better. I wanted to hear him. It was easy to understand how he had gathered a following. Men with fears seek those who are fearless. This was such a man. This was a man without fear. The fearlessness showed in his face. He did not need approval—even that of those with authority in Jerusalem. He did not fear us. He did not need us. His eyes seemed to look right through us. "Say more," I thought. "Say more. I would hear more of what you say."

But he said nothing. All others except Nicodemus averted his gaze. The Baptizer began to turn away.

Nicodemus took a few steps forward, then stopped and spoke. There was earnestness in his voice. "Are you the one who is to come?"

The Baptizer stopped and looked back.

The others in our group halted.

The Baptizer tilted his head as if to consider what to make of the one who had asked the question. His demeanor softened, as did his voice. He took the tone of a teacher. Perhaps he recognized the sincerity of the question. He came close enough to speak without shouting. "I baptize with water for repentance." He motioned to the water behind him. "But he who is coming after me is mightier than I, whose sandals I am not worthy to carry. He will baptize you—not with water but with the Holy Spirit and with fire." He paused for a moment and looked at the hills around us, as if searching for the promised one at that moment. "His winnowing fork is in his hand, and he will clear his threshing floor and gather his wheat into the barn. But the chaff—" He brought his eyes back from the hills to those of us standing there. "The chaff he will burn with unquenchable fire."

All of us stood silently for a moment until the Baptizer calmly turned away and walked back into the water. Nicodemus's eyes went to the hills, as if he also was looking for the one who was coming.

We all remained silent for another long moment. Then we turned back.

The dinner at Herod's palace that night was a more somber affair than the previous night. Ananus did not attend. The others said little and ate little. Each of us had been shaken. The Sadducees dismissed themselves first and a few moments later the Pharisees did likewise, except for Nicodemus. He had eaten little all evening. Even now, with the hall empty save for the two of us, and the palace servants taking the plates away, he still seemed immersed in his own world of thoughts.

I moved from my position at the other end of the table to a place near Nicodemus. He smiled and motioned for me to sit.

"There is something on your mind, master Nicodemus."

He nodded. "John and I have little in common—yet much in common."

The irony of his statement seemed to take the weariness from his face for a moment. His eyes brightened. "I reside in a palace on the edge of Jerusalem while John has the desert and the hills as his home; I sleep on a soft bed with soft cushions while John huddles on the ground. A dozen fine robes hang near the bed I sleep in, while he adorns himself with camel hair and leather. I eat the choicest food while John subsists on insects and honey. My associates are the members of the Sanhedrin, the most influential Jews with the Roman authorities. And John . . . you saw those who were following him."

He squinted his eyes as if to look into his own soul.

"This is what we have in common, John the Baptizer and I." He paused for a moment. "Both of us live in anticipation of the one who will redeem Israel. We both cling to that hope. Both of us recognize our nation has lost its way, and we both know only the Anointed One, the Messiah, can bring us back into our covenant with God."

He took a deep breath and turned to me. "Tell me, Malchus. Do we have more or less in common with each other?"

I said nothing.

He smiled. "John preaches repentance—which Israel truly needs, but does a man hear about repentance in the Sanhedrin? No." He took a deep breath. "I believe, however, along with John, that Israel needs to repent."

Nicodemus worked his hands together as if he were forming his thoughts through his fingertips.

"I have told you what John and I have in common: Now I will tell you how John and I are least alike—and it is a sad comparison." He paused for a moment. "John is a man of courage. I am not. John speaks clearly and with conviction without concern for the consequences. I, however, seek compromise. That is the distinction between us. Yes, we have much in common; our convictions are similar, but in the end—in the most essential thing, courage, we are not much alike."

Chapter 30

Claudia's Arrival

The information was not public, but it was known in the house of Annas.

Pilate had informed no one in Judea that his wife, Claudia Procula, was coming to Caesarea to join him. Nevertheless, Annas's informers in Rome had learned of the plan and alerted Annas.

"The shaved-face Roman has sent for his wife," Eleazer said to his brothers. "Could he not be satisfied with the slave-girls as Valerius Gratus was?"

Agony and hope came jointly with that news, for those twin emotions were—to me— always tied to Sabrina. Would Sabrina accompany Claudia to Judea? I tried to dismiss the question. It would be better, I told myself, if she stayed in Rome. If she were in Caesarea, she would be too much on my mind. Better that she stay in Rome. There I would not see her. If she were in Caesarea, she would accompany Claudia to Jerusalem for the festivals. And her presence would increase my agony and remind me of the hopelessness of my hope.

A year and a half had passed since I saw her at the quay in Puteoli. In those restless hours on my bed—which all men endure, I suppose—the memory of that last brief interaction would come back to me.

What did she look like? I could not make her face out in my mind. And Claudia? What was her face like? Women's faces—I could never make them clear in my mind. The faces of the women whose lives had intersected mine were blurred in my memory. The memory of my mother's face had been supplanted by the face of the lady. In my memory her face had become mingled with that of my mother. But now, no matter how hard I tried, the face of the lady would not come back to me. I could imagine her long black hair and how it fell over me as she attended my neck. But I could not make out her face. Neither her face nor my mother's face are held in my memory. My memory holds only the sounds of their wailings.

What of Claudia's face? I remember her countenance but not her features. When Claudia looked at me at the slave market, and I caught her eyes, she was more than a woman looking to buy a slave. Hers was a gentle face without contempt or indifference. Rather, I saw sadness and compassion. It was the face of a woman who herself had known tragedy. But it was Sabrina's face I sought. I saw her face, and she saw mine with an immediate identification, as if her eyes were saying, "Yes, I am a slave like you. And yes, like you, I know I am not made for slavery."

I determined to point my thoughts to something more useful. But I could not take my own advice. Despite my determination otherwise, the girl haunted my thoughts.

When Claudia arrived, there was no ceremony. Pilate wanted no publicity for his wife's coming, but the information circulated among the Roman troops, and I overheard one of them say, "She brought the copper-haired beauty from the islands with her."

I absorbed the news. Sabrina was now nearby.

Chapter 31

The Leper

I was near the Nicanor Gate when I heard the voices—intemperate, angry voices. I looked toward the Court of Priests, from where the sounds came. There, in the shadow of the great golden candlestick that rises to the height of three men, a crowd had gathered, and from there the competing voices rose. I pressed through the crowd. Five men, *amharetzin*, if I could tell by their clothing, were arguing with an officiating priest. Another dozen priests stood behind him. "He told us to come to you!" one of the *amharetz* shouted." The priests held up their hands to calm the man down and mumbled something I could not hear.

I saw Zuriel. "What is wrong?" I asked.

"Look there," he pointed to a man sitting on a bench by himself. The man sat, elbows on his knees, looking around as if he were trying to make sense of what was going on. "That one, the one saying nothing, the one sitting on the bench, he—" Zuriel stopped.

"Go on," I said.

"The five shaking their fists and shouting at the priests are the man's brothers and cousins. They claim the man on the bench had leprosy. But now he's healed—by a prophet in the Galilee."

"He told us to come to you!" one of the men repeated.

I shook my head at Zuriel to make him realize I didn't understand.

"This Galilean prophet who did the healing told the *amharetzin* to show himself to the priests. Moses gave instructions about what a man should do when he was healed from leprosy. The priests say they have never performed that ceremony. And they question whether the man ever had leprosy."

"I tell you again," one of the brothers shouted. "My brother was unclean. He lived alone in the hills as Moses required. But now he is clean. Jesus bar-Joseph, the rabbi from Nazareth, healed him."

Jesus bar-Joseph. It was the first time I ever heard the name of the Galilean rabbi. Little did I know how many more times I would hear that name.

"Cousin," one of the other amharetzin said, reprimanding the other. "He told us to say nothing about this to anyone."

"Who can keep from telling such a thing? Has such a thing ever happened in Israel before? A leper has been healed. How can we avoid telling such a thing?" He showed the priest two bags. "We have brought the offering—two doves, cedar wood, scarlet yarn, and hyssop, just as Moses commanded."

Asriel the scribe had been summoned. He looked at the *amharetzin* with scorn. The officiating priest took him aside, explained the matter, and asked for his judgement. A scroll from the library was offered. Asriel seemed reluctant to read it, but he began, running his finger over the lines of text, "This shall be the law of the leper for the day of his cleansing. He shall be brought to the priest..."

The instructions were lengthy. As Asriel continued to read, Zuriel and I walked over to the man on the bench.

"He had pity on me," the man said as we approached. "I was not supposed to come near him—but I did. I was desperate. I have been sick many years. I asked him if he could make me well—and he did." Sadness and wonder were mixed in his face. "He had pity on me. He touched me. No man had touched me in many years. Many years. And when he did..." The man held out his arms and his legs to show his skin.

The reading concluded, and the argument picked up again. "He told us to come to you!" the brother repeated. "He told us to follow the law of Moses!"

"Return to the Galilee!" Asriel shouted. "You are foolish peasants! Concern yourselves with the matters in your village. You know nothing of the law of Moses."

The man's brother stepped toward Asriel, but Zuriel moved between them. He put his hand on the shoulder of the brother to calm him. He asked Asriel and the priest to come aside for a moment.

"They are foolish peasants," Asriel said. "And you, Zuriel, are intruding on a question of the Law. That is not your authority."

"I will not learn my duty from you, scribe Asriel. I know my duty, and I know my authority. My authority requires me to keep the peace at the temple, and I will do that." He turned to the priest, "What is the request of these men?"

The priest looked at Asriel before he answered, "They claim that their brother was a leper and now he has been healed and . . . and they want us to perform the ceremony Moses prescribed."

"Is there such a ceremony?" Zuriel asked.

"Moses wrote of it. The scribe Asriel has just read it. But we have no way of verifying that this man had leprosy."

"Did Moses write that you must verify?" Zuriel asked.

The priest's eyes flickered. He turned his head slightly to the side as one would when considering a question he had not before considered. "But we have never performed this ceremony, and as far as we know, no priest has ever performed the ceremony. Moses wrote of it, but it is unknown since Moses."

"If you performed the ceremony—you would be the first." Zuriel replied.

Asriel started to protest, but the priest held up his hand to quiet him. "Zuriel has brought wisdom to this discussion. We should consider this wisdom." The priest paused before he spoke again. "But the instructions require that the man should stay here at the temple for eight days."

Zuriel said nothing.

"Let me speak to the other priests." He returned to the other priests and huddled them together to explain. Then he turned to the brothers and cousins. "This son of Israel," he nodded toward the man on the bench, "will stay in the courts of the temple for eight days to follow the admonitions of Moses."

The brothers and cousins hugged each other and hugged the one who had been healed, and then he was led away by the priests. The crowd dispersed. Only Asriel lingered, anger and bitterness in his face.

The report of the incident came to Annas quickly, as did all events at the temple. For him it may have been the first time that he had heard the name of the rabbi from Galilee, Jesus bar-Joseph. But he would soon hear it again, and he would hear it often.

Chapter 32

Antipas and Herodias

"Aretas is offended. He may retaliate. It could mean war." It was one of the eldest of the council members who spoke. I had just arrived at the house of Annas, answering his summons. A dozen donkeys stood tethered outside. Inside the house perhaps twenty members of the Sanhedrin had convened. Joseph and Nicodemus were among them.

Two scribes sat in the corner at tables, their pens ready. Annas sat at the front of the gathering, his face impassive as always. His sons stood at the door of the hall as I entered.

"Aretas is a proud man, a proud king," the old man went on. "He will not suffer this indignity." There were grunts of acknowledgement in the room.

Caiaphas saw me and came over, concern showing on his face. He took me just outside the door and explained. "Antipas enticed his brother's wife, Herodias, to join him at his palace at Sepphoris. Phasaelis, the wife of Antipas, heard of the plan and has returned to her father, Aretas, in Nabatea."

I recalled Manaen's letter and the concern he had while the two half-brothers were in Rome.

Ananus leaned near, smirking, "Did she require two donkeys for her escape? Would one only be adequate for her bulk?" He laughed at his own joke, as did his brothers. He went on, "Some have asked, since the canyons at Petra are reputed to be narrow, can she enter that way, or will she have to go over the mountains to return to her father's house?" He and his brothers laughed again.

Caiaphas led me away from the door. "My brothers-in-law find humor where there is danger," he said sternly. "Aretas will not let this slight go unpunished. The Nabateans are a proud people. Antipas himself carries Nabatean blood, but he is a fool. If Aretas brings an army against Antipas, we in Judea, although we are not involved, will certainly suffer. We border both kingdoms."

"What is the will of the council?" I asked.

"The first thought was to send a delegation to Aretas, condemning Antipas's actions, but advising restraint. That idea was rejected. Wiser members cautioned that a delegation might only accentuate the embarrassment, so a letter is being drafted instead."

"Am I to deliver that letter?"

"No," Caiaphas replied. "Someone else will deliver the letter to Aretas. However, you will deliver a different letter—to Antipas."

He looked at me for my response, but I said nothing.

"The delegation you lead will be small, only enough temple guards to make sure you are safe."

Caiaphas had suggested six other men for the journey, but I took only two. Eldad and Nathan were both good riders and knew their weapons, enough to keep the brigands away. We took only one day to prepare for the journey, and we set out when the sky was finding its first light. Our first destination was Antipatris, now a familiar stop for me. I was interested to hear the rumors among the soldiers. The Romans, we all knew, would be concerned about the Nabateans' response to the humiliation of Phasaelis. The Romans wanted their vassal states—especially those that shared a border—to dwell in peace. Wars disrupted the collection of taxes. But a proud king like Aretas could not let his daughter's shame go unpunished. The Romans were on alert. Both those kings had small armies—not large enough to threaten the Romans but adequate to create problems if they faced each other.

We were five miles from Antipatris when I saw the dust of approaching horses coming toward us. My men put their hands to their swords, but I held my arm in the air to assure them these were not brigands. Robbers would never create such dust. My expectation was that it was a Roman contingency coming to greet us. I had sent a quick rider to Antipatris the previous day to inform the Romans we were coming. But I did not expect to be greeted on the road.

As the horses came nearer and slowed to a trot, I heard a familiar voice.

"Hail, Malchus!"

"Marius! Can that be you?" I shouted. "Again you have surprised me."

We slid from our horses and embraced.

"It is good to see you, my friend," I said.

"There is much to discuss," Marius replied, holding both my arms. "Let us first get you inside the compound. You and your men will have more food than you can eat."

After our horses were stabled and we found our beds, he had a meal of roasted lamb waiting for us, laying on a bed of herbs. After we had eaten our fill, I excused the guards. They gave their thanks to Marius and went to their beds, leaving the two of us alone.

"What does Pilate say of Antipas?" I asked.

"He says Antipas is a fool, but he is not yet ready to confront Antipas directly." He swirled the wine in his cup. "However, he wants Antipas to be aware of Rome's displeasure. Pilate has allowed me to take twenty of my cavalrymen to escort you to Sepphoris."

"You will join us tomorrow?"

"Yes. But we will deliver no written message. You and your guards will do that. Rome will send a message not that Antipas reads, but one he sees—twenty Roman cavalrymen in full battle array.

"Will Antipas heed Pilate's warning?"

"Perhaps to stop future foolishness . . . but the damage is done. Phasaelis has returned to her father." He took a drink from his cup. "This message is also for Aretas, to let him know that Rome does not approve of Antipas's actions. Perhaps Aretas will not give vent to his anger and embarrassment, at least not immediately."

We sat in silence for some time. "I have seen Sabrina," he said.

Something quickened inside me, but I said nothing.

"Only two days ago," he went on. "I am in the palace regularly. When I was there to receive instructions for this assignment, Claudia sought me out. She asked me about you." He stopped himself. "Do you have any interest?"

Nothing can come of it. Sabrina is a slave. I am a slave. What hope do we have?"

"Claudia asked—"

"Tell me no more. There is no hope. She is a slave in the house of Pontius Pilate. I am a slave in the house of Joseph Caiaphas. That cannot change—"

"Listen for a moment," Marius interrupted. "Claudia chose you once. She now wishes to choose you again—to bring you into her household."

I stared at him. "Bring me into *her* household?"

He nodded.

"Do you think Annas would agree to that?"

"It may be difficult. You have made yourself valuable to Annas and Caiaphas. Yes, they would be reluctant to release you. But Annas will not live forever. Caiaphas is not strong. And Claudia is not without influence on Pilate."

"Marius my friend, you wish me well, and I am grateful for that. But for the moment this is not something we can pursue."

That night, on my bed, I reflected on that conversation. My words were more resolute than my heart. Two voices in my mind argued with each other. One affirmed the words I said to Marius, but the other wanted to believe the chance was possible. Perhaps, as Marius had said, Claudia could convince Pontius Pilate to purchase me from Caiaphas. Perhaps Sabrina and I could be joined together. But then the other voice would say it was impossible. The two voices were still arguing when I drifted into sleep.

"My men and my horses need a challenge," Marius said the next morning as cinched our bags on our horses. He had roused me from my bed an hour before sunrise and had my breakfast waiting. "I want to make the trip to Sepphoris by nightfall." He smiled. "I have a bet with the blacksmith. He says it is not possible to reach Sepphoris by sunset. He will owe me a new saddle when I prove him wrong."

"And if you do not make it by dark," I asked him. "Will you owe the blacksmith a saddle?"

He laughed. "One cannot consider defeat, can he? But my concern is for you and your men. Can you keep up?"

"Our horses are no match for Roman war horses. We cannot hope to keep pace. But one of the guards is from Galilee. He knows these roads. We will find you in Sepphoris."

Marius saluted me and he and his men took off in a gallop.

The three of us took a slower pace that day as we made our way north across the Jezreel Valley and through the rolling hills of the lower Galilee where they steepened.

I turned in my saddle to look at the sun on my left, the orange orb hanging just above the low hills between us and the sea, throwing its color against the thin clouds. When I did, I noticed Eldad pointing toward the hills to our right, talking with Nathan. I slowed my mount to allow him to come alongside me.

"Nazareth is there," he said.

"Nazareth?"

"Do you remember the man who was healed of leprosy?"

"Yes, of course."

"The one who healed him, Jesus bar-Joseph, is from that village."

I nodded to Eldad and urged my horse on. But I looked over my shoulder at that hill several times until it was out of sight.

Less than an hour later, as we came to a small stream, we found two of Marius's cavalrymen tending to their horses.

"Both horses are limping slightly," one of them explained. "Marius instructed us to wait for you here and then go on to Sepphoris in the morning."

"Will Marius win his bet?" I asked.

The cavalryman smiled. "If it can be done, Marius will do it."

As we finished our meal, Eldad pushed another branch into the fire. Sparks flew upward and disappeared. As he sat down, I asked him a question, "You and Nathan had much conversation today. What is it you talked about?"

The fire threw light on his face as Eldad laughed. "We are Jews! What do Jews always talk about? We talk about the Law. But we also talk about the Messiah. That is what Jews talk about."

I said nothing and waited for him to go on.

He looked directly into the fire. "We wait for the Messiah. He is the one who will bring freedom. He is the one who will deliver Israel."

He took a stick and stirred the fire. "Some think the Messiah walks among us. Our prophets told us to look to Bethlehem Ephratah for him. Thirty years ago there were some signs in Bethlehem—signs that some say indicate the Messiah was born there. You have heard the story, I'm sure."

I nodded. "I know the story. The magi from the East."

Elday looked into the fire. "Yes. So we ask, did Herod kill the one he intended to kill? That is one of a thousand discussions we Jews have about the Messiah. That is what Nathan and I talk about."

"You pointed to Nazareth."

Eldad nodded. "That is the village of Jesus bar-Joseph, the one who healed the leper. He has healed many others, according to reports. That has made some ask if he could be the one we expect."

This was more than I had heard. "What do you think?"

He smiled. "If you ask Nathan," he nodded toward his associate who was now asleep, "he will tell you it is not likely. In fact, he will tell you it is impossible. He will sneer and say, 'A messiah from Nazareth? A messiah whose disciples are from a poor village? A messiah with *amharetzin* as followers? How could he deliver Israel from the Romans?' That is what Nathan asks."

"And how do you reply?"

He smiled again. "I am without answers, Malchus. I have only questions. And my question is not how such a messiah could deliver Israel from the Romans. Rather, my question is, how could he heal a leper? And how can one with such power be ignored?"

The flames illuminated Eldad's face as he looked directly at me. We both stared into the fire for some time until I rose and patted him on the shoulder. "Take your rest, my friend. We will have an interesting day tomorrow."

At mid-day we arrived at Sepphoris. Marius and his cavalrymen were resting in the shade of the scrubby oaks that surrounded Antipas' palace.

"Does the blacksmith owe you a saddle?" I asked Marius as I dismounted.

"There will be an argument," he smiled. "The question will be which sunset—the one behind the hills or the one into the sea? The hills are high in Galilee. I had not considered that when I made the wager. The sun had fallen behind those hills when we arrived here—but it certainly had not dropped into the Great Sea. Will you take my position, my friend?"

"As you said, it is an argument for you and the blacksmith."

He laughed and embraced me. "You are just in time. The tetrarch is making plans to depart the palace. He will go to Machaerus, across the river. I suspect he knew you were coming and hoped to avoid receiving the letter you carry."

"He has spies, just like Annas."

"He would have been gone by tomorrow, or at least by the next day, so I'm glad we hastened."

"Yes," I acknowledged, looking at the palace, "I'm certain he did not expect us to arrive so soon."

"Malchus, do you remember when we were in Rome, how Manaen spoke of Chuza?"

"Antipas's servant?"

"Yes, although 'servant' may no longer be apt. It appears he is the chief steward for the tetrarch, responsible for all his properties."

"Yes, I remember him. Manaen always spoke highly of him. Is he here?"

"He greeted us as we arrived. And he sent us food this morning and promised to provide more later today."

"Did he speak of Antipas?"

"Only briefly. We had little opportunity to talk, but he said that Herodias and her daughter are in the palace. He presumes they will accompany Antipas when he goes to Machaerus." He paused for a moment and smiled.

"Why do you smile?"

He shook his head. "Women. Women have such power over us, don't they, Malchus? Look at Antipas. He is risking war because of a woman. He may lose his kingdom—and his life—because he is enthralled by a woman."

"When can I deliver the message?" I asked.

"Chuza will answer that question. By the way, when he and I spoke, he asked about you. He is also aware that Manaen intends to come to Judea. He said that Manaen mentioned you in his most recent letter."

"Would that Manaen had arrived sooner, perhaps to prevent his foster-brother from this folly," I said.

"As I recall, Manaen, for all his efforts, told us that Antipas and his brother rarely heeded his advice," Marius replied.

"What you say is true."

Two hours later, the palace gate opened, and several carts laden with food rolled out, attended by servants. "That is Chuza," Marius said, pointing to the one who was leading the procession. "That must be his wife beside him."

As the food was being distributed to the soldiers, the lady came toward us. "I am Joanna," the lady said, making a small bow. "You must be Malchus," she said to me. "And you must be Marius, if I can trust Manaen's descriptions."

"I speak for both of us," Marius said, bowing his head slightly, "Manaen often spoke of you and your husband. He has great affection for you."

"And we for him." She looked behind her toward Chuza, who was directing the servants. "My husband and I would like to talk with both of you if possible."

A few moments later we were seated in the shade of the scrub oaks next to Marius's tent.

"Tell me about Antipas," Marius said. "What are his plans?"

Chuza looked at Joanna before he spoke. "We know little more than others. Antipas, these days, gives little attention to his farms or even his building projects, so he requires no reports from us. Most of what we know we hear from the house servants. A few months ago, I met with Antipas almost every day. Now? It has been nearly a week since I have seen him." He paused for a moment. "This woman has consumed him. Herodias and her daughter have taken residence here, but only temporarily. Very soon they plan to cross the river to the palace in Machaerus."

"All the house servants are preparing for the move," Joanna said. "The animals are being readied, and dozens of crates are already loaded."

"Do you think," Marius asked, "when Manaen arrives, that Antipas will take his counsel?"

The couple looked at each other before Joanna spoke. "We see little reason for that expectation. Manaen, for all his efforts, was never able to restrain his two foster-brothers." Joanna looked at her husband again before she continued. "However, Manaen is returning to Judea not only because of Antipas. He also has another reason. We believe . . . We believe he is coming because he expects the Anointed One."

We all sat in brief silence.

Chuza said, "I assume you know of what we speak."

"Of course." Marius smiled. "No one could live in this country without hearing that a great deliverer is coming who will kill all us Romans and set up a new kingdom for the Jews."

"Yes," Joanna acknowledged. "That is what many Jews pray for—and expect. However, what if the common expectation is wrong? What if this deliverer and his kingdom are different from what we have expected?"

"Go on," Marius said.

Joanna looked at her husband before she continued. "I went to Gennesaret. Manaen sent a letter and requested me to go. He seems to have had some premonition about a prophet that is preaching in Galilee."

"Is this the one who healed the leper?" Marius asked. "The one who is called Jesus bar-Joseph?"

"It is." Joanna confirmed.

"And you heard him?"

"I did." Her eyes had a far-away look.

As I recall, these many years later, that conversation under the scrub-oaks at Sepphoris, I wonder at the insensitivity of my heart. Nothing said that day prodded my stubborn soul. I had no interest in a deliverer for Israel. I had no interest in one who healed lepers. I had no interest in one who told odd stories—yet for all my lack of interest in him, he was very interested in me. That irony, in later years, was not lost on me. I, who spent all those years at the temple among those who were looking for God, was myself uninterested in seeking him. Yet the one whom I did not seek, sought me . . . and he found me.

Joanna gathered her thoughts before she continued. "He speaks as one having authority." She looked at each of us to make sure we heard her point. "All who heard him said the same. When I first heard him, I realized there was something different about the way he spoke, but I was not sure what, until someone near me said, 'He speaks as one having authority.' 'Yes,' I said to myself, 'that is what is different. This one is not like the scribes or the Pharisees or the rabbis.'"

"And what did this Jesus bar-Joseph say?" Marius asked.

A smile came to Joanna's face. "I wish I remembered every word that came from his mouth, for his words touched my heart. Fear, regret, hope, all of these emotions came to my heart."

"But what did he say?" Marius persisted.

"He told stories." Joanna let out a small laugh. "He told stories—but not ordinary stories. Well, I suppose they were ordinary stories, but they were not ordinary in the way they touched my heart."

She looked at each of us. No one spoke.

"He told a story about a son who took his father's inheritance and wasted it in a foreign land. The son was reduced to eating what was thrown to the pigs, so he decided to come home and ask to be a hired hand at his father's estate. But when he returned, his father was waiting for him—and arranged a great feast for him. The father rejoiced that his son had returned." She paused for a moment and then repeated slowly, "The father rejoiced." She seemed to search her thoughts. "I'm sorry I cannot tell the story as well as it was told the day I heard it. But that was the sense of it. I believe Jesus bar-Joseph would have us understand that the father in the story is like God, that he is willing to forgive those who return to him."

Marius's face was alert. "It is a wonderful story. Were there others? Tell us more."

Before Joanna could reply, I interrupted. "I'm sure there are more stories, and I'm sure there will be a time to hear them, but I have been given a task, and it is important that I make every effort to fulfill it."

Chuza spoke, "My master, I am afraid, has already determined—determined accurately, it would seem—your purpose here. He has instructed me to inform you that he is readying himself for a journey, and he is very sorry he cannot receive the high priest's delegation."

"In that event," I said, "I ask Marius of the Roman legions to attest that I have delivered the message from Caiaphas the high priest to Chuza, the steward of Herod Antipas." I handed the document to Chuza.

"I do so attest," Marius said. "And I will so attest in the company of the high priest."

He turned to Chuza. "Will Antipas read this letter?"

"He will read it. But he will ignore it. He is enthralled by Herodias, and the damage he has done cannot be remedied. I can guess the letter's contents. It is an injunction that Herod Antipas refrain from this relationship with Herodias."

I nodded.

"But the damage is done. Phasaelis has returned to Nabataea—to her father. Aretas, I imagine, is already planning revenge. He is a proud man among a proud people. Only the Romans," he nodded to Marius, "are able to keep Aretas and the Nabataeans from bringing an army against Antipas. He has suffered an insufferable humiliation. He will not, in my estimation, let it pass."

No one spoke for a moment.

I broke the silence. "My duty has been discharged. Marius, we are free to return to Jerusalem."

Joanna spoke quickly, "My master may fail to receive you, but you will not return to Jerusalem until my husband and I have extended our hospitality for the night. The palace may be closed to you, but we have other rooms, not as lavish but adequate, and we will make every effort to make you comfortable and rested before you begin your return journey."

"My lady," Marius said with a broad smile, "I am a Roman soldier and am accustomed to taking orders. I hereby acknowledge my orders and promise my obedience. Direct us to our quarters."

We began to disperse but then Marius spoke again, "My friends, before you go I must tell you of a report I heard about from my fellow Roman soldier, Atticus, who commands a century posted outside Capernaum. He gave me the report himself. According to him, Jesus bar-Joseph healed his servant, a young man more like a son than a servant. Atticus is known for his honor and integrity, as well as his generosity. There are soldiers whom I would not trust for any report, but Atticus has my full trust. He told me his servant was dying—and he was desperate for the boy. He had heard about Jesus' healing the leprous man, so he went to him and pleaded with him to restore his servant.

'I had tears in my eyes when I came to the rabbi,' he told me. 'I, a Roman soldier, commander of a century, pleading with a Jewish rabbi for help—with *tears* in my eyes. I begged him for the life of my servant, but I told him I was not even worthy for him to come inside my house. I told him I was a man with authority, but not a man with authority over disease. I asked him just to speak a word, and I was sure the servant would be healed. Jesus looked at me for a moment, and I quivered when I saw the affection in his face. He turned back to the crowd following him and lauded me for my faith. But in truth I wonder if it was faith or desperation that brought me to him. Jesus never spoke to me. He simply nodded, and in that nod there was somehow confirmation and dismissal, and somehow I knew my request had been granted. I ran back to my house and found my servant sitting on the edge of his bed, taking water and requesting food.'"

Marius paused. "That is the story that Atticus the Roman centurion in Capernaum told."

"We have heard the same." Joanna said. Atticus is well known among the Jews for his kindness and generosity, and we do not doubt his honesty."

"Atticus," Chuza said, "recognized the same thing that others of us have observed—that Jesus bar-Joseph not only speaks with authority, but also commands authority."

The others nodded in agreement, and then we went to our quarters.

At Sepphoris the sun falls early over the hills that rise on the west between the Galilee and the Great Sea. It had just dropped over the peaks that buffer the Plain of Sharon, throwing shades of purple and orange across the sky, when Marius came to summon me from my quarters. "Come look," he said, with a smile on his face.

Outside, all the men in his troop stood looking toward Antipas's palace. There on the lowest porch I could see a woman—or a girl—dancing near the edge of the railing. Her outer robe was draped on the balustrade and only her thin linen tunic covered her young body. No music accompanied her except the metal cymbals on her fingers. She moved fluidly, and the thin tunic flowed with her dance.

Marius's cavalrymen enjoyed the show and swapped leering comments among themselves.

"It is the daughter of Herodias." Marius said. "Salome. Chuza said she likes to dance—especially when she has an audience."

"She has an audience today," I replied.

Salome came nearer to the edge of the rail and looked down, her tunic clinging to her body as she gyrated her hips, bringing groans of appreciation from the soldiers.

"I hope this dance ends soon," Marius said. "Otherwise, my men may be difficult to control."

Salome's dance went on for some time until she ended the performance in a frenzy of finger cymbals and gyrations. The men cheered as Salome sauntered by the edge of the rail to pick up her stola, nodding to her audience.

We were fed well that night. Chuza and Joanna lingered after our meal. She did her best to recount one more story from the Galilean rabbi, and we talked about Manaen's coming.

"I expect him on the first boat the weather allows," Chuza said. He looked at Marius.

What is it in the hearts of men and women that make them receptive to the truth of God? Some men and women seemed ready to hear the news about the Messiah as soon as it arrived. Marius, Chu-

za, and Joanna were among these. I was not. My senses were dull to the news. I had no interest in this Nazarene preacher, this moralist, this miracle-worker. For me it took the hacking of my head before what was apparent to others became apparent to me.

We departed Sepphoris the next morning and lingered for an extra night at Antipatris at Marius's insistence. He gave me a strong embrace as I departed the next morning. I would not see him the remainder of that winter.

Through that winter the talk in the streets and in the temple was tense. The men of the city were concerned about Aretas. "It was wrong of Antipas," men said, "wrong of him to take his brother's wife." "Will it lead to war?" some asked. "The Romans will not allow a war," others countered. "Neither of them—Aretas nor Antipas—have enough soldiers to contend with the Romans." And although neither men had a significant army, all knew that Aretas's anger boiled at the humiliation of his daughter, and would seek revenge. Pontius Pilate, realizing the tension, added forces in the south to discourage the Nabateans from coming north, and we all watched carefully to see what would develop.

As the city waited, more reports came from the Galilee about the rabbi from Nazareth. Throngs followed him, some coming from great distances to be healed or to hear his teaching. Stephen, the young student of the law, was among those from Jerusalem who heard the rabbi. "He says we should love our enemies," Stephen reported to Nicodemus and Joseph. "He also says a tree is known by its fruit—and that it is a *woe* to us when all people speak well of us, for so did those in the old days speak of the false prophets."

"It is unusual teaching," Joseph said.

"Indeed," Nicodemus concurred.

Chapter 33

The Pool of Bethesda

A few days before Passover I found Nicodemus and Joseph huddled together in the porticoes. Their demeanor was more serious than usual.

"Shalom," I said. "I shall not disturb you,"

Nicodemus stood and motioned with his hand. "Come near, Malchus. You are always welcome—and there is something we should tell you."

"Yes," Joseph concurred.

"You should also know the information I am providing to Joseph," Nicodemus continued. "The rabbi from the Galilee, Jesus bar-Joseph, is in Jerusalem."

Joseph nodded.

"By whose report?" I asked.

"By my report," Nicodemus replied. "I spoke with him last night. Stephen bar-Jonas arranged it."

Joseph again nodded his confirmation.

"There is much I would like to tell you about that conversation." Nicodemus paused, looking into the distance. "But it is adequate to say that I am a shaken man." He paused again, working his hands together as he thought. "At some time I will tell you of the conversation. But for now it is important that you know the rabbi is in the city—and that there are those in my own sect who wish him killed."

"For now," Joseph said, "we do not believe Annas has commissioned his death—but I sense it would be a convenience to him if he were killed."

"Yes," Nicodemus added, "My Pharisee brothers are infuriated. They say he does not adhere to the Sabbath traditions. They say he speaks heresies. Some would like to have his heresies—as they call them—purged from Israel. And that is why you and Zuriel should know that the rabbi is in the city, and he is in some danger. Both Joseph and I have counseled patience—but we know that counsel may be ignored."

"I will report this to Zuriel," I said.

"Thank you," Nicodemus said. "Please make every effort to keep Jesus bar-Joseph safe. My conversation with him shook me. It—" he was unable to finish his thought.

Joseph stood. "My friend, you have spoken of the Sabbath. It approaches." He looked at the sky to gauge the angle of the sun. "In a few hours we will gather for the Sabbath meal. Both of us should return to our homes."

I dismissed myself, and sought out Zuriel, and gave him the information.

"Joseph and Nicodemus are among the best men in Israel," Zuriel said. "We should honor their wishes. I will dispatch two of my best guards to watch this rabbi and protect him."

The next day, at the sixth hour, when the sun was at its highest, I was summoned by Zuriel and met him near the Nicanor Gate.

"An odd thing." He looked confused. "My guards found the Galilean rabbi and his disciples near the Gate of the Sheep. They followed him to the Pools of Bethesda where the sick and lame and blind gather." He hesitated.

"Go on," I said.

"There is a crippled man who has been there many years. How many I do not know, but many times I have seen him at the pool." Once again he paused.

"What is it?"

"My guards tell me the man is walking about. He has been healed."

"Healed?"

"Yes, healed. When he left the pool, some of the scribes told him it was unlawful for him to carry his bed on the Sabbath. But he responded, 'The one who healed me told me to take up my bed. What else could I do?'"

"Where is the rabbi now?" I asked.

Before Zuriel could answer, Asriel, other scribes, and several Pharisees came rushing up. "He must be arrested!" Asriel said.

"Of whom do you speak?" Zuriel answered coldly.

"Do not show your insolence. You know of whom I speak. I speak of the Galilean who has no regard for our traditions, the one who violates our Sabbath."

"And speaks blasphemy!" one of the Pharisees added. "He said he was sent by God."

"Jesus bar-Joseph and his followers have left the city," Zuriel replied.

"Send your officers to arrest him," Asriel said.

"My officers, as you know," Zuriel answered, talking as if explaining an issue to a child, "have great duties at the temple. They are needed here. I cannot spare them at this time. However, I would be willing to issue you a writ authorizing you to arrest the Galilean. But as you consider it, you might think of his followers. They were not an insignificant number, and you may have seen how attentively they listened to him as he spoke. And you might consider how they might respond if you tried to arrest him."

The Pharisees and the scribes looked at each other.

"Shall I write the authorization?" Zuriel asked.

"Your insolence knows no bounds, Zuriel, captain of the temple guards," Asriel said. "The high priest will learn of your insolence and of your unwillingness to uphold the laws of our nation."

The men turned and walked away, grumbling among themselves.

"I think," I said, "the threat of Asriel is an empty one. You have little to fear, my friend, of any difficulties from the high priest."

Zuriel smiled. "Annas likes Asriel less than I. He will not intervene—not as long as the goats and lambs are being purchased and the coins are being exchanged."

In the end, nothing further came of the incident, although it increased the curiosity in Jerusalem concerning the rabbi from the Galilee.

"Antipas has arrested the Baptizer." Zuriel brought the news. We stood at the wall of the temple overlooking the Kidron Valley. Pockets of snow lay in the crevices of the hill just below the olive grove. Thin rivulets of water formed streaks on the bank feeding into the Kidron. The *tink, tink, tink* of the silversmiths' hammers rose from their shops along the valley. In the grove a man and his young son stacked dead branches from the olive trees in their hand-cart.

"He criticized Antipas for taking his brother's wife," Zuriel continued. "He should have kept silent."

John, I thought to myself, was not a man who kept silent. A man who would hurl a rock in the direction of the son of the high priest would not hesitate to criticize the tetrarch for stealing his brother's wife.

"Antipas has brought John to the palace at Machaerus," Zuriel added, "beyond the river, where the tetrarch and his new wife have sought sanctuary from criticism."

We stood side by side looking across the valley, saying nothing. The sky was low, gray and somber, a sky befitting the news we had received.

"Look," Zuriel said, pointing across the valley. "The almond trees are wiser than us, I think. Do you see the blossoms?"

I squinted my eyes as I searched the string of almond trees lying below the olive grove. The first few blossoms, their white matching the white of the snow pockets, were beginning to bloom.

"The almonds have hope." Zuriel said. "Even when there is no reason to think that spring will come, they still put out their blossoms."

I put my hand on Zuriel's back. "I wish I were as hopeful as the almond tree."

"The almond blossoms tell us one more thing," Zuriel said. "Passover is approaching. It is when I see the first blossoms that I notify the priests to send their representatives to the villages to repair the roads and bridges. It is time to prepare for Passover."

Chapter 34

A Kingdom is Announced

"These are true citizens of Israel!" Joseph the Arimathean laughed.

Two goats, tethered too closely in the pen at the Court of the Gentiles, butted their heads together.

"Look how they contend with each other!" He snickered. "Perhaps one is a Sadducee and the other is a Pharisee!" He burst out laughing.

Nicodemus smiled—a weary and wise smile. "You have spoken accurately, my friend." The two goats bashed their heads against each other again. "Ah, the Pharisee got the better of the Sadducee that time."

The promise of the almond trees, mentioned by Zuriel, had been fulfilled. The last pockets of melted snow turned the banks of the valley into mud. Above them the olive trees were gaining their green and sending out tiny white blossoms.

"You know where we sit," Nicodemus said to me. "Join us when you can. Young Stephen has again been to the Galilee and brings a report."

Less than an hour later I made my way to the place.

"It is a dangerous thing—to talk about a new kingdom." It was Amos, one of the Pharisees known for his calm demeanor, who spoke. He and a handful of others, including some Sadducees, had joined Joseph and Nicodemus on the benches of the Royal Portico.

"Yet," Stephen answered. "When you hear him speak of this kingdom, it will set a spark alight in your heart." He stood before the men, giving his report. "I cannot tell you much about this kingdom, but I know it does not depend on an army to be established. It is most intriguing."

"And why, master Stephen," Amos asked, "would you be intrigued by this Galilean rabbi and what he says about a kingdom?"

Stephen smiled. "A difficult question. I have asked it of myself a hundred times, and I have yet to answer it adequately." He looked around at the men who had gathered. "You men know me. My father sent me here to Jerusalem eight years ago when I was only twelve. He sent me that I should learn from the greatest teachers in our nation. His dream for me was that I learn the Law of Israel and that I teach it to others. For eight years I have received the instruction of the wisest men in Israel. Could one count the hours that I have spent under their tutelage? I think not. I have learned the Torah. I have learned the prophets. I have studied the opinions of the sages. I have examined the decisions of the scholars. However . . ."

"What?" Amos asked.

"Yet the teaching of Jesus bar-Joseph is different."

"In what way is it different?" Amos asked. "Tell us how the teaching of Jesus bar-Joseph differs from the teaching of the experts in the law."

Stephen looked around at the men waiting for his answer. "I wish for each of you the opportunity to hear Jesus bar-Joseph himself, for I am not able to adequately convey what he says—or how he says it. But let me make an effort. Let me start this way—If I were sitting with other students at the feet of one of the rabbis here in Jerusalem— as I have done many times—and our topic was sin and repentance, my teacher would refer his students to the Talmud, particularly the *Berakhoth*, the commentary on prayers and benedictions, or to the *Abhodah Zarah*, with its discussion of idolatry, or perhaps he would direct us to the *Vayyikra Babba,* in the *Midrash,* and its examination of the laws of Leviticus. After we had read these instructions, we would be directed to discuss what the sage Hillel, or rabbi Shammai, or Yohanan ben Zakkia said in his commentary of these topics. We would be asked how each of these men, and others, contributed to our better understanding of sin and repentance. That discussion would lead to a *further* discussion, perhaps," pointing to the temple behind him, "of the importance of sacrifice for sin to be atoned."

He paused for a moment, collecting his thoughts.

"All my teachers—and I have had many—defer to other teachers. They refer to other scholars to verify their opinion. They all cite various positions on the subject. But Jesus bar-Joseph does none of this. He makes no such references. He quotes no scholars nor does he speak of the opinions of either Sadducees or Pharisees. Rather—and let me say this carefully—he speaks as if he were speaking the thoughts of our heavenly Father."

The men looked at each other to gauge each other's reaction.

Stephen went on. "He not only teaches differently than the scribes and rabbis. He also conducts himself differently. A few days ago, in Capernaum, Simon the Pharisee invited Jesus bar-Joseph and others, including me, to his house for a meal. I do not know Simon's motive, but it is not unlikely that the invitation came at the suggestion of some here in the city."

"Not unlikely at all," Nicodemus said. "Many among our party are suspicious of him and are concerned about the crowds that follow him and seek to trap him in something that would incriminate him."

Stephen went on. "Shortly after he arrived and took his place, there was a commotion at the door, and a woman, a prostitute, broke free from those trying to restrain her, and entered the house. A prostitute! The Pharisees clamored to get away from her. They backed up to the walls, whispering curses at the woman. But Jesus kept his place, reclining at the table. The woman brought a flask, full of ointment. She knelt at Jesus' feet and began crying and wiping his feet with her hair. She applied the ointment, all the time sobbing, her body convulsing as she rubbed the ointment on his feet. Whispers went along the wall where the Pharisees had taken refuge. 'Surely he knows this woman is a sinner.' And 'If he were a prophet, he would surely know.' Jesus looked up and spoke. 'I have something to say.' Simon replied. 'Say it, Rabbi.'

'A certain money-lender had two debtors. One owed five hundred denarii, and the other fifty denarii. When they could not pay, he cancelled the debt of both.' The woman continued to weep and continued to rub the lotion on Jesus' feet. He looked at the men cringing at the wall and asked, 'Which of those two men will love him more?'

Simon answered, 'The one, I suppose, for whom he cancelled the larger debt.'

'You have judged correctly,' Jesus said.

Then he turned toward the woman, whose sobbing continued. 'Do you see this woman, Simon? When I entered your house, you gave me no water for my feet, but she has wet my feet with her tears and wiped them with her hair. You greeted me with no kiss, but she has kissed my feet. You did not anoint my head with oil, but she has anointed my feet with her ointment. Therefore, I tell you, her sins, which are many, are forgiven—for she loved much. But he who is forgiven little, loves little.'"

Stephen paused and narrowed his eyes as if he were seeing the event again. "Murmurs ran through those who were pressed up against the wall. 'Who is this, that even forgives sin?' Jesus looked at each of those men, but they averted their eyes. They could not return his gaze. He put his hand on the shoulder of the sobbing woman and said, 'Your faith has saved you. Go in peace.'" Stephen went quiet.

After a moment Amos spoke, "What are we to make of this? Does this Jesus bar-Joseph claim to be the Anointed? Does he claim he can deliver Israel? Does he call himself a king?"

"You have more questions than I have answers, brother Amos," Stephen replied. "Perhaps he will attend the Passover. If so, you can hear him for yourself—and ask whatever questions you may have."

The men were still in discussion as I left them. Stephen's report concerned me. If the Galilean rabbi came to the Passover, there might be trouble. Zuriel should be alerted.

"By the power of the demons he casts out demons!" Asriel's shrill voice filled the hall.

A slanting afternoon sun angling through the high windows threw muted reflections off the marble columns and onto the squares of the floor of the Hall of Hewn Stones—illuminating the concern and confusion on the faces of the men gathered. More than half the seventy seats of the Sanhedrin in this half-circle room were occupied. Nicodemus and Joseph were both in the hall—but on opposite sides of the room. I had accompanied Caiaphas and Annas from their houses to the temple, where they had taken their places on the raised dais at the front of the hall.

A delegation had been sent from the Sanhedrin to investigate this new prophet, and now Asriel stood before its members giving his report. Sitting nearby, waiting his turn to report, was Stephen, who had joined the delegation.

"He profanes our holy day. He has no regard for the Sabbath. His disciples gathered grain on the Sabbath. And on the same Sabbath he performed a healing."

Some of the Sadducees rolled their eyes, but the Pharisees grunted their approval.

"By the power of the demons he casts out demons!" he repeated.

The reports had been regular. Jesus bar-Joseph had increased his following—several thousand people now gathered when he preached.

"I hope," Ananus said to his brothers, loud enough to be heard by those around him, "that Stephen does not smell of fish guts when he gives his report. The Galilean has surrounded himself with fishermen, I have heard."

One of the Sadducees stood and asked Asriel a question: "Did you observe these men gathering grain on the Sabbath? Did you witness this healing on the Sabbath? Did you see these things yourself?"

"My Sabbaths are spent in prayer and fasting, not following some false prophet who cares nothing for the traditions of our ancestors," Asriel snarled.

"So you cannot attest to this healing of which you speak," the Sadducee went on.

He looked at Stephen. "I have summoned a witness."

Before Stephen could be called, Annas leaned over to Caiaphas and whispered something. Caiaphas then asked, "This prophet, this son of a carpenter, from what you have determined—does he speak of a kingdom?"

"It is reported he speaks often of a kingdom," Asriel replied.

A buzz went through the hall as the council members commented to each other.

"We will hear from Stephen bar-Jonas," Caiaphas said.

As Stephen came forward, one of the Pharisees shouted, "What blasphemy does the Galilean spout these days? Does he call himself a prophet? A prophet from the Galilee? Around him he has gathered a few smelly fishermen. And a tax collector. And at least one insurrectionist. How can he call himself a prophet?"

Stephen waited until all the denunciations had ended. He then acknowledged the council. "Brothers and fathers, please hear me. To what my brother Asriel has reported, I can attest. I saw the man who was healed. His arm hung useless to his side until Jesus bar-Joseph told him to stretch it out—and his arm became whole. He raised both arms and gave glory to God for his healing."

"Did this take place on the Sabbath?" Caiaphas asked.

"Yes, as my brother has reported, this occurred on the Sabbath."

A Pharisee stood and was recognized by Caiaphas. "Asriel holds that this man heals and casts out demons by the power of the demons. What do you say of that?"

"The rabbi was asked the same question. My answer would be the same as his: 'If Satan casts out Satan, he is divided against himself. How then will his kingdom stand?'"

Smiles of amusement came to the faces of a few in the hall, but Asriel's jaw clenched tighter.

"This rabbi has spoken of a kingdom," Caiaphas said. "Does he purport to gather his followers and form a new kingdom?"

"If so," a thin smile formed on Stephen's face, "it seems he has chosen the wrong people for his followers. A more unlikely group to form a new kingdom I cannot imagine. Most are common people, the *amharetzin,* who are desperate to find hope in the world. They do not seem to be ones who would form a kingdom."

The Pharisee, still standing, asked, "What do these people—those who follow this rabbi—say about him?"

Stephen paused before he replied: "They are amazed by him. Amazement is the common response—not just at the healings, but also at his teaching. He teaches differently from the other rabbis...." His voice trailed off as if he were trying to collect his thoughts.

"And how," the Pharisee went on, "is this rabbi's teaching different?"

"The people say he does not—" he looked at Asriel warily "—teach like the scribes. Instead he teaches with authority."

"He has no authority!" Asriel erupted. "No authority has been conferred on him! He does not follow the fasts! He does not honor the Sabbath! He does not follow the teaching of our forefathers! He has an unclean spirit!"

Caiaphas raised both his hands to calm Asriel. Annas leaned over to him, said something, and Caiaphas asked, "We have a question about those who follow him. Do these consider him to be the Anointed One—the one who will deliver Israel?"

"Many ask this question. It is often on the lips of the followers."

Again Annas leaned in to Caiaphas, and Caiaphas asked Stephen, "And what of the rabbi? What does he say? Does he consider himself the redeemer of Israel? Does he call himself the Anointed One?"

All movement in the hall ceased. Every man went quiet. Stephen looked around the hall. "I have not heard Jesus bar-Joseph call himself the Anointed One. Instead he refers to himself as 'the Son of Man.'"

I looked at Annas when Stephen spoke. He winced as if his face had been slapped. His eyes went from side to side in the room, examining the response of the council. They had formed clusters and were arguing among themselves. The words "Son of Man" came from the lips of many.

"I have brought the scroll of Daniel," Stephen said loudly, trying to gain the council's attention. When the noise subsided, he unrolled the scroll and read:

> And behold, with the clouds of heaven there came
> one like the Son of Man,
> and he came to the Ancient of Days and was present-
> ed before him.
> And to him was given dominion and glory and a
> kingdom, that all peoples,
> nations, and languages should serve him; his domin-
> ion is an everlasting dominion,
> which shall not pass away, and his kingdom one that
> shall not be destroyed.

The council members all began to talk at once, some in great agitation. Caiaphas, after some moments gained control of the hall.

"He should be arrested!" a Pharisee shouted, and a few others voiced their approval. The noise in the hall swelled again.

Then Joseph stood and tapped his walking stick on the smooth stones. He rarely spoke in the council and his fellow council members were surprised that he stood. "My fellow members of the Sanhedrin, I counsel patience." He paused to look around the hall. "Our nation, since we came out of Egypt, has had difficulties—and we have difficulties now. Our Roman ruler has his own difficulties, as all of us know. He does not know what the next few months hold for him, and neither do we. We must pray that whatever happens in Rome and among the Romans, that we do not suffer because of their intrigues. And while the Romans have their intrigues, we have our own. Antipas, our former king's son, has taken his brother's wife and in so doing, angered the Nabateans. Will the Nabateans wage war? That is the question on many lips in Jerusalem. In a few weeks we will celebrate the Passover. For all the glory we take in that celebration, we all know that as the city is swelled with people, some, like the Zelotes, would use the celebration to disturb the peace and bring the wrath of the Romans on us. I counsel patience. These are times of tension. Let us not add unnecessarily to that tension. This Galilean rabbi has created a following—this we acknowledge—but he and his followers have done nothing to warrant arrest. Such action could aggravate those followers and lead to unrest. This is no time for the people of Israel to add to the unrest in our land. The Romans have enough concerns. We should not add to them. I counsel patience."

As he sat down, clusters of the members of the Sanhedrin began talking among each other. Annas looked at Caiaphas and nodded. At the prompt from his father-in-law, Caiaphas stood, "Joseph of Arimathea has advised patience and we will follow his counsel in this matter. The council of the Sanhedrin is now dismissed."

As I followed Caiaphas out of the hall, a few of the Sanhedrin clustered in the back with Asriel. Not all, it appeared, agreed with Joseph's advice.

The note I received from Manaen was brief:

Manaen to Malchus.

Greetings and peace to you.

I am in Caesarea. I came quickly when I learned that Antipas had imprisoned John the Baptizer. I am sorry to have given you no prior notice of my arrival. I hope to see you soon, but first I must go to Sepphoris, where I will see Chuza and Joanna and learn what I can from their reports. I then hope to go across the river to Machaerus to see Antipas as soon as possible. Antipas has not listened to my counsel before, but perhaps he will hear my appeal for him to release John the Baptizer. My efforts to convince him to abandon his relationship with Herodias, his brother's wife, had no effect. However, I hope he will listen to me and release John. I must make the effort. But before I go to see Antipas, Pilate wants to consult with the Sanhedrin. I am sending requests to a few members. Nicodemus is among them. I have also requested that you accompany that delegation. I hope to see you soon in Caesarea.

Chapter 35

The Caesarea Delegation

A few days later, a delegation that included me, Nicodemus, and a few other members of the Sanhedrin arrived in Antipatris on our way to Caesarea at the request of the prefect. Marius was assigned to accompany us on the final day of our trip.

We had finished our evening meal. Marius had servants arrange pillows around a fire in the courtyard and then dismissed himself to check on the horses.

"Brother Nicodemus, your face speaks of something your lips are reluctant to say." It was Amos, the oldest member of the group who spoke. "Are we not your brothers? Should we not help you bear the burden your face betrays? Is there not something you have to say to us?"

The melancholy Nicodemus carried was constant, but on this day it seemed more evident. A reluctant smile came to his face, illuminated by the fire, and he nodded his head in agreement. "My brother, I am grateful for your concern. Yes, I suppose I bear a burden, and a man should not bear burdens alone when he has brothers with strong arms beside him. Every donkey has a limit as to what he can carry. When he has more than he can carry, he should look around at the other donkeys to see if they are willing to take a portion of the load."

"Yes, Nicodemus," Amos said. Your fellow donkeys would be honored to assume some of your burden." Laughter came from the group.

He paused for a moment and looked around at the other members of the Sanhedrin. "I have not spoken of this before, but perhaps now is the time for me to tell of this. In Jerusalem we are hearing much about this Galilean, the rabbi—if rabbi is the proper title—from

Nazareth, Jesus bar-Joseph. I spoke with him. It was just before Passover. I had heard of his miracles in the Galilee, and I sought an opportunity to speak with him. Stephen bar-Jonas, the one who is called 'the impertinent one,' who has been often to the Galilee to hear Jesus bar-Joseph, arranged the meeting." He paused. "Like all of you," he looked around at the faces illuminated by the fire, "I have always prayed for the Deliverer, the Anointed One, the one who will redeem Israel. Last year, as Malchus can attest, he and I and others, including the youngest son of the high priest, journeyed to the Jordan River, just above the point where the waters spill into the Sea of Asphalt. As all of you know, that was the site where the son of Zacharias, the one called John the Baptizer, carried out his preaching. It was an interesting trip." He paused and a smile came to his lips. "The Baptizer did not easily suffer insolence, did he, Malchus?" I nodded in agreement. "And he was not unwilling to fling a stone at an arrogant man, no matter whose son he was. Am I right?" He smiled and I nodded again.

Nicodemus took a deep breath. "I made that journey to ask one question, and one question only. However, I thought the opportunity to ask that question had been lost as our group scrambled away from the river, hoping to avoid the stones the Baptizer held. But I paused for a moment. I persevered to ask him, "Are you the Redeemer of Israel?" His answer was certain. He made no such claim, yet if I understood him correctly, and I believe I did, he intimated that the Redeemer might, *even now*, be among us."

The men around the fire looked at each other.

"We are implored to be 'watchmen on the walls,' are we not?" Nicodemus went on. "We are required to be alert. We, who count ourselves as Israelites, should heed the promises made to us. Our scriptures promise a Redeemer, and that promise sustains us. You know that I have always sought to find the one who would redeem Israel. Will he come in our lifetime? I cannot say, yet a watchman on the wall should always be alert. All of you have gray beards. All of you can remember the odd occurrences thirty years ago when those magi came from the east and met with Herod. All of you know what the prophet said, 'But you, O Bethlehem Ephratah, who are too little to be among the clans of Judah, from you shall come forth for me one who is to be ruler of Israel, whose coming forth is from of old, from ancient days.'"

Some of the council members formed the words on their lips as Nicodemus recited the passage.

"Whatever the magi reported to Herod, apparently it struck fear in his heart. All of you can remember the massacre."

Nicodemus squinted his eyes as if he were reimagining the conversation only a few weeks earlier. "Do not worry, my brothers. I will get to the point of my story and after all, we have much wood for the fire." Nicodemus took a deep breath. "We, Jesus bar-Joseph and I met at night. That was my request." He smiled. "After all, I am a member of the Great Council! I am a ruler of Israel! What would my brothers in the Sanhedrin—including all of you—think of me if it were known that I was mingling with someone who was, according to our council, a blasphemer and a false teacher?"

At that moment Marius returned and took a seat beside me.

"I should warn you, Marius," Nicodemus continued, "our conversation is touching on the prospect of Israel's Redeemer. Most of our brothers in the Great Council pray that he will come and drive out the Romans and restore Israel to the Jews. However," he paused to motion to the men around the fire, an impish smile on his face. "You have little worries about our delegation—these gray-beards you see are little threat to the empire."

The Jews laughed and Nicodemus went on. "It was two nights before Passover. We met at the steps below the Huldah gates at the beginning of the second watch. Jesus bar-Joseph was waiting for me when I arrived. His disciples were nearby under the olive trees that grow on the terraces below the gates. The Passover moon had slipped up over the Mount of Olives, and a few men were traversing the area. I was concerned I would be recognized. I pulled my hood closer around my face as I approached the rabbi. He noticed my nervousness and—" Nicodemus paused, trying to organize his thoughts. He looked around at those around the fire. "I have thought many times about that moment. I saw his face and—I will tell you clearly I was arrested by his countenance. What did I see in his face? Bemusement? . . . mercy? . . . pity? All of those? Perhaps. I am uncertain. But I am certain of this: the conversation I had planned, the conversation I had rehearsed, the conversation I expected—never took place."

He looked around again at his listeners. "And who were the parties to this conversation?—only two. I, Nicodemus, was one member. Who is Nicodemus? Nicodemus is a Pharisee. Nicodemus is a member of the Great Council. Nicodemus has been trained by the great teachers of the Law. Nicodemus is a rich man. How many among the Jews hold more land and more flocks and more houses than Nicodemus? Can they be counted on one hand?" The men around the fire nodded in agreement.

"And the other one in this conversation, who was he? An *amharetzin*, a Galilean, a rabbi with no training, a carpenter's son from a poor village. Which of the two in this conversation should have been ill at ease, I ask you?" Nicodemus looked around at his listeners. "The obvious answer is not the correct answer. When I saw his face, full of bemusement, yet not judgement, I was disconcerted. I was ill at ease. Then his expression changed from bemusement to—is there such a thing as stern graciousness? That was what I saw in his face as he waited for me to begin the conversation. I had rehearsed my conversation, but I stuttered for a moment before I could say the words I had practiced: 'Rabbi, it seems you are a teacher come from

God, for no one could perform these miracles unless God is with him.'

Nicodemus chuckled to himself. "I thought I was clever, asking for an answer without asking a question. I did not directly say he was sent from God, but in my thinking he had no other recourse than to either confirm or deny that he was sent from God. That was the little trap I had set with my clever words."

"What did he say?" Amos asked.

A smile came across Nicodemus's face as he looked into the fire. "He told me . . . that I must be born again."

The council members looked at each other in confusion.

Nicodemus raised his hand. "You are confused. I understand. But your confusion cannot possibly match my confusion at that moment. I have not known such discomfort before. It was greater even than when I once stood before Herod."

The others kept their eyes on Nicodemus.

"This encounter with the Galilean rabbi was different. It was not the same fear I felt when I stood before Herod. It was a different discomfort. I sensed no need to flee from him. On the contrary, there was much inside me that made me want to embrace him. Nevertheless, I felt threatened. How is it possible to be threatened but not be afraid? I cannot tell you, but there was something troubling about this discourse, an uneasiness I could not immediately identify. Then it came to me. I suddenly realized why I felt so uneasy. *It was because he seemed to know me.* In some way, this man whom I had never met—knew everything about me. He knew the question I had asked was not a genuine question. He knew it was a dishonest question. And he knew more about me than just the hypocrisy of my question. He seemed to know *me*! I was shaken. I was not thinking clearly. Perhaps I should have said, 'You did not address my question.' That would have been a reasonable response, but I had no control over this conversation. The trap I had set caught me instead.

An awkward response—some effort to struggle against the snare, I suppose, came out of my mouth: 'How can a man be born when he is old? Can he enter a second time into his mother's womb and be born?' The reply of Jesus bar-Joseph came quickly: 'Truly, truly I say to you, unless one is born of water and the Spirit, he cannot enter the kingdom of God.'"

Nicodemus went quiet for a moment as he recalled the event. "He said more—which I have committed to ink and papyrus. You are welcome to read it when you wish. He spoke of the kingdom of God, of the Spirit of God, of the judgement of God, and of eternal life." Nicodemus looked around at the men surrounding the fire. "Eternal life," Nicodemus repeated himself, looking directly into the fire. "Eternal life—at that moment there was no question in my mind that Jesus bar-Joseph, who referred to himself as 'the Son of Man,' was informing me that he was the one who could confer this eternal life."

No one spoke, and Nicodemus continued. "I came away from that conversation shaken, and I remain shaken. Have I, the one who has always claimed to seek the kingdom of God, found it? If so, what am I to do about it? Am I willing to face the scorn of the Sanhedrin to say these things publicly? I will tell you plainly, my brothers—I am enchanted by this Galilean rabbi, but I am not sure I have the courage to come alongside him."

There was silence around the fire for a moment until Nicodemus spoke again. "The words that return to me are these, the question the Galilean asked me: 'Are you the teacher of Israel, and yet you do not understand these things?'" Nicodemus looked at the faces around the fire. "It is a good question. I purport to be a teacher. I am a member of the great council. The nation of Israel considers me a leader, do they not? Yet, do I really understand the workings of our God? I do not have an answer."

The men were silent.

Nicodemus stood. "Tomorrow we will go to Caesarea to see the governor. I wish all of you a good night."

As Nicodemus turned away from the fire, he talked to himself under his breath, "Are you the teacher of Israel?"

Manaen greeted the delegation as we arrived in Caesarea. Once the necessary formalities were out of the way and we were shown our quarters, Manaen came to my room.

"How is Gavriel?" I asked. "Still absorbed in his books?"

"He is probably unaware I left Rome," Manaen laughed. "I exaggerate of course, but Gavriel will find all he needs in his books."

"Will you stay in Judea?" I asked.

"We will discuss that later," he answered. "But now we should talk about the audience with Pilate in the morning. I have recommended to Pilate that there should be an official response from Rome to the Sanhedrin concerning Antipas's behavior."

"Please do not forget John, the one they call the Baptizer," Nicodemus said. "He is a courageous man and does not deserve his imprisonment."

"Be sure, brother Nicodemus, that he will not be forgotten. I will advocate very strongly that Antipas grant his release."

I stood again in the reception hall of Pilate's palace in Caesarea on the coast of the Great Sea. The sea-breezes rustled the curtains on the open windows, and beyond them the blue-green water of the shallows met the deep blue of the deeper sea, and as the sea aroma filled my nose, I was reminded of the days Pilate and I had sailed together from Rome to Caesarea.

Three years had passed. Sailing from Rome to Caesarea seemed both like yesterday and yet, like a lifetime ago. Was I that person who sailed into this port three years earlier? Was I the person who trained in Rome? Was I the person who served as a slave on the estate? Was I the person who was taken as a boy from his home? Was I that person? That person, it seemed, had become someone else.

I stepped closer to the windows to gather more of the sea-breeze. On the open portico fronting the ocean, Pilate was dismissing his barber after his daily shave. As the barber gathered his tools, Claudia Procula stepped onto the porch and kissed her husband on his forehead. And then—it was just a glimpse as the curtains caught the breeze and spread for an instant—Sabrina stood at the door. The breeze subsided, and she was gone from view. I took a step toward the window to gain a better angle. The curtains fluttered open, and I saw her again. She seemed to me both a servant and a goddess. She stood a few paces from her mistress—in appropriate deference, waiting for Claudia to conclude her morning greeting to her husband—yet her posture was not servile. Her hands were folded in front of her as she waited, yet she stood with a measure of pride. The same breeze that tugged at the curtains also tugged at her robe, outlining her young body. Her hair was pinned, but wisps—the color of honey and bronze, played around her forehead. The breeze changed. The curtains blotted her out. Just as suddenly a small current tossed the curtains open, and I could see her again. Her chin was erect. Her posture was stately, but not arrogant.

Would a goddess have a better bearing?

As if she had some premonition of being watched, her head turned slowly toward the window. She was near enough that I could catch the blue of her eyes, near to the color of the shallows just below us. We looked at each other, and I felt a fragility in my soul I had never known before. I—who had confronted the slaver and killed men with my bow, was trained by the Roman army to be a master of weapons with a sword on my hip—felt a vulnerability in my soul I had never before known. Our eyes held for only a few seconds until the fickle breeze obscured our view again.

The wind changed, and along with Claudia, she walked away, but she turned her head slightly, looking back over her shoulder to the window where I stood. The curtain fell and then she was gone.

A man should have hope in his life. It is, I believe, a necessity of our existence. But how can a slave have hope? A germ of hope is born into every man, but slavery eventually grinds it down. A slave must always suppress the instinct of hope, for his slavery will allow little opportunity. And that glimpse of Sabrina that perhaps should have given me hope instead filled me with despair. I was a slave. I would always be a slave—or so I thought.

Pilate entered the hall. His eyes met mine, and those eyes seemed weary as he gave me an almost imperceptible nod of acknowledgement. No one else would have noticed that nod, it was so slight. However, men with shared history are apt to acknowledge each other, and he did so. I did not exceed my station and kept my acknowledgment equally imperceptible. "Greetings to the members of the Great Council of the Jews," Pilate said in a monotone, "and to the representative of the Temple Guard," he added, nodding in my direction. "Rome extends its best wishes to those who provide counsel and security for the people of this land. Please be seated."

Little of the conversation that followed do I recall. My mind stayed at the window where I had seen Sabrina. The recollection of the last time I had seen her as I boarded the ship at Puteoli three years before came back to me. And now I had seen her eyes again. We had never spoken a word to each other, and yet I wanted to believe there was some true communication between us. But the more realistic part of me determined it was just a dream.

Pilate's words brought me out of my thoughts. "We are resolved then that we will remain vigilant. We will not allow the unwise actions of others to destroy the peace of the nation."

The discussion had run something along the lines of how the prefect and the Sanhedrin should respond to the threat of instability that Antipas's marriage to Herodias had produced and the resulting tension with Aretas. It was determined that Manaen should go immediately across the Jordan River to Machaerus and counsel him to not further antagonize Aretas.

Pontius stood and we did the same. "Please extend to the Great Council of the Jews the acknowledgement of Rome to their great wisdom and leadership." We were dismissed.

As we left Pilate's hall, Manaen said, "I will leave tomorrow. I will stop at Sepphoris to learn any news from Chuza and Joanna and then proceed to Machaerus. I will deliver Pilate's warning, but my greater purpose will be to appeal for the release of the Baptizer. Wish me well."

Chapter 36

The Death of John

"The Baptizer is dead," a spice-seller said to a butcher as he trimmed the fat from the flanks of a freshly killed goat. "Antipas had his head lopped off." The butcher's shoulders drooped at hearing the news, but he said nothing. A sandal-maker from a nearby booth came, and hearing the news, cursed Antipas. Others shrugged their shoulders and went back to their work. By the end of the day, all in Jerusalem had heard the news, and the city went back to its routine. If John had stirred hope among some, that hope now seemed extinguished.

The news angered me more than I expected. John did not deserve this death. My mind went back to the river, to that day in the valley among the tamarisk trees along the river when he tossed the rock at our feet. He was a man I would like to have known better. A strong and honest man had been killed by a weak and dishonest man. Why I was angry over the death of this one man, I could not say. Jerusalem, Judea, Rome—all were unjust. The world was full of injustice. I saw injustices every day, but this injustice pierced my soul.

My feelings told me that my soul was not completely dead. Some moral sense still lay deep inside, still alive. The death of John stirred an anger in me that was different from anger I had known previously. I had only known anger toward those who had hurt me, not to another. But this death gave me anger toward Antipas.

Toward John I sensed some kind of kinship, an identification I could not explain. Never had I met a man I so admired immediately. When I saw him at the river, I saw a man indifferent to other men's opinions and values. I sensed he was a man given to unwavering convictions that were not subject to human review.

He was a man who, in a sense, had already died—at least to the ambitions of the world. So I suppose he met his death courageously. His was a life he had already surrendered. He would not have resisted the executioner.

These are realizations that have come to me in later years. At the initial news of John's death, I had none of these realizations. I sensed only anger—anger that a good man, a man with the conviction to call other men to repentance, a man with the courage to fling a stone at the impertinent son of the high priest and not worry about the consequences, a man with the courage to defy the tetrarch when he took his brother's wife and not worry about the consequences. That man was now dead, and no one seemed to care.

Nicodemus lamented that he lacked the courage of John the Baptizer. But now I asked "What did John's courage accomplish? Did it serve only to get him killed?" I had no answer for my questions, but there was anger in my soul.

A note came from Manaen, confirming what I already knew.

> Manaen to Malchus.
>
> Greetings.
>
> I have failed. My sorrow is great. John, the son of Zechariah, is dead. Antipas would not hear me. His soldiers would not permit me to pass the river. My soul is grieved. I know you join me in my mourning, for I heard you held the Baptizer in high regard. I am sorry I was not able to rescue him. I have returned to Sepphoris, where I am the guest of Chuza and Joan-

na. Passover approaches. I hope soon to come to Jerusalem.

Manaen did not come to Jerusalem for Passover. He changed his mind. Neither did Jesus bar-Joseph, as many had expected. Both stayed in the Galilee. For Jesus bar-Joseph, it seemed a wise decision to avoid Jerusalem. The clamor for his arrest, as his following increased, grew stronger among the Pharisees. "He insults us and violates our traditions," they told Annas. They hoped he would come to Jerusalem for the Passover, so he could be killed, but he remained in the Galilee. He reportedly said, "My time has not yet come."

For that I was grateful. It would have meant his death. The men who were to kill him I saw. My eyes were trained for such things. A man at worship and a man with murder in his heart have different expressions on their faces and a different way of walking. Zuriel saw them too. Three of them moved through the crowds. There may have been others outside the temple, and some along the road—all looking for the best opportunity to kill the prophet from Galilee.

Annas, I realized, must have approved the idea. He had acquiesced to the demands of the Pharisees, and I knew why. I heard Asriel talking to Caiaphas, "Does Annas want another sect like the Essenes to develop? The Essenes do not pay the temple tax. They do not make the sacrifices. They do not honor our traditions. Should we allow others to do the same—to defy the laws? This Galilean now has many hundreds of followers. If they will not follow the admonitions of our forefathers in honoring the Sabbath, neither will they follow the admonitions of our forefathers to honor the temple."

It was a clever argument. I'm sure Annas gave it careful consideration. He had little concern about keeping the Sabbath, but he had great concern about honoring the temple and the sacrifices, on which his income depended. If he allowed one Galilean faction to dishonor the traditions, similar factions could develop as well. What would keep the nation of Israel from being splintered into dozens of factions, each with its own interpretation of the laws of Moses—and few of them purchasing the sacrifices that filled the coffers of Annas and his sons?

Decisions. All men make decisions. Annas was no different. Kill the rabbi and risk a riot—or let the rabbi live and risk the revolt of the people. He would have received counsel for each of the options. Those whose voices were the most strident—calling for the death of Jesus—had the accusation of blasphemy. But in truth, Annas had little concern about blasphemy; Annas cared for the perpetuation of his power—and his revenue. If the Galilean's supporters continued to grow, his power and his revenue were threatened. In the end, Annas made his decision: The Galilean dead was less of a threat than the Galilean alive. That was the decision of Annas.

Many scribes and Pharisees came and went at the house of Annas the days before Passover, offering advice on this topic. When I saw the three men in the temple, I knew Annas had made his decision—*the prophet was to be killed.*

But he did not come to the city.

I overheard a whisper among the sons of Annas. "He is in the Galilee. He will not come to the feast." Jesus bar-Joseph, for the time being, had thwarted the plans to kill him. The collaborators dared not kill him in the Galilee, where he had his greatest number of followers. In Jerusalem it was possible. In Jerusalem, during the festival, in the crush of the crowds, some brief commotion, a quick knife thrust, straight into the heart—the rabbi is killed, but there is no one to blame, and the Passover goes on. That was the plan. I'm sure of it.

How did he know he should not come to the Passover? Was he alerted? Did he sense it himself? I do not know, but I found myself grateful that the murder had been avoided.

Passover concluded. The scribes and Pharisees were frustrated over their failure to curtail the preaching of the Galilean rabbi, and his following continued to grow.

Chapter 37
The Interim

The summer sun pushed down on the temple mount, heating the pavement-stones with a heat I felt through my sandals. A few supplicants—but only a few, mostly women with sick children—made sacrifices. The rabbis conducted their classes at first light and dismissed their students early before the sun could summon its greatest strength. The old men likewise congregated early to hear the gossip and then went home to sleep under their grapevines until the worst of the heat had dissipated. The animals penned near the booths suffered and complained and many died. The Kidron thinned, its waters trickling sluggishly between the temple and the Mount of Olives, where swallows swooped in to catch the insects that had gathered along the mud. A few wildflowers, fragile and pale, defied the sun. The primroses waited until the sun was low to open their yellow flowers. The bees however, seemed indifferent to the heat, and their buzzing was audible in the fields as they went about their labors.

Along the hill that runs toward Bethany, swaths of blue lupines filled the shaded valley. They, it seemed, had borrowed blue from the sky and now rose up in profusion, knee-high, to give the color, now condensed and richer, back to the heavens where it belonged.

The summer eventually relented, and we prepared for the Day of Atonement. Caiaphas performed his duties with minimal hesitations, but as always, with little energy, though the officiating priests were less irritated with him than in previous years. The Feast of Booths followed only five days after the Day of Atonement, and we were making preparation when we heard the news from Rome . . .

Chapter 38

News from Rome

At first it was just a rumor, but unlike most rumors in Jerusalem, this rumor was confirmed. Sejanus was dead.

The rumor circulated the first day after the Feast of Booths. For eight nights the Jews had slept on their roof-tops under their shelters, remembering their forefathers' flight from Egypt, but the celebration was now over. The boys of the families were throwing the olive and palm branches, now dried and brown, down to the street to be carried off when the whispers started. For every ten rumors in Jerusalem, nine are disproved. But this one was true.

"My men and I are on our way to the south," Marius told me as he received me at the Antonia Fortress. "Pilate wants a report from the troops he has stationed there to watch Aretas."

"A rumor—" I started.

"It is not a rumor. Sejanus is dead. Do not doubt it. The day before I departed, a ship from Rome arrived, carrying the usual items— bronzeware, silk, tin items—but a tax representative was onboard also, who had come to gather the prefect's records. I spoke with him myself on the quay.

'Tricked into coming to the Senate,' he told me. 'Thought he was going to be made emperor. Strangled to death instead. He thought the letter from Tiberius that was read to the Senate was going to make him the successor to Tiberius. But instead, it accused him of treachery. He was arrested and taken to Tullianum prison. No one leaves Tullianum alive. He didn't have many hours to regret his ambition. The executioners came soon and put the rope around his neck and choked the life from him. His body was dragged with hooks through the streets, and a great crowd gathered to cheer. The carcass was taken to the Gemonian Stairs, where it was thrown down the stairs and dumped into the Tiber, but not before many of his victims' families came to kick and beat the body. Yes, Lucius Aelius Sejanus, the equestrian who aspired to royalty, who wished to become emperor, is dead. His wife and children and many of his friends are dead also. His ambition finally caught up with him.' The tax administrator looked around to see if anyone else was near and then he said, 'Tiberius may be deranged—but he's not stupid. He finally determined that Sejanus aspired to become emperor—and was killing anyone who stood in his way.'"

Marius paused.

"What does this mean for—"

"For Pilate?" Marius completed my question. "There could be no news worse than this. Pilate was closely allied to Sejanus in Rome, and it was Sejanus who recommended Pilate for the prefectorship here in Judea."

Sejanus, the equestrian who rose through the ranks to become the leader of Rome, the patron of Pontius Pilate, the one who presumed to be emperor of Rome, was dead. How would we in Jerusalem be affected?

Rumors in Jerusalem, whether true or untrue, seem to take residence on the breezes that blow through the narrow streets. A word spoken inside the walls of Jerusalem moves quickly—as if on birds' wings—through the shops and alleys and households. "It is the end of Rome," one hopeful, but unrealistic shop-owner whispered.

"It may not be the end of Rome," came a reply, "but it's the end of Pilate."

How would this affect Pilate? That was the question that now went through the minds of the Jews. Pilate had been appointed by Sejanus and been loyal to him. He had tied his ambitions to Sejanus. How would that loyalty and that ambition serve him now?

Caiaphas had spoken openly with me when he was away from his father-in-law. "Annas takes pleasure in Pilate's dilemma." He paused for a moment as if he were working out the situation in his own mind. "He would like Pilate weakened. Weakened, but not replaced." He shook his head and smiled. "Annas had me send a letter of condolence to the governor expressing our nation's sorrow for the passing of Sejanus. *Passing*," he laughed, turning the word over slowly. "He was strangled! And they dragged his body through the city. *Passing*," he repeated, and snickered again. "Is Pontius Pilate, the prefect of Rome, sitting in his fortress along the sea in Caesarea, concerned that the same fate awaits him?"

Whatever worries Pontius Pilate may have had about his future, for the time being they were his alone. For at least the duration of the winter, he would receive no news. The *mare clausum*, as the Romans called it, had arrived. The sea-lanes, in respect of the winds that blew down from the north, had closed. They would not open until the spring. What news the first boat from Rome would bring him, he would have to wait to see.

In the house of Annas, for a few weeks after Sejanus's death, as the sons of Annas gathered, Pilate's name was often mentioned, "He will meet the same fate as Sejanus," Ananus proffered. "Perhaps not," Theophilus countered. "Perhaps Tiberius prefers a frightened governor." Annas himself said nothing about Pilate, and after a few weeks none in the house mentioned his name. The discussion of Pilate in the streets and shops waned, perhaps because all the possibilities had been exhausted. There was nothing more for anyone to say. And there was nothing for anyone to do but wait. So we waited—as did Pilate. All of us, and surely Pilate, expected news with the first boat from Rome in the spring. Until then we would wait.

Chapter 39

Harsh Words

"Harsh words," Joseph said. "Those are harsh words the rabbi speaks."

I stayed to hear the Arimathean say more.

The rains came early that fall, enough to loosen the dust from the court's stones, but not enough to rinse it away, creating a thin layer of pasty mud on the temple pavement. Nicodemus and Joseph had brought extra cushions and the afternoon rain, more mist than rain, did not seem to concern them. Concerns greater than the weather were on their minds.

"Indeed," Nicodemus replied. "'Fools and hypocrites' he called them. These are words that give impetus to his enemies. I trust that Jesus bar-Joseph knows he has enemies among my fellow Pharisees. His words may create still more."

The recent reports from the north about the Galilean rabbi had been consistent. He had recently pronounced woes on the Pharisees, accusing them of greed and wickedness. He called them fools. He said they were like "unmarked graves" that the unwary could fall into.

"None of this can I deny," Nicodemus said. "What Jesus bar-Joseph says of most Pharisees is, unfortunately, not inaccurate."

"Yet his words create more enemies," Joseph added. "Asriel and others—including some Sadducees, have made no secret that they are calling for his death."

"Although Annas probably enjoys the denigration of the Pharisees, it is the size of the crowds that follow Jesus that troubles him."

"Thousands now gather when he preaches."

"Yes," Nicodemus went on. "And I am like Annas in this way: I am less concerned about what Jesus bar-Joseph says about the Pharisees than what he says about himself. According to the reports, he continues to refer to himself as 'the Son of Man.' Annas cannot allow a new sect to develop, especially one that does not follow the traditions."

"Is that the purpose of Jesus bar-Joseph?" Joseph asked. "To develop a following? To oppose the high priest? To oppose the scribes and Pharisees? He speaks often of a kingdom. Does he plan to make himself the king of a new kingdom?"

"I do not know," Nicodemus replied. "But, as I have said, after my conversation with him, I am a shaken, unsettled man. I still have sleepless nights. The words he spoke to me: 'You must be born again' are like needles in my soul." Nicodemus looked directly at Joseph and then at me. "Will Jesus bar-Joseph declare a kingdom and make himself king? I do not know. But if he were to declare that kingdom and summon me to become a citizen of it, I cannot be sure I would not respond."

A cool wet wind had kept the commerce at the booths minimal and the attendants were glad at the end of the day when they were able to shutter their booths for the evening. I also was glad when the booths closed, for I had received word that Marius had come to Jerusalem and was at the fortress.

"Greetings, my friend!" Marius said as he handed me warm cider. We sat near a fire in the large hall.

"Likewise, greetings," I responded as I took a sip from the cup. I hung my wet cloak on a peg. "What duty brings you to Jerusalem?"

He laughed. "These days my duties are whatever I make them to be. I made up an imaginary need requiring me to come to Jerusalem, and Pilate agreed to it."

"There is much talk about Pilate in Jerusalem."

"It is the same among the troops in Antipatris and Caesarea—as it is here in the fortress and the other postings."

"Do you often see Pilate?"

Marius considered the question before he answered. "I go to Caesarea regularly, but I rarely see the prefect, at least not in an official capacity. He has quit reviewing the troops, and he seems disinterested in their training. He has withdrawn to the palace and does not come to the barracks. However, last week I saw him on his balcony. Only a few days ago, an hour before sunrise, when I came to the stables to take my horse for an early ride, I saw him. He was standing outside the Tiberium, the temple he had dedicated to the emperor. It was cool, but his arms were bare, and he had his hand on the inscription stone that has the emperor's name and his own."

Marius took a long drink of the cider before he continued. "It will be another two months before a ship departs from Puteoli, yet I am told Pilate stands on his balcony each morning looking across the sea."

"When the ships come, what do you expect?"

"I am no prophet," Marius smiled. "I cannot predict the future. The politics of Rome are unpredictable."

Chapter 40

The Feast of Lots

Marius, after a week in Jerusalem, returned to Antipatris to wait for further orders. Pilate waited in Caesarea. And it seemed all Jerusalem waited—waited for a word from Rome, a word that could not come until the winds quit on the Great Sea. A month passed.

Some snow had fallen the day when I received the note from Marius. The olive trees held the white on their crowns, but underneath them the sheltered barley stubble formed brown circles under each tree. Around the temple courts the snow had blown into knee-high drifts in the corners. The temple guards stood near their braziers to keep warm. They had little duty, for few supplicants had come to the temple this morning.

I was surprised to hear that Marius had returned to Jerusalem. He had escorted Claudia for the Feast of Lots. After the evening sacrifice, I met him at the fortress.

"Claudia has been restless in the palace in Caesarea," Marius said. "She asked permission from Pilate to come to the city for the feast. He agreed."

"Did that surprise you?"

Marius thought for a moment. "Pilate is wise to listen to his wife's wishes right now. She is, after all, the grand-daughter of Caesar, Tiberius' predecessor. Tiberius had affection for her at one time. He may still. I'm sure Pilate hopes so. She may be the only thing that protects him from Tiberius."

"Does Claudia speak of her husband?" I asked.

"Not to me. We had some conversation on the way to the city, but it was not about her husband. It was about Jesus bar-Joseph. She has heard him speak. About six weeks ago I accompanied her and her attendants to Capernaum, to hear the rabbi speak."

"Pilate agreed to this?"

"He agreed to allow her to visit Sepphoris and the Sea of Gennesaret. That was her request, but her real aim was to hear the prophet."

"Was she noticed?"

"No. She and her servant girl are both adequate riders, so we avoided a carriage and gave them some Jewish clothing. Besides, there were many hundreds gathered, including a few dozen scribes and Pharisees from the Galilee and from Jerusalem." He smiled. "Those scribes and Pharisees were not prepared for what they heard."

"What did they hear?"

"I will tell you tomorrow." He stood. "I have been asked to give a report to your Jewish friends Nicodemus and Joseph. You can hear that report."

"I bring you greetings from Manaen," Marius told Nicodemus and Joseph as we gathered in the court of the Gentiles. It seemed odd to see him in a common robe rather than his centurion's uniform.

"What can you tell us of our brother Manaen?" Nicodemus asked.

"He stays in Sepphoris. Chuza and Joanna are there as well. But he goes often to Capernaum to hear Jesus bar-Joseph. He still regrets that he was unable to gain John the Baptizer's release."

"He bears no responsibility," Joseph said.

"I have said the same," Marius said.

"Tell us—" Nicodemus said, "What does Manaen say of Jesus bar-Joseph? His opinion is well-respected with me and my brother Joseph."

"He says to tell you that his response, like that of all who have heard him with honest hearts, is that of amazement. 'What he teaches,' Manaen said, 'rings with truth in my heart.'"

"Did you yourself hear the rabbi?" Joseph asked.

"I did," Marius responded. "And I too was amazed at how the prophet carried himself. As a Roman soldier, I know something of authority and recognize when a man carries it. He was asked a question. It was from one of your scribes, one who should have authority. The question was: 'What must I do to inherit eternal life?'"

"It may have been asked to trick Jesus," Joseph said.

"Jesus' answer was unexpected. Apparently, you Jews are required by your law to love God and love your neighbor. That was what Jesus said was required."

"It is our great commandment," Nicodemus said.

"The scribe asked another question: 'Who is my neighbor?' His answer was to tell a story."

"We have heard that he often tells stories," Joseph said.

"The story was about a man—a Jew—robbed and beaten and left for dead by brigands. Both a priest and a Levite passed by the victim as he lay beside the road, but a Samaritan had compassion on the man and took care of him."

"This rabbi surely made no friends among the priests that day," Joseph said. "Speaking well of a Samaritan!"

"Indeed, there was murmuring and grumbling among the religious leaders, but many of the common people seemed to appreciate the story. It appears they have more resentment for the scribes and Pharisees than for the Samaritans."

"I must hear this Jesus myself," Joseph said. "He has unsettled Nicodemus and he has unsettled others. Why should I be exempt from being unsettled? I am asking the same question others are asking: 'Is this the Promised One?' He seems to speak in riddles, yet his riddles, these parables he tells, have an intriguing appeal. Even if I don't understand them entirely, they find a place in my heart. I hear he is accused of not speaking plainly. Perhaps it is not the fault of the speaker, but the fault of the listeners. Perhaps there is a dullness of heart that prevents our hearing."

No one seemed to be able to add to Joseph's words, so we began our goodbyes.

"Before we leave each other," Marius said to me, "I have been instructed by Claudia Procula that she would like to speak with you tomorrow."

"With me? Why would the prefect's wife wish to speak with me?"

He smiled. "Are you asking me to determine a woman's motives? I do not know why Claudia wants to speak with you, but she has an investment in you. Perhaps she feels some responsibility for you. But I do not know. You are to meet her tomorrow at the sixth hour in the palace courtyard. You can learn her motives for yourself."

My mind was still unsettled when I was admitted to Herod's palace. A servant led me into the courtyard through a path bordered by orange trees and stone columns. A stream of water ran beside us and then under us as we crossed a small foot-bridge. A few slaves whisked leaves from the marble pathway and gathered them into baskets. Although I had been in the palace itself a few times, I had never been in the courtyard. We came to a pool where the water spilled out of the mouths of bronze fish into a shallow basin where papyrus stalks ringed the pool. Pigeons splashed in the shallow water. The path had several deviations which led to porticoes sheltered by groves of trees. The servant motioned for me to follow him along one of the side paths. Overhanging willow limbs brushed my face on the narrow path which, after a few steps, opened to a circular area ringed by marble columns with benches and tables. Trailing flowers spilled from urns mounted on the walls, adding sweet scents to the air.

My mind raced. Why has Claudia sought this conversation? But the greater question was: Will Sabrina accompany her?

Footsteps came on the paving stones. Two female palace slaves brought trays of fruit and a chilled pitcher, which they placed on the marble table. They motioned to me to come and then dismissed themselves.

Then footsteps came again. It was Claudia—and Sabrina.

Sabrina walked beside Claudia, not behind her, and her steps were graceful and confident.

She does not walk like a slave, I thought to myself.

I, who had been a student of men's strides, having watched thousands of men walking in the temple, observing the stuttering timidity in the hesitant steps of slave—saw nothing of that in this young woman's pace.

Her dress was the color of the cream that lays on top of ewe's milk, the borders worked in blue, matching the sky color of her eyes. Held by delicate silver clasps, a sash in the same blue girded her waist and draped nearly to the floor. Her hair, streaked the color of honey, lay softly over her shoulders. Her sandals whisked gracefully on the stone floor as she walked.

"Greetings to you, Malchus," Claudia said as she approached.

I lowered my head. "My lady."

"It has been five years since you departed Rome and now nearly three years I have been in Caesarea, yet it is the first time I have spoken with you since—"

"Since you purchased me in the slave market."

I tried to keep my eyes on Claudia as I spoke, but I found myself looking toward Sabrina. She kept her eyes averted.

"You have my gratitude," I continued. "I have often wished for the opportunity to express my gratitude. I will always be grateful to you for rescuing me at the slave market."

She smiled. "This is Sabrina."

I lowered my head slightly but said nothing. Sabrina likewise bent at the waist, but said nothing. Wisps of hair, like finely worked bronze, curled on her forehead, trickled down to the edges of her eyes.

"Please have a seat at the table, Malchus."

"If my lady would not mind, I believe it would be presumptuous for me to sit with the wife of the prefect."

"As you wish. However, I will sit."

Sabrina helped Claudia arrange her robe as she sat, and then she bowed slightly, her eyes catching mine for a brief second as she dismissed herself to walk to the farthest wall, where she began to examine the vine blossoms.

"I asked Sabrina to excuse herself from our conversation but not to leave the courtyard. It would be inappropriate for the wife of the prefect to be alone in the courtyard with a—" She caught herself. "With a young man."

She sipped the wine and then looked at me. "I would like to talk to you about Sabrina. Her history has some similarities to yours. I found her in the slave market. She was among a group brought from the north after one of the battles in the islands. I was only eighteen at the time and she was hardly twelve, but I persuaded my grandmother to purchase her for me. For many years I have been accused of treating Sabrina as if she were my sister. It is an accusation to which I cannot claim innocence."

Claudia paused for a moment as if some private memory came to her.

"I will speak plainly, Malchus... I seek a husband for Sabrina. Would you consent—if there were an opportunity—to take Sabrina for your wife? If so, I will have my husband speak with the high priest about releasing you to our house. There, I have spoken plainly. Can you provide an equally plain response?"

The same sense of despair—of hopelessness—when I saw Sabrina just the previous day came on me again. I had ordered my life to have no hope. And the prospect that the woman who stood across the courtyard could become my wife created a hope with no hope of fulfillment.

I could say nothing.

"Well," Claudia said. "Have you nothing to say?"

I stepped toward Claudia. It surprised her and I saw fear in her face. I stood closer than was appropriate. My chest heaved. I sought the words I needed. Claudia looked around as if she were going to call for the palace guards. I stood near her face and pulled back the hair at my temple. "Look at this, my lady. Do you see this? Do you see the wedge cut in my ear? Do you know what it means? Of course you do. I am a slave to the Jews. A slave to the Jews does not have a will of his own. He is not able to 'give consent' as you say it, no matter how much he desires. His will is submerged in the will of his master. He can do only what his master dictates. Why ask me a question when I have no capability of answering? I am a slave!"

My last remark, spoken too loudly, was heard by Sabrina across the courtyard and she took a few steps in our direction until Claudia raised her hand.

I stepped back from Claudia and caught my composure. "Forgive me, my lady. I have spoken unwisely. It is to you I owe a debt of gratitude I can never repay. Your intentions are worthy. I know that. Yet I am in the custody of Annas, and I know his heart well enough to know he would never consent to my release. What could you offer him? Slaves? Money? He has no need of either. Your idea, no matter how noble your intent, has no possibility of success. Nevertheless, I appreciate your effort and again I apologize for my words."

Claudia's eyes took on a look that I recognized—but I could not immediately identify. Then it came to me. It was the expression of pity and tenderness that had often been in the eyes of the lady of the plantation as she looked at me.

As I have grown older, I have seen this instinct among women, or at least among good women—the instinct, when confronted with a boy or man in a desperate situation, to rescue, to nurture, to protect. Perhaps it is stronger among women who are childless, as Claudia was and as the lady was, as if having no child of her own to nurture and protect, must necessarily find one outside her household.

"Malchus, please accept my offer to sit."

She poured cold water in a silver cup and gave it to me as I sat down. "Your apology is accepted. And perhaps you are right. Perhaps Annas will not entertain my husband's offer. Of the outcome of such an offer, I can predict nothing. But Malchus, we must do what we can and not lose hope."

She paused and looked around the courtyard. There was some hesitation in her face. "You spoke of slavery. Does slavery have only one form? I have no wedge cut in my ear, that is true, but does that mean I am truly free? You were in Rome long enough to know what was said about me, were you not?

I said nothing.

"'The girl with a grandfather but no father.' That is what the Romans whispered when I went by. Despite the fact that Augustus was my grandfather, I was an embarrassment to the imperial family, and my youth was spent in seclusion. I will not speak of hardships. I had none, and I am certain yours were significant. But I was rarely allowed to leave my mother's house. I often heard discussions my mother had with others about me—what to do with me as I came of age. That discussion ran through all the royal houses, I am sure. 'What to do with Claudia?' It seemed to be a question without an answer. Eventually it was decided that I should be married to Pilate. It was a convenient solution for all. I, although of royal blood, yet unable to name my father, was not appropriate material to marry another in the royal line. However, Pilate, like his advocate and fellow equestrian Sejanus, was ambitious, and I was an appropriate prize for a man looking to improve himself in Rome's hierarchy. And of course, the added benefit was, contrary to custom, I was allowed to come to Palestine to join Pilate. I was removed from Rome and from Rome's scrutiny and gossip. The royal family would not have to suffer the snickers of the Roman people every time I presented myself."

She paused again, narrowing her eyes. "I will tell you of another one who knows slavery. Every morning my husband goes to the balcony and looks over the sea for sails with the imperial insignia."

Her face became even more sober. "He has a medallion. On that medallion is written *'Friend of Caesar.'* You know of it, I'm sure. Tiberius conferred it in the final ceremonies as my husband was about to sail for Caesarea. Each morning, at first light, he steps out on the balcony that looks out over the sea. He does not know that I often watch him as he scans the horizon, looking for the sail that might bring a summons for him to return to Rome. He takes that medallion with him as he stands in the early morning breeze, working it over in his hand, sometimes looking at it intently, reading the inscribed words *'Friend of Caesar.'*"

A wry smile came to her face. "The friendship of Caesar can be irregular, can it not? Sejanus, after all, was referred to by Tiberius as *socius laborum,* 'my partner in my toils.' What was the result of that partnership for Sejanus? He was strangled to death by order of the one who was his supposed partner."

The smile on her face increased. "Partnerships and friendships. Partnerships and friendships. Of these we should be careful." She paused. "You have said you are not a free man. It is true. But let me ask you this: Is my husband a free man?"

"I am not—"

"I withdraw my question. It is not appropriate. I cannot ask you to evaluate the status of the Roman prefect, but hear me, Malchus, there is more than one form of slavery. If you could look into the eyes of my husband, as I do, you would not see the countenance of a free man. His slavery is of a different sort than yours—but it is slavery nonetheless."

She nodded toward Sabrina, who began walking toward us. I was again caught by the grace and confidence of her steps.

"What will become of my request I cannot say," Claudia said as I watched Sabrina. "But your eyes tell me I must make the effort."

That effort came to the conclusion I expected. Annas declined Claudia's request. Marius would tell me that I had made myself too valuable to the high priest's family. Perhaps, but it was also Annas's nature to defy the Romans, even on the occasions that it made political sense. Though I had repeatedly counseled myself to give no hope to the expectation that Annas would agree to the proposal, hope is essential to a man. And I found I had not heeded my own counsel. A fragment of hope, despite my counsel to myself, had not been killed— and when Caiaphas informed me of his father-in-law's refusal of Pilate's request, I took the news as would have been expected of a man of the temple guard, trained by the Roman army. But that night alone in my room at the temple, I succumbed to the agony of realizing that the desire I denied indeed existed and was now crushed. I broke the vow I had made as a boy—that I would never cry. For the first time since that day, tears came to my eyes as I realized that a hope I would not acknowledge was now dead.

Chapter 41

The First Ship from Rome

Passover concluded. Jerusalem, and the temple, returned to its routines. The pilgrims returned to their villages, and the residents of Jerusalem, now rid of the tens of thousands of temporary citizens, got back into the rhythm of their everyday lives. It was then that the message came: "A Roman ship, the first of the season, is in the harbor at Caesarea!" Every citizen in the city heard of it within hours.

"Has Pilate been recalled? Did he kill himself rather than be executed?" were the questions running through the streets.

The question festered another day before it could be answered. Yes, the first Roman ship of the season was in the harbor—but no Roman representative was onboard. It was a private ship, owned by an enterprising and daring captain. "My men are courageous," the captain said when he arrived at the quay. "We do not wait for the Ides of May, when the timid raise their sails. We came along the coast for protection from the winds. It takes longer, but we are here. We are the first to Judea, and we will be the first to return to Rome."

If Pilate's pulse had quickened when he first saw the ship's sail on the horizon, as it got closer, he would have seen it was not a trireme and did not display the golden eagle of the empire. It was not a ship commissioned by the emperor. That would have given him relief. No Roman soldiers would be aboard this ship. In fact, there were no passengers on board at all—and no cargo. It carried only rocks—as ballast. "Rome is hungry," the pilot said, laughing, standing on the quay. "She needs dates and olives and figs. In exchange, she sends you rocks!"

But the conversation in Caesarea, and soon in Jerusalem, was not about the rocks onboard the ship. The conversation was about what was not on the ship—Roman soldiers. Pilate, for the moment, was not subject to being recalled to Rome. The news ran through the streets of Jerusalem. "What does this mean?" people asked. Every man had an opinion.

"The next ship will have soldiers on it. Tiberius is torturing Pilate by making him wait," said a man leaning in the stall of a spice shop.

"Perhaps," the proprietor answered. "But who knows the mind of Tiberius?"

Three days passed before the next ship entered the harbor at Caesarea, but, like the previous ship, it did not carry the Roman soldiers that Pilate dreaded. Lightly laden with glassware and trinkets, it was ready to take on the foodstuff the residents of Rome needed. Within the week, ships began arriving regularly, but all were commercial vessels. None bore the Roman eagle on its flagstaff.

The days grew longer, and dozens of ships came in and out of the harbor at Caesarea, but none had the delegation aboard that Pilate feared.

"Has the prefect taken a breath yet?" a man asked, laughing, as he slid from his donkey. "A lesser man," came the reply, "would have suffocated by now. Six months is a long time for a man to hold his breath!"

The summer passed with few events.

Annas sent a few teams to the Galilee to spy on Jesus bar-Joseph and his band of followers, but the rabbi seemed more elusive than in previous months. At times these spies could not find the rabbi at all.

"Perhaps the so-called prophet from Galilee is not the threat we thought," I overheard Eleazer say to his father. "He failed to come to Passover because of his fear, and now he hides in remote places."

Annas listened, but said nothing.

Chapter 42
The Bethany Report

In a city accustomed to rumors and reports, this report, even so, stunned the people in Jerusalem.

A cool winter wind had blown across the Kidron that morning, rippling the water in the shallow stream. We were two months from Passover. The temple priests had just concluded the morning sacrifice when a synagogue leader from Bethany came to announce: "A dead man is alive! Jesus bar-Joseph raised Lazarus from the dead."

The news ran through the temple, and in a few hours it had passed through the streets of Jerusalem. The report was discounted at first. But Bethany was only a couple of hours away, and many came to attest to the event.

The temple guards, like others in the city, were troubled by the news. "I hope he comes no closer. If he can bring a dead man to life, he can kill a man as well."

"Is this the Anointed One?" some asked. "Is he the one who is promised to Israel?"

The Sanhedrin quickly called a council. I accompanied Caiaphas to the session. "What are we to do?" one of the members asked. "This man performs many signs. If we let him go on like this, everyone will believe in him, and the Romans will come and take away our place and our nation."

Arguments broke out throughout the council, until Caiaphas, with unexpected boldness shouted out, "You know nothing at all. Nor do you understand that it is better for you that one man should die for the people, not that the whole nation should perish."

The temple guards, along with the Roman garrison, were put on alert—in case Jesus bar-Joseph made the short journey from Bethany to Jerusalem. But he did not come.

Pilate, however, came to Jerusalem. He had little choice. The Roman prefect could not avoid the greatest holiday in the calendar of the nation he governed. And perhaps he had taken some courage that no ship had arrived with orders for him to return to Rome.

He stayed at Herod's palace for Passover, his custom when Claudia accompanied him. When alone he played the part of a soldier and stayed at Fortress Antonia. The apartments in the fortress were not without their luxuries, yet nothing in Jerusalem could compare to the palace of Herod. Indeed, if the emperors in Rome could have seen the accommodations Herod had built for himself, they would have been jealous, for nothing in Rome surpassed the palace in Jerusalem. So not only could Claudia enjoy the luxuries and spacious gardens of Herod's palace, it also insulated Claudia and her female attendants from the soldiers in the barracks.

My orders were to take a contingent of the temple guard to receive Pilate and his train near Jaffa Gate, just outside the city walls. There the responsibility for Pilate's train would be transferred from the Roman soldiers to the temple guards. Pilate could have insisted his soldiers take him directly to the palace, but he had learned a painful lesson about Jewish sensibilities. Roman soldiers inside the city walls were an unnecessary offense to the Jews. Better to dismiss his forces outside the city walls and send them to join the garrison at Fortress Antonia—and avoid the possibility of trouble in the streets.

Pilate rode his white stallion beside Marius and six others from his cavalry unit, with a century of soldiers—a larger force than necessary, but Pilate knew it was important to project an image of strength. Behind the cavalry unit and in front of the foot soldiers was an ornate coach, curtains drawn. I recognized it as Claudia's. Sabrina was certainly inside, but I could not think about that now.

"Your royal prefect," I announced with my strongest voice. "The high priest Joseph Caiaphas sends you greetings. He welcomes you to Jerusalem to celebrate the Passover of the Jews."

A thin smile came to his face.

Emotion did not come readily to the face of Pilate. A lifetime of wariness, as he had worked himself up through the ranks of the Roman army had forced him to keep impassive and wary. Those wary eyes, gray as steel, sheltered a cautious spirit. Yet, as he looked at me, the slightest bit of humanity came to his face, showing both amusement and irony. He seemed to say, 'You and I have a history together, do we not?' I too could recognize the irony of our association, But neither Pilate nor I could imagine that our lives in the next few days would be further entwined in events that would forever change the world.

The worries of a man's heart, if they are severe and sustaining, will find expression on his face, as Pilate's face clearly demonstrated. The strain of his worries over the previous months etched lines in his face I had not seen before. He was an older man than the man who sailed with me to Judea.

The thin smile still on his face, Pilate nodded in the perfunctory manner common to him, acknowledging my announcement.

"Allow me," I said, "to lead you to your quarters."

I could not avoid taking a quick glance at the first carriage. There was no value in seeking an inaccessible treasure. More grief would be the only outcome of seeing her again. Yet my sight returned to the carriage. The curtains were barely open. A woman's face, probably Claudia's, peered out the slit in those curtains.

We rode the short distance to Jaffa Gate, where Pilate dismissed his soldiers, except for Marius and his men. At my command, the gatekeeper opened the gate. I entered first. Pilate rode just behind me. Suddenly Pilate's horse whinnied loudly. I turned to see the white stallion rearing high. Pilate held desperately to the reins, leaning forward to avoid being toppled. A black splotch stained the horse's flanks, and remnants of a rotten onion fell to the pavement. Hardly ten paces away a man reached into a basket and drew out another onion. He threw again but missed. I ran to him and caught his arm before he could throw a third time. I fell on him and pinned his arms. I recognized him. He was well known around Jaffa Gate—infested by demons, many said, known for his wild eyes and wild talk. I had often seen him walking quickly through the streets, waving his arms and talking incoherently. His hair and beard foul with dirt, he was a man who slept in the gutters and ate from garbage piles. As I held him, he babbled, "Romans, Romans. Kill the Romans."

Marius came beside me quickly, pulled the man up and held his arms behind him. The man offered no resistance. I put my sword away. He was no threat. Pilate, after gaining control of his horse, came with sword in hand. His face was flushed, and he gripped his sword tightly. I expected to see the man's throat slit. I stepped back. The man continued to babble, "Kill the Romans. Kill the Romans." Pilate put the blade to the man's throat and kicked the basket. Onions, the size of a small child's fist, some black and rotten, rolled onto the pavement. I stood near enough to see Pilate's gray eyes, wide open and furious. The deranged man raised his chin in compliance as if to facilitate the slitting of his throat. Pilate's sword hand twitched and then relaxed.

Pilate stepped back—his face contorted as the foul odor of the man filled our nostrils. He looked around and then looked back at the demented man. He took a further step back to escape the odor.

Pilate's arms relaxed. He looked around again as if to assess the situation and put his sword back in his sheath.

"Release him," Pilate said.

Marius did as instructed. The deranged man looked at all of us with contempt and began picking up the onions, muttering, "Kill the Romans." With his onions regathered, he said one more time, as if to no one, "Kill the Romans," and then walked away.

Pilate surprised us that day. Had this deranged man thrown a rotten onion at Pilate in his first year as prefect, when Pilate was committed to asserting Roman authority on Judea, would the man have escaped with his life? Or had the contingent of Roman soldiers witnessed the event, would he have felt compelled to uphold Roman dignity by slitting the man's throat? I do not know the answer to my questions, but the incident reminded me of the moment on the ship as we were crossing the sea from Rome to Caesarea, and the dolphins appeared alongside. In one of those rare moments when the prefect demonstrated some humanity apart from his demeanor as Roman prefect. But neither could Marius nor I have known that in a few days the humanity Pilate had just demonstrated would be tested to the greatest degree.

As soon as Pilate and his entourage were settled in Herod's palace, I received a summons to come to the house of Annas. An argument was going among the sons of Annas. "He stays in Bethany. As he comes to Jerusalem we will apprehend him. A few dozen of our guards could easily capture him."

"Capture is not what we seek. The people will riot. Do not discount the numbers of his followers. He must be killed."

"Will you also kill the hundreds of his followers, including many women, who will be alongside him on the road?"

An unusual tension filled the city that week. The week of Passover was always filled with tension, but this time was unusual. With every pilgrim who arrived, the tension increased. Within that tension was a sense of expectation, of anticipation. It seemed the whole city carried a nervousness filled with anticipation. Anticipation of what? No one knew, but all sensed it.

Chapter 43

The Booths

The smoke from the fire of the previous night's sacrifice mixed with the smoke of the campfires on the hills and hung like a thin, gray ribbon over the Kidron. Soon the morning sun would break over the olive trees on the hillside and throw its light against the bronze pillars and golden doors of the temple. The priests would follow the morning ceremonies, the trumpets would sound, and the lamb would be sacrificed as a new day began in Jerusalem. Passover was a week away, but even so, some pilgrims were already camped in the hills around the city, and some were gathering outside the gates waiting to enter and purchase their sacrifice.

Buzzards circled silently in a limitless sky. During the next few days, they would feed well. The refuse of thousands of sacrifices would allow them to gorge. My eyes came lower. Along the parapets of the fortress stood Roman soldiers. Their number was greater than on ordinary days, but that number would become even greater in the next few days in anticipation of Passover.

"The Nazarene is coming," Zuriel told me. "He left Bethany two hours ago. More than a thousand accompany him. The report is going through the city. Many more will come. We must be ready. I have alerted the guards."

Hardly an hour later Zuriel came back. "The crowd is great, but the guards are ready. The Nazarene is on the road coming down the hill beside the olive trees."

A tumult rose outside the walls. "Hosanna! Hosanna! Blessed is the king who comes in the name of the Lord."

"The crowd is calling him a king," Zuriel said. "These are dangerous words. Be on the alert."

The chants became louder. Although I could not see the crowd, I knew they were crossing the bridge that spanned the Kidron to the Eastern Gate, which led directly to the temple. Two hundred paces away I saw the crowd as they entered. Above and behind them, the Roman soldiers came to the walls to look down on this commotion.

A strange sensation came over me. What caused it, I am not sure. Perhaps the steady drone of many conversations was hushed.

I saw him.

He stood facing the temple, its golden doors rising up before him, then he turned his head toward the Court of the Gentiles—toward me. He began walking toward the Court of the Gentiles—toward me.

The memory of his movement across those smooth stones is still vivid in my mind. The image of his advancing toward the stalls, cord in hand, face purposeful, strong legs pushing against his brown robe as he came near, will always remain in my memory.

The temple itself, behind him, formed his backdrop, the smoke from the sacrifices wafting upward, the morning sun gleaming from the gold-plated doors, as he moved urgently, insistently, toward the booths of the sons of Annas in the Court of the Gentiles. Ten times ten thousand had I seen men walk in the temple courts—but no man before walked like this. No one had ever stridden the temple as he did. The purpose and pace in his steps had never before been known.

Toward the booths. Toward me . . .

The stride he maintained was out of place. People mill about and move slowly at the temple. They do not walk like this man walked.

Across the Court of the Gentiles he came, and I watched every step. It is no short distance across the courtyard, and this man strode as though he owned every stone.

A ripple of anticipation ran through me. I sensed something important was about to happen.

In his right hand he held knotted cords. He seemed prepared to use them. Every step was strong and purposeful as he came toward the money-changers. His face was set like a stone, his eyes drawn toward his task. His hair hung on his shoulders, bouncing in rhythm to his stride. There was freshness to his movement. In the Court of the Gentiles men skulk as if intimidated or trudge as if weighed down. But not this man—not this stride. This man walked as if he knew his own heart—as if he knew his purpose, as if he knew where he was going, as if he knew what he would do when he got there. Unless one knows the temple and has grown accustomed to the rhythm of the movement on the mount, he cannot understand what an affront this man and his stride made. Perhaps it is part fear of God and part fear of man that constrains motion on the mount. However, I know unusual movement brings attention and suspicion. Yet this man went across the stones as if he owned them.

Heads turned toward him, at first a few, then dozens and hundreds.

He came closer.

I did nothing. Why, I cannot explain. My duty was to maintain order at the temple, and it was obvious this man was about to disrupt that order—yet I did nothing. The anticipation I felt prickled the hair on the back of my neck.

Something wonderful is going to happen.

The man's pace did not diminish as he came closer. His face was resolute, yet if there was rage in his countenance, I could not see it. The sun was slightly behind him, and he stepped on his own shadow as he neared the traders' stalls.

I hugged a column near the outer wall, out of the way, but near enough to watch. The traders were stacking their coins and haggling among themselves, oblivious to the one who came toward them.

Crash! The first table went over. Coins spilled on the stones. Doves flew from broken cages. *Crash!* Sheep broke their tethers and ran. *Crash*! Another table went flying, the legs breaking against the stone walls. The trader at the next booth spread his arms to protect his goods. The knotted cords came down with fury, throwing coins in all directions. The trader abandoned his table, and it too shattered against the wall. The crashes continued. A hundred men or more watched this spectacle, but none offered resistance. Uncommon strength and uncommon anger were mixed in this man, and none on the mount that day would stand in his way. From table to table he went, throwing them over, spilling their contents, until none was left standing.

How I wanted to join him!

Yes, I wanted to join him! Why, I did not know. Something suppressed took great delight in this scene, and I also wanted to throw the tables to the ground. Why? I could not explain my inclination. But I also wanted to bring my anger to the traders' tables and smash them against the stones.

Feathers filled the air. Dozens of doves had found their freedom and fluttered around the temple. Sheep ran free, bleating, seeking escape. When every table was broken, the man finally paused and looked around. His followers stood in a cluster nearby, their faces full of amazement and fear. He wiped his hair from his face. Sweat poured from his brow. He still held the cords in his hands. His chest heaved from his exertion. There was an uncanny silence. No one moved. The sky was clear, and there seemed to be no sound in the universe except for this man's breathing. Then he spoke, filling the temple mount with his voice: "My house shall be called a house of prayer for all peoples!" His voice found resonance against the great stones and echoed through the temple. "But you"—he pointed at the sons of Annas, the knotted cords still in his hand, "have made it a den of thieves!"

A sheep bleated, but otherwise it was silent on the mount.

A rare moment of intense stillness came to the temple, as if everything in the world had momentarily stopped. The traders huddled in silence at a safe distance. Zoreb, the fattest of the lot, had fallen in his escape, and now he sought refuge behind an overturned table. He seemed fearful of standing—afraid this cord-carrying invader would attack him. But the Nazarene attacked no one. His wrath was spent on the tables and the stalls. None of the sellers had dared confront the Nazarene.

It was fear that restrained the sellers, but for me—I felt no fear, so I had no explanation for my reluctance. But somewhere in the deepest part of me, I felt a rising joy. Whoever this man was, and for whatever reason he had done this thing, I was glad of it.

I was commissioned to keep the peace of the temple. The peace of the temple had just been upset—yet I did nothing.

It was not fear that restrained me. Something else restrained me. Something inside me said, *This man has the authority to do what he is doing.*

Zoreb looked at me, imploring me to do something. I pretended I did not see him. The prophet's followers were also silent. A few doves, confused in their freedom, fluttered overhead, breaking the silence.

Then the Galilean dropped his outstretched arm and slowly turned his head in my direction. I could not move. My throat went dry. Time seemed to stop. His head kept turning. I could not move. When he looked at me, he did not say a word.

His eyes found mine and held me in his gaze.

When I saw his face, my heart was arrested. At that moment I would have gone to war for him.

He never spoke a word to me, but I knew who he was, and I knew he looked at me for one reason—to summon me. His eyes called me to join him. Somehow, without a spoken word, I knew he had a place for me, and I would no longer be a slave.

Had a trumpet sounded, the call could not have been clearer. He called me to join him. And I felt in my heart what soldiers must feel as they quicken themselves the moment before battle. Every nerve in my body was attentive. I had been summoned. And I was ready to respond.

The summons was certain, though it was not immediate. A few momentous days would pass before I would come alongside him. But that day in the temple is when I first encountered the master. And like all others who encountered him, we mark our days in relation to the encounter. We had days before we met him, and we have had days after we met him. But the encounter with him frames all our days.

What now? What will he do now? I felt the same anticipation as the thousands behind him. He had told the Pharisees the rocks were likely to cry out. If they had, I would have been only a little surprised.

A man's memories can become jumbled as they pile up in his mind. The events of my life that are vivid in my mind—my capture by the slaver, my years at the estate and the lady's tender care, the death of the slaver, my time in Rome—all of those memories pale in comparison to what I witnessed that day in the temple when the Galilean rabbi came striding, overturned the tables, and shook my soul when he looked into my eyes. All memories have facts attached to them— but they also have sensations and emotions. Even now I can hear the sounds of the crashing tables, the coins spilling onto the pavement, the squawk of doves and bleating of sheep. These details are fresh, even now. But just as vivid are the sensations of that moment. Some- how I knew Jesus was doing the right thing—and I wanted to join him.

But I did not join him. But neither did I constrain him, as was my duty. For this I realized I would be held accountable, yet for some reason I did not care. The threats of Annas and his sons felt insignificant. Why? I asked myself. Why am I indifferent to the threats of my masters? And the answer came instinctively: Because I now had a new master.

I cannot say I felt less like a slave. Except at this point most slaves are not offered the opportunity to choose their master.

Yet a further question came: Did I choose him or did he choose me?

Chapter 44

The Aftermath

The questions were still on my mind when I received the summons—as I knew I would—to the house of Annas. His sons were in an agitated conversation when I entered.

Ananus pointed at me and shouted, "And where was the temple guard when that Galilean *amharetzin* was destroying our booths?"

To my surprise Caiaphas came to my defense. "Thousands of *amharetzin*—he enunciated the word slowly as if to mock Ananus— were nearby. If the Galilean had been attacked, what do you think would have happened? The Galilean has the favor of the people. Do you think the same thing can be said about our house?"

Annas narrowed his eyes at this remark. Questions about the legitimacy of his house to perform the high priestly functions were often uttered across Jerusalem—by both the common people and also by some of the priests, but he was offended to hear it from his own son-in-law. While his sons squabbled about some insignificant loss of revenue at the temple booths, Annas was considering a greater threat—that his house might be supplanted as the high priestly house. The preservation of his position—and that of his sons and his son-in-law—as the high priestly family was, I knew, was often on his mind. There had been previous threats to that position, but those threats had been handled. However, this Galilean miracle-working rabbi worried him.

Annas raised his hand. The various discussions among the brothers subsided. They turned their attention to the patriarch. He spoke slowly, barely above a whisper. "This Galilean apparently has charmed the people with his words. We will use his words against him. We will call for the scribes to test this so-called rabbi."

"It is a good plan," Eleazer said. "Once the people hear the Galilean villager stumble on the questions he is asked, they will lose their confidence in him."

"And once he is deserted," Ananus said, with malice in his face, "then we can do away with him."

I was dismissed from the gathering. My instinct was to send a message to Jesus and his disciples, to warn them that the high priest was sending the best theologians in the city, the best debaters, to confront him and capture him in some inconsistency in order to make him appear foolish before his followers.

But I also had another concern: What if the scribes are successful? What if they produce confusion in Jesus bar-Joseph? What if he is caught in some inconsistency? What if he indeed stumbles in a confrontation? What if his followers become demoralized by the answers he provides? What if they laugh at his response? I wanted none of these things to be true, but the questions concerned me. How am I to account for the sensations I felt yesterday when Jesus bar-Joseph confronted me? If he is embarrassed tomorrow by the scribes, will I still feel the same?

Those doubts swirled in my mind as I went to sleep.

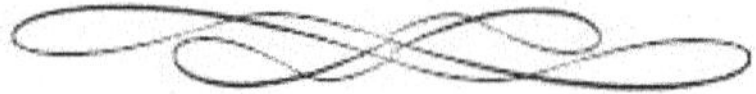

The crowds at the temple courtyard the next morning were greater than I had ever seen four days before Passover. The vast expanse was packed with pilgrims as well as the residents of the city. The word about Jesus' entering the city on a donkey the day before and his driving out the moneychangers and overturning the sellers' tables had passed quickly through the city. And now the crowds had come to see what would happen next. Clusters of men were in animated conversations. Hundreds of women were there as well, pushed to the edges of the Women's Court because of the number of pilgrims and locals who had gathered in the courtyards.

"He rode a donkey," an old man said, "just as Solomon did when David conferred the kingdom on him. Perhaps this son of David will assume the kingship that is promised."

"He has healed many people," another man said. "You cannot discount those reports."

"The messiah cannot come from the Galilee, can he?" another asked.

"Did you hear what he did to the booths of the house of Annas?" One man snickered and others joined him, but they checked their laughter quickly and looked around them to see if their conversation had been overheard. It was not wise to be critical of the high priest.

One group was not talking. In the corner of the Court of Israel, near the porticoes, stood eight men, noticeable because of their fine clothing, surveying the courtyard. I recognized them. These were the scribes and Pharisees Annas had recruited to confute Jesus. At the opposite corner was another group of Sadducees who were also waiting their chance to interrogate Jesus.

The doubts of the previous night returned. The scribes were the best trained of the Pharisees in Jerusalem. Their entire lives were consumed by the study of the Jewish Scriptures. How could the son of a carpenter from a small village in the Galilee hope to avoid embarrassment by such a delegation? The Sadducees were likewise the best debaters from their group.

"Malchus!"

My thoughts were interrupted, and Manaen came pushing through the crowd toward me.

"Manaen," I greeted him. "I would like to embrace you, but I am wearing the uniform of the temple guard."

"I understand. Save your embrace for later. We have much to discuss." He looked around. "It is my first Passover in many years. The crowd is massive."

"More than twice the crowd of last year. The Galilean rabbi has stirred up a great deal of interest. Did you hear about his coming to the temple yesterday?"

"I arrived last night. But I heard the story. Were you here? Did he indeed attack the booths of Annas?"

"What you have heard is true. I witnessed the entire event."

"And I also heard that he entered the city on a donkey. My mind went to the account of David directing Solomon to enter the city in a similar fashion to signify that Solomon, not Adonijah, was the authentic heir to the kingdom. The Messiah we have been promised will come from the line of David and he will renew the Davidic kingdom. It appears Jesus bar-Joseph was very intentional in planning his entry. Those who know the Scriptures will understand this."

A messenger came to me. "Jesus bar-Joseph remains in Bethany," he informed me.

Manaen smiled as the messenger walked away. "Annas watches everything carefully, does he not?"

"Each hour I get a report from one of his spies. For a quick-footed messenger it is less than two hours' walk from Bethany to the temple. Annas wants to give his interrogators ample opportunity to prepare."

There were signs of restlessness among the crowd. "The Galilean is afraid. He is not coming." Someone said."

"If he were a man of fear, he would not have attacked the booths of Annas," came a reply.

"I must go," Manaen said. "Nicodemus has asked me to join him and Joseph of Arimathea. Both are concerned about the safety of Jesus if he comes to the city again." He nodded to me and disappeared into the crowd.

Jesus bar-Joseph did not appear, and the crowds began to dissipate. Shortly after the Roman water clock signified the *hora tertia,* the third hour, I received a report that Jesus lingered in Bethany.

"He is not coming," a man said with a sigh.

"Will he come tomorrow?" another asked.

"We should not expect it," another added. "He would be wise to return to the Galilee."

I agreed. It would indeed be wise for Jesus to leave Jerusalem. Those who had opposed Annas did not survive long. And none of them had confronted Annas as boldly as Jesus had done with the moneychangers. The only thing keeping Jesus alive was the support of the crowds. But if he were embarrassed by the scribes or by Sadducees, the crowds would abandon him to the wrath of Annas.

My instinct called me to be the protector of Jesus bar-Joseph, but I felt powerless.

A steel-gray motionless sky lingered that afternoon. The sun, hidden somewhere behind the clouds, seemed reluctant to go down that day. That brought to mind the legend I had heard as a boy about Helios, who rode his sun chariot across the sky, eventually relinquishing his duties to his sister Selene. I did not hold any confidence in that legend then or now, but I realized that anticipation slows down time. My hope of Jesus' coming to the temple that day was now over, and the late afternoon seemed to stand still. Only a few handfuls of men remained in the courtyard, some looking wistfully at the gates in the reluctant hope that Jesus might come at the last moment. The emotion I saw in their faces was the same I sensed in my heart.

He has not come today. He may not come at all.

I went to sleep with those doubts on my mind.

One of the guards woke me two hours before sunrise as I had directed. I dressed myself and made my way to the temple courtyard. The clouds of the previous evening had lifted, and the sky sparkled with stars. Several dozen priests were already at work, preparing for the days' sacrifices. Hundreds of goats and sheep and pigeons would be sacrificed this day and their blood splashed on the altar.

I pulled my cloak around my shoulders to protect against the cool early morning air and made my way out the Eastern Gate and outside the temple. This was the gate by which Jesus entered only two days earlier. Would he return? I wished to see him, yet I knew it would be wiser for him to stay away. Annas sought to kill him, that was clear.

"Greetings Malchus," Marius said as I approached the Antonia Fortress. "Come inside."

He led me to a well-lit room with cushions filling the edges of the room. A servant brought mulled wine as we reclined.

Marius sipped his cup and worked the wine around his teeth. "I suppose you are now unclean," he smiled, "now that you have entered a Gentile's house."

"Annas and his sons care little about my uncleanness. They leave that concern to the Pharisees."

"Yes, I know." Marius answered, "I also know what concerns Annas—as you do. And I have heard reports about what happened at his booths the day before yesterday. I was told you were there. What can you tell me? Did Jesus indeed throw over the tables?"

I took a deep breath.

"Will you tell me or not? I do want to hear."

"I was there. I saw it all."

"You have a smile on your face." Marius said. "It is rare to see a smile on the face of Malchus. I am glad to see it."

I nodded. "I found joy in seeing the tables overturned, in the panic of the moneychangers, in the spilling of the coins on the stones, in the doves and sheep breaking free. All of this gave me great joy."

"You did not try to stop this?"

"My instinct was the opposite. I wanted to join the destruction rather than stop it."

"Did Annas and his sons reprimand you?"

"Caiaphas came to my defense. He said, and I suppose it is true, that if the other guards and I had tried to stop Jesus, two thousand men, or more, would have come to his defense."

We were quiet for a moment, and then Marius asked, "Is there more you can tell me?"

I took another sip of the wine. "I wish you could have seen him as he came across the pavement toward the stalls. I have seen thousands of men in the temple courtyard, but I have never seen a man walk like this man. I am still trying to make sense of what I saw. Jesus seemed in some way to have authority, to have jurisdiction over the temple— as if he owned it, as if it were his."

"It is the same report everywhere," Marius said. "The common Jews all say he does not speak like the scribes and Pharisees, who cushion all their commands in layers of rulings and opinions of others, but that he speaks with clear authority. It was what my friend in Capernaum noticed more than a year ago. He remains convinced that Jesus, without even coming to his house, healed his servant."

I nodded but said nothing.

"Malchus, my friend, have you told me all of the events of that day? It seems there may be more you have not told."

I paused before I answered. "It is as you say. There is more to tell—but how to tell it I do not know."

"I will wait."

"What I have not yet said is that . . . I hardly know how to say this, but as he came near, he looked at me, and it was not just a glance. He looked directly at me, and he looked at me intently. In some way I sensed that he knew me—and that he was summoning me to something. What that is I do not know. But I knew at that moment, and I know now, I remain ready to respond to that summons."

We were quiet for a moment, and then I continued, "Today I had opposing emotions. I wanted Jesus to return to the temple so that in some way I could get a better understanding of what he meant when he looked at me, and yet . . ."

"Yet you feared for him."

"Yes. When Jesus was in the Galilee, he was a concern to Annas but not an immediate threat. Now Jesus has attacked Annas at the very heart of his authority. Annas knows an uprising among the people, especially here in Jerusalem, could result in the Romans' suspending the sacrifices or responding to those Jews—of whom there are many—who would like to see the house of Annas replaced by others."

"This is true," Marius said. "Annas and his family were given the high priest's role by Quirinius, legate at that time, only thirty years ago. Rome could decide—if they thought it would better mollify the Jews—to appoint another high priestly family. All to say, Annas has good reason to be wary. What was given to him can be taken away."

"For that reason, Annas and his sons, along with some members of the Sanhedrin, are plotting to kill Jesus."

"But they fear the people, do they not?" Marius replied.

"Indeed, and well they should. You heard of the crowd in the temple only two days ago. And you heard of those who cheered when Jesus disrupted the selling of the sacrifices. I sometimes wonder who the common people resent the most, you Romans or their Jewish leaders."

Marius smiled and asked, "Do you think he will come today?"

"The better part of me hopes not. Although Annas fears the people, he is devious. He will seek a way to rid himself of this one who threatens his power."

"He is coming!" The messenger was out of breath and panted heavily. He was one of several of Annas's spies who were watching the road from Bethany.

"Go on," I said.

"He and his disciples left Bethany. A large throng follows him. They are on the road to Jerusalem."

I thanked him and dismissed him. I then sent word to Zuriel and the temple guards to stay alert.

The word of Jesus' coming was passing through the crowd. Clusters of men whispered among themselves, and many of them gathered near the Eastern Gate, the place he had entered two days earlier.

I stationed myself between the Eastern Gate and the stalls. Annas and his sons were concerned that Jesus would come again to disrupt the selling of the animals. What would I do if he did? I'm sure I would have thrown my sword aside—but I did not have to make that decision.

A commotion arose to my left. A group of men were coming up from the Huldah Gates, and Jesus was at the center. Some cheers went up.

On an ordinary day there would have been several clusters of students with their teachers in various sites around the courtyard, discussing the laws of Moses. But this morning the crowd had swelled to fill the courtyard, and all the groups and teachers had abandoned their lessons and were waiting to hear Jesus.

I kept my position for a moment as Jesus found a place to stand. Then the men Annas had chosen to confound Jesus moved in his direction. They pushed through the crowd and came to the front. I made my way closer so I could hear.

Asriel raised his hands to have the crowd be quiet. Beside him stood other scribes in fine clothes, standing among the common people. "Tell us—" he said as he waved his hand across the crowd, "—by what authority do you do these things? Who is it that gave you this authority?" As he took a step back, he smiled at his associates as if to congratulate himself.

Jesus' answer came quickly, almost before Asriel had concluded: "I also will ask *you* a question." A murmur went through the crowd. They were amused that Jesus spoke so directly to an eminent scribe. "Was the baptism of John from heaven or from man?"

Another murmur went through the crowd and smiles came to the faces of many. Every man knew the dilemma. If the scribes answered that the baptism of John was from heaven, the logical response was: "Why then did you not believe him?" However, because of their fear of the crowd—most of whom considered John a prophet and resented Antipas for killing him—they could not answer "from man," for that would have stirred up the crowd even more.

The scribes huddled together for some time before Asriel replied quietly, "We do not know."

A humming murmur went through the crowd as the response was passed from the front to the back and then there was complete quiet. No one moved. Jesus looked intently at Asriel, who fidgeted slightly. It seemed the sky itself went silent.

Finally Jesus spoke: "Neither will I tell you by what authority I do these things."

A great cheer, mixed with laughter, erupted from the throng. The noise filled the courtyard. The common people's resentment of the religious authorities found expression in their laughter. The scribes, who had laid a trap, had instead been trapped. The common people were delirious.

Two fears had concerned me. The first was that Jesus would have been confounded by these debaters. I could not have imagined how the debaters themselves would have been so confounded. I was relieved beyond my hope. But my other fear was that Jesus would put himself in additional danger. Even at that moment I was certain that some of Annas's spies were running toward his house to give him a report on this confrontation. That report would serve to make Jesus even more onerous to Annas—and Annas more committed to having him killed. That fear now intensified.

As the cluster of scribes left the courtyard, some of the men in the crowd came near them and shouted their derision: "Neither will I tell you!"

After the scribes left the courtyard, the crowd went quiet again as Jesus told a parable: "A man planted a vineyard and let it out to tenants and went into another country for a long while. When the time came, he sent a servant to the tenants, so that they would give him some of the fruit of the vineyard. But the tenants beat him and sent him away empty-handed. And he sent another servant. But they also beat and treated him shamefully and sent him away empty-handed. And he sent yet a third. This one also they wounded and cast out. Then the owner of the vineyard said, 'What shall I do? I will send my beloved son. Perhaps they will respect him.' But when the tenants saw him, they said to themselves, 'This is the heir. Let us kill him, so that the inheritance may be ours.' And they threw him out of the vineyard and killed him. What then will the owner of the vineyard do to them? He will come and destroy those tenants and give the vineyard to others."

When they heard this, they said, "Surely not!"

The parable troubled many in the crowd. What did it mean? Who will be replaced? And who will replace them? Are the high priests the ones to be replaced? "Surely it is not our nation that will be replaced," one man said.

The arguments still simmered when a second group of scribes moved to the front of the crowd. One of them stepped up, and speaking more to the crowd than to Jesus himself, said, "Teacher, we know that you speak and teach rightly, and show no partiality, but truly teach the way of God."

Murmurs ran through the crowd, for they could sense the insincerity.

The scribe waited for the grumbles to subside. "Tell us," he went on. "Is it lawful for us to give tribute to Caesar or not?"

It was a well-directed question. If Jesus claimed to be the Messiah, the Anointed One, the Deliverer, he must in their minds overthrow the Romans and restore Israel to its sovereign status—which would mean he must oppose the paying of taxes to occupiers. To say yes, pay the tax, would disqualify him as Messiah. However, if he were to suggest that Jews should not pay their taxes, that word would be immediately transferred to the Roman authorities, and all knew he would immediately be arrested as an insurrectionist.

As before, hundreds of animated conversations filled the temple.

"There is no answer to this question," I heard a man near me say, some despondency in his tone.

I agreed. How could Jesus answer this question? One answer would make him an ally of the Roman, and disqualify him as the Messiah, and the other answer would make him an enemy of Rome, which would mean his immediate arrest. I, like those around me, saw no way out of this quandary.

When the noise of the conversations began to subside, Jesus spoke directly to the scribe who had questioned him. "Show me a denarius."

The scribe seemed confused. He looked around him at his fellow scribes.

"He has no coin purse!" A man laughed. "His servant carries his coins."

One of the other scribes produced a coin from his purse and handed it to the scribe standing beside Jesus. That scribe still seemed confused.

"Look at the coin," Jesus told the scribe, who held it up to his eyes. "Whose image is on it? And what inscription does it have?"

The scribe looked around at the crowd, confusion still evident in his face.

"Answer the question!" someone shouted.

"Caesar's," he eventually said.

"Then render to Caesar the things that are Caesar's and to God the things that are God's."

The crowd maintained its silence for a few seconds as they absorbed Jesus's words. Then they began repeating his words "Render to Caesar . . ." nodding in approval. The noise swelled again as the crowd voiced their appreciation for Jesus' answer, but the scribes sulked away. They too would certainly bear a report to Annas and his sons, and it would serve only to add to their fury.

"Can there be any doubt—" I turned to see Manaen, who had made his way through the crowd "—that this is the Messiah?" he asked.

Before I could answer, he went on. "I fear for him. His words serve only to put himself in greater danger from Annas. What does Annas say? What are his plans?"

"He fears the crowds. That alone keeps him from having Jesus killed. But I do not know his plans. I do not hear the words spoken when he is in council with his sons and the chief priests, but it is evident his plan was to bring Jesus to ridicule."

"Which instead brought ridicule on the scribes and priests. And indeed Annas should fear the crowds. After today, they are even more enchanted by Jesus bar-Joseph." Annas and the scribes and priests have been unable to turn the crowd against Jesus—and the contempt for the priests is evident among those here today. Yes, Annas has good reason to be concerned—but here is my question, Malchus. Where does this lead? Jesus speaks often of the kingdom of God. How will he usher in that kingdom? Will he do it now? Or will he, after the Passover, just return to the Galilee? And yes, the crowds provide his protection now. But what about later? I do not trust the perseverance of any crowd." His face showed his worry as he surveyed the throng in the courtyard.

"I must report to Marius. He entreated me to inform him if Jesus returned to the temple."

I left through the Priests' Gate and walked quickly by the *mikvahs*. The lines at the ritual baths were ordinarily long, but on this day they were empty. As I made my way through the narrow streets up the hill toward Herod's palace, I realized the shopkeepers' stalls were not active. The pilgrims were not at the stalls. They were at the temple to hear Jesus.

Chapter 45

Claudia Procula's Report

The guards admitted me through the palace gate and Marius met me as I entered. "I am anxious to hear your report, but hold it for a moment. There is another who also wishes to hear. Follow me."

Marius led me through the same walkways of the palace gardens I had followed a few days before. Claudia Procula sat at the same table where we had met before. The fountain gurgled like it was telling secrets.

She motioned for us to sit on the benches. "I am unattended," she said. "This is a violation of protocol—the wife of the Roman prefect in the company of a Roman soldier and—"

"—a slave," I said.

She smiled. "This is a conversation we have had previously, is it not?"

I knew the reason Claudia was unattended. Her effort to purchase me from Annas and join me with Sabrina had failed, and she did not want me to have to endure the reminder of that failure by seeing Sabrina again. I should have been more appreciative of her sensitivity.

"I cannot stay long," she said. "Malchus, please tell me what you can about Jesus at the temple today. When I heard him in the Galilee, his words touched places in my heart I did not know existed. I have longed to hear him again—and I considered disguising myself and going to the temple myself, such was my longing—but that would have been unwise. But I must know what he said. What can you tell me?"

I looked at Marius. "I also am anxious to hear," he said.

"The scribes and priests," I began, "tried to trap him with their questions." I recounted the confrontations at the temple, with Jesus confounding his interrogators and delighting the crowd as he responded to the questions about the nature of John's ministry—whether it was of God or not—and about paying tribute to Rome." They listened attentively until I finished.

"And the crowd—how did they react?" Marius asked.

"They took great pleasure in the humiliation of the priests. They, to a man, are on the side of Jesus."

"Is he safe?" Claudia asked.

"His only safety," I answered, "is in the approval of the crowds. Annas recognizes the threat to his priesthood—to his livelihood—and seeks to have Jesus killed. It is the people's support that keeps Annas from his plan."

"Should Pilate be notified of Annas's plan? If Jesus were killed, a riot could take place."

We looked at Claudia.

She gathered her thoughts. "My husband is a tormented man. The sea-lanes will open again in a few weeks. Will the favorable winds bring the ships with the delegation that recalls him—*us*—to Rome? They did not come last year, but Tiberius can be unpredictable—and patient. My husband and his career were entwined with Sejanus. No doubt there are those in Rome—those who hated Sejanus—who are giving Tiberius counsel to rid the empire of all who aligned themselves with Sejanus. No one more than my husband better fits that description."

We waited for a moment as Claudia paused.

"My husband brought his medallion with him," she went on. "I have mentioned it before. Sejanus presented it to my husband just before he sailed here to Judea. *Amicus Caesaris*, it says, 'Friend of Caesar.'" She smiled ruefully. "If only we could be assured of that friendship. The friendship of Caesar, as Sejanus would attest—if he were alive—is not to be guaranteed by a medallion."

She paused again. "Yes, my husband should be informed. A riot in Jerusalem would provide Tiberias more reason to recall him. He should be informed."

"I will go now to inform him," Marius said.

"I am due at the house of Annas," I said, "to report on the day's activities at the temple."

Chapter 46

The Traitor

I came quickly to the house of Annas which stands only a few hundred paces from Herod's palace. When I came through the gate, I was surprised to see Zuriel in the outer courtyard. He seemed troubled.

"The temple priests—" he nodded toward the rooms above us, "—are here. One of the disciples of the Galilean rabbi is with them."

Before I could ask any questions, he went on. "His name is Judas. He is one of the followers of Jesus. This one stayed behind when Jesus and the others left the temple. He came to the priests and said he wished to talk with the high priest. The temple priests compelled me to bring him here."

"To what purpose?" I asked.

"I do not know, Malchus, but the sons of Annas seem pleased."

I tried to make sense of Zuriel's report, but I could not. I felt unsettled. Something in my spirit sensed this news was foreboding.

At that moment one of the council members, an ally of Annas's, arrived and quickly went into the house. Just behind him, another of the inner circle, riding a donkey led by a servant, arrived and went inside.

"Whatever this news," Zuriel said, "it is important. Annas does not gather his closest advisors without good reason."

I nodded in agreement. But what could this news be? And why did I sense such turmoil?

A murmur of voices came through the open windows above. I could make no sense of the conversation, but the meeting did not last long. After only perhaps a half hour men came down the stone stairs.

Ananus was the first to emerge from the house. Behind him was Judas, walking very tentatively. He looked around carefully before he came into the courtyard. In his hand was a bag—a bag of coins.

I looked at Judas. If a man's walk can express his heart, even more so his countenance. This was the face of a traitor.

Judas held the money-bag with both hands, his nervous eyes moving back and forth across the courtyard.

Jesus has been betrayed. His own disciple has betrayed him.

Judas folded the money-bag into the sash around his waist, still looking around him. He stood for a few seconds until Ananus nodded to him, as if to dismiss him. Judas, unsure of himself, took one final look around and then set off down the stone steps by himself.

"Assemble twenty of your best men." Ananus said to me, "No, make it forty. Put them at the ready, but wait at the temple until you are summoned." I paused for a moment trying to grasp what was taking place. "Did you hear my instructions, *slave?*" Ananus shouted. Instinctively, my hand went to the hilt of my sword and Ananus stepped back, stumbling for a second before he caught himself.

Zuriel stepped between Ananus and me and took me by the shoulders, leading me away. "The guards will not like this duty," he whispered as we walked away from the house of Annas back toward the temple. "Many of them have heard Jesus bar-Joseph with willing ears. Others are fearful of him because of the reports of the miracles he has done. The raising of Lazarus in Bethany is much on their minds. They whisper among themselves asking if this miracle came from God or from Beelzebub. They are much afraid."

"What you say is true. I suggest you select the men, but do not tell them the mission. There will be time for that later."

"Malchus," Caiaphas called to me. He stood with his brothers-in-law. They were in discussion—apparently about these new developments. "Remain here."

I spoke to Zuriel, "As I said, select your men but do not tell them the mission."

Caiaphas and his brothers-in-law went inside the house. I was sure they were consulting with Annas. After only a few minutes Caiaphas came out and said, "Go to the palace. Inform the prefect that the high priest requests an audience with him on a matter of great urgency."

"I repeat," Caiaphas said, "tell Pilate this is a matter of great urgency. Go quickly."

It would be a few weeks later when I would learn what was taking place at this time only a few minutes' walk from the house of Annas, at the house of John Mark's mother—where Jesus had gathered his disciples for the Passover meal. Peter would tell me about it. "He washed our feet," he said, as his eyes glistened over. "He washed our feet."

Claudia was with Pilate when I was admitted to the palace. I bowed to her as she nodded to me. Pilate sat in his curule chair, sipping wine from a silver goblet.

"Honorable prefect, Joseph Caiaphas the high priest requests an audience with you on a matter of urgency."

Pilate said nothing at first. He seemed to study my request. He took a sip from the goblet and worked the wine around his teeth. "Hmm." He tilted his head. "A matter of urgency. The high priest—" He twirled the wine in the goblet. "—has a matter of urgency."

Claudia looked at me. She sensed there was something wrong. There were questions on her face, questions I could not answer in front of her husband.

"Did the high priest indicate the nature of this 'matter of urgency'?" Pilate asked.

"I was given no other instruction—only to request an audience as soon as possible."

"Well-answered," Pilate said. "Answered like a soldier." He pointed at me with the cup in his hand. "You should have been a soldier, Malchus. Yes, I know you came to Rome as a slave, and the law says slaves cannot become soldiers, but Rome always finds ways to achieve its purposes. You would have been a fine soldier, Malchus. You impressed everyone on the training field. When you snapped the shoulder of that brute Brasus, that amazed the entire barracks. Sejanus and I—"

He caught himself as he called Sejanus's name.

He brought the silver cup to his face and wiped his cheek with it. The late afternoon light spilled through the open windows, and the silver cup highlighted his gray eyes, which seemed to look into eternity.

His voice softened. "I should have remained a soldier myself. The life of a soldier is less complicated than the life of a politician." A thin smile came to his face. "You have brought a request, and I will honor it. But—" He looked at me and smiled. "Patience is a great virtue, is it not, Malchus? Shouldn't we help Annas develop that virtue."

Pilate went quiet for a moment, narrowing his eyes, processing his own thoughts. I looked again at Claudia, her face full of questions.

"Since we are waiting," Pilate said, "I will insist you be seated."

I started to object, but Pilate stopped me. "For the moment we will both be soldiers. My command is that you be seated."

As I took a seat Pilate refilled his goblet then filled another and gave it to me. "Did you know Antipas is in Jerusalem?"

I nodded.

He pointed toward the open window. "He stays at the Hasmonean palace, hardly five hundred paces outside the walls of this palace. What gall the man shows to come here at Passover! He remembers his childhood, I suppose. As a child, I have been told, he stayed here, in this palace—Herod's palace—with his father and mother during the Passover. He seeks that again. I know about his efforts in Rome. He longs for the day when he can stay here during Passover." Pilate's eyes tightened. "But be sure of this, Malchus, I will do everything I can to make sure Antipas never spends a night on this site." A deep frown came on his face. "He sends reports to Rome about my 'mismanagement,' pleading with the emperor to restore his father's position to him. Ha! A man who stole his brother's wife, a man who alienated the king of the Nabataens, a man who lopped off the head of the Jewish prophet—this is the man who purports to become king of the Jews."

He looked out the open window.

"He, Antipas, would be king," he muttered to himself. "Yet I must make efforts to pacify him. He has supporters, wealthy supporters. They call themselves 'the Herodians,' mostly relatives and friends of the late 'Herod the Great,' as he is called. They became wealthy because of their affiliation with Herod, and they seek the day when one of his offspring might become king again. That is their hope—so Antipas sends regular messengers to Rome to complain about me and to try to curry favor with Tiberius."

Pilate turned the cup in his hand, looking at the wine. A wry smile came to his face and he looked at Claudia. "My dear, I am afraid the tetrarch Antipas is envious of your opulent surroundings. His hope, I am sure, is that he and his new wife will use these accommodations next Passover. Perhaps his step-daughter will dance here in this room." He waved his arm across the open room. "She is quite the dancer we have been told." He smiled at his own humor and drank the last of the wine in his cup.

"Ah, yes," Pilate said as he put the goblet on a table. "We must pacify Antipas, and we must pacify Annas. Both hate me—as I hate them—but all of us are compelled by Rome to pacify each other. Rome must have its taxes—so we all must follow the pretenses we have set. We must all pacify each other."

He turned to me. "Tell your high priest Joseph Caiaphas that I would be *delighted* to grant him an audience. He may come to the palace at his convenience."

I bowed and started to leave, but stopped, "Prefect, excuse me, but there is one additional request."

Pilate opened his hands as if to say, "What is the request?"

"Would you be willing to meet the high priest in your courtyard?"

A smile came to Pilate's face. "Aha. Of course. The high priest could not suffer *defilement* at Passover by entering the house of a *barbarian,* could he? Tell him, of course, the prefect of Rome will meet the high priest of Israel in the courtyard."

Caiaphas and Annas and his sons were waiting when I returned. I told Caiaphas, "The prefect will meet you in his courtyard at your convenience."

He nodded and looked at Annas.

"I will go also," Annas said. The brothers looked at each other. Annas had not left his house in several months. As the brothers looked at each other, I looked at Annas. His countenance—a countenance which terrified children—was more intense than usual.

Ananus stepped forward. "I will have your sedan chair readied, father."

Less than an hour later, Annas, Caiaphas, and I waited in one of the gathering areas of the courtyard of Herod's palace. Myrtles framed the open area with taller palms above, and water trickled through a marble channel beside us. Three slaves attended us as we sat. One added wood to a fire-pit, but the flame helped little against the early evening chill. Annas refused the blanket offered to him. He wanted his priestly robes visible. He also refused the wine the slaves offered him. Caiaphas did the same.

Both Caiaphas and I glanced up at the windows of the palace. The curtains were drawn, but we could see light and movement of shadows behind the curtains. As Pilate had indicated, he would have the priests learn patience. Annas and Caiaphas could wait. What their request was, Pilate did not know, but he sensed he had the high priest in a good position. He would let the high priest seethe in the cool air for a while. Urgency was an uncommon trait for Annas, a man of deliberation and calculation, and he seemed willing to suffer this humiliation for whatever purpose he had in mind.

Neither Annas nor Caiaphas nor I spoke as we waited. The silence gave me some moments to piece together the events of the last few days.

Was it only three days ago that Jesus confronted me in the temple? Was it only a day ago that he confounded the scribes in the courtyard?

And now I—who had pledged in my heart that I would bear arms for the one who confronted me and confounded the scribes—seemed to be acting as an agent to betray him. I quickly determined my purpose: I would learn the plans of the high priest and relay them to Jesus. *But what of his disciples? Were others of the disciples involved in this betrayal? Whom could I trust with this information? How could I get the information to Jesus? Where was he at this hour?*

I wished Manaen were with me. He would know what to do.

The palace slave added more branches to the fire. The flames lit up the underside of the myrtles that branched over us, and the sparks lifted up over our heads and disappeared. I looked at Annas. Whether there was contempt in his face for Pilate's delay I could not tell. His was a face always filled with contempt.

Caiaphas took a step closer to the fire and looked up at the windows of the palace. At that moment we heard the palace gates open, and the soldiers saluted. Then Pilate, alone, walked briskly through the shadowed pathway.

"Greetings to the high priests of Israel," he said cheerily. "I am grateful to be in Jerusalem to celebrate the Passover of the Jews."

"The prefect of Rome is welcome in Jerusalem," Caiaphas responded. "If the priests or the Council of the Sanhedrin can do anything to make his stay in Jerusalem more comfortable, please let us know."

"As my son-in-law has said," Annas added flatly, "the prefect of Rome is welcome in Jerusalem."

"I wish," Pilate responded, his voice heavy with hidden intent, "I could offer you the warmth of my inner chambers."

Hatred and hypocrisy were heavy in the air—heavier than the aroma of the hyssop plants that bordered the marble walkways. The words that came from Pilate's mouth were conciliatory, but I knew what he wanted to say: 'You are a vile, despicable, hypocritical, scheming old man, who considers me an infidel, who, if you even touched me or entered my house, you would be contaminated. You are a man who will do anything, or murder anyone, to keep your title and keep the revenue that flows from your temple booths. I know you hate me, Annas, but be sure of this: I hate you equally.'

Likewise, the voice of Annas was flat and unemotional, but all knew his true opinion of Pilate: 'You are a barbarian and an infidel, and you are the representative of the occupiers of our land. And while you show arrogance toward me at this moment—I know your position. You are afraid. You are afraid of Tiberius, afraid you will end up like Sejanus—and you have real reason for that fear. I will endure your arrogance this evening, but I will find a way to turn your fear against you. Yes, I know you hate me, but be sure of this: I hate you equally."

Pilate nodded to the three slaves, who bowed and dismissed themselves. I saw Annas look at Caiaphas and I knew I was to be dismissed also.

"Malchus," Caiaphas said, "Make certain Zuriel has secured the guards. Assemble them at my house."

I bowed, then turned to Pilate, acknowledged him, and walked toward the outer gate.

I was near the gate when I heard my name whispered from the dense myrtle trees, "Malchus." Claudia stepped out of the shadows.

"My lady."

"Tell me Malchus. What is this meeting?"

"Jesus has been betrayed. One of his disciples has turned against him. I have been instructed to gather a contingent of temple guards."

"For what purpose?"

"To arrest Jesus."

"What part does my husband have in this?"

"I do not know, my lady. There is much I do not know. I need Manaen's counsel. Could you get a message to him?"

"I will send a servant. What is the message?"

"Only what I have just reported, that Jesus has been betrayed to Annas."

"I will arrange it." I looked at her face and she looked at me. She seemed to be saying, *"We understand each other. We have the same calling. We are both summoned to follow the same one."* I thought for a moment she might embrace me, but she stopped herself and slipped away through the dark pathways. When she had gone, I made my way toward the temple.

Chapter 47

Gethsemane

"The men are assembled—my best men, forty of them, but they are curious about their mission," Zuriel said.

"Better they not know yet," I responded.

Forty temple guards going directly through the city at this time of the evening would create undue attention. We took the route out the Huldah gates and down the new road I had helped construct, "Pilate's Road," as some Jews called it. We passed beside the Pool of Siloam on our descent. The Gihon Spring gurgled as it emptied into the pool.

"Jesus healed the blind beggar here," one of the guards said to another.

"On the Sabbath, wasn't it?" the other responded. "An irritation to the Pharisees."

We went out through the South Gate and turned back up the hill outside the city walls, the Valley of Gihon on our left as we trudged up the steep hill and re-entered the city at the gate near the house of Caiaphas.

Angry voices came from inside. I halted the guards and entered. The sons of Annas were arguing among themselves. A few of the Sanhedrin stood nearby, carrying clubs. A few paces away, against the stones of Caiaphas' house, in the dim light I saw the face of Judas. He stood alone. "You will be the one to go," Eleazar said to Ananus, and the other brothers agreed.

"I am the youngest," Ananus whimpered. "Why should I be the one to go?"

Caiaphas stood outside the circle of the arguing brothers, and I stepped up to him. He answered my questions before I could ask. "The Galilean is to be arrested. He is at the Mount of Olives. Annas has required that one of his sons accompany the guards. They cast lots. The lot fell on Ananus, but he tries to refuse."

"Some of the guards may refuse as well," I told him. "Many of them admire the Galilean—and all of them fear him."

"They must obey. Annas has spoken. Jesus bar-Joseph must be arrested. Annas will suffer no treason. The guards will follow their orders. That one," he pointed to Judas who stood alone, "will identify him."

Judas stood against the wall of the house with his head down. My sword hand quivered involuntarily. *Should I lop off this traitor's head now? Or should I wait until we are on the path?*

I took Zuriel by the shoulders. "The guards must be told of their duty."

He nodded in agreement. "I will inform them. And I will remind them of their pledge. They took the oath to follow the orders of the high priest."

I heard the protests of the guards when Zuriel gave the orders, and I saw the fear on their faces as they whispered among each other as they entered Caiaphas' courtyard.

Every second man was to carry a torch and when they were all lit, the courtyard seemed ablaze. Judas, the traitor, still stood by himself against the wall of the house, his head down, the flames throwing his shadow against the wall. Ananus made one final appeal to his brothers to be released from this duty, but he found no sympathy among them. Zuriel put Judas and Ananus at the front of the group as we left the compound. I stayed in the back. I had to ensure none of the guards slipped off. These were the best of the guards, but the torches showed the fear in their faces.

There is a coldness that sometimes comes to a man's bones that is not borne by the air around him. I felt it as we descended. The others felt it as well.

As we headed down the incline outside the walls, we formed a long line of light in the otherwise dark night. I looked across the valley to the Mount of Olives, where Judas reported that Jesus and his disciples were staying. The hill was dark. The cook-fires of the pilgrims had gone cold. The pilgrims were asleep. We turned left at the corner of the temple, its high walls looming above us. At the base the torches threw distorted shadows of the reluctant soldiers against the smooth stones. As we turned up the incline of the Kidron, the light of the torches filled a section of the dark valley but as we looked across to the grove, there was only blackness.

Perhaps the followers of Jesus will see these torches and flee. That was my hope. If they saw the torches, they would surely know the purpose of those who carried them. My mind went back again to the previous day when Jesus came toward the booths—toward me—and looked directly at me.

Our pace was slow, weighed down by our collective reluctance. One of the guards turned to look at me—incrimination and fear in his face. *What are you doing? Where are you leading us? Do you take us to our death?* he seemed to ask. I had no assurance to offer.

We entered the edge of the olive grove. As we passed the great gnarled trunks of those ancient trees, they seemed to form malevolent faces in the torchlight. Zuriel's voice whispered, "halt." In a moment he was beside me. "Judas says they are at the olive press. It is near. Come to the front."

I avoided the faces of the guards as I walked past them. Some of these men had fought Zelotes hand-to-hand without fear, but what I saw was not fear. It was worse than fear. It was terror I saw on their faces.

I came to the front of the line and saw the outline of the olive press against the night sky.

"Is this the place?" Zuriel whispered to Judas.

He nodded.

Zuriel looked at me and I at him. "Bring the guards forward," he said.

How many hundred times have I told the events of that night? How many hundred times more have I recounted those events in my mind? Yet they are no less vivid in my mind today—the torches throwing light on the olive press and the trees . . .the confused disciples roused from their sleep . . .the kiss of Judas . . .the fisherman lunging toward Ananus . . .Ananus slinking behind me . . .the sword striking the side of my head . . .crumbling to my feet . . .the sensation of warm blood dripping down my neck . . .and then, the touch of Jesus to my head. All of that remains clear. None of that has lost its clarity in my memory.

The hand of Jesus was still on my head when he caught them in their hypocrisy, "Have you come out as against a robber, with swords and clubs to capture me? Day after day I was with you in the temple, teaching, and you did not seize me."

I raised my head to see his disciples looking at each other and then slinking away into the darkness. Jesus offered his hands—hands which had just healed me, hands that still carried my blood—to the guards, who tied them with leather ropes. Zuriel came and knelt beside me.

"He touched me," I said. "He touched me. My ear. My head. There was blood. Then—" I spoke incoherently, yet I had never felt more certain of anything in my life.

I had been healed.

Ananus, seeing Jesus was bound and his disciples gone, took new courage. He slapped Jesus across the face.

I sprang to my feet, my blade in my hand, the strength of a bull in my arms. Zuriel pulled at me to restrain me, but six men of Zuriel's strength could not have held me. I escaped his hold and a noise came from my throat I did not recognize—deep and loud, more like an animal than a man. Ananus stumbled as he saw me coming toward him, my sword in both hands above my head. I was about to bring the blade down on this impudent, cowardly son of a corrupt priest. I intended to split him from the top of his head to his waist—such was the strength I felt. Then—I saw Jesus' face. *Not now. Not this,* his face seemed to say. *I have something else for you.* He had instructed Peter to put away his sword and he gave me the same instruction—without saying a word. My shoulders and my arms quivered and, at the gaze of Jesus, the tension went out of them.

Zuriel took control. "To the house of Annas. Quickly!" The guards responded. Zuriel came to me. He helped me put my sword in its sheath. My fingers were still tight on the handle. Ananus lay on the ground, whimpering. I saw disgust in the faces of the guards. Some seemed inclined to finish what I had intended.

No words were spoken as we left the grove. Neither was anything said as we crossed the Kidron and made the ascent to the house of Annas. Ananus often looked suspiciously over his shoulder to make sure I was not near him.

We had walked in fear from the house of Annas to the olive grove. We returned in confusion. A few of the guards looked at me, the torchlight showing the questions on their faces. Before their eyes asked, *To what are you taking us?* Now their eyes showed different questions. *What have I witnessed? What have I seen?*

Jesus, at the front of the line, his hands tied in front of him, kept pace with the guards beside him. I wanted to run to the front and ask: *What is it you wish me to do? You have summoned me. What is my duty?*

We came to the gate and entered the courtyard. The sons of Annas were on the porch above us. Zuriel and two guards took Jesus inside the house. I tried to follow, but Zuriel raised his hand to stop me.

I moved away and sat with my back against the wall. I put my hand on my head, trying to make sense of the touch I had felt in the garden.

Some of the temple guards were watching me. They seemed relieved that their duty was over, but still confused. *What is next?* they seemed to ask. I could not help them. I had the same question.

The servants of Annas's household were awakened. Chaya was among them. She brought water while others built fires in the fire pits in the courtyard. I shivered in the cool night air. Pulling my cloak around me, I looked up at the windows of the room where Jesus had been taken. Some feeble yellow light, spattered with shadows, came from the windows. There was movement in the room, but I could hear nothing of what was being said inside.

Time passed. How long? I can't be sure. Perhaps an hour. Probably less. Chaya brought bread, but I refused. "You should eat," she said, but I felt no hunger.

Zuriel emerged from Caiaphas' house and found me. "You must flee. Ananus has reported the events in the grove. Annas and his sons are conspiring to kill you."

"I cannot flee," I protested. "Not when he—" I pointed to the windows "—is in danger. He healed me. I cannot abandon him."

"Listen to me, Malchus. Your lungs will not draw a hundred more breaths. They intend to kill you *now*. What purpose does it serve you or the Galilean rabbi for you to die here? Go."

I knew he was right. And I knew where I should go. I clasped Zuriel by the shoulders. "You have been a strong friend."

"Go. Go while you can."

Chapter 48

Escape

I pulled my cloak tightly around my shoulders and started quickly toward the gate. As I passed one of the fire-pits, my eyes were arrested—a huddled figure, head down, around the fire. *Is it possible? Are those the arms of the man who swung the sword at me?* I stopped and bent over. His hood was pulled around his head, and at first I could not see his face—then, very slowly, he turned slightly. I recognized the eyes—but they were now different. The enraged, angry eyes I had seen two hours earlier in the grove had changed. These eyes were now full of grief, of fear, of remorse. The eyes had changed, but they belonged to the same man. I was sure of it.

I turned back to Zuriel who was watching me, but he urged me to leave. I took one last look at the huddled figure around the fire. His eyes came up to mine for just a moment. Our eyes locked. We recognized each other. Then I started walking briskly toward the house of Joseph.

The fisherman and I would later talk often of that moment. Both of us had sworn allegiance to Jesus, and yet both of us were fearful. "What sort of man was I?" Peter would ask, "Ready to fight the temple guards in one moment—then cowed by Chaya, the servant girl just hours later. I failed him, Yet he forgave me, Malchus. He forgave me."

The house of Joseph—that was my destination. That was my best decision. Manaen was there. I needed sanctuary, and Manaen and the others needed to know Jesus had been arrested. The Roman guards at Herod's palace stopped me as I came near. "I am on the business of the priest," I told them. They let me pass. I looked up at the unlit windows of the rooms of the palace. Somewhere up there Sabrina slept, but this was not the time for such thoughts. At the Jaffa Gate I repeated my claim to be on the business of the high priest, and they let me pass out of the city.

Stillness. It is the stillness of that moment that comes back to me. No breeze disturbed the air and no sound intruded on it. Neither man nor animal stirred. The Passover moon was high and white, but it was motionless in the wide sky. The universe, it seemed, had paused for a moment. I looked back at Jaffa Gate. Four years earlier, along with a great retinue of Romans, I arrived at this gate and entered the city for the first time. We arrived in full daylight with great pomp. Now I left the city by the same gate, in the darkness, alone. And in my spirit I sensed—I would never enter the city again.

I looked at the sky—three hours, perhaps less, before sunrise. How long would it take me to get to the house of Joseph? More than an hour. Perhaps I should have taken one of Annas's mules, I thought. My mind was racing. I brought no water, and I had failed to drink all evening. I put my hand to my head and remembered the touch of Jesus on it.

I ascended the ridge that runs above the valley outside Jaffa Gate and began the descent on the other side. I had another, higher, ridge to cross before I came to the plains that would lead me to the estate.

At a bend in the path two men came quickly out of the rocks behind me. I turned and faced them and pulled my sword from its sheath. In the full moonlight we could see each other clearly—they with their knives and me with my sword. They thought better of their intentions. They backed away and I proceeded up the hill.

When I reached the crest of the hill, the sky behind me was gaining some color, the slightest bit of yellow below the silver and gray clouds above Moab. Within two hours, a priest would stand at the corner of the temple and shout, "Behold, the sky is lit up as far as Hebron," a lamb would be sacrificed, and the day in Jerusalem would begin like any other.

What would this day bring for Jesus? I did not know the answer, but I had to get to the house of Joseph. He and Manaen and Nicodemus must be alerted. Perhaps they could avert a tragedy.

"Water, I need water," I announced to the servant who came to the gate. A few minutes later I sat with Joseph and Manaen in the atrium of Joseph's house and told them of the events. "Annas now holds Jesus at his house. Some of the Sanhedrin are there with him."

"Annas cannot conduct a trial at night!" Joseph said. "The code of the Sanhedrin forbids it. The law is clear. Only in the daylight can a trial be held."

"But will he break the law if his money and power are threatened?" Manaen asked.

Joseph nodded. "He will."

"What does Annas hope to gain?" Manaen asked. "He has no authority to put Jesus to death. The Romans do not allow it. How then does this trial serve his purpose? His ambition is to have Jesus killed. Why then has he conducted this sham trial?"

"I can answer your question," I answered. "Annas and Caiaphas met with Pontius Pilate at Herod's palace just a few hours before the guards went to the olive grove."

"Ah!" both men said in unison.

"That makes it clear. The priests have made an arrangement with Pilate," Manaen said.

Joseph nodded again. "Annas will ask the Romans to do what he is not allowed to do—put Jesus to death."

"And if I can read Annas's purpose," Manaen added, "his plan must unfold quickly—before sundown and the Sabbath."

"He must be stopped," Joseph said. "There are honorable men in the Sanhedrin who must be notified, men who will oppose Annas. Nicodemus is one of those. He must be notified—and any others with him."

"Send word to those men quickly," Manaen responded.

"I will dispatch runners as soon as I can write the notes," Joseph said.

"I will go to Herod's palace," Manaen said. "I will seek to see Pontius Pilate. He must be warned of the plans of Annas."

"I will accompany you," I said.

"No, Malchus," Manaen replied. "You are now a hunted man. Your presence would make the matter worse."

"What Manaen says is true." Joseph added. "You must stay away."

They departed quickly with no more conversation. I was left alone. A servant girl brought bread, wine, pullet eggs, and fruit. I declined. I went to the porch and watched as Joseph and Manaen mounted mules and started toward the city. The sun had broken free of the mountains of Moab in the east. No clouds impeded its rays as it shone directly in our faces as it rose over the hill of Zion and the city of Jerusalem.

For a thousand lifetimes, I suppose, the sun had risen above the hills of Moab, bringing light to the mountain once called Mt. Moriah. But this day would be different. This day the sun would witness something never before known.

Shielding my eyes, I watched the men until they were out of sight. I watched a while longer, pacing back and forth on the porch, wondering what was taking place in Jerusalem. Eventually I went inside and took a quince from the bowl the servant girl had left. Until I began eating I did not realize my hunger. I finished all that had been brought, and the servant girl brought more, which I also consumed. I went back to the porch. It was now mid-morning. Joseph should have met Annas by now. *Perhaps he can bring some influence on Annas.* Manaen should have alerted Nicodemus by now. *Those two men have influence. Those two men can convince the Sanhedrin to release Jesus.*

When the servant girl came to take the dishes away, she sensed my weariness and motioned to the cushions along the wall. As suddenly as hunger had come over me, so did my fatigue. I found a place in the cushions and soon fell asleep.

Have I slept until evening? The room was dark. I went to the porch. The servant girl stood looking in the direction of Jerusalem, a concerned look on her face. The sky was oddly dark, but it was not the darkness of evening. Thicker clouds than I had ever seen, low and unmoving—clouds that seemed to have the weight of boulders— hovered over us. For four years I had looked at the sky above the city, but never had I seen a black sky like this.

All men, I suppose, have moments of despair. What brings that despair we cannot always know. We cannot always attribute that despair. What about these clouds caused my despair?

I fought the impulse to go to the city. I wanted to be there, to see what was happening, but what I had been told was true—I would not be unnoticed.

The clouds, which seemed they would crush us if they came lower, lingered for some time. When they cleared, I went outside, restless. I walked through Joseph's gardens, into the lemon grove, trying to make sense of the last two days—the moment at the temple when Jesus, coming toward the moneychangers, looked directly at me. And then last night when his eyes caught mine again as I was about to kill Ananus.

How am I to make sense of these things?

My hand went involuntarily to my head and ear. The memory of that healing—that sensation when Jesus touched me, was still fresh.

I will never be able to explain the sensation when Jesus' hand went to my bleeding head. I no longer try.

There are times when a man's posture—the way he holds his shoulders, the pace of his step—tells the news before his lips can form the words. When I saw Manaen and Simon approaching, before either man spoke, I knew the report.

"We failed, Malchus. We failed." Manaen called to me as he approached. "He has been crucified."

Chapter 49
The Reports

"His blood remains," Simon said, pointing at his shoulder. He sat slumped, barely raising his head. A red stain ran across his robe. The pain in his eyes was a pain I had never before seen, even in our months in the quarry. He looked at his shoulder again, taking the fabric in his fingers. "His blood remains," he repeated.

"We failed," Manaen said. "Jesus was crucified."

Manaen, Simon, and I sat in the cedar-paneled hall of Joseph's house. It was the hour for the Sabbath meal, and the meal had been prepared on the low tables near us—the roasted lamb, the bitter herbs, the unleavened bread—but no one took the food. At the windows a few bees buzzed in the lemon branches, using the last of the day's sunlight.

"Simon," Manaen explained, "was compelled to carry the cross for Jesus. The Romans pulled him from the crowd."

Simon nodded and looked at his shoulder again. The bloodstains remained. His hands still carried some stains as well. "His knees buckled under him," Simon said, shaking his head. "He had been beaten. His back . . .his back . . .it was bloody, mangled—he could not bear the weight."

"The Romans, I suppose, wanted a strong man, so they pulled him from our side," Manaean explained.

"Where is Joseph? Where is Nicodemus" I asked.

"At Herod's palace," Manaen answered. "Joseph has offered a tomb for the burial of Jesus," They are asking Pilate for the body of Jesus."

The room went quiet.

Manaen went to the window and looked toward the city. I looked at him as he looked out the open window. "I failed," he said, clasping his hands together. "I failed John and now I have failed Jesus."

"You have no blame," I said. "There was nothing you could do."

Some minutes later we heard voices at the gate. Joseph and Nicodemus returned. In a few minutes they joined us. Both men wore weariness and sorrow in their faces. Manaen embraced both men and all of them sobbed. Each man then took a seat on the cushions. Their shoulders were slumped. They said nothing.

The last rays of the afternoon sun slid up the walls and disappeared.

"I suppose I am defiled," Nicodemus said. "My Pharisee friends would say so. My journey was concluded before the sun fell on the Sabbath. Yet it does not concern me."

Servants came and lit the candles that ringed the room.

No one spoke for some time until Manaen raised his head and took a deep breath. He looked around at each of us. "We had such hope, didn't we? Didn't we hope that he was the one who would redeem Israel? Weren't we convinced by his healings, by his miracles? More so, weren't we convinced by his words?"

Manaen moved his head from side to side. "It was his words, wasn't it? His words had life in them. When he spoke of the kingdom—the kingdom of God—didn't our hearts burn to become citizens of such a kingdom? Didn't those words give us hope? Didn't we want to serve such a king?"

The others nodded in agreement.

"But now —" Manaen went on. "—where is our hope? His lips can no longer speak of hope or—" He broke into sobs.

Joseph brought him water and sat beside him. "Tell us what happened. What happened at the trial?"

Manaen held the cup of water in his hand. Joseph pushed it to his lips and he took a sip.

"*Trial*?" A rueful smile came to Manaen's face. "It was no trial. Jesus was offered no trial. But I will tell you what I saw—and what I heard." He looked out the window toward Jerusalem as he gathered his thoughts.

"Even as Pilate conducted the interrogation, I held hope that Jesus would be released. And once released, he would assume his role as the deliverer of Israel."

"You must tell us about the trial," Nicodemus said.

"Pilate made an effort to make it a trial, but it was no trial."

"Tell us, Manaen," Nicodemus said quietly. "Tell us what happened."

Manaen composed himself. "I arrived at Herod's palace only moments after the council members and the sons of Annas had delivered Jesus to Pilate. A crowd, which was growing larger, had gathered on the pavement in the large courtyard. A servant of the household, whom I knew, admitted me to the palace. Inside, I saw Claudia in the hallway, the kohl around her eyes in streaks on her cheeks. 'I warned him,' she told me, wiping her eyes, 'I warned my husband. I told him I have suffered greatly in a dream because of that man. Have nothing to do with that righteous man, I told him.'

At that moment a noise behind me distracted me. I turned to look as Roman soldiers brought Jesus through the hall. His face was bloody, but his countenance was composed. When they passed, I looked for Claudia, but she was gone.

Pilate's servant came through the hall and put the prefect's curule on the balcony overlooking the crowd on the pavement just below. But Pilate made the crowd wait. The curule sat empty on the porch. Pilate did not come. Murmurs ran through the crowd. Neither Annas nor Caiaphas were among those on the pavement. But all the sons of Annas were immediately below the balcony. Their irritation and impatience was evident. They had only hours to achieve their purposes.

Still they waited. The curule remained empty. The shadow line on the walls moved slowly down the beveled stones as the sun moved higher in the sky. But Pilate did not appear. Jesus and the soldiers who held him were not in my sight, but I knew they must be in the wings of the balcony, not only out of my sight but also out of sight of the crowd on the pavement below. The sons of Annas shuffled their feet in agitation as the sunlight came into the courtyard. With every degree the sun moved higher, it made their effort more difficult. The grumbles and murmurs of the crowd grew louder. Finally, Pontius Pilate came through the hall, walking like a man going to war. He wore his civilian tunic, but his gait was military. Around his neck hung the medallion he always wore. He came to the balcony and surveyed the crowd below him—as they, in degrees, quieted at his appearance. Pilate stood for some moments, looking over the silent crowd. Most of them averted their eyes. Pilate took his seat. His lips were tight. His eyes were narrowed. He said nothing. Then he motioned to the wing of the balcony. Two soldiers brought Jesus to the view of the crowd. 'Blasphemer,' a few murmured. Pilate stood and raised his arm to silence the crowd. He looked at Jesus, who stood beside him, and then directly at the sons of Annas, who stood at the front of the crowd, but spoke loudly enough for all the crowd to hear: 'What accusation do you bring against this man?'"

Manaen paused for a moment and looked around at us. "The sons of Annas looked at each other in confusion. They were unprepared for this question. They looked at each other, perplexed. They had not expected this. Pilate had asked them to make a formal accusation— the first step in a Roman trial—but the sons of Annas were caught off guard. I suddenly realized, *They thought they had an agreement. They thought they already had Pilate's concession. They had not planned a formal accusation. What had changed?*

"The sons of Annas talked among themselves, then Eleazar addressed Pilate, 'If this man were not doing evil, we would not have delivered him over to you.'

Pilate pursed his lips and responded dismissively, 'Then take him yourselves and judge him by your own law.'"

Who can account for the effect of the whispers of a woman in a husband's ear? No man with a wife will deny it. As it is true for most men, it was true for Pontius Pilate, the prefect for Rome. "Have nothing to do with that righteous man," she told him. "I have suffered greatly in a dream because of him." And now as he sat on his balcony, Jesus standing nearby, he looked over the pavement, crowded with the Jews. These people disgusted him. Nothing in him moved him to cooperate with this mob. Expediency would have counseled him to accede to their demands and placate them, but no natural impulses ran in that direction, and the admonition of his wife would not leave him—but the words of his wife, "Have nothing to do with that righteous man . . ." lingered in his mind.

Manaen went on. "Pilate stood as if he were leaving the balcony. Someone in the crowd shouted, 'He calls himself a king.' Pilate smirked. He turned to Jesus, 'Are you the King of the Jews?' The answer he received would stun Pilate. I saw it in his face.

Jesus raised his head and spoke quietly, 'Do you say this of your own accord, or did others say it to you about me?'"

Manaen stopped again. He looked at us. "What was it I saw on Pilate's face? Astonishment? Confusion? Fear? All of those, I think. His head went to the side slightly as if he were trying to make sense of what he had just heard. Whatever Pilate expected as an answer to his question, he, the prefect of Judea, representative of Rome, appointed as judge of this trial, did not expect to be asked a question by the one on trial.

Pilate shifted his weight. He was unsettled. Did his mind go back to his wife's warning? Did he, at that moment, realize he was dealing with a different kind of man—a 'righteous' man, as Claudia called him. Did he, I wonder, think of the reports he had heard—of Jesus healing the blind man, of his raising Lazarus from the dead? Was that what caused his countenance to shift? Whatever it was, the arrogance was gone. The contempt he had shown as he spoke to the sons of Annas was gone. Confusion replaced the arrogance and the contempt. He looked at Jesus carefully, his eyes narrowed, trying to make sense of what he had heard. The murmurs of the crowd outside grew louder. Pilate looked out from the balcony and then back at Jesus.

Returning to the porch, he called out to the crowd, 'I find no guilt in this man.' But Eleazar called back, 'He calls himself a king and he forbids us to pay tribute to Caesar. He should be crucified.' Some in the crowd, holding in their hands the coins that Eleazar and his brothers had distributed, began chanting, 'Crucify him! Crucify him!'

Pilate turned back to Jesus, 'Are you a king?'

'You have said so,' was the reply.

Pilate hesitated for a moment and then addressed the crowd, offering, according to custom at Passover, to release Jesus, but Eleazar answered. 'He stirs up the people both in Judea and Galilee.'

Pilate stepped back from the porch and summoned one of his aides. They conferred for a few moments before he returned to the porch and spoke directly to the sons of Annas, 'I am informed that this man is a Galilean. Therefore he belongs to the jurisdiction of the tetrarch of Galilee and Perea. Herod Antipas is in the city. I will send this man to him for judgement.'

The sons of Annas started to protest, but Pilate stepped away from the porch and directed his soldiers to take Jesus to Herod Antipas. I slipped out of the palace and ran toward the Hasmonean Palace, ahead of the crowd, who crowded around the Roman soldiers escorting Jesus.

When I reached the Hasmonean Palace, I asked for Chuza, who came to the gate and admitted me. I gave him and Joanna a quick report, informing them that the Romans were bringing Jesus to Antipas. Joanna provided a servant's tunic, and we went into the great hall as Antipas was being escorted into the room and onto his seat on the dais. Twenty of his soldiers were arrayed around him. The sons of Annas, a few other priests, some of the scribes, and a few members of the Sanhedrin were admitted, but the crowd remained outside. There were a few others, perhaps eight or ten, who were leaders of the Herodian party, who were provided seats to the side of Antipas.

Antipas himself seemed slightly nervous as Jesus was brought in. He looked at Jesus intently for some time before he spoke. 'I have heard much of you. Will you do a sign for us today?'

Jesus did not reply.

'Have you nothing to say?' Antipas asked. 'It is said you have done much teaching. What will you teach us today?'

Jesus remained silent. Antipas raised his eyebrows, and a smirk came to his face. He addressed the audience, 'Is this the one who calls himself a king?' The crowd laughed and then the sons of Annas began shouting, 'He is a blasphemer!' A chorus of other accusations came from the crowd. Antipas raised his hand to silence the crowd. He looked at Jesus. 'Will you make a defense to these accusations?' But there was no reply."

Manaen paused for a moment, squinting his eyes. "I was reminded of what the prophet Isaiah said, 'He was oppressed, and he was afflicted, yet he opened not his mouth; he was led like a sheep to the slaughter, and as a sheep is silent before the shearer is silent, he opened not his mouth.'"

Manaen went quiet for a while. None of us spoke as he collected his thoughts. "Antipas seemed nervous, even fearful, when Jesus was first admitted, but he gradually gained courage when Jesus said nothing. Antipas had a tattered old robe brought out. 'Should not a king have a royal robe?' he asked the audience as he held it up. Laughter filled the hall. One of the soldiers put the robe around Jesus and mockingly bowed before him. More laughter filled the room. But Jesus, who until that moment had kept his eyes down, raised his head and looked directly at Antipas. When he did, the countenance of Antipas changed. He was unsettled. I could see it in his face. He waved his arms to dismiss the proceedings and left the dais quickly."

I too have known the gaze of Jesus. There are no soul-secrets to be withheld from the scrutiny of that gaze—of that I am sure. What did Antipas sense when the eyes of Jesus came to him? Did he see the irony of his seeking a kingdom—while mocking one who professed to have a kingdom? Antipas had come to Jerusalem in the hopes of becoming a king, but now he looked into the eyes of one who was truly a king.

Manaen continued. "More jeering followed Jesus as he was led out of the hall. Some spat on him. The sons of Annas, realizing the urgency of their effort, parted the crowd so that the soldiers could return Jesus to Pilate.

Pilate made several pleas to the crowd to have Jesus released, but they would not hear it. Pilate seemed resolute. I thought he would confound Annas and release Jesus, but—"

Manaen went quiet.

"What happened?" Joseph asked.

"A voice came from the crowd—one of the Herodians, I think—speaking in Latin. It was a strong voice. It seemed a practiced statement: *Si hunc dimittis no es amicus Caesaris*—'If you release this man,' the voice said, 'you are not Caesar's friend.'

As if a short-sword had been plunged into his ribs, Pilate winced in pain. The color went out of his face, his shoulders fell, and his hand went involuntarily to the medallion at his throat. 'Crucify him. Crucify him.' the crowd began to shout."

What went through Pilate's mind at that moment? I do not profess to be a reader of men's minds, but certainly he had to consider the precariousness of his position. His champion and advocate Sejanus was dead. Both Annas and Antipas had representatives in Rome who maligned him. He knew that a ship from Rome could arrive at Caesarea any day to recall him. Was Tiberius waiting for only one more bad report? Could the Herodians convince Tiberius that Jesus was indeed preaching resistance to Rome—and that Pilate failed to quell the rebellion? Were those the questions that went through his mind at that moment?

Manaen continued, "Pilate turned and looked back at the doorway where Claudia had stood earlier. She was not there. The crowd's chant, prompted by the sons of Annas, resumed, louder this time, 'Crucify him! Crucify him!' Those voices, in the end, prevailed. Pilate had a bowl of water brought out and he washed his hands before the crowd, telling them 'I am innocent of this man's blood.'"

Manaen went quiet.

"You know the rest," he said after some moments.

All nodded but no one spoke. Simon looked at the blood on his shoulder.

"Yet...yet..." Manaen said, as if he were just framing his thoughts, "although I have no reason for hope, yet, for some reason, I still sense it. The words Jesus spoke gave me hope when I heard them. I still feel that hope in the deepest part of my heart. His last words on the cross—loud words, for he summoned some final strength—were, 'It is finished!' What does that mean? I do not know, but they were not the words of one who had failed."

Joseph spoke, "We have done what we could. We prepared his body and placed it in my family's tomb. Now we must think of what to do now." He turned to me. "Malchus, you must leave Jerusalem. Your life is in danger. Annas and his sons will not allow you to live. I have family in Damascus. You must go there. I have thought about this. It is the best choice for you. You must leave at first light. Annas will not seek you on the Sabbath. By the next day you should be free of his search. However, you must be careful to keep your head covered. If someone sees the wedge in your ear, they will try to capture you for the bounty."

"I have no wedge in my ear."

All in the room looked at me oddly. I raised my hair. "Look."

"Your ear!" they exclaimed, coming closer. "How?"

"He healed me. The fisherman hacked my ear in the olive grove, but Jesus put his hand to it and healed it. My ear is complete."

The men looked at each other and then again at my ear—my whole ear.

"If this becomes known to Annas," Joseph said, "he will have more reason to require your death. More reason for you to leave quickly."

Of the trip to Damascus I have little memory. My mind, as I rode on the horse Joseph provided, was occupied with the events of the days just before. I often put my hand to my head to confirm my heal-ing. Simon rode with me for the first half day, but if we spoke to each other at all, I do not recall the words. Eventually I sent him back. We embraced as friends who never expect to see each other again. But we did not know the future.

Chapter 50
Reports from Galilee

The first report I discounted.

It came from a Galilean from Capernaum who professed to know Peter and the other followers of Jesus. I had been in Damascus, staying with the cousins of Joseph for a week when I heard him. "He's alive," the Galilean said. "Jesus is alive."

Another report came the next day, two men from Bethany. "His disciples attest to it. Jesus appeared to them. God has raised him from the dead."

Could it be true? I did not doubt it. Whatever I sensed when he touched me in the olive grove—whatever that was, it was something powerful, perhaps even something adequately powerful to raise one from the dead. In the deepest part of my soul, I knew it was true.

My intuition was confirmed. Simon came to Damascus. "I saw him, Malchus," he said. "I saw him. I heard him. Jesus, the one whose cross I carried, spoke to me. He took me by the shoulders. He is raised from the dead."

What I sensed in my spirit, Simon's account affirmed.

"Annas and his sons now seek my life," Simon said. "It is known that I carried his cross—and that I have told of his resurrection. Joseph sent me here. We are brothers again," he said, smiling, "Annas seeks us both."

More came from Jerusalem, some, like Simon and me, threatened by Annas and the Sanhedrin. Chuza and Joanna joined us. We, the few dozen who declared ourselves followers of Jesus, began gathering at the house of Ananias, a Jewish scholar well-known among those in Jerusalem. A conflict with Annas and the Sanhedrin years earlier had forced him to move to Damascus. "God sometimes surprises us, does he not?" he asked us. "We expected him to prove his power by overthrowing the Romans. But instead he has proven his power by overthrowing death." He smiled through a white beard. "Overthrowing the Romans would have been, in comparison, a small effort."

Our fellowship grew. We met regularly, and Ananias taught us from the Scriptures. "We should not have been surprised at these events," he said. "The prophet Isaiah told us to expect what we have witnessed: 'Surely he has borne our griefs and carried our sorrows; yet we esteemed him stricken, smitten by God and afflicted But he was pierced for our transgressions; he was crushed for our iniquities; upon him was the chastisement that brought us peace, and with his wounds we were healed.'"

Others came from Jerusalem—some only to visit and to encourage us. Others stayed. One of the scribes came. "All you have heard is true," he told our gathering. "Jesus is the Redeemer for which our nation has awaited. The Scriptures are clear. He is the one who was promised. He has fulfilled what the prophets foretold. The council has forbidden that this message be proclaimed—yet Peter, the one cowed by a servant girl in the high priest's courtyard when he denied he knew Jesus," the scribe looked at me and I nodded in acknowledgement, "has defied the council and is preaching name of Jesus with great boldness. Many hundreds have responded to this message."

Our fellowship grew as well. Many from Damascus heard our stories and joined us. More from Jerusalem and the Galilee came—convinced that Jesus was the Deliverer that God had promised. Still more came from Jerusalem.

Then one came that I did not expect.

Who can account for the hopes and events of a man's life? Who can explain a man's hopes when he has no reason for those hopes? When a man has put past hopes away and dismissed those hopes, why should there be any expectation that such hopes might be realized?

I embraced Marius as soon as his feet were free of his stirrups. "Welcome to Damascus, my friend," I said. "It is good to see you after these weeks."

"And good to see you as well," he answered. "We have much to discuss."

An odd expression was fixed on his face, a thin smile—the look of a man who is holding a secret. Behind him were three more mounts. Two of his fellow cavalry-men stood beside their horses, but on the other horse was another figure—completely shrouded.

"Come," Marius said, pulling my arm, leading me toward the shrouded figure. We came near.

From the sleeves of the robe, small delicate hands, the color and luster of porcelain—as if porcelain had come to life—emerged and reached for the hood. The morning sunlight caught the copper hair as it spilled from its restraints.

Sabrina.

"Claudia has released me," she said, looking directly at me. "If you will have me, I will stay here. If not—"

"Sabrina!" Joanna shouted from behind me. She ran toward Sabrina and reached to help her from the horse, but Sabrina held her off. Sabrina looked at me.

"I cannot dismount until—"

"Yes! Yes! Yes!" was all I could say. I was a pitiful fool. Ten thousand thoughts flooded my mind, but no other words would form on my lips.

Joanna helped Sabrina from her horse. Others came to greet her. I was undone. I was grateful, but I was without words. I looked at Marius. A wide grin covered his face.

The wedding, only a week later, was a joyous affair, planned and executed by Joanna. All our fellowship attended. We had wine and music, and Ananias reminded us that God, many generations ago, had ordained marriage, just as he had ordained that he would provide a Redeemer—and that promise had just been fulfilled. The next few weeks were akin to delirium. My joy with Sabrina was matched by the joy of the fellowship with the other believers.

Three weeks later that joy was tempered. Manaen came to Damascus. "Stephen is dead," he told us. "He was stoned to death by the council. The name of our Lord was on his lips when he died."

After we had expressed our grief, our fellowship began asking, "What will this mean?" What does it mean for the believers in Jerusalem? And what does it mean for us?"

"Annas is emboldened by the death of Stephen," Manaen said. "He and the council seek to root out all who follow our movement." Manaen looked at us as he paused. "There is no safety in Jerusalem—and soon there will be no safety here in Damascus. Saul of Tarsus has returned to the city. He is a zealous Pharisee. He assisted in the death of Stephen, and he has now asked the Sanhedrin for a commission to come to Damascus. His intent is to arrest us or kill us."

Manaen looked at me. "Your name is on the list to be arrested—as is mine, as is Simon's, as is Chuza's and Joanna's. Saul will soon be on his way. It is wise for us to leave the city."

"Where shall we go?"

"North, to Antioch," Manaen replied. "I have friends in the city. We should be safe there."

The story of Saul of Tarsus is better told by Luke than by me. I will not tell that story. I will say only this: Saul indeed came to Damascus, but like many of us—like me—he was confronted by One who summons us to a different destiny that we imagined. Saul—like me—was surprised by the confrontation. What Saul sought he did not find. But what he found was far better than what he sought.

We implored Ananias to join us, to go with us to Antioch, but he refused. "I will stay in Damascus," he said. "I sense that God is not through with me yet. Perhaps he has more for me to do in Damascus."

Ananias was correct. The Lord had other purposes for him in Damascus. Saul, the accuser of the brethren, the persecutor of *The Way,* became one of the brethren and a member of *The Way* in the house of Ananias. Ananias was wise to stay in Damascus. Most in our movement, however, came to Antioch. For nearly thirty years we have been here. For those of us who now call ourselves *Christians,* Antioch has become our home, our destiny. It is a place of great joy. We thrive in this community of believers. Sabrina and I have shared a love we never thought possible. Our daughter's daughter, who plays at my feet, was born here, carries the copper of her grandmother's hair on her head. She has recently taken her first steps. The world she will walk in is different from the one I knew only thirty years earlier. Our movement, our good news, has taken root in many places.

Paul, our brother, who has taken the message to many places, is imprisoned in Caesarea—but his spirit is irrepressible. "I am crucified with Christ," he wrote to the believers in Galatia, "and I no longer live, but Christ lives in me. And the real life I now have within this body is a result of my trusting in the Son of God, who loved me and gave himself for me."

Paul's preaching has taken the message, the message about the kingdom of God, to many places—to Adramyttium, Ephesus, Troas, Apollonia, Berea, Philippi, Thessaloniki, Corinth—in all these places, even Athens, this good news has found hearts that seemed to have been prepared to hear this "good news". Peter has taken this message to Rome, Andrew to Scythia, Thomas to Bharat, Thaddeus to Persia, and James to Egypt.

In each of those places, the story of Jesus and the kingdom has been embraced—and those that have embraced it have taken it to others, who likewise have received it. In every place it has gone, the message has found willing hearers.

Can this message be confined? Can it be contained? It seems destined to grow.

Epilogue

What will become of us—we who are the followers of Jesus? Does history have a place for our story? That part of the story remains to be written.

The story I have told is a story of kingdoms—of one authentic kingdom and many inauthentic ones. I have told of kings—of false kings, heads of false kingdoms—and I have told of a true king, the head of a true kingdom. I have told of those who in arrogance and ambition and evil, sought earthly kingdoms, and the one who in grace and mercy and humility, established an everlasting kingdom. That is the story I have told. It is both a true story and a story of truth.

It is a story in which I had a small part—a story that is ongoing—a story that will have no end. It is my story.

I am Malchus.

About the Author

A native Kentuckian who holds a B.A. in English from Mississippi State University, D. Charles King and his wife Lynne, former residents of the Holy Land, now make their home in South Carolina.